By Edward Hoagland

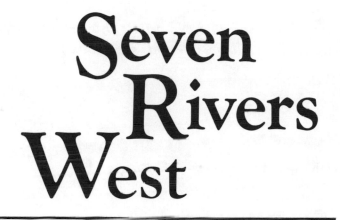

Seven Rivers West

Edward Hoagland

SUMMIT BOOKS NEW YORK

This novel is an invention. No people or tribes, no rivers or mountains, no villages or events are drawn from life.

Sections of this work have appeared in *Esquire.*

Copyright © 1986 by Edward Hoagland
All rights reserved
including the right of reproduction
in whole or in part in any form
Published by SUMMIT BOOKS
A Division of Simon & Schuster, Inc.
Simon & Schuster Building
1230 Avenue of the Americas
New York, New York 10020
SUMMIT BOOKS and colophon are trademarks
of Simon & Schuster, Inc.

Manufactured in the United States of America
10 9 8 7 6 5 4 3 2 1

Library of Congress Cataloging in Publication Data
Hoagland, Edward.
    Seven rivers west.

    I. Title.
PS3558.0334S48   1986   813'.54   86-5815
ISBN: 0-671-60753-7

For Howard Mosher
and
Suzanne Mantell

CONTENTS

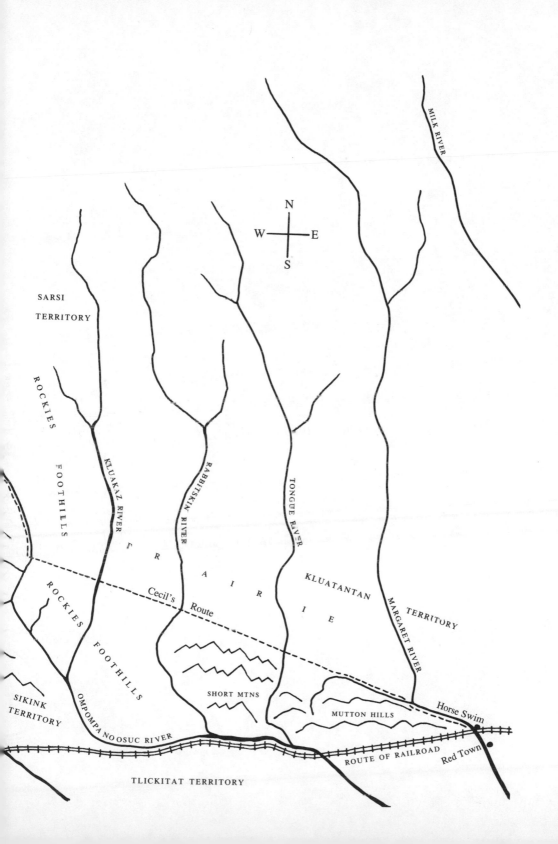

Part 1

Horse
Swim

1

HORSE SWIM

The ice was still going off the river in bobbing tiles and platters when Cecil Roop hooked a snapping turtle as big as a saddle, using a rabbit's foot for bait. He had cut its head off and the bottom shell but was gazing at its heart and lungs, which continued to palpitate, and was holding onto one cold and clawy paw, which felt like a monkey's and kept pulling away whenever he considered how to cook the thing.

"Now if that was a porcupine you'd know what to do with it," his friend Sutton teased him, sauntering over.

"Can I cook him in the shell?"

"No, it comes apart and your meat's in the ashes then."

Cecil was a skinny, durable-looking man from Massachusetts with long legs, a short body and a red mustache. He had a gentle, dogged air and his head would tilt insistently as if for emphasis as he talked. Six weeks ago he'd caught the Albany and Chicago train; then from Chicago another one to the railhead at Cameron on the Dakota plains, where he'd invested in two horses and a few other purchases and, after waiting around, had picked up with five companions, including Sutton, who also wanted to head north. The railroad that reached Cameron had run out of money, so many of the workers who had gathered there to lay track all summer were talking about trying to intercept another construction gang that they had heard of up in Canadian territory. Cecil himself harbored further ambitions. He hoped to catch and train a grizzly bear and go back East with it to show on the vaudeville circuit, and Sutton, who was in his late forties—twenty years older than Cecil—and a retired circus bandsman and performer, was sympathetic to that crazy idea.

"There's still snow on the ground, but I been missing turtle. I sure had no notion such a tasty monster was swimming in godawful Eskimo country," he said. A stout man from Louisiana, Sutton seemed to grow even stouter, his voice changing as his mouth began to water. He went so far as to volunteer his gold pan as a cooking utensil, and he dug a pepper shaker and a vial of vinegar out of his kit and waded in the icy river shallows, plucking underwater plants he could hardly see. After examining these, they saved several and kindled a fire of twigs and simmered the augmented turtle on its back for about an hour.

Sutton was after gold. Together they had ridden two hundred-and-fifty or three hundred miles from Cameron before fetching up at this old packtrain crossing on the Margaret River, named Horse Swim, which had in fact been uninhabited until the beginning of March, about the time Cecil had left home. They were sitting pretty—Cecil comfortably camped in his cozy gray tent in the shallow snow, with a scattering of gear and his one painty horse and his one sorrel picketed beside him, earning a dollar a day, although the job involved nothing more than occupying four building lots that, along with a dozen others, had been pegged out by a Mr. Leo Driggs on a homestead claim of a hundred sixty acres which had already twice changed hands and afterwards been divided among eleven speculators who thought they had reason to believe that the new Winnipeg and Pacific Railway was going to cross the Margaret at this old-time horse ford and that a city would grow up on the site.

Cecil had throw lines in the river for catfish, and would have liked to hunt, except that the antelope had hightailed it. Coming from the flour-scoop valleys of New England, he had never seen such horizons, and on the ride from Cameron the several dogs he'd brought along to warn them about Indians or grizzlies hiding in the willows had rousted up two buffaloes that had been a thrill to chase and as murky rich as beer-boiled beef to eat. He'd grown up with an axe in his hands, had logged on the Penobscot and the Androscoggin, had many winters behind him of trapping fur or handling teams of sled horses, and in the Maine woods, as a sideline to logging, had captured a good number of black bear cubs, using hounds or foot snares, and had sold them to barbers and tavern keepers for a drawing card to cage out in front of the shop. As a boy, he'd tramped the hardwood ridges of the Berkshires with his father, hunting for ginseng roots to sell. Those summers they had slept out for weeks at a time, or, with his mother and two sisters and two brothers, had followed the lumber camps in Vermont and New Hampshire with a wagonload of beehives, putting the boxes wherever the bees could make a quantity of honey from the fireweed and other flowers that sprang up after trees were felled.

At home they'd operated a cedar still, cutting cedar boughs and steaming the oil out of them for a liniment company in Boston, until "C. R." Roop, as Cecil Jr.'s father was called, gradually won a bit of a reputation as a medicine man who could cure skin cancers with a secret ointment he had developed. Eventually C. R. traveled alone, abandoning his family for as long as half the year to visit patients, with his provisions tied in a sack that was cinched in the middle and carried over his shoulder or over his horse's withers—the meat and soda biscuits for his supper at one end and his infusions, oils and herbs at the other. Because of his notoriety, it became as trying as it had been a pleasure earlier to be one of his sons, both a relief and unsettling for Cecil to find that everybody in his hometown regarded him as more ordinary than his uncanny, queer-headed old man.

But there was no pain now, so far from home, to being the son of such a man. Although for all of C. R.'s resourcefulness he'd died of a cancer himself—curled up in a ball in a maple-sap tub on top of a sugarhouse stove, trying to steam the bite of the cancer out of him— Cecil, besides a talent with an axe and at peddling his father's leftover physics, had learned from him a certain worldly nimbleness in traveling. He could work on an empty stomach in the bitterest cold, building a barn or vetting a cow, when he was short of money. Mo-

seying into a strange town with a horse to trade, he would whittle a
stick and look at the ground, letting the locals talk themselves out
before striking a deal with anybody. Always he had possessed a special knack with animals, surpassing his father's, which he hoped to
depend on here. Some people in Horse Swim had begun calling him
"Dog" Roop because he was invariably accompanied by a couple of
dogs, plus a trick terrier that leapt in and out of a deep and
capacious pocket he had sewn on the left side of his coat. Yet he
didn't stand out as an eccentric in the same way his father would
have, and was equally known for having fixed Walter Sutton's nose
after a fight by sticking his forefinger up one nostril and his middle
finger up the other and straightening it so it healed right.

When the turtle's claws could be twitched off, Sutton said the first
stage of preparing the meat was done. They let the pan cool and the
juices collect, shooing away various panhandlers who had been drawn
by the aroma, except for their boss, Mr. Driggs, and a one-armed,
white-haired bootlegger and desert rat named Left-handed Roy, who
was willing to contribute a flask of corn lightning to the festivities.
Roy had no teeth but had perfected a means of cooking even his buffalo meat into a porridge. He had lost his right arm while prospecting down in Colorado ten years ago and had one eardrum gone
from what he'd heard at Antietam fifteen years before that; yet he'd
carried his distillery tubing all this way so he could boil whiskey
where nobody else had ever boiled whiskey. "Indian cleaner," he
called it—the new tent saloon, Soak's Heaven, sold the regular brands.

Sutton sliced lengthwise steaks from the turtle's legs, which they
broiled on a spit, and skinned the neck, which furnished a pale meat
that was shaped like and nearly as transparent as the glass in a bottle and later formed the base of a good gumbo. He stripped out what
was inedible inside the shell but fried the liver, which lay next to the
neck, and saved the small intestines and all the mossy fluids, pouring
them into a stewpot along with maybe twelve pounds of miscellaneous morsels, and placed this brew on the fire for two more hours,
till you could practically drink the luscious blackish, grayish meat
and yeasty liquid. Then he and Cecil toasted one another.

Without saying so, they were eyeing the possibility of teaming up
again for a much riskier ride than the trip from Cameron had been.

An "old crawdad" from the bayous, as he described himself, and a gator hunter before he'd taken up the trumpet and gone to work on the Mississippi riverboats and had joined his first circus, Sutton was used to living in a hut slapped together out of mud and sticks. Here in Horse Swim he'd chopped a sodhouse from the ground with a pick and had fired a clay oven with a short chimney which, burning driftwood, made his living arrangements snugger than most. The same people who called Cecil "Dog" called Sutton "Frenchy" because of his darkish tint and the slight thickening he said his French mamma had given to his English, although his father had been a seaman from Baltimore. To Cecil, he sounded like the French Canadians who farmed in New England, and like Cecil, he wasn't interested as much in the approach of the track layers or the plan for the future town as by the rumors of huge mountains, only to be imagined, several weeks' travel to the west of where they were. Though everybody was anticipating that first glimpse of the Front Range of the Rockies, many in this crew collecting on the Margaret hoped to enter with a troop of soldiers for protection, as part of the army of railroad navvies on the move that was presently reported to number a thousand strong.

Six weeks ago not a blessed soul had been at Horse Swim, but now another batch of entrepreneurs was squatting across the river on another platted site for a town, and a third had bet on land next to a stretch of shallows upstream. South of Horse Swim, at a point where a wooded creek debouched into the Margaret River, a community of Kluatantan Indians was situated; and *this* might be the best natural setting for a county seat to develop—or at least Cecil liked to kid Mr. Driggs that the Margaret there, being deeper, flowing between shady, stable banks, could be just what the bridge builders were after.

Driggs was a high-shouldered, puffing individual with a soup strainer trembling on his upper lip, a wall eye and a rattled shuffle. He had a wife and children in Ontario but no big bankroll, and the mood on this slushy prairie flat had turned so nervous he was suffering breathing troubles. It augured badly that no government registrar had shown up to record anybody's claims. In the meantime he was afraid new speculators might ride in and try to jump his claim or even that some of the claim sitters like Cecil and Sutton would try to grab an allotment when the day came to sign and then sign over the papers.

When he talked about the possibility that the railroad might slant past to the south, missing Horse Swim, he put one hand up to his throat and squeezed his shoulders together. Or maybe the Margaret wasn't slated for a depot at all, no matter what route the tracks followed. Or maybe the present property layout might not be honored in the crunch because richer and sharper men than anybody on the river had obtained land grants in advance without ever leaving Montreal. He and other members of the Horse Swim Landholders Association had started buying rabbits and prairie chickens from a Kluatantan squaw to keep their claim sitters happy, although he said that last year he had hedgehopped in the same way in front of the surveying team, speculating on building lots with boundaries blazed among the cottonwoods and aspen trees and paths for streets mowed through the buffalo grass alongside a wild river. But when the track layers slogged through, they had kept right on, to build the station on the other side where some sodbuster had been subsisting for years, and made him rich instead.

The Kluatantans had not proved troublesome and hadn't been disarmed thus far, though in a land rush that swung toward them they could turn tough, as Driggs warned. Indeed, a wandering Gros Ventre Indian had just been captured, when a packer recognized him as the one who, according to the packer, had shot a partner of his near Bozeman after an argument over a mess of ducks shot for the pot.

Twenty or thirty packers were camping by the river after delivering goods to Horse Swim, and they made for a rough and mostly Southern contingent always ready for a card game or a fight. The bootlegger—cat-eyed, gray-headed—who ran Soak's Heaven had set up shop in his prairie schooner and a tent pitched beside them, with extra caches of swag stuffed inside dead horses and other trailside carcasses as much as eighty miles back (or so the word went); supposedly he had sent a courier to empty them.

With hand-scrawled signs he had advertised a dance for the evening that "will be a caution to corns and cockroaches." But when Cecil and Sutton got to it, replete from eating turtle, they found that the main event was going to be the hanging of the Indian. To Cecil, this man had a face like a Turk; and even as they arrived he was being lifted onto the rump of an ox, where he stood surrounded by horsemen, shaking his head, denying the crime, although without the benefit of knowing English.

"You lie, you dirty shit!" the packer who'd identified him yelled.

The hangman was a cowboy wearing a rattlesnake skin for a tie. He rapidly prepared to resolve the matter. The Indian soon seemed to give up hope. He started asking in both Indian talk and with the language of his hands to be shot instead of hung. Then his hands were tied, and—even as somebody explained to Cecil that the reason he had wanted to be shot was so his spirit could escape from his body through his throat—a great holler went up because it was his penis that rose as he choked.

Cecil and Sutton squinted at each other in dismay and astonishment, it had been so very quick and final and yet inconclusive. Several participants were laughing loudly; several glaring at the laughers. Cecil felt the incongruity of looking on with his terrier poking its head out of his coat pocket, cheerful as a cricket, and rain fell now to break up the dance anyway.

He got a little shaky whenever something overly wretched happened on this trip, because he hadn't left home with the good will of his family—he'd left in a rush and a rage, not just the misery of his marriage bed, but two young kids.

"You go home with a yellow bear on a leash all trained for a show and some gold in your pants and they'll hire you a band," Sutton assured him. Sutton had been a drifter for so long that he had the knack of offering friendship without really giving much of anything, a self-containment in a league with Cecil's father's but more tolerant. He was not a man to try to medicate anybody. Nevertheless, he observed for Cecil's sake, "Sometimes they won't take a cock. They'll swallow a pill and sleep with the kids instead."

Which was unfortunately true. Cecil's wife Sara had told him they got nightmares and wet the bed if she didn't, or she had fallen asleep with them after their bedside story without intending to, she'd said. Or if she did climb under the covers with him, she might start snoring softly just as he moved toward her, then wake up but begin talking to him in a voice as low as a man's, unmanning him. He was glad to hear his memories echoed so that they seemed less singular and less his fault, but on the other hand, he had lately dreamt of her calling to him across the spring skies, angry and yet still plaintive and affectionate; had seen her simulacrum in the distance walking to catch up with him—wiry, feisty and yet still fragile.

Sutton had a strong back, a square chest and a brown beard to go with his fat stomach, which he liked to rub as if he valued a plump belly. He said in fact that it had been his "meal ticket" occasionally in the circus when he had jumped into washtubs and rain barrels from high up, as a stunt. Cecil asked how he could stay fat when he was riding around on the ass end of a mule at the wrong side of nowhere and everybody else was getting scrawny.

"Overeating."

"Overeating? How can you overeat when you're eating beans out of a box and firebread?"

"Tonight we're eating turtle. But it ain't what you eat, it's how much."

Cecil had acquired a dented army bugle from an overburdened wagoneer and let Sutton toot on this. He blew such bell-toned ribbony riffs on what was just a stumpy instrument that Cecil had traded a pint of purgative for, the Soak's Heaven bunch wanted to get the party rolling again.

With the bugle on his knee, Sutton said that he'd missed the 1849 Rush from being only a kid and there might not be another one until it was too late for him, so he wanted to prospect in the mountains while he still had the legs for it. He'd grown sick of performing, yet spoke of those showboat trips with drawling nostalgia. In the morning he had practiced his trumpet by the paddle wheel where nobody could hear him, and they would tie up at a landing after lunch, keeping the boiler fired and hooking the calliope to it so the neighborhood would know. If a farmer gave them a lift in his wagon to the nearest store, they would play a few five-minute concerts on the porch during the afternoon, until by evening you'd see all through the swamps the wagon lanterns of families that were coming to the show.

He'd bought his riding mule from the last impresario who had employed him, in a mud show that had gone broke outside St. Louis. They'd sold their big top and their elephant and tiger, but when the buyer was slow to pay for these and they were stuck and couldn't keep buying hay for their hippo—the hippo and the owner both sweating blood—they'd turned the hippo loose into the Mississippi and wished her luck; and he felt he'd been turned loose too.

Night and day there were card games to watch, and a farrier and a gunsmith working, and the incessant dickering of the real estate magnates. A dozen hide hunters—heavy, meat-fed men wearing canvas suits stiff with buffalo blood—dropped in looking for a drink and a little fun. Half-breeds or Northerners, bear huggers, hermits and solitaries, they simmered less but maybe exploded more often than the packers—the Johnny Rebs—did.

"Nothing but bugs and blood last season. Nothing but bald-headed prairie," the boss told Cecil.

"No mountains?"

"We seen the mountains but we didn't go in the mountains. No buffalo in the mountains and I didn't want to go in the mountains."

Gaunt or ghostly-looking newcomers arrived alone daily, including a chatty chap on a Roman-nosed horse who claimed he had come clear from Texas, and wore his hair long to cover the fact that the tops of his ears had been clipped, a horse thief's stigma. Besides that, he was not anybody to link up with, because he left a stool twitching with tapeworms behind him. Everyone kept a close eye on him at first, until he had lost at cards and lost a couple of fights without attempting to kill the men who had beaten him.

An Indian with yellow streaks on his cheeks showed up for a purchase, then disappeared like a will-o'-the-wisp, the man who had been the likeliest to know what lay beyond them. Full-bloods seldom ventured into Horse Swim after what had happened to the Gros Ventre unless they were in the hire of a white hunter or packer. Cecil and Sutton spoke to any that they could, though they were getting a reputation as Injun lovers, and Cecil, collecting his daily dollar, felt foolish to have ridden into town with such a scanty load when a bag of turnip seeds or tenpenny nails, a bundle of shovels, a roll of oilcloth or barbed wire would have quadrupled in price from the railhead at Cameron to here. Extra horses to carry the stuff would have sold profitably too.

For money, he did have the square-cornered blue bottles of his father's decoctions and cordials and efflorescences which he had brought West. He had bought his pied-colored mare Kitty for a gallon of fig juice and three of castor oil—and Sutton, with a set of iron shoe lasts and three cured steer hides to work with, likewise wasn't pinched for cash. A flatboatman had inaugurated what was to be a regular freight and passenger service on the Margaret, and hired people to lay out a towpath. Driggs and the rest of the speculators gazed at the dirty beaches of the Margaret and visualized haberdasheries and tobacconists, but part of the puzzle was that nobody could be sure that some of them weren't agents for investors far from this scene, or (to skip that question) how much land the railroad was going to get for its station and switching yard, besides the bonus subsections the company was entitled to take and resell by the terms of its charter. If, as Driggs and his colleagues liked to imagine, Horse Swim might be slated for a territorial capital, then when the surveyors showed up they would grab wholesale chunks of acreage for government buildings and warehouses, and squeeze out some of the early birds in favor of later arrivals.

Cecil said he wouldn't mind helping to build the water tower— that would be a proud sight—although the only coopering he'd done was fashioning an occasional butter tub or cider barrel.

"Twenty thousand gallons' worth. Nothing's going to be taller than that. You could ride ten miles and still see it behind you." He painted "Horse Swim" with his finger.

"I may jump off it. Make some real money. You know, we're doin' good enough for here, but we're going to need to buy a lot of gear if we go out for gold or to catch you a yellow bear," said Sutton.

They did some work for an English couple who set up a canvas bunkhouse that slept sixty people on pallets of pinewood, and fed twice that many—griddle cakes with molasses for breakfast, buffalo for lunch and supper—having hired themselves a hunter. But the tenting was tattered because they had leapfrogged ahead of the railroad last summer too. After the wind blew hard, Sutton lowered the structure section by section and stitched the rips in the canvas, and when people with some cash watched him ply his sailor's needle, they would ask him for a pair of shoes.

The first hatch of blackflies gave everybody something to complain about, but the sky, if you lay on your back, was a king's purple. In the absence of hills and trees, Cecil felt peculiarly subject to whatever was going on overhead. A rain could seem grueling, but he got awfully happy when the clouds streaming by from the faraway mountains were piled briskly high with fantastic animals, gala warriors, silvery horsemen. And the river, uncapped of its ice, was a surging whale of a presence, forcing you to imagine where it came from. Cecil had never seen the Atlantic except at Boston Harbor, and from this perspective, having journeyed all the way from the Eastern Seaboard, felt like a fool for that. He had begun to cherish the hope of riding finally through to the Pacific with his dancing bears, gathering more as he went along and stopping to train them, like Grizzly Adams had done in the California Sierras—though Grizzly Adams had seldom bothered to return to civilization to exhibit his.

He showed Sutton the tangle of fur traps he had bought in Chicago. Two dozen number ones for mink and muskrat. Two dozen number twos for fox and fisher. Two dozen number fours for beaver had set him back sixteen-fifty, though with these last, which weighed three pounds apiece, he wanted to make do for wolves and wolverines as well, and to catch a deer on occasion for his dinnerplate. He'd bought one six-dollar number-five trap, weighing seventeen pounds, with jaws a foot wide, for any special situation that might arise. A regular grizzly or moose trap weighed three times as much as the number five and was priced by Newhouse twice as high, but was too big a load to carry. Besides, his coils of snaring wire would catch any creature dead or alive.

When the ground was bare of snow a convoy of oxcarts arrived, screaming excruciatingly because the wheels could not be oiled or they would seize up in the mud. Oxen were stronger and more sure-footed than a cart horse, less given to sickness, but Cecil had never worked with them in Maine because their strength was in the neck, not in the shoulders and chest, so they couldn't apply it to uphill pulling as well as a horse.

Woken from a nap by the shriek of the wheels, he noticed two boys walking beside the nearest covered wagon, which carried some straw-strewn crates of broody hens in back and had a milk cow roped behind. The woman on the wagon box wore a sun hat, boots and dress. It was the starch in her potato water that kept her hat so stiff and nice, she told him when he asked. But she was deaf from the wheels, and it was a bitter business for her husband and her to find that so much ground was spoken for even before the land recorder had gotten here. Blinking sweat out of her eyes with a disjointed smile, she wanted advice on where to camp. Her husband emerged from inside with a fish pole. They were the Stephanssons, he said, his fluffy mustache bobbing, and showed Cecil the repairs he'd jury-rigged on both axles. The canvas wagon-siding bellied with the wind, and when Cecil glanced in he saw oil lamps, some hardware and their bed.

He pointed at a spot of grass which he'd been saving for Kitty and the sorrel horse and gave the man an eel to cut for bait. The kids, after weeks of eating pinto beans and bannock bread, were wild to taste a pan of fish. The parents kept saying that they had beaten the immigrant train. They'd ridden partway with their wagon and goods but had left the train to outdistance the other passengers. Two shiploads of Germans were aboard, and the railroad had been dropping off three hundred of them every twenty miles with a carload of hire-purchase harrows and plows, some auction-house nags, and ten thousand bags of Red Fife wheat seed, as new track was laid.

Ellen Stephansson began grating corn and pumping Cecil for information, leaning left and right, with her sand-brown hair lying loose about her neck as if to belie the grip displayed in her hands.

He told her what he could and gradually blurted more—not only that the gold he was hunting for wore a fur coat but that he'd been married for seven years himself, that the child he'd married his wife for had been carried off by quinsy and sometimes he still heard her crying raggedly and coughing.

"And she didn't like you too much after that? Will she like you better if you get killed?"

He laughed. "It wasn't that bad, no. I'm giving it a rest. Try my luck. I'm not going to get killed. The funny thing is, I'm not scared of the bears. In my dreams I'm scared of the mountains."

"You're scared of what lives in the mountains," she said, with a cousinly smile.

He pooh-poohed that, although a hunter had hauled in a large plains grizzly the other day which, though gutted, was otherwise intact, and it had sprawled across the staggering horse like a drunken gorilla that had passed out but at any minute might sit up with that meat-grinder mouth, those nostrils like drainpipes, and roar. He explained how he had sold bear cubs back East—one, to a firehouse, that he had trained to stand up and balance a ball on its nose.

"I'll learn as I go." Whistling, Cecil got the several dogs that were hanging around to rush over and sit down, the coyote-y mutt named Smoky tugging gently with his incisors at his sideburns. A lot of different dogs rambled by every day to visit the two that Cecil had so far adopted, and they seemed to stay, although he didn't go to great lengths to persuade them to, apart from accepting their presence and enforcing a sort of pack discipline around his tent which intrigued them and which they enjoyed. He didn't pet them inordinately but did have a way of employing his hands like a dog's teeth and tongue while reaching itchy places they could not scratch, and rubbed their eyes gently with the heel of his hand or inserted his finger slowly into their ears to remove the wax, a sensation they didn't entirely like but which was addictive. It was claimed about him that he made dogs out of his horses too, sweet-talking them, and that he could steal the affections of any man's mongrel if he and it were left alone.

None of that would go very far in training a bear, Sutton said. You could buy 'em from Syria or Russia or Hungary, all Gypsy-trained, with scars on their feet from the heated irons they had been tutored with. The best trainer Sutton had ever worked with had used the technique of sailing over on the boat with his animals. "That was a month at sea—everybody speaking Persian to him. He just had his elephant to talk to, and by God, his elephant goddamned well had him! When it was seasick he was seasick right along with it. If it was thirsty he was thirsty. If it was lonesome and missed the food it was used to, so did he. That's how you make friends with an animal. That elephant and him—he stayed in St. Louis to take care of her, he stuck by her when she needed him. And he was the one that made us let that hippo go instead of selling her tusks and selling her meat as a novelty."

Cecil agreed that if he snared a "white bear," as the Indians called the grizzlies, when the bear tried to go to sleep when winter started— there in the cage he would build for it next to his cabin in the mountains—he would keep it awake round the clock, feed it dabs of fish, give it water, slap it when it slipped into a state of semihibernation, until all of its reactions to him were jumbled, just like you'd work with a hawk that you were trying to tame.

"I hear they tear people's cabins apart. I don't know why he's going to sit still in your cage for you," said Sutton.

"I mean a cub."

"Cubs, yeah, let's do it!"

He was like a thin man inside a fat man at moments like this, when he was paying attention, and his aplomb, as Cecil realized, was more than your average bandstand trumpeter's. He had a gliding, exact walk, disdainful gray eyes like a daredevil's, and a peculiar limberness, rubbing his forearms with a focused air like an acrobat on a trapeze bar. He said he'd wrestled gators as a boy but never a bear, although they had had those piney-woods bears that in a muskrat marsh would catch a snap trap on every toe.

"It's hell when you've set out a couple of hundred traps. The bear'll walk away wearing about ten of them. We were huntin' gators anyway on the bayou at night, shining a gas light. Got fifty cents a skin and might get fifteen or twenty in a night—and you're wrestlin' them anyhow when you shoot them and they sink. You have to go in after 'em; so you might as well do it in the daylight for money. I'm going to do that jump," he said, and began training for it daily with back and belly exercises.

When a railroader got fired, he hiked to Horse Swim now as often as not, instead of heading East. And the survey chief in angling past a certain knoll seemed to have tipped his hand as to where he planned to bridge the Margaret. By raft and buggy the whole conglomeration of squatters who had pitched their hopes on the townsite upstream came tumbling down to Horse Swim to try to jimmy out the weak sisters. But everybody in the Landholders Association linked up in proper style, readying affidavits, wearing weapons, and so on.

At night one of the fishplate tiers who'd quit the railway produced his flute and joined in with a Scandinavian mouth organist and a Nova Scotian fiddle player who had a hacking cough that punctuated the music and who said he'd "come West for a kill or cure." Mrs. Stephansson sold bean soup with bacon in it for six cents a bowl, and Left-handed Roy peddled his devil's brew, which Sutton had found some mint for at the edge of the river so he could call it a julep. Sutton tooted on the bugle at these blasts, too, as a means of keeping an eye out for new faces. Whether they wound up with an Indian or a white man, they needed to obtain a guide, and there were always campfires on the opposite bank, burning like a crimson riddle, while moon mists feathered the ribbed water in between.

You could buy a pair of socks, a meerschaum pipe, a concertina, if you wanted to. Every patch of dirt for half a mile on the east side of the river had its canvas roped up to advertise a storefront, half constructed, or space to lease to set one up. Yet ring-necked geese and pintail ducks still hurtled by, migrating north—whereupon every gunslinger unslung his firearm.

Because Cecil was selling soothing syrups, people called him "Doc" as well as "Dog"; and like a doctor, he was roused one night when a Swiss gentleman was shot in the bunkhouse for snoring. The Texan who had done it swaggered about on legs as bowed as a horse collar—as proud of being that crazy as he was ashamed. Lingeringly, he packed his clothes to leave and stopped to warm a cup of tea, shamefaced but with a tight, small smile. Meanwhile the Swiss man was reclining against three pillows on his blood-soaked bed, rubbing his beard to keep his hands away from his chest, where the wound was.

"Is there any law here? Why did he do that?" he asked in a hollow voice, as if oblivious to the gunman. "Is there any medicine?"

he asked Cecil, who had nothing effective for pain. "Is there a grave-yard? No churchyard yet? You're not going to bury me with that poor Indian? Am I the first grave?"

The blacksmith announced that he could do surgery, but Cecil and Ellen Stephansson found the bullet in the mattress, luckily. Cleaning the wound, they promised the fellow that if it didn't mortify he wasn't going to die.

"It sounded like a sawmill in here. Why did he pick me?" He chuckled humorlessly, as did the Texan—the one man bleaching steadily, the other flushing darker. Sutton rigged a curtain to afford him privacy, and he remained so quizzically philosophical for the remainder of that day that he appeared to be resting comfortably. The Texan swam the river to camp on the other side, where his comrades, shouldering their rifles with the muzzles down, warned that nobody should dare follow him.

Nobody did. Nor did anybody want to nurse the dying patient, so Ellen undertook that task. He turned out to be a dry-goods merchant with a complete inventory in a freight car rolling westward, and when he passed away modestly but painfully of blood poisoning, she and her husband gained by his signature the rights to his property in transit and quit scratching around for land to farm. He was buried by the river at a bend where it had been reported that a traveler had drowned last year, although the cross was gone.

Another death also occurred. A boy driving a team and wagon was thrown in front of the wheels and crushed when his animals bolted during a hailstorm, though he too lasted a few nights and days. A committee built a little church; and Cecil, in on the boy's suffering, saw himself squashed by a bear, shot by gunmen in the mountains, standing on the hindquarters of an ox with a rope around his neck like the Gros Ventre, in rapid-fire dreams. He woke at night with his gums bleeding from bad nerves.

But he'd appropriated the Swiss's duck dog, a black, good-natured retriever, to add to his terrier and two big malemutes he'd swapped for in Cameron named Moose and White Eye. And he was learning cowboy tricks with horseflesh, such as the running dismount, and rode with no bit, only a loop around the nose of his pretty Kitty, who responded to digs of his toes. He was accustomed to husky woods horses, whose broad necks and rumps he'd liked to lean against, and to a picky sort of woods riding in country where a sprinting cow pony would have broken her neck. Yet he loved the three-stride turns she could negotiate, and also the rougher beat of his studhorse, Fred, whose sorrel flanks were splashed with black as well as brown, who carried one ear forward and one ear back, and who might make a buffalo horse, as a friendly hide hunter informed him. He traded his father's silver pocket watch—which he did not expect to need any time soon—to a Manitoba wrangler for a prime red burly duffel horse which he figured ought to round out his outfit.

2

RED TOWN

But they wanted to wait for the railroad for more supplies, and needed a guide. The hanging of the Gros Ventre—so quick that even in retrospect it didn't seem they could have interfered—had frightened off any other stray Indians they might have hired. Though they were doing fine in town, they knew they'd die in no time, lost and alone on the prairies.

Nobody trifled with Cecil, because when other people showed off their shooting, he did stunts with his axe. He could throw it to hit a mouse, or whisk his supper kindling into splints a quarter of an inch thick with what looked like a full swing. But he missed his family when he handled it; the familiar motions stirred his memories of the woods and therefore home. When he woke in the wee hours he yearned for his children, sure he'd made an idiot's mistake. He wondered if he didn't lack a decent love for them, to have run off as he had, when any sensible man whose marriage was a mess would just have scouted out a widow in the next town to visit on the sly while continuing to live at home.

Sutton, to toughen himself for his jump, went for a swim each noon, and had been wheedling tips about placer mining from old one-armed Roy, who despite his lush's ruby nose and cheesy skin

was eager to go with them. Sutton kept his private history to himself, except to mention that his relatives had included a few Jay-
hawkers during the War Between the States, and besides he'd poked
around in Yankeeland so much he was half Yankee, on top of his
daddy having been one.

"My daddy quit being a Yankee. He even dabbled in slaves a little bit. He traveled the back country with them. But he was a Yankee when he swam ashore. It was in the forties, when his ship went
down. My mamma took him in, and she wouldn't let him keep on
being no Yankee!" He said that, as for him, he tended to like a
Southern woman best—that they liked men—but thought a Yankee
man made maybe a better friend than most Rebs.

"One gun more," Roy argued in his own favor; and Cecil was inclined to take him along, enjoying his stories of his corn patch on a
sweet-water river in the Arizona Territory, with a rifle pit he'd dug
in the middle of it to hop into when the Chiricahua Apaches prowled
through.

"I had some water jugs buried there. Had some jerky. Had my
melons planted next to it."

"Where was this at?" Sutton said.

"In the Cahuillas."

"And you tell me they couldn't have sat you out?"

"They could have, only they'da hadda lay around and they didn't
want to do that. They was on their way to winter and wasn't cutting
anybody's throat." Every spring and fall the same ones had come
through, the same way that a bear would do on his way to sleep in
his cave. "Two families, right through the yard, wouldn't stop for
nothin'. I was adobe, they couldn't burn me out, but you didn't want
to be chopping corn with no place to jump into when those bucks
and bitches came through. No grass grows under them. They ride a
horse till he plays out and then they'll eat him for the taste his fear
puts into him and after that they'll run as fast as he could have till
you get close. Then they hide in the grass, which is what's worst. Nobody hides like a Chiricahua. He's flat on his back with his bow
drawn in hip-high grass that you can't see through till you're on top
of him and he's got his arrow in your throat," he concluded, with
chuckling bravado.

However, with mostly Easterners showing up on the Margaret and the Kluatantans giving every white man a wide berth, they decided by late April that they must visit the village of Red Town, as the whites called it.

Riding down made for a lovely jaunt over miles of fresh-smelling bunchgrass that tickled the horses' fetlocks, through thickets of wolf willow at eye level to a mounted man. Cecil had brought along three dogs—Smoky, Moose and White Eye—to see how well they minded him, but when the infinite horizon had swallowed Horse Swim, he grew anxious enough to appreciate the extra protection too, and was glad for the addition of Roy's presence. The Kluatantans were not as formidable by reputation as the Oglalas and Arapahos and other tribes to the south, and he had known and worked with a few Indians in New England, but this was utterly different.

"This is an Indian world."

"What do you mean, an Indian's world? It's anybody's goldamned world. That attitude won't get you anywhere," Roy told him—adding unexpectedly, "I love it. Love the puddles. Love the creeks."

"I like that there's no trees, but I'll wish there was trees if they start giving us trouble," said Cecil.

"Well I didn't really like watching that guy swing, but now it's better that they hung him. And you wanta ride a thousand miles, and we're just riding ten?" Roy glanced over at Sutton, who was silent but grinning mildly.

Nobody spoke when the dogs quit chasing ground squirrels and stood sniffing. A winding line of cottonwoods ahead that marked a creek bed ended in a large grove by the river that lent an air of permanence to the cluster of round tan tipis under it, which they spotted one by one as they drew nearer.

They expected a lookout would either stop them or greet them. Pausing uneasily to fire a shot in salutation, they waited, trying to count the tents. There didn't seem to be enough to justify all the talk about this place back in Horse Swim.

"Has anybody *been* here?" Cecil said.

They picked a beaten path and approached unobtrusively, tying their dogs and horses beside the one log cabin, which appeared quite odd-looking under the circumstances because of its rectangularity, and was collapsing. The village dogs raised a cautious ruckus, and a woman who had been scraping a hide with her back to them hurried out of sight. They noticed several kids crouched next to the creek that watered the trees, but a man who had been sitting by the kids got up and walked away.

The crossed tops of the lodgepoles poking through each tipi's smoke hole endowed these tall, well-kept dwellings with an airier feeling than Cecil's tent had. There were about a baker's dozen of them, and perhaps as many rings of stones remaining on the ground where others had been pitched. The ground, though cleaner than at Horse Swim, smelled of meat and drying skins—skins pinned flesh-side-out on slanted racks facing the sun like flying antelopes. Two platforms set on posts provided storage space for food, and other sacks were suspended from convenient limbs out of the dogs' reach. Two ponies were tethered to a wind-thrown tree.

"Hey, my friends, I have business with you!" Sutton hollered.

He tapped on the cabin's unhinged door. "This was the trader's." He and Roy disputed whether the sod was washing off the roof because the rafters were crumbling or if the rafters had crumbled because the sod was washing off. They left their rifles in their saddle scabbards and sat down in a traderly manner, lighting a fire for tea, and took their pipes and pouches out—though, stupidly, they had forgotten to bring anything to trade.

When they had brewed a pot, Roy called out in what he said was Chiricahua to the kids. Sutton tried some Chickasaw words that he remembered, and Cecil, something in Seneca. None were accurate, of course. But one boy, who wore a dried kingfisher in his hair, was trying to shoot another kingfisher. The bird rattled at him and dodged angrily, so that his arrow dropped into the creek. When he swam to retrieve it, he lost the bird in his hair and had to swim back again for that. His fussing made everybody laugh, and when he came to warm up at the fire with a drink of tea, this development brought his mother to find out what the white men had given him. When he told her it was sweetened she had a cup, as did the rest of the kids, and one of the men who'd been observing from indoors was roused to shout at her.

He stalked over, wanting none of the stuff. He spat out a mouthful after tasting it to be certain they weren't foisting any rotgut on his youngsters. Nor had he horses to sell, he said in English. Nor did he want to buy their horses or guns or shirts or pants.

"Nothing from you." He waved to include their boots and hats and bedrolls, strapped behind their saddles.

His name was Billy Buckskin, and he had long hair parted in the middle, rheumy but intelligent eyes, and a countenance much weatherworn for a man still straight and young, although it was creased appealingly with smile lines. Besides, he looked familiar, as if he'd visited Horse Swim. He knew Roy cooked red-eye for a living, and his pants were hide but his shirt was wool.

"You cutting trees? No trees here. We don't sell trees."

"No sir, that's not what we're after," said Cecil. Though cottonwood bark was a winter food for Indian ponies, he'd been intrigued to see that within a perimeter of a quarter-mile of the village no trees had been stripped. Apparently loggers from Horse Swim had done some piecemeal cutting farther off, however. There were signs that they'd been twitching out the straighter aspens and peach-leaf willows and the cottonwoods that were already girdled, with a team of fat-hoofed horses with iron shoes.

"You know what they do, these fellas?" Billy Buckskin went on. "They tell me a man sold those trees to them. He did live here—yes. They say he's our 'chief,' but he ain't no 'chief.' They say he's got their money in his pocket, and how can I prove he didn't sell those trees to them when he's gone now? They're lying, but if I fight with them you're going to string me up. Ain't that so?"

The three whites stared at him. Sutton remarked that that wasn't right. "You got a sweetheart of a spot. We're not here to grab it away from you."

"We don't have no power—it's a zoo over there," said Roy, jerking his thumb towards Horse Swim.

Sutton refilled his mug and offered it to Billy Buckskin, who refused both that and a pipe, as blunt as a white man.

"You see, we can ask who's cutting your land, but we can't shoot them any more than you can shoot them," Cecil said.

"You must have more places like this," Roy threw in, sounding

the wrong note. Everyone was silent. Cecil, watching the handful
of Indians in sight, tried to imagine fighting or being taken prisoner
by them, but they were too shy or indifferent and too few. He reminded himself that packtrains had been slogging through the
vicinity for forty years.

"You run out of places and you run out of people. I seen them
with measles. I seen them try to wash those red spots off," Billy
Buckskin muttered bitterly. He told the kids to clear out and they
chased after the kingfisher again. He accepted a pinch of tobacco,
put it under his lower lip, and gave another to the woman, who was
darker-skinned. She left. Other Kluatantans had now emerged to go
about their business. Sutton decided to come to the point.

"We're going to the mountains. And that's so far we want somebody to help us."

Billy, though surprised, was unbending. "This is a naked country.
Not much food for so many people. But anybody that wants to work
for you already works for you. Don't you know that?"

When Sutton asked what the trader whose cabin this was would
have done about the logging, he snorted. "He would have charged.
I don't think he liked white men too much. We don't care if they
don't like white men—or why would they come?—but he didn't
like *us*." He waved as if to dissipate a stink.

Cecil inquired about big bears in the region, but he ignored that
question.

"We don't know the mountains. Nobody knows the mountains
here. You talk to Margaret."

"What?"

"Talk to Margaret." He pointed at a sort of bark hut, wider but
lower-set than the tipis.

They were flabbergasted. "Margaret of the Margaret River?
There's a Margaret?" Cecil said.

But Billy, reaching for and gulping Sutton's mug of tea, stood up.
"He was a squaw man. She smokes white men."

"Smokes 'em is good, huh?" Roy coughed and rubbed the nub of
his stump. It did have a cannibal ring. He'd wanted to break out a
bottle of booze for purposes of persuasion earlier and Sutton had

prevented him. Now he did, for himself, as Billy retreated and they sized up Margaret's habitation. A black rabbit hound that was tied in front began to bark.

"They can always make more Indians," Roy said with a laugh, dismissing Billy's complaints.

When they went over, she appeared—a husky woman of indeterminate middle age with a broad, mild face and deep, close-set eyes, who looked rumpled, as if she had been napping. She closed them again, as though not to take in too much; then turned toward the creek and the activity at the other tents while waiting for her visitors to explain what they wanted. Such matter-of-factness was pleasing, after the scuttling manner of the other women, and Cecil, recognizing more and more the demoralized flavor of the encampment, remembered an Indian friend in Massachusetts who had told him that the best thing to do was go and live among the white men instead of hanging on in the old village as it died.

But she wasn't sorry-looking. Indeed, her face bones had a cast unlike Billy's—which Sutton mentioned later on as being interesting, because a trader's lady might have traveled in with him from another tribe and territory. He was watching for a "long-haired dictionary," a lady translator and bed partner.

"Is he dead, your husband?" He pointed to the derelict cabin.

She said yes. His name, according to her pronunciation of it, was "Mick" or "Mike."

"Did he name the river for you or did he name you for the river?"

She shrugged ruefully, as though the honor was unwelcome in Red Town. *"Ninstints* is what they call this river. Slow River."

"But he called you Margaret first and then he called it the Margaret and told the packers to?"

"That's what he did." Red Town was really called *Ninstints* also, she said.

Although she wasn't the squaw that Driggs had bought his rabbits from—a young carrot-colored girl who was keeping company with a carpenter now—Cecil asked whether she wasn't that one's mother, because a row of rabbits was hanging between poles. Yes, she said, standing with her hands clasped at her waist, intrigued but still barring the door. She showed them her meat rack of wind-dried cutlets. "Indian icebox."

Cecil asked if she'd been to the cities.

"Oh yes," she said, though it was difficult to guess whether she just meant she'd gone to the old trappers' rendezvous. She wore a fawnskin skirt and a red cotton shawl. Her teeth, when she smiled, looked ground down as if they'd chewed on their share of skins for vests and leggings, and she had earth-colored skin, and yet an attitude bespeaking a thorough familiarity with white men. Billy Buckskin too was used to dealing with outsiders such as them. "Mick" or "Mike" had fired him. "Then he skun mules."

"And Billy doesn't like you?"

"He doesn't, no."

She had a touch of the shaman to her, an unsettling way of closing her eyes for a moment after looking at Cecil, as if for his own protection as well as because she was unimpressed. He was reminded of a Gypsy woman in a wagon train that had trundled through Pittsfield every fall when he was small.

A couple of kids were showing off, shooting arrows through a hoop. Billy would probably have told them to stop, in front of such unwelcome visitors, but Margaret prompted them to demonstrate a more dramatic game—pulling the lights of a buffalo behind a pony and shooting arrows into these. Once they had the pony out, they planted an arrow in the ground with a moccasin tied to it and took turns tearing past, plugging that.

"How about these Scandihoovians that are cutting on your creek? Do you know them?" Sutton asked.

"I can hear them. Roughnecks."

She consented to show them the stumps; then came to their fire for a cup of tea with a fillip poured in by Roy, though she wouldn't speak about where else the Kluatantans had settlements. "Don't try to get me drunk." She said the village was "falling down around our ears," that her son fed her. "But I'm not one of these people and they don't forget it." Billy Buckskin was one of her husband's sons, too, by another woman, she admitted, relaxing, picking tea leaves off her tongue and fingering her gray-streaked hair.

Ninstints was now an unhappy place. "They got to clear out, but they don't want to."

Sutton offered to take her to the mountains if she wished.

"And what'll you pay? Do you think it's something new for us to meet a white man who wants us to bring him to the gold?" She practically jeered. But because although he was surprised, he wasn't mad, she softened—her face growing larger, browner, richly Chinese—and told them she was from a tribe from the southern mountains called the Crows and that her father had traded her to Mike for two horses many years ago. "But even then I think Mike thought we were going to show him where the gold was—that we were going to throw that in," she said.

They laughed with her, Sutton inviting her to come and see the railroad anyway and look in on him.

She asked if he had a dollar. When he shook his head, she got up and turned toward her hut. He followed, however, and stepped past her, lifting the wolfskin flap when she sought to prevent him from entering. She touched him, in agreement, moving him in. Cecil was amused but soon afterwards pushed inside too, hearing Sutton moan—could she have stabbed him? Sutton was sitting on the edge of the wooden bed and Margaret had knelt in front of him. He was holding her shoulder lightly while feeling for a coin in his poke with his other hand.

They dawdled late into the afternoon in order to give her a chance to satisfy Cecil and Roy in a leisurely way, as though no money was changing hands, but she refused. Instead she showed them Mike's horse, a "soldier pony"—a cavalry horse—which seemed still vigorous, and his Sharp's Big Fifty buffalo gun. "Nothing but the best."

His coats were hanging up; there was a trunk of mementos. Her widow's pride kept them respectful, and she led them to the maze of wicker fish traps she had by the creek which in the fall at the time of the whitefish spawning run would be "feeding your town," she said.

"Well, if you come to town we'll put you to work. Or if you like the mountains where we're going, we'll take you along," Sutton said.

"I'll put *you* to work." She pointed at the pile of traps.

3

THE RAILHEAD

Pulling down bundles of firewood from a girdled tree to tie behind their saddles, they rode home in fine spirits, catching a badger alive along the way. Twice Cecil swam Kitty through pools they came to, pleased how she plunged in. She had a taste for this that could prove valuable, and a barrel breadbasket for buoyancy, and she would stand for him day or night when he got off.

They staked the badger outside Sutton's friends' bunkhouse—which, as it happened, had been sold while they were gone. Under the new owners it went by the name of the Old Judge Saloon. The "Judge" was the head of a Flathead Indian preserved in a pickle jar set on the bar, and the bar was outdoors because, as a sign announced: "Grizzlys Milk to All Bronk Peelers Who Make Me a House." Grizzlys Milk was whiskey stirred into sugared canned milk, so, not surprisingly, the walls of the annex were already up. The covered wagon parked there had LIVE HOOSIER scrawled on it in charcoal; and another wagon I HAVE SEEN THE ELE-PHANT, in axle grease.

Two Territorial policemen in green uniforms had shown up, and a gang of teamsters with mauls and miners' candlesticks, coal oil and cooking oil, cigars and sowbelly, dynamite and spaghetti mops. Somebody had tacked up a notice that the railroad was bringing in a mob of Chinamen (though it was coming from the East); the other news was that some unlucky Frenchman had got bit by a black widow spider while sitting on his thunder mug.

Local wisdom had it that the Horse Swim landowners had picked their spot too well. If the railroad didn't swallow them the government would. Yet Mr. Driggs had an offer of $11,000 for his lots, although his claim was unrecorded still. A businessman with no lumber in hand put up an advertisement that he was a dealer in lumber, and people began to place orders with him. Two women, Lotte and Zoe, who had traveled with the teamsters turned out not to be the wives of anybody in particular but "pretty waiters" employed to work at the Old Judge. They wore tit guns in their bodices and black spots on their powdered cheeks and had high singsong voices and a talent for catching tips thrown to them by squeezing their breasts together, in the California style.

It made for a bold show. Everywhere you looked you saw cash changing hands or IOUs. Sutton, who admitted that the only gold he'd ever seen was either in a double eagle or a lady's ring, bought a magnet and a pound of mercury for cleanups in his sluice box. They needed money and he began playing cards, with Cecil backing him up in case of trouble at the rim of the firelight, where he developed a taste for writing letters.

"I'm here to catch you a bear you couldn't dream of," Cecil wrote his kids—his daughter Ottilie and his son Sam. "He's going to stand on his head. He's going to pull a cart, when I come back."

He also practiced rabbit calls with a blade of grass pressed between his thumbs until the card sharks yelled at him. By these squeals and squeaks he collected an assortment of dogs whose owners didn't realize they might soon leave town with him. He was piecing together a pack for the trip, and wanted sled dogs, dogs to chase or retrieve, fighting dogs for cannon fodder in the encounters with grizzlies that he expected, dogs to follow scent on the ground and dogs to scent the wind. They should be ready to lay down their lives to save him but be able to provide for themselves in the meantime by gobbling prairie dogs, wood rats, rock chucks as they trotted along, or survive on the buffalo fish and catfish heads he threw them. Dogs that had traveled this far were sturdy creatures and had made themselves a good pal to somebody already.

Smoky, who was smoke-colored and affectionate but suffered from epilepsy, had long paw pads like a wolf and liked to hide and race around the rest like the speedster he was and pounce at them. A Missouri cowboy had traded him for a big box of lozenges. Moose was a winter-ready, self-reliant, blue-brown dog whose last owner had signed on with the railroad. Cecil called him Moose because of his shoulders, but Sutton called him Buffalo because he'd ended up in possession of the buffaloes' heads on their ride from Cameron; went for the heads of carrion, too, seizing this item of a carcass to tug along as if it had been especially left for him. None of the other dogs could oppose him, though he was not a bully otherwise. Less moody than Smoky or White Eye, he loved Cecil with his whole heart, and Cecil spent a minute tussling with him most afternoons to stretch the kinks out of his own joints.

White Eye, the second husky, had been juggled among so many masters he had lost his sense of being attached. The first was said to have been a settler who had got bushwhacked. Then a Sioux had had him; and the bluecoats after they had killed the Sioux. And a passing packer had taken him over to use for bear medicine at campsites. In Cameron he had started to bite people. You needed to point at him as he slid toward you and produce a sound like a donkey engine—*"tut-tut-tut-tut"*—to stop him. Cecil had adopted him to prevent him from being shot. And a new dog, Coffee, was coffee-colored and deer-sized and had a collie's tail but an airedale's face. She was so gentle she let him train his trick terrier to leap onto her back and balance as she dog-trotted.

By sticking by each other, Cecil and Sutton acquired *hombre* reputations. Cecil could throw his axe like a bowie knife, as well as plaster people's sores and cuts or drench a horse, and Sutton, although one of the older citizens, was always working on a rooftree. He told the bigwigs he would be glad to on their opera house—the first they'd heard about an opera house. The higher he worked, the more meticulous he was, and he would lie up there after he finished, balancing like a mountain lion. He hadn't boasted publicly about his

circus stunts, but quite abruptly he told Driggs and the rest that
when the scaffolding for the water tower was done he'd jump off of
the top of it into a foot of water in a horse trough to celebrate the
railroad's arrival, if they paid him handsomely enough. "Forty feet
to one foot of water!"

Unfortunately, Driggs held out too long, hoping to up the bid for
his land—whereupon it became known that the Winnipeg and
Pacific Railroad was going to miss Horse Swim by three miles on
the Red Town side. The entire town, four hundred souls, dashed
down at sunrise, only to discover that representatives of the government and railroad had pegged out the key half-mile and that an
equivalent parcel of properties had been clinched by several agents
for a syndicate in Montreal for subdivision and sale, although a pair
of latecomers had horned in by dumb luck when they stumbled on
the moonlit scene.

The land recorder was there, dotting the *i*'s and crossing the *t*'s,
prepared to register any claim and to ride to Horse Swim and pace
out those boundaries as well, which were not valueless. He was a
precise individual in a black suit, wing collar, and string tie, with a
waxed mustache, pince-nez, and railroadman's timepiece and chain.
When the aggrieved speculators set up a howl in front of his tent,
he was unfazed, pointing out that he'd had no more to do with the
choice of a townsite than a dentist does with how a toothache gets
started.

"Don't holler to me. I live on my salary. Any adjudication, once it
is put in my hands, is going to be handled impartially."

Driggs, bunkoed this year all over again, took to his bed to sleep
off his disappointment, but soon among many citizens a content-
ment developed that the investors who had been their neighbors,
after "bucking the tiger," were miserable. Nobody who had been
leasing a dab of ground for a roast beef and cider stand or a notions
shop was hurting too much. They just loaded their dunnage on a
horse and moved down, bringing their boards and their poles with
them. All Horse Swim was quarried for wood for the new town,
which was to be named Bledsoeville, after a former governor-
general. Most people called it New Horse Swim, however—then
Horse Swim, for short—and there was so much to do—a depot and

water tower to build, and four thirst parlors, two livery stables, a church, the Margaret River Lodging House, and the Winnipeg and Pacific Hotel—that the bitter ring went out of even the name.

The railroad men already knew who was who, and to have befriended the Stephanssons did no one any harm. Ellen and her husband were ticketed to manage the hotel and had lots of hiring to do, as if just possibly they'd been spies. Cecil and Sutton got jobs on the water tower, as they'd wished, Sutton doing belly flops and swimming in the cold river before he went to work. "Bangin' my belly," he said. "It's so I won't flinch. If you flinch on the way down, you miss, and if you miss, you die."

The employment opportunities lent an open-ended spirit to what was going on, and the church was for a preacher who had hiked from the railhead, now scarcely twenty miles away. He hopped on a box of nails and blustered till he had the crowd ashamed they hadn't put a decent church in the first town, which was carrying things too far, as he discovered the next morning when he started baptizing souls in the river and several layabouts went upcurrent and threw in garbage, logs and dogs to disrupt the proceedings. One of these bad guys had the nerve to demand that the Reverend Zweig—his face red, his hair yellow, his eyeglasses broken and taped—apologize to his dog Scabs for kicking him. A brawl that lasted half the day was precipitated, with the hide hunters and ox whackers against the settlers, the Easterners, the Christers.

Cecil sometimes loafed at the land recorder's office in the evening to watch him wind up his proceedings. Instead of rubber-stamping the various applications, the recorder made each claimant identify himself and tell his story, and when the tale was right, it could be neighborly. A farmer, flat-nosed, mild-mouthed, registering a quarter section of prairie muck, while two boys arm-wrestled off in the corner and his small daughter, sitting beside his wife, cradled a live Leghorn chicken as if it were a doll, could wax eloquent.

Cecil, listening once, became more curious about a jug-eared, white-haired stranger with his head thrown back who was also listening. He was wrinklier but fitter than Left-handed Roy, his beard streaked white and black, and had no cloth at all in his clothes, which were expertly stitched with sinew. Cecil came alert, yet sat

loose, betraying no active interest, while he glanced at the man's
leather hand-sack, which was all of a piece and which he decided
must be a buffalo's or a moose's scrotum. When the hearing ended,
Cecil eavesdropped enough to catch him asking the "Judge" whether
the government was buying gold yet. He displayed a single cartridge casing packed with the stuff, sealed with candle wax.

The land recorder stiffened with a visible rectitude. He told him
softly that the government would do so after the first train brought
more officials in, eyeing Cecil as the only person who had overheard what was being said. He told him nothing else—not to sell it
and not *not* to sell it at one of the bars—and Cecil wasted no time
getting outside to look for the old fellow's horses.

They were easy to pick out, both carpeted with winter hair and
being of a chunky, mountain type.

"Good snow horses. That's what I want. They're like the firehouse
horses where I come from. Not the legs like a deer like these Texas
horses." He chatted with the man when he emerged.

"You like them stubby legs?"

"I'd like for you to see the ponies I have. They've got pretty colors
on them, but I don't know how good they're going to be when we
go in the snow."

The gentleman, after favoring Cecil with a fishy stare, pulled on
a boat-shaped beaver-skin hat. His only apparent armament was an
old-style water-stained Winchester .44-40 long gun, which he carried on his shoulder like a mule switch. But he seemed to notice
that Cecil, too, boasted no gun belt, as most of the characters did
who wanted to cause a stir around town—instead flourished an axe
with the head like the head of a cane in his hand—and that four
formidably obliging dogs that had been waiting now collected about
him, plus a fifth that darted out of nowhere and sprang up into his
pocket. He looked at the railroad station, already framed up; at the
skeleton of the water tower, tall against the sunset; and a sign—
GRIZZLYS MILK FORTH DRINK FREE—written in tar on a
board at the Old Judge. Across the street was Soak's Heaven—WE
CHEAT THE OTHER SUCKER AND PASS THE SAVINGS
ON TO YOU—and another establishment, Stiff's Rest:

STIFF'S REST
10 BARRELS WEDDING WHISKEY
WONT FLOAT TALLOW
1ST BBL FREE

Cecil wanted to offer him a drink but waited for him to suggest
it, so as not to appear too eager, and the old stranger did seem to
want a drink but took hold of his horses' halters.

"How far?"

"Two steps."

"Lemme see them in that case." He volunteered his name, which
was Charley Biskner.

Sutton—who had camped with Cecil by the tower—to his credit,
promptly recognized the man for what he was.

"Sir," he said, getting up from seasoning a delicious-smelling
roux. He took in the two horses' extraordinary coats of fur, the
spruce-root sewing on the pack bags that they wore, and the rumens
and reticulums from various ruminants that were attached to these,
each for some particular or eccentric purpose, and the lumps in the
old-timer's own moose-skin garments where diverse stoppered items
were pinned—bottles and tin boxes for matches, needles, pills, and
other treasures he must have almost run out of and intended to re-
plenish here.

"Goddam, that's an outfit like we need." Sutton introduced himself and gave a disquisition on how the tower was being built and
how he hoped to earn a hatful of money by jumping off of it, so
drawling and easy that the implausible sounded possible. He said he
was even training his mule to stand on his stomach, which should
be hard because he'd have to land on it."

"You'd die if you didn't? That is a trick," admitted Charley Biskner, though standing back a bit. "Your partner here caught an eye-
ful, looking at my poke."

"Well, whatever he saw, I haven't."

"What do you see?"

"I see a man who came from over there"—Sutton smiled, pointing
to the west—"instead of over there"—pointing east.

Cecil said, "I saw you had a little gold, but I didn't want to steal it. We're going to the mountains." He didn't need to explain that to rob him would defeat their purpose.

Biskner hesitated. "It's poor pickings where I am, and quite a ride." Then he looked for a box to sit on and soon was sharing their supper. Once he tasted how good that was, he ate gleefully, dipping soda biscuits in the pot liquor.

"You're feeding a man of the bush. Open a roadhouse, if you can cook like this!"

He had a weak, unused-sounding voice, faintly British in flavor, and active, liver-spotted hands. Though he claimed that he felt giddy at being back in civilization, he seemed to possess an old man's full portion of equanimity, and after Cecil's dogs had bounded over one another on command and gone to lie facing the fire from different directions, he watched Sutton recline under Laddie the mule's front hooves, and inspected a number of newspaper clippings about his circus feats—equally interested in the news to be read on the back of these.

"If you're thieves you're not run-of-the-mill." He picketed his horses and threw down his bedroll. "I like your dogs. You have a safe camp." The dozens of fires delighted him. "You know, I haven't seen a railroad for seventeen years. I ought to go out tomorrow and watch them lay the track."

In a state that gradually approached rapture at the town's bright, night buzz and bustle, he wanted a drink. They gave him a tour of the card games and whatnot and were heading for Soak's Heaven.

"Stay here," he said. "Give me some money so I won't have to open my poke. Come and get me if I don't come back."

In the morning over coffee he told them he had found a buyer for his fox skins, so he'd have some cash. "Nothing changes as fast as the mirror does. They don't make mirrors like they used to, do they? Not at all. Can't buy none of the old kind."

Cecil asked if he had heard about this hubbub from the Indians.

"I did. I usually go the other way."

"You mean to the coast?"

"We don't bring them clear to salt water," Biskner said, speaking of his catch of furs. "We sell them at a village on the river about halfway down. The riverboat comes up about twice a year, so you can buy stuff. It's still a hell of a hump, as hard as getting here was. It's not my river. It's three rivers down." He scratched with a stick in the dirt a river joining other rivers as the water flowed toward where the sea was.

"These aren't the Kluatantans?"

"No, no, not Kluatantans. There's a couple of tribes between me and the Kluatantans. Mine are Thloadennis. And we trade with the Hainainos, way over to the west of me, halfway from the high peaks to the ocean. I've never met many Kluatantans, except for prisoners. They tell me—my Indians do—that they have splattered like a bird's egg that you throw against a rock—the Kluatantans have—from what's been happening to them around here."

He scratched a map of tribes with parallel lines: "Kluatantans. Sarsis. Tlickitats. Thloadennis. Sikinks. Hainainos. And more beyond them. More mountains. And more mountains. Takes the steamboat two weeks to get upriver from salt water to the Hainainos." He moved his hand over the lines and tribes. "Squaw Paradise, right here." He grinned, indicating his own Thloadenniland, and scrubbed out everything he had drawn.

A newspaper correspondent from Chicago had arrived, and some of the boys staged a horse race to impress him. Cecil, riding Kitty, got a snootful of dust in the midst of the crush. But what pleased him was the instant understanding with which she acted on the signals of his hands on her neck. She, Fred the sorrel, and the red packhorse were tied next to Sutton's saddle mule and Biskner's two shaggy brown payload horses, all of them politicking and bobbing their heads and also getting acquainted with the dogs they would be traveling with, which were staked in a string like sled dogs opposite them, living on fish from a new trotline Sutton had strung in the river during his swims.

Though Biskner hadn't set foot on this stretch of the Margaret before, he recognized more than one of the half-breeds who were lolling around, as drunk as puffed-up pigeons, and whom he said must have been beached here by a white packer who'd used to work through the route of The Swim toward his mountains, and had been eking out an existence in three wickiups across from Red Town ever

since. Even without drinking, he was unaccustomed to tempering
his emotions, often as oblivious as if he was talking to himself.
His voice choked, his eyes teared up, when he mentioned how they
all had waited for this event twenty years ago. The beaver trappers,
settlers and prospectors who had been thinly spread from here to
tarnation had rarely encountered each other but had needed a better
method of transportation than métis' packtrains for whatever they
found or raised or grew.

"It came too late for them. For an old billy goat onion eater like
me, of course, it doesn't matter. But they just left the country. Any
man who wanted a family, wanted stores, wanted a school." He had
lost fine friends.

Though oddly shy with individuals he hadn't spoken to before—
pursing his lips, widening his eyes in reaction to their comments,
like somebody who had forgotten how diverse a bunch of people
can be—he wouldn't drink privately and wouldn't drink Indian
burner, only the regular brands with the crowd at the Old Judge,
where a glass chandelier and a double-thick flooring of buffalo rugs
had been installed and there were pigs' feet and peanuts to eat and
a great teakwood bar was on order. He loved "city life," springing
up to point with his hide knife at any new muleteer galloping into
the town square with appropriate fuss and feathers, or a dentist-
wigmaker's two-story house wagon with three baggage carts that
rolled to a stop in front of Stiff's Rest. The wagonman, wearing a
Prince Albert beard and a mustache that winged out from under his
sallow nose, disembarked and displayed a crateful of hippo ivory
he had brought to whittle false teeth out of, and sackfuls of human
hair from Europe and the Orient.

More plains parties delivered salt-cured buffalo hides for the train
to haul, and two old beaver men Biskner said he remembered from
the previous era were among the hunters, together with a few ob-
vious "curly wolves" (as real outlaws were called), riflemen who
competed all afternoon at snuffing out a candle at eighty yards.
When an outfit describing itself as the Milk River Cattle Company
drove six thousand mossy-horned, bawling beeves to the Margaret's
banks, the price of meat suddenly plummeted and another day of
horse races and gunfire at bean cans was staged to welcome the trail

boss and his sixteen punchers. Biskner, Cecil, Roy and Sutton entered the latter contest and performed about in that order, Roy's gimpy style of gumption having more charm for Cecil than for Biskner, who regarded him rather bleakly as a man who ought to have stayed home and soon might die.

Charley—they were switching to his first name from "Biskner"—as he roamed the settlement, fell in with this new trail boss, a man with little feet, a wheeze, a corded throat and mocking eyes, who carried a whip as well as a pistol everywhere and accompanied whatever he said with gestures of his trigger finger. Though they didn't know each other's haunts and didn't talk a lot, they enjoyed the same jokes, drank sparingly in the same company, and went and watched the brickworks going up, or a crew as numerous as for the water tower swinging picks to dig a borrow pit for the town levee. The cowman kept a string of five ponies for his own locomotion, so he liked this hub of horseflesh for its zany variety, as much as observing the parade of human rough diamonds and leavings. He despised only the outlaws and Indians. He would listen politely when Charley bragged about living in Squaw Paradise on the Memphramagog River in the wild mountains, but when he saw an Indian face he would ride over and point with his whip butt or trail rifle at the closest horse turd and say, "That's where an Indian shat. And look, that's where he shat again."

Abruptly in early May the surveyors arrived, to ragged cheers. The party chief strode along nimbly, with a trim haircut and no beard, smiling at the crowd without actually glancing at them, like a celebrity. He had chainmen, rodmen and transitmen to assist him, all better tempered than another batch of railroad men who had been sent ahead to build the sectionhouse. The plumb bobs on his transits were of polished brass, and he was pitching pointed stakes into the ground in alignment with the Gunter's chain, carrying a compass attached to a five-foot staff. He was elegant in his tan shirt and pants, trailed by a lovely blond matched pair of trotters hitched to a democrat, with cheesecloth screening over their noses to ward off the flies.

Snacking on river-water soup and "cowboy trout," as he called his bacon, he praised the virtues of driftwood over buffalo chips to cook with. He was clipped and cool to the investors' agents and other power players, who could be replaced much more easily than him, but was genuinely courteous to the construction foremen, and the cattle boss, the land recorder and anybody else with down-to-earth responsibilities. When a couple of stalwarts of the Old Horse Swim Landholders Association rushed to berate him, he didn't give them the satisfaction of getting mad.

"Gentlemen, we didn't take much of the prairie away from you. I had my marching orders, but if you'll just ship in about a gross of baby trees, you'll have a garden spot in no time. What counts is if you love it. That, and a sweathouse. I like a sweathouse."

He saw Charley grin at that, and grinned back. "I'm Elmer Meecham. Where do you live at?"

Charley pointed, and Meecham stared both there and at Charley again, who was notable for his Indian dress and for not slapping at the blackflies as much as other people did.

"Can you speak Tlickitat?"

Charley shrugged. "I can say 'Pass the salt.' I don't live with them. I live behind them. Their valley's like a trench—that's why it's good for you. Mine is north of that and mine is like a jumble."

"Do you want to work for me? I can pay you wages or I could pay you prize money."

"Prize money?" Charley said, as though the words had a vague ring of piracy. "No, they know you're coming. They'll pull back."

Meecham had two eastern Indians in his cadre of assistants, wore a carved Indian soapstone figure on his watch chain, and was said to sleep in a tipi when he was on the march, so he was not an Indian hater. But he did wonder whether he should expect an attack.

"No, I don't see them fighting you. Them sidehills are so steep your people will stay where they belong. They're going to miss the fishing and in the winter they'll want to come down for the elk, but the elk'll have to leave too, so they'll end up trailing along after the elk and come up and bother me in the Main Range."

Meecham pressed his offer in a casual and friendly manner, while every drunk and sober citizen strolled by. He made it plain, however, that this was a one-night stand for him, that he and the supervising civil engineer often met with rubber-neckers even out here, and that behind them an irresistible force was massing, and rivers, mountains, angry Indians and disgruntled speculators would all give way, whether or not he had the help of local old-timers such as Charley. Their hauling animals alone ate nine hundred bushels of oats a day; the steel tracks had come from the Krupp works in Germany to New Orleans and through St. Paul.

Building the Margaret River Bridge required considerable computation, although as far as possible it would be a duplicate of the Milk River Bridge two hundred miles back. He and the engineer and several lesser lights, as well as the telegraph operator—waiting now for poles and wire—huddled over the mathematics of the task at their camp by the water tower, which they shared by evening with the seventy-five-man bridging crew who hurried into town, the timbers for cribwork, pilings, sleepers and ties following in lengthy eight-horse wagonloads throughout the night.

Meecham, lounging late in a camp chair with a beefsteak that hung over the edge of his oversized plate, with pancake bread, and black tea in his cup, and a chess game going with the engineer, said, "The Peg is like the Milk. Shouldn't have too much of a bother with it." No, he'd not seen the Pacific. Hoped to, but couldn't promise himself that treat. "It's like a relay race. One bloke carries it so far, and then another so far again, and another jabs in from the opposite side of the compass. First we'll reach the Short Mountains and then the Valley of the Tlickitats and the further ranges after that." He'd got into the Shorts a year ago on his preliminary hike, he told Cecil and Charley, and another surveyor, his deputy, whom he called "the Major," or "the head-knockers," "the flying column," "the flying squadron," was scouting a passage for him ahead of that. "He's the genius. He's the major who wins the battles and I'm the general who follows after him and hogs the credit for what he's done.

"The job's open for you if you catch up with us," he told Charley. Charley pointed out that there were other old-time beaver men around, but Meecham answered equably that he hadn't seen one that he liked as much.

Cecil asked if he encountered many bears.

"When there's only two or three of us we do. But we sure don't shoot 'em. Makes them mad to shoot 'em." He promised he would try to obtain for Cecil the use of a baggage car to bring his bears home if he caught any giant ones. And he responded with the same genuine and generous sort of busy-man's curiosity to the news of Sutton's impending "jump for life"—examining the horse trough he would land in, listening to his explanation of how he would hit the shallow water on his belly and bounce up like a ball; Sutton blew it out like a blowfish to astonishing proportions—and then he shamed the members of the new Merchants Association who were standing about into going to the gunsmith's and buying a Sunday gun with a walnut stock inlaid with mother-of-pearl to put up for the stunt. He also agreed with Sutton that New Horse Swim should build an opera house, but expressed the view that any town with such a sport as him didn't really need an opera house.

Next morning at sunup, with a piece of fried bread in his hand and rain streaming down in bluish ribbons in the distance, he left so that the scraping crew, who were constructing the roadbed, would not catch up with him.

4

THE JUMP

The cowboys whooped it up with another bronc race over the buffalo grass and wild flowers, and Cecil and three Scandinavians competed at wood chopping and axe throwing. They won the chop; he won the throw. Although they wouldn't birl with him, they did know the strong man's trick of holding a six-pound axe in one outstretched fist and twitching the blade up and down above one's nose.

"Hey, you've got some murder in your bones," Sutton crowed. "But I'm going to take all the rest of the mouse out of you. I'm going to teach you showmanship so you'll be able to show off those yaller bears."

Red Town's groves were being cut wholesale for building logs, and Cecil saw Billy Buckskin, drunk and vomiting in the square. Margaret turned up too with bales of dried river fish, willow withes strung through their gill holes, bundled upon her soldier pony, as if they were muskrat skins for sale. She looked compact and muscular because of the work and the ride—her skin smooth, her expression uningratiating—but Cecil glimpsed better than before the practical advantages of taking an Indian wife.

"We sell our trees and our fish, and then in the winter what will we sell?" she said, claiming that Billy Buckskin was even talking of war. "But who would fight? It's all half-breeds, I tell him. He didn't like that. The old men are gone and the young men are gone. My son left too, but I wouldn't go."

With her fish to peddle, she laughed, however, when Sutton pretended to grope in his pocket for a coin to give her. "I'm going to get you to smoke *me,* white man!"

Charley, who was a squaw man "from the word go," as he put it, told her he had run into her husband once in the Sarsis' country and had "clocked" him when they had had some words but that he had seemed like a good fellow. It was just dumb luck he had hit the Margaret so close to the End of Track, he said. "I always trust the Maggie. You don't need victuals on the Maggie; you can dress out a perch for breakfast and a dolly varden for lunch. Put a little sour grass on it when you fry it up. I know the upper river, always had a happy experience there. It's a sweetheart, hard to drown in, not fast, no bogs.

"So you lost a flipper?" he asked Roy, dubious about his handicap, though afflicted meanwhile with a bad cough himself. Roy admitted that yes, he was flying on one wing.

"Awful hard to swim like that," Charley said. He nodded toward his horses. "That coat makes them float, fills right up with air like a caribou's. They were born in the snow, both of them. It lifts them when they swim."

His own river, the Memphramagog, was still sweeter, under Bootjack Peak, but he didn't offer to describe his place beyond saying it was potato ground. "You don't have to weed; they smother the weeds. I've dug nine feet down and never struck enough gravel to shine my shovel. You can't see the ground for the potato plants," he muttered, with his eyes aglitter at the possibilities for farming. "I'm not a metals man."

The grading gang, two hundred strong, came dundering into New Horse Swim just as the bridge builders completed their span. Employing six-mule teams pulling wooden scrapers, they raised an embankment for the roadbed four feet high and ditched it out for twenty yards on either side. Only a day behind this operation, three hundred men with one hundred seventy horses and a whole corps of wagons arrived pulling and unloading heaps of rails, spikes and ties, as well as numberless telegraph poles and big spools of wire, because three hours behind the tie outfit, twenty-five men were stringing the telegraph line.

The track layers strode the proud roadbed as if it were a royal avenue and made believe to ignore the crowd. Measuring two-foot intervals, they laid the ties, then laid each pair of rails on top of them and hammered spikes into the fishplates that fastened rail to tie. With their esprit and by long habit they were able to work without visible hurry but never pausing, and while the entire town gazed on, they crossed the just-completed bridge before nightfall, finishing their daily allotment of three miles.

The first locomotive, the "puffing billy," painted blue with its name, *Western Zephyr,* in red lettering much dirtied, and a balloon-shaped smokestack rising six feet over the engineer's cab, thereupon wailed, screeched, hissed, whistled, clanged and shuddered up to the varnished depot, which was hung with Christmas bunting. The tang of coal soot, piston grease, tamarack ties and salt pork all scented the air, and the telegraph puncher immediately went on duty in one of the railroad cars strung east from the Margaret.

Office cars, freight cars, sleeping cars, mess cars, flatcars, repair cars, and laundry lines, tent flies, bonfires. Altogether, this self-sufficient army was far less intrigued by Horse Swim than Horse Swim was interested in it. It was as populous and the railroad navvies knew that the mere whisper they were coming had brought Horse Swim into existence. Italian crews and Germans, Britishers and Irishers and Yankees—they generally ignored the knots of ox whackers and cowboys swaggering past their separate bivouacs, as well as the more modest citizens like Cecil, who was selling fish for Margaret and trotting his dogs through their repertoire of tricks as an excuse to gossip. Roy served red-eye, Sutton got rid of half a dozen pairs of medium-sized shoes, Charley borrowed clippers and called to mind how to cut hair; and although they bought the fish, the red-eye and the shoes, the railroaders were inclined to answer and not ask questions, and what they knew was the terrain they'd covered, and maybe Europe, too, but not the unknown country that loomed ahead.

The different bivouacs were mistrustful of one another, but the construction superintendent, a hard, bent, diminutive man with a voice like an elephant's trumpet, made no distinctions or concessions. He spoke rapid-fire English, and if the orders he gave were somehow carried out, he didn't care whether the people who did them understood the language and could speak it back. For several weeks he had refused transportation to anybody who quit, but now that they had reached this populated spot with new men lining up for work, he announced that anybody who wanted to could climb in a flatcar and roll east "when the *Zephyr* goes for sticks."

There was gunfire that night, but the Winnipeg and Pacific's own doctor handled the casualties. With booze, the gangs of trackmen put on a range war for a couple of minutes—Yankees and Germans and Irishers—until the locomotive steamed up and down with its headlight on them and the superintendent yelling imprecations above the screaming whistle and wheels. The card games were a zoo of unfamiliar faces, yet even so, Sutton, usually cautious at cards, saw his prudence fail him and lost the two well-shod and fattened packhorses which he'd collected for his previous winnings and for which he had already sewn individual fittings.

Next morning, with a vengeance, he was fortifying his back and shoulders, doing belly flops into the Margaret, bulging his middle as he hit the water and blowing like a whale to vent the pressure. Cecil meanwhile amused Charley by hypnotizing frogs from the river by stroking their undersides. When Charley didn't understand what that might have to do with hounding homicidal bears, he persuaded a range bull from the Milk River herd to approach him to have its forehead scratched.

"I wish the fish would do it"—Cecil laughed—"but we're crooks with animals. They trust you and then what happens?"

"They trust you and you ride them into a snowstorm, you ride them into quicksand," Charley agreed.

A siding was laid and an entrepreneur named Jack Willey, after managing to get four boxcars loaded with dry goods and toolware sited next to the Winnipeg and Pacific Hotel, advertised a good-will sale for late afternoon. He had his own cylinder press, and as soon as the flyers appeared, Sutton chased him down and for fifty dollars in trade goods offered to jump off of the water jug just beforehand so that the crowd that congregated for the jump would stick together and move from one event to the other.

Mr. Willey was relaxing in Ellen Stephansson's saloon with an arm in a sling and his neck supported by a neck brace and his left big toe, black and blue, poking out from a hole he had cut in his boot, which also had a sheath knife tucked in it. A sly and shifty man with an ill-fitting grin, he was undiminished in his energies despite these infirmities. He glanced at the Stephanssons to see if Sutton was for real; then suggested five bucks would more than pay for any benefit to him.

Ellen, who was mindful of who had been her friends in Old Horse Swim, interceded, however. She sent for the straw boss at the water tower, the Merchants Association head, the chief cop, the land recorder, the railroad construction and section superintendents, and the new bank's manager and provided complimentary drinks so they could oil their tongues and plan a proper celebration. After batting pros and cons about, they decided to give everyone a two-hour holiday at suppertime, have some speeches, and do it all today so the track layers could move out bright and early tomorrow. Sutton in the meantime began huddling in a hustlers' alliance with Mr. Willey. Side by side they muttered to each other, sizing people up without moving their lips.

Sutton was to make most of his money from bets and from a purse of greenbacks, coins and chits tossed into the construction superintendent's ten-gallon hat by a grateful public at the event. He sent Roy to ride quickly to Red Town to "bring the old woman if she went back," and Cecil to circulate around and wager whatever they had against whoever would bet odds on his death. In a black shirt and cut-off trousers, he poured a depth of water that measured from the heel of his hand to his armpit into the horse trough, which he'd first had carried from the water tower to the square in front of the hotel. He did his last exercises there, wearing a shrewd and baiting look and with a spring in his step, as though he might be the agent for the man who was risking his life, and not the man himself.

Then he had the wagon with the trough riding on it return to the tower, and climbed up and hammered a board platform to stand on, and tacked a Union Jack above. He also started the donkey engine at the water pump, just for the attention its noise got, and climbed to the platform again to inspect his arrangements, inviting people to come up on the wagon and see how shallow the water was, but vouchsafing no explanation for how he hoped to dive so far and survive.

The difficulty for Cecil in nailing down commitments was that he had so little collateral to bet with and couldn't ask Charley to stake part of his gold dust in their behalf. Risking his own grubstake, he realized how much he was counting on the company of his friend anyway—that he would be reluctant to ride off alone with Charley or Roy for any purpose more ambitious than sight-seeing. Most of the original Horse Swim personalities wouldn't bet against Sutton's life, if only for reasons of sentiment; they said they'd fatten the kitty instead. The Milk River cattle boys, possibly because they took so many tumbles themselves and scrambled up safely afterwards, seemed to be believers, too, but put up even money that he was going to break something.

"If it's a *finger,* you pay," they said.

This issue was arcane enough that Cecil went to check. The trough was not much wider than Sutton's arms would reach when he flung them out, and if one smacked the edge it would be shattered, and god knows how they would travel if that happened. But Sutton claimed he wouldn't even bust a finger. He told Cecil to take any odds of better than two to one that he was going to die.

Margaret showed up with a basket of crayfish, which she'd remembered from their visit was a favorite of Sutton's. Although she was sedate and dignified once she had her feet on the ground, she was a lively rider, almost girlish, the way she held her legs straight down. Her horse was iron-colored, heavyset, and had an honorable touch of asthma, like an aging cavalry mount that had been brought into the territory by a white man, but it had also acquired the sulky, hard-bitten, underprivileged air of a real Indian pony. She said only a few were left of the Red Town herd and she didn't believe the Indian boy watching them with a quiver of arrows on his back would be able to prevent the whites from stealing the rest for long.

Cecil suggested she call her beast Mike, after her husband.

Startled, she decided to laugh.

"What was Mike like?" he asked, a little jealous.

"Oh, sometimes he was mean. Most of the time he wasn't," she said, both leery and exhilarated, looking at the dozen things going on at once.

Mr. Willey had removed his neck brace and the sling under his arm, like a man changing costumes. He clambered onto the wagon with the horse trough on it in front of the water tower and smiled confidingly.

"Say, boys, if you screwed up where you came from, here's a new town that you can try and be a decent citizen in. We're giving it a Limey's name so's all the Limeys'll take good care of us. Bledsoeville. God bless you and God bless us and God bless him. We've got some boys who can shoot the red off a blackbird's wing and also some the sheriff chased out of the last place they lived in, but here's a fellow that knows how to do something that nobody else does—nobody anywhere. Give him a neighbor's attention, please."

He held up the walnut-wood, mother-of-pearl Sunday gun, and the Stephanssons' stablehand led out a pig-colored packhorse that Sutton had won and then had lost at cards and now was going to be part of his prize. People were running to witness the feat, while Sutton lit up a smoke and sat on his heels to allow them time. Stretching one leg out, he touched his nose to his knee for exercise, and accepted a slug of whiskey, and lifted his shirt to demonstrate how he rippled his stomach muscles to help it down. He did a handstand, and stood on his elbows for a while.

"Bangin' my belly. But that water is going to take the punishment, not me," he informed the closest well-wishers. "I take my time going off because I like it up there and I may not have another chance. It's a long way down. That water glows below you like a crystal ball, but you're not real sure what it says."

Cecil, having placed all of their money in bets, walked around the crowd with his hat in hand. He wagered this money, too, on the outcome, giving the land recorder the cash to hold. If anybody was hooting for blood, it may have been some of the railroad men.

Shouldering one another, they didn't know who was jumping from where to what, but—Poles and French Canadians and Austrians—were glad to have some action to drink to instead of glowering up-track or down-track at Irishers and Italians and whatnot they couldn't talk to; and they were ready to bet on a very bad end for whichever local clown was going to perform.

Charley, whose first beamish delight at being in the city had waned—who was saying he missed the meat of his caribou, and who had become somewhat oblivious to what went on in the streets, though he pricked up his ears whenever four talky geese winged overhead—got angry.

"What is this? Those bastards think our chum's going to kill himself?" He hardly paused. To Cecil's astonishment, he unlimbered his wallet and took pinches of gold dust and rolled them into cigarette papers and offered these to cover bets of such a sort. It signified that he was counting more particularly on Sutton to survive. He would need protection, heading home, now that it would become general knowledge that he had gold.

Sutton, still at ground level, blew out his ribbed, roly-poly stomach one more time. But, as he climbed the ladder, he seemed to shed weight. In his black shirt, poising in earnest on the diving board, he looked limber, and the sun threw his shadow far out. Half a thousand people had collected, and Cecil, stationed with Roy and Charley next to the wagon, had been inviting them to step up and feel for themselves how shallow the water was. A procession of spectators did so, gazing up at Sutton near the rim of the tower, forty feet higher than the wagon bed. For all his grace and assurance, he reminded Cecil dismayingly of the Gros Ventre standing on the gaudy yellow behind of the thirsty-tongued oxen a month ago, both of them wearing ropes around their necks.

"All bets down?" Sutton yelled.

Mr. Willey launched into a spiel about the sale he was holding. . . . "Straightaway after we see whether our good neighbor breaks his neck. But now let's watch this brave man who's come all the way out here so's he could jump sixty feet into a narrow barrel. You are seeing a headliner, gentlemen. You may be plenty sharp with your ponies or your sledgehammers. You may be a good wagon boss. But this fellow has come straight from performances with the Forepaugh Circus in Chicago and St. Louie to jump seventy feet into that narrow grave with two drinks of water in it."

"All bets down? Goin' to get you wet," Sutton warned.

"No fooling, folks. I've never seen this anywhere," added Mr. Willey with a telling nod.

Sutton, staring off at the prairie, asked a final time about the bets—until he heard Willey's sharp auction-house voice say yes. Then, spreading his arms and looking down, he fixed upon the dab of water like a hawk above a rabbit, locking in.

"All bets in hand. All away," he said. He dived outwards, as flat as a descending swan, belly foremost but falling unbelievably fast, holding his spread-eagled position clear down to the tremendous smack he made on the water, an impact which not just his belly but his arched chest, arms, thighs, hands, feet, neck and chin absorbed. He hit so hard that Cecil staggered when hit by the sheet of water that was thrown out by the concussion, as though he himself was injured. Many in the crowd were soaked; many checked themselves for injuries. And the hatfuls of money were soaked.

Sutton delayed standing up, but when he did, rubbing his stinging stomach, the water poured off him, shining like a set of medals. Removing his shirt so that the sun could dry him, and streaming water, he raised his arms to show that he was alive and whole. After he hopped down from the bed of the wagon, that wetness still marked him magically.

"Ol' partner, I guess we're on our way," he murmured to Cecil, massaging the sting from his stomach. A bunch of gunsels were firing off their thumb-busters, and Cecil had brought along the beat-up bugle to blow. Most of those who'd bet against the feat hadn't entirely understood what they would see and were so flabbergasted by the reality of it they hadn't begun hurting yet.

"Holy Jesus!" Charley bubbled, already picturing what his Thloadennis might be willing to do for somebody who turned up on their river and could accomplish such a stunt.

"Now all you neighbors, there's not a town west of London, England, that's watched a thrill like that," shouted Mr. Willey, while Sutton pumped the hands of navvies, bosses, dignitaries, settlers, accepting the cheers with that manner of somebody who lives by them and yet after an interval pretends to turn them aside. Till the sun dried him he was a marked man, and when the hatfuls of coin and currency had been handed over, he went around buying back assorted pieces of property he had had to sell to pay for his losses at poker.

There were speeches at the siding, a jeroboam of champagne for those next to the speakers' bench, and two cowboys did Ocean Waves, Zigzags and Butterflies with their waxed lariats.

"Boys, the dust on the stuff is free. We won't charge you for that. Don't miss the boat. Who'll say five dollars and go? Factory new. This is Christmas in May. You start her and we'll stop her. I don't mind dying poor, but I want to die honest. I'll give you the profit on her, boys. These sod-busters turn a furrow two foot wide," Willey perorated from the station platform with the assistance of a hired hand who rolled out wheelbarrows piled with ploughshares and colters.

A team of horses was hitched against a yoke of oxen, a test the oxen of course won; and Cecil threw his seven dogs against a single Percheron and lost. Then there was a tug-of-war in which supposedly a hundred railroad men were to be pitted against a hundred locals (if anybody could be said to be local). But extra section-hands and extra sod-heavers kept joining the pull, and though the locals weren't outnumbered, neither were they used to pulling together. The rope passed over a fire, to compel the team that lost to suffer for it, and the railroad men were winning the pull. The Horse Swimmers had just begun a helpless rush into the fire, when the rope broke and half of them fell down and one man broke his collarbone.

"Boys, I may be paid to yell, but I'm not here to rook ya," Willey confided in the meantime. "We were way under the money on those Queensware bowls. Now we got stovepipes. Don't rent the sonofabitch—we want to sell her! Boys, it's only money. Awfully cheap at that price. Yes! Yes! Yes!" he wheedled and needled as sharp as a whiplash as each bid rose. Intense or giddy as though in combat, a farmer would decide no. "Oh, I lost him! Mark it cheap. We lost on that one. I'm going to need a drink tonight. If we go much further

under the money I'm going to lose my job," Willey complained to
the crowd. When one of the settlers emitted a laugh, he leaned forward gleefully—"I'll bet you your farm!" But even as he spoke, the
Western Zephyr was puffing into town again with a line of boxcars
consigned to the bootlegger who ran Soak's Heaven.

Cecil pegged the pig-colored, short-necked freighting horse with
Sutton's mule and his own sorrel Fred and packhorse Red and Roy's
cayuse and Charley's hammer-headed, stubby-legged pair, and rode
Kitty out a couple of miles to take another look at Horse Swim's
common herd of maybe twenty dozen miscellaneous beasts that
weren't being used. A few cowboys were usually hanging around
to tell him which might be for sale and kid him that the only reason he was in the market at all was for a bride price when he got to
where the Injuns lived.

He'd brought oats and circulated on foot among the animals that
would stand still for the sake of munching those. Some nuzzled
him, and he leaned gently against the chests of the likeliest of them,
listening to the beat of their bloodstreams, sniffing their discomforts,
the pain of their bit sores and aching gaskins, and sidestepping the
kickers and the biters meanwhile.

"You want a dobbin, not a workhorse," one of the cowboys protested. But Cecil herded the animals that caught his interest on
Kitty, watching for lameness, and saddled and loped several and
tried them at a foxlike trot, and finished at sundown by singling
out three that were good enough that the same puncher admitted they
were going to cost him something.

Sutton, the toast of the town, was cherubically drunk, sitting with
Margaret, Charley and Roy at the Stephanssons' eatery. Margaret,
rather like Charley on his first night in town, seemed both wary and
happy, though trying to preserve a solemn demeanor. As a trader's
wife, she had learned her capacity in liquor and was sipping hers.
Apparently her daughter had obtained a chance for her to work as
a translator for the railroad in the months ahead, and Margaret was
carefully teasing Sutton to the effect that she might do that. Roy,
who was raspier when he was in his cups, agreed that that sounded
best, but Sutton ignored the whole proposition grandly.

Charley as an old squaw man accepted Margaret's presence immediately; in fact was sorry to hear that her pretty daughter was going to stay behind. The girl, who sat at another table with her carpenter friend, had long black hair and a likable mouth. She had Indian features but was paler than an Indian woman; her skin looked bleached, unnatural, wraithlike, next to Margaret's strong fig-color. It blurred her in a way, at least to Cecil's eye, though he also liked her looks. Dressed in a blue shirt and pressed pink cotton pants from Willey's supplies, she had a becoming air of prosperity and wasn't too shy to say she had admired Sutton's jump.

Sutton embarrassed everybody by telling Cecil that when Margaret had "smoked" him after his triumph, "she spit just like you'd spit tobacco in a spittoon."

Margaret had to laugh—he was, after all, making fun of himself as much as her—but stood up, sleepy, with a comfortable look, as if she would be able to swallow not simply him but herself and him, and allowed him to hug her hips.

"We're leaving in the forenoon. Come back," he said.

Very late that night, at camp, Charley poured the gold out of his cartridge casings to dispel for them the mystery of how much he had. Four years' worth, as he stated thickly, and a dollar a day for those years.

"That's what I aim for. It's like wages. There ain't too much of it—no pay strike where I live. You pan a week and you'll get seven dollars."

When Roy, although swaying, inquired how he could be sure there was no concentration roundabout, Charley insisted that it had been looked at. The sluices, the long toms, the trestles, "the water-works" which would turn such a project into more than a low-pay show, he hadn't gotten around to. He was a trapper, and by the fire-light, with a load of drink in all of them, he made each man swear the Trapper's Oath.

"It's not *of your time,*" he conceded loudly. "But it matters to me. And we're all drunk so we must be careful."

Telling them to take their shoes off, he had them stand with their rifles at their sides. With two or three false starts and some confusion, he demonstrated how he wanted each man to balance on one leg and hook the big toe of the other one over the trigger of his gun while covering the muzzle with his mouth.

"Tastes like a coffin. Now," he announced. "Are you too drunk? We don't want to lose one. Can you lunkheads do that without shooting your damn head off?"

All asserted that they could.

"Do it."

They tried the position, after watching again what a deep bite of the barrel he took—until the muzzle must have touched his tonsils. Then when he was satisfied that they had learned that part, he rested his chin on the muzzle, still with his big toe hooked across the trigger, and instructed them to pledge as follows:

"I swear I'll blow my brains out if I ever double-cross anybody at this fire here!"

Individually and vociferously, each repeated the vow, in the hot orange leaping light, with their chins touching their guns, and mouthed their muzzle barrels both before and afterwards.

In the morning, quite chipper—although he said a friend of his had gone to town one year and drunk so much "his bladder stopped on him. It burst; he died"—he accepted a taste of Roy's red-eye "to get the rat out of my mouth." He avowed to Cecil, "I've seen 'em do it. You don't believe me? It might not be infallible in civilization, but if you toss some yo-yo out in the bush who's left his buddy with a broken leg and taken all the kit and catch and grub they had, and he goes off alone all winter in the snow and all summer in mosquito season, he's going to remember what he said he'd do. Can't throw his ammunition away or he'll starve. So he'll keep remembering it so many times that sooner or later he'll put a bullet in and bite that gun mouth just like he promised he'd do."

Charley had doubled the money he'd wagered on Sutton, so after transacting a private arrangement with the banker, he shopped and stowed away his numerous purchases, as attentive as a magpie. Flour, rice, sugar, tea, coffee, salt for pickling, a Peacemaker revolver and a short saddle-rifle, fishline, matches, a cauldron and smaller pots, three hundred fifty candles, many spools of thread and bolts of cotton, some wire screening and tin sheeting, an oil lamp he intended to try with bear grease, two suits of long johns, a demijohn of brandy, a four-gallon keg of double-strength Barbados rum, several crates of dynamite, a padlock and hinges, and various boxwood, horn and ivory combs and paperback mirrors and flints, awls, scissors and chisels for the Indians who visited him.

His special pleasure was the sacks of seeds he bought—sifting them and smelling them. His turnips and pole beans had been getting scruffy and his onions, "a trapper's caviar," had shrunk to pebbles from inbreeding. It gratified him that these were "Atlantic provisions," not from the Pacific boats that sometimes after a year's delay supplied the trader on the Hainaino River whom he ordinarily did business with. He mentioned that he often had a problem finding enough horse feed for just his two during the winter and said they shouldn't plan on moving into his valley but head elsewhere once they had reached the mountains. Nevertheless, Cecil brought in the extra animals he had chosen and bought a fourth, a cat-hammed buckskin, to carry Roy's gear.

Roy's still had been smashed by unknown parties during the night—either another bootlegger or a Temperance man—so he started beating his gums, bewailing his fate, and proclaiming how tough and fit he was, afraid that Charley, sober, might strand him here, not believing he could survive a trip towards the high peaks and over to the western side. He was "a single-blanket, jackass-hauling prospector," he said. "A pick and a pack and a burro's back. Where I come from you climb for water and dig for wood. You build your fire with roots because that's all there is for vegetation in the desert, and you climb for water because it bakes away before it ever has a chance to run downhill."

Charley grunted sourly that he was not a miner, himself; he was a trapper.

Emulating him, they added roofing paper, window paper, mattocks, adzes, pinch bars, a mouth organ, a dutch oven and a collapsible stove of thickened tin and sheet iron to their stores, as well as plenty of skillets and hatchets, hats and woollen items of clothing, and loads of petty goods for trading. Then Margaret, soldierly on her brown soldier-horse, led a white pony they hadn't seen before, which carried her bedroll and possessions, to join them. She had her husband's Sharp's Big Fifty buffalo gun and also an older Spencer rifle and a funny, antiquated, five-barreled pistol called a Pepperbox. Because her daughter had ridden with her from Red Town leading a dappled beast bundled with bales of meat and fish and dusty furs, Cecil hoped for a moment that the girl had changed her mind—but no, the two of them had divided what they owned and she was going to stay in town, sell what she had, and make a new life with her Scotch carpenter.

"We had a big to-do, a big parley. Everybody's left. Everybody had to decide what they wanted to do. It won't be long before *Ninstints* burns up," Margaret told them dramatically. The settlers were already setting their lines of property stakes within sight of it. "They're angry that they're scared of us."

Roy muttered that he'd like to know what white man that white horse of hers had used to belong to and where his sorry grave was. But Sutton laughed at that idea, and Charley said, "The West is a great place for turnover."

Even in the rush of packing they regretted the notice their departure was attracting from Horse Swim's curly wolves and sharpshooters and crop-eared loafers—unsavory buckaroos that looked "so crooked they couldn't piss a straight hole in the snow," as Charley put it, though he was marveling, too, at what a foursome of odd ducks he'd linked up with. "Probably it's inevitable, a queer old soul like me that's run off to the mountains." Four hundred miles to the west at a crossing on a river called the Rabbitskin was a convenient place to stop and wait for anybody that was trailing them. "Meantime," he said, "I'm the golden goose that ain't laid his egg yet. Any man'd be a fool to shoot me till he knows where I live."

In the afternoon, when they had finally saddled up and were prepared to lead all the horses over the railroad bridge—Charley having bought another one right off Main Street—Cecil, he, Sutton, Roy and Margaret rode into the square, feeling hungry-looking from having skipped their lunch, and drew up at the benches in front of Soak's Heaven where the worst outlaws hung out.

"Awful rough, boys!" Roy hollered at them, with his pistol out. The rest held a rifle in each hand.

"If you track us we got the powder to put you under," Sutton said to this group that he most disliked from all the midnight card games.

Cecil, flourishing his two rifles as upright as umbrellas and with a grin so wicked that he loved the feel of it, told them, "It would be my real pleasure." And although he could see the broken veins in the nose of the grifter he was speaking to, the discouragement in the man's rheumy eyes and humped back, and the actual skull his face would rot into during the course of a summer's weather on the open plains where there would be no obstacle to killing him, it was true.

Old Charley, pursing his wrinkles, said, "I have got about a thousand Indians that will want to talk to you between here and where I go."

"Well la-de-da. Says Hiawatha," one of these Texans—all beard and sideburns—standing up with both hands on his gun belt, yelled back at him.

But there were quick, affectionate goodbyes from a number of citizens.

Part 2

The
Prairie

5

THE MARGARET

The smell of raw tar on the bridge made the horses sneeze, but everybody was grateful not to have to swim. Just beyond the west bank of the Maggie were wire fences and sod houses, then a few miles of stakes and tents, and then only prairie. Margaret was singing softly, though her position among them, Cecil thought, was as precarious as Roy's.

Charley, once he got well clear of the big city, sat up straight in his saddle and began to crow. His rhubarb grew as big around as your wrists. His parsnips were as sweet as candy and he made wine from them, he said. His carrots swelled so fat he had to dig them up before they started strutting around like Margaret's rabbit hound.

Cecil was glad to see his own dogs form a phalanx in front of the horses with an excitement equal to his. Smoky talked to him not with barks but in a human style—"Oooh, oooh, oooh"—and much as he'd expected, a mutt convention of other dogs dashed out of New Horse Swim, abandoning house and home for the adventure of racing after them. Besides, the bridging crew had turned over a pet white billy goat that had been their mascot to Sutton in celebration of his feat; and the Milk River Cattle Company foreman, a steer that mooed as it walked or bawled as it trotted.

A cloudburst soaked them, with a nagging chilly breeze that tagged after it as if to dampen their enthusiasm. Yet they traveled smartly, Charley being so accustomed to riding alone he couldn't bear the sight of anybody in front of him. He even shouted at the villages of prairie dogs to clear out of his way. Eager to be home, he said he had a lake near him so large that only caribou lived along one shore and only elk along the other, and at the outlet, so he claimed, you could pick up chunks of coal from broken ledges of the stuff hanging overhead and make your night fire of them.

At sunset they toasted one another with branch water, after butchering the steer, which had proven to be a nuisance. All this meat produced a sanguine mood, and the moon was like a sickle. Charley had scooped up a tricolored kitten for luck as they left town. They'd also been given a camp mouser cat, which crouched on top of the pig-colored packhorse's load on the move and had faced down the dogs with its back to the fire when they called a halt. Besides Cecil's two stalwart malemutes, White Eye and Moose, and the coyote-sized, smoke-colored Smoky, and Coffee, a loving but snappish airedale-collie cross, and the heavy-furred, mild, dark retriever named Sally that he had adopted lately, and a shepherd whose loyalties Cecil had succeeded in preempting only in the past day or so from the German grocer who owned him, there were five or six other stray dogs prancing and slinking around—a tattered, gay, short-haired, short-legged collection he doubted would survive very well in the mountains and would have liked to send back except that their passions had been aroused. His trick terrier rode in his jacket pocket or with its front feet planted on the saddle horn. On the ground, it liked harassing Moose by threatening to nip his lips and ears, before leaping safely into Cecil's pocket again.

Charley chatted about the water meadow in front of his cabin where the hay grew tall and which he drowned every couple of years by damming the brook to kill the seedling trees. He told about his first walk into the mountains from the Pacific; how on the beach the surf had been taller than he was even on a sunny day; and how a whale had stranded itself near his first camp and so many grizzlies had come to eat off it he had had to move. He would always remember the whitecaps washing half over them as they chewed on the blubber and fins. He had lived in a cave for a month or two after hiking inland for about three weeks and meeting his first wild Indians. This was on a side river called the Grease, and he had brought in a bad case of grippe which killed a good many of his hosts, but he cured the rest with paregoric, turpentine, moonshine and sweat baths.

"I was better than the medicine man. They didn't understand I was responsible for it, because if a man breaks his arm, you don't break your arm from being with him. They believed it's a bad song in you that makes you sick. You had to sing it out. And that made for lots of widows. But I was doing fine until they found a dead white man on the Hainaino who had tipped over on his raft and drowned, and when they went over him with a fine-tooth comb, they saw that he had crabs and scabs and a cock and balls on him just the same as them. So after that they didn't look at me like I was different."

He'd once fallen asleep on a skin-boat trip down the Grease River himself and had gone over a dang-garn falls but had crawled out of the water in satisfactory shape; then the next day had stepped on a rotten log and broken his goddamned ankle. "It's the little stumbles that kill you."

And what if Charley did die suddenly? Cecil wondered. Would they turn back? An old man still so much in the midst of life could die in an instant when you least expected it.

Logy the next morning from eating heavily and sleeping deeply, they were silent in the enormous landscape. But Charley on his shaggy pony—which turned roan-colored as the sun rose—flapped his arms whenever marsh birds took flight ahead of them. Wordlessly he caught the waltz-master's beat of a heron's wings and the profile of its neck bent back prudishly, as well as the flittering rush of the plentiful ducks, the bowsprit look of the sandhill cranes, and the projectile speed of the loons, whose necks were stretched out like a goose's when they flew but who held their heads lower than the capsule of their bodies.

Sutton had slept with Margaret, though she pretended that he hadn't. She was happy, however, and seemed to have accepted Charley wholeheartedly as their guide. When Cecil asked her if Charley reminded her of her husband on the trail, she said not at all.

"Mike always went with the Indians. He let them show him. He never went alone."

That second night they found a grove of balm-of-gilead trees where they could enjoy a log bonfire and bake a crane Cecil had shot, as well as corn-dodger bread, in the hot embers. The horizon was steel blue, extending coldly toward the years of exploring that Cecil envisioned lay in store for him, and yet he couldn't have conjured up anyplace he would rather have been. He had dawdled too long, postponing this trip, and in his striped hickory shirt, soft green woodsman's hat, droopy in the brim, and gray wool pants reinforced with a patch of colt's hide in the seat, with a new navy six-shooter and a lever-action Winchester sighted for game at a quarter-mile, he looked the part he wanted to play. Although he mostly pictured the traveling rather than the grizzly-wrestling that might occur, he knew that every fifty miles of slippery grass he rode over was going to engender an increasing recklessness in him.

Charley's custom was to grab a couple hours' start at dawn before sitting down pleasantly to breakfast after the sun had dried the dew—searing a strip of beefsteak and heating tea. He had a funny scarecrow's sunshade made of bark on willow withes that he attached to his saddle, rain or shine, for the midmorning ride. And when he needed to relieve himself, he did so with an important air, like a wolf marking a bush, and picked some vantage point for the purpose if he could, gazing about, as a bobcat would. He allowed time again for a sensible lunch, with a nap afterwards for the sake of his heart, and picked wild leeks at the streamsides to chew with his meat, saying he used to cook sweet-flag root with birch-tree sugar for his lady friends, but now that he was just an old onion-eater he didn't care how his breath smelled. Being sturdy in old age he believed was a sign of how well you were built throughout, not just your heart.

"You get a canker in you if you get down-in-the-mouth. You know how bad it tastes after you throw up? Well, that's what's inside you if you get discouraged, waiting to rot you out."

They'd paralleled the Margaret's west bank for four days, and then a tributary for about as long, swinging close to the water at night for the comfort of a driftwood fire, but didn't have to stop to

hunt, because by suppertime they would have come across a goose or
two with a broken wing and Roy, who had the only shotgun, would
have shot some rabbits in front of the dogs to boil with potatoes—
saving the rinds of these to plant. Sutton fished at dusk if he wasn't
too tired or the flies too fierce. He caught the oily little panfish
known as lamplighters, and fat-tailed trout that in an access of enthusiasm had slapped the hook into their mouths. Rubbing himself
as he had before his jump, he said he could live off the fat on his
belly like a bear all winter no matter where they ended up. He
loved the ponds they passed; would look at a pond with sunlight on
it, the wind nicking the surface, and might rein up and swim with
the dogs if the air was warm—he finally adopted the duck dog as
his own.

Circling ponds that were alive with birds, they found the grass at
the edges crackly with eggshells. The dogs gobbled addled eggs that
had failed to hatch and motherless ducklings in the shallows; also
baby ground squirrels, gophers and other tidbits the lobo wolves and
prairie foxes were not numerous enough to keep track of at this busy
season of the year. At one they noticed a corral of brush and stones
such as the Kluatantans employed at midsummer moulting time to
catch the waterfowl that were unable to fly. Farther along, a lightning fire had burned miles of creek bank before petering out, and in
the midst of this blackened ground the prominent nest of two cranes
remained, situated on the still-steaming mound of wet vegetable ma-
terial they had constructed to support it. Indeed, a parent was still
loyally brooding the roasted eggs and only reluctantly, with mournful croaks, flew away.

The three-colored kitten died from a fall from the pack box where
it had been stowed, but the tiger mouser, being fully grown and
careful to establish fastidious relations with the steed on whose high
load she rode, regularly pounced off to devour small rodents that
fled from under the horses' feet, then sprang back on. And the white
billy goat, by his prissy, tough and humorous ways, had likewise
chipped out a niche for himself. He'd learned never to break into a
run in front of the dogs, only to trot behind them, so that they didn't
get the idea that his haunches were meat. Moose had taken a liking
to him. Moose menaced him head-on, even mouthing the back of

his neck, while the billy hooked Moose again and again in the throat with his horns. Moose, with his eyes glittering at this, liked it strong but not too strong, and would sidle off when his throat hurt, and dive in low like a sheep dog to have another go, grabbing the goat's leg in his mouth. But the billy answered this tactic with side hooks to the ribs.

Their aim was to strike the Ompompanoosuc, another trunk river like the Maggie into whose upper reaches Biskner said his Memphramagog flowed. A trail as faint as a wisp occasionally indicated where an Indian band had crossed, and other whispery paths forked off toward the Short Mountains, whose hunchbacked profile could be seen to the southwest, or to former buffalo camps which had witnessed more traffic when the first hide hunters had arrived.

They'd seen scanty evidence of buffalo, till early one morning Cecil kicked Kitty hard and caught up with a cow and calf as they ran and laid his rifle into the cow's ear and blasted her.

They camped on the spot to dress her out, wrestling her legs up and down while Charley cut from the jaw to the tail on the belly side, though Margaret argued for skinning her Indian-style, from the hump down. Margaret and Sutton set up a frame to dry what they wanted to carry with them, and Cecil managed to rope the frightened calf with a greenhorn's throw. Tying its stubborn legs, he breathed into its nostrils awhile, at Margaret's suggestion, on the chance that the next day it might be willing to follow him like a new mother. The skin soaked in a tub of ashes and brains to make parfleche.

Cecil hefted the weighty head, the horns, the beard and the hooves of the dead buffalo. With her head crushing his knees, he could feel within his own eyes the angles of vision she must have had and imagine her powers of hearing and scent. Her eyes looked dead, but not her nostrils or her ears, and even a man's dim nose could fathom what a horse or a dog smelled when asked to pursue so formidable a beast.

Having spitted the ribs on sticks leaning over the fire and watched these char, they gnawed on them with meat-drunk grins. The grateful dogs, several of whom were already limping, consumed the suet and the offal until they couldn't lift their heads from their paws.

Barefoot, Cecil went to check on the horses' hobbles and on their back trail, although no gold hunters would be likely to be pressing after Charley so soon. He felt as proprietary about the trip as if it had been undertaken solely for him, yet lonesome, too, when they broke the routine to rest for a day. He wanted to tell his kids about shooting the buffalo, and when he came back and tried to feed grass to the red-furred calf and it sucked his fingers, he thought about them some more, because they would have liked to play with it.

"Means something to me, that buffalo! My first alone," he told Charley.

"By gosh, I guess so. You got a lot of firsts ahead of you. When I walked in from the coast I had seals and porpoises swimming right alongside me. I was walking and they were swimming, but they were headed where I was and the rivers are steeper on that side, you know, so you have the feeling there's more behind it that you're on your way to. Little rivers coming in morning, noon and night, which can be a nuisance, but you'd see a dozen eagles in the trees anywhere in salmon season, and the porpoises chasing the salmon, and seals plopped on the rocks as fat as turtles, watching the porpoises hop, and those great big red bears everywhere, red from eating salmon, ripping out into the water to try and grab themselves a seal."

Cecil was going to suggest that at least the clouds couldn't have been better than the shapes here—which were engaging each other in a drama of lions and giants—but Charley went on, almost as though to steal Cecil's thunder: "I don't guess I've been happier—that pure water washing all the poisons out of me from the filthy foundry, and I'd been eating oysters on the beach."

He said he'd arrived in the West as pale as porridge from Fredericton, New Brunswick, where he'd labored, like his father, in a pipe foundry and the filings had tangled up his lungs. "I was losing weight like it was water. It's funny how your old man can work at something and never be bothered by it, but the doctor will tell you it's going to kill you." Besides that reason for being miserable, he said he had proposed to a young lady that she marry him and she'd turned him down. "And I went right round to the big knickknack shop next to the bank and bought the best damn rocking chair they had and had it delivered to her so she could rock her life away, and I went and caught a ship and I've never been that miserable since."

It had been on Kettle Island, at the mouth of his seal and salmon river, where he'd run into the first Indian lady who had caught his fancy. "She was the trader's wife. She was a Haida crossed with Russian blood and she could make a piano talk or lay out a dandy meal for everybody, and after that she'd put her husband's feet in her lap and cut his toenails for him in front of everybody." So that was where he'd got the idea of looking for a few Indian girls who were willing to do the same for him when he got to the Thloadennis' territory, he said.

Cecil went to check on the horses again, tired of the old man's vanity and envious of his friend Sutton for Margaret's company. How would the winter work out when they all got cabin fever together? Sutton rode like a cool rock-bottom soul with a good traveler's hardy slouch, yet he could be overtaken by slowpoke spells— a sort of toadish gloom—that didn't accord with Cecil's desire for steady progress. There was a hole in him somewhere, a whiff of gnomish sadness when he thought he was unobserved. Him and his mismatched brown beard, bald head, hairy chest and glum, bald stomach.

Sorry that he hadn't worn his shoes, Cecil was rubbing his bruised feet beyond the knoll when Margaret joined him. He was surprised, but she sat down without a word and let him hug her, laughing only at how hungry he was as he did so, as well as what she called his "protection"—their audience of half a dozen meat-sated dogs.

"Always seems to be somebody around to say the old days were the best," he complained to her, asking if they were still in Kluatantan country and whether she had been this far out from Red Town before.

"We are. I didn't come out, no; I'd had my ride." She meant her original ride from her ancestral mountains as a girl.

"Are you scared of the next Indians?" he asked, and waved in a westerly direction.

She laughed again. "I'm not scared of Indians. You're the one who's scared of Indians. I'm scared of white men. If I was scared of Indians I would be with the Indians."

"You're scared of the white man, so you're with a bunch of white men?"

"Sure. What better place?"

"Aren't you afraid we'll ditch you?"

"I don't think you're going to ditch me," she replied, smiling at how assiduously he was rubbing her backside.

"But if we bump up against some Indians, they aren't liable to be any more friendly to you."

"No, but I'm safer with you than my son Johnny is with the people he's with if they run into any white men."

"Why are you safer?" He was astonished she was so positive.

"Why am I safer with the white men? I think the white men are going to kill all the Indians that don't live with them, and maybe plenty of *us* Indians too. I've been with white men since I was a girl."

"And that's why you're alive?"

Fending off his hands with her elbows, she shrugged in amusement, as though that was putting it too strongly.

"Maybe, maybe not. I'm not afraid of the Indians if there is plenty of food to go around and nobody gets too crazy with their guns. You guys won't, will you? Three out of four of you are pretty old guys, if I just keep *you* calm."

She carried her moccasins and they walked a ways to an eddy in the creek and dangled their feet, watching a snag in the current bobbing like an otter's head.

"But is that why you left when you were a girl?" Cecil asked.

"So I could be safer? No, I didn't know that—how could I know that? I liked Mike better than the men where I was and my father liked him and wanted horses from him and I thought I wanted to be rich." She fingered her wrist as though remembering a bracelet there.

Cecil laid his head in her lap, lying on his back, and hugged her in silence with his arms over his head—her hips in a leather skirt. Although she stroked his chest and fingered his mustache, the surge of comfort he felt was deeper than because of that, and she hummed as if expressing what he felt. Yet, still startled by what she'd said about dangerous white men, he asked, "Was he different from us?"

"You mean my husband? Oh, he came out to sell a few flints to
the Indians, not after gold really. No gold here, and not much fur
on the flatland, and a lot of that is bum fur. Fur likes the trees. He
wanted the peaceful life, is what he said."

"So if he didn't come to get rich and kill all the Indians, why did
you say once that he treated you bad?"

"I didn't say I liked you better. I said you can protect me, like your
friends protect you." She laughed in exasperation and grasped his
hair.

Cecil, who had turned on his side with his face next to her stomach, couldn't bring himself to sit up and quarrel with her, but he
did mildly repeat his question about why this admirable man had
been difficult.

"Maybe I stretched it, and maybe it *was* on account of his not going to the mountains and giving it a try, the same as you. He knew
that's what he was supposed to do. He stewed, he hit the bottle, he
had his moods, he liked to have more than one woman around, and
he'd give me a black eye every year or two. But he never killed anybody in his life and he didn't love his rifle like you fellows do. He
saw all the beavermen and prospectors come through, but I think he
liked us Indians."

When she said her feet were cold, Cecil sat cross-legged and she
stuck them in his lap for him to dry with his shirttails. "Maybe I
would like more than one man, too."

"So why didn't you go to Horse Swim if you wanted to stay with
the white men?"

"I like 'em, I don't like 'em. I know 'em, I don't know 'em. I was
used to that little trading post and all the people that showed up
there."

"And how about Horse Swim?"

"Plenty of kinds of people in Horse Swim. I went over with my
daughter one time and I even knew some of them from when we
had the Post, but I didn't know what I would do if we moved there."

"And your son's not trigger-happy? Or Billy Buckskin? Only us?"

"It's better with the white men," she insisted. "Where can he go
with the Indians that the whites aren't going to follow them? You
can go to St. Louie. No Indian's going to come after you there."

Cecil figured nevertheless that Billy was as likely to bushwhack a stranger as any white man, but he didn't say so. He was inserting his fingers between her toes, while she teased him that he must trim her toenails, too—watching him blush but not get mad.

"I hear you sold Indian medicine back East. What was that?"

"My father did. Wizard Oil. Indian Tonic. Indian Restorative. Iris Juice. He had a root he'd dug up. I would have brought it along except it's five feet tall. It was from a swamp lily and it looks like a young boy, with the elbows on him and the head and all. Little heinie, little dong. He nailed that lily root to the wagon so we wouldn't have to explain to people what we were in town for."

"And that explained it?"

"It left so much to explain that nobody asked. They just bought what we had."

She lay back in the grass and hitched her skirt up to her hips. "Come on if you're ready to, squaw man. I'm not afraid of you."

Afterward, grasping his mustache again, she asked him, "Am I an easy lay?"—her ordinarily rather somber face breaking into a grin like a girl's. "You can see why I might have gone to the bad if I had moved to Horse Swim."

He was laughing and of course had forgotten that her hair was gray-streaked and smelled of squaw-wood smoke and that the plump neck he had kissed was wrinkled like that of a woman twenty years older than any former lady friend of his. But the thought of Sutton was another matter. He decided that he knew two things: Sutton hadn't sent her to him, but he hadn't minded her coming, either.

"You're not jealous of each other?" she teased, watching these doubts cross his face. Walking back, he was reassured because she herself seemed unworried that she had endangered her position with them. It dawned on him that Sutton had actually meant what he'd said about having been a nigger dealer's son and about how the gentleness or politeness he had learned to use with them should work well with Indians also. There must have been loads of women coming and going about the farm, interchangeable, nobody jealous.

Sure enough, although he didn't wink at Cecil, Sutton made no fuss. It was Cecil who, that night, felt jealous.

•

White pelicans, green-tailed magpies and black-headed gulls congregated on the creek banks, and whenever the horses splashed across
a marsh, a whole skyful of gadwall, pintail and shoveler ducks was
scared up, flapping. The rivulets between the ponds had acquired a
westward focus, which was a sign they might be reaching the drainage of the Ompompanoosuc River. Under the prodigious clouds
their own trek seemed minuscule, except that they were headed
dramatically against the flow of the wind, so that to look up when
the sky turned solid with cold clouds fleeing from the mountains
they intended to enter was intimidating.

Otherwise, in the noon sunshine, Cecil rode barefoot, with the
tallgrass flower heads tickling the soles of his feet, watching Kitty's
ears cock and twitch and her nose ride the news conveyed on the
breezes. A humpetty bog buffalo lurched to its feet and lumbered
away over the mud. A coyote veered clear of the dogs, scatting like a
cat but with a humorous glint in its backwards glance, like a burglar
sideslipping the police.

The shiny-skinned buffalo calf hadn't lasted very long. Bewildered,
rebuffed by the horses, it got kicked painfully in the ear when it
tried to tag along behind them and thereafter clung close to the goat,
much to the goat's dissatisfaction, until, exhausted by its terror and
lagging absently, it was cut off by Moose and White Eye and Smoky
and, in a sad, swift scuffle, killed. A short-legged, nameless brown
dog had also dropped behind and not caught up, the sort of dog that
even a coyote could have accounted for. Another of the last-minute
volunteers, choking helplessly on a bird bone, had had to be shot—
its coat so thin it probably wouldn't have survived the winter anyhow. Earlier, one of the shrewder littler dogs, sensing the drift of
what might happen to it if it didn't turn back before the cavalcade
got too far out of Horse Swim, had made a run for it.

They skirted and then camped at the north edge of the Mutton
Hills, as Charley called these first, sheep-backed foothills. Past the
cluster of the Muttons they struck the Tongue River, which drained
the Short Mountains, as well as the Muttons, and was named for all
of the buffalo tongues that had been consumed hereabouts. On average it was a hundred yards wide, and they searched for a safe ford

that would keep them close to their line of travel, although Charley said the Tongue itself would link up with the Ompompanoosuc in good time. Roy was worried about the swim, but Charley was cheery as they camped, because the bend in front of their tent site seethed with pike and whitefish.

The whole region had been a resort for antelope and Kluatantans hunting them, according to Margaret, and Cecil, heeding her advice, tied the dogs in camp and fastened a strip of flannel to a pole. Together they went on foot to a ripple of higher ground a mile away to try and see whether by waving this they could decoy some of the dainty creatures close enough to shoot. The bucks stamped their feet and scrammed at the sight of the flag, however. While she and Cecil were squirming nearer to a cluster of does and fawns, he found himself gripping her breasts and hips in famished fashion again. Laughing, she rolled on top of him and said she had a sister who, like her, had gone off with the white men.

"I wonder where she is right now. Maybe she got all the way to St. Louie. Hers was supposed to come and be partners with mine, you know. They were going to join up with us. These partnerships!" she said, to indicate how many white men she'd seen come and go, but added that she had never cheated on Mike.

"I'm glad of that."

The river, emitting a windy roar, wound southward, and the mists moving on it intensified their mutual feeling of mystery when, after exploring further, they discovered a bankhouse twenty feet over the water in a high cut where a bunch of hide hunters must have wintered. These gentlemen had excavated space for two rooms, roofing their diggings with driftwood and sod, had installed a trapdoor, and walled the open side above the cutbank with more driftwood limbs and sod and brush. Close by, there was a wagon shed built of heaped brush, with wagon ruts leading out onto the prairie, a storage cellar, a raised log cache and traces of three tipi rings. Although the view upriver was sinuous and lovely, the currents circled sullenly upon themselves as if they would make for hard swimming, when looked at directly from above, and the scene in the dooryard was grim, what with buffalo bones stacked high like a woodpile and corduroyed in mudholes on the wagon paths. A comedian among the skinners had constructed the letters *DAN* eight feet long on the ground from skulls he'd carefully fitted together like stones.

"Number-one work," said Margaret sarcastically. They climbed down inside the house, finding torn calico and scraps of hide, a broken table, a bent bedstead, a mush pot peppered with pistol holes. Peering for "signs of a woman's hand," she got the creeps instead from the bold prints of wolves that had poked low and high, chewing on the table legs, pawing up the floor, climbing to mouth the earthen shelves. Nesting in the ceiling were pack rats which neither the wolves nor the men had been able to dislodge. She pointed to some bullet nicks where—probably as they lay in bed—the men had tried. Yet, after all the scavenging the wolves had done, the rocks and river flotsam below the house still stunk of meat.

Margaret had her rifle with her and set off from camp once they were outside again, while Cecil continued down-current. The late sun put a feathery sheen on the river, and he soon caught sight of a brindled wolf in back of a roll of ground. A gray one was skulking behind the first, as well as a third wolf, which was whitish brown, although because they were using every fold of terrain to conceal themselves, he didn't put the combination together for a while. No doubt they were so prudent because the hide men had shot at them. They were investigating rather than stalking him, and though he felt quite naked without the protection of his dogs, he wasn't seriously scared.

They carried their heads low, as befitted an animal with heavy jaws, but had endless leg power—could wheel or dash sideways in a crouch or standing up, then light out with legs in a blur like the blades of a windmill; and never a sound. Apparently they presumed that because he was smarter than them and a better buffalo killer, a wolf that dogged him could glean his leavings. Indeed, it was true. Noticing a lark's nest in the grass, he had stepped over to have a look, but when he went on and then glanced back, both nest and nestlings, to his dismay, were being crunched up.

These were his first wolves—he was excited. Yet they were immediately as familiar as if he had encountered bushel loads before. They were already part of the mob of wildlife he'd imagined here.

And the river's flat racket—a noise like tin sheeting being rattled—bolstered his stride as if its very strength was his, though if he watched it narrowly he felt dizzy, because the slant of the light on the water caused the currents to slide backwards, to his eye.

He reached another of the hidemen's skinning sites, and, wandering uneasily through this boneyard, thought for a moment that he had encountered his first live grizzly. A large, stern shape as black as death and with a hump for its shoulders and a mane of hair was standing in front of the low sun, which obscured its identity. He dropped to a shooting position to be ready for anything, with his ears burning and ringing, his scalp tingling, his fingers trembling on the trigger guard. None of his imaginings had prepared him for how afraid he was.

The creature stirred but didn't charge, and gradually he perceived that it was grazing. As big as any bear, it turned out to be a stray buffalo—a lorn survivor. He was too absorbed in studying it to make meat out of it until, by the time he might have done so, he realized that actually there was a bear around. He didn't know where, but, by intuition or by somehow seeing her without knowing it or by smelling her in spite of the charnel stench of the surroundings, he sat tight, waiting until he finally spotted her foraging among the skeletons on the periphery, bashing out enough room between them to crouch in comfort and crack a marrowbone.

She was smaller than the living buffalo and shrew-shaped at a distance, and because the buffalo bones themselves were so sizable, her coloring was what distinguished her from a lesser scavenger—the dished face frosty brown, the rump like maple sugar, the splash of curdled yellow cream spreading from her armpit up one shoulder. Blackish fur masked her eyes, but not like a raccoon's expression—more in the manner of a person who looked haggard and insomniac. She was short-sighted, and having the advantage of the wind, he stole closer. As he did this, the larger and the hairier she grew, the more she gathered about her a queerly human air of dislocation or desperation. As had become the case with one of the bears in Maine that he had trained, she impressed him as being more like a human in a state of savagery—a sort of castaway—than like a beast who passingly resembled a man.

The buffalo with the lion's mane was not perturbed by the bear's macabre activities, was more watchful of Cecil, and, as he knew, would soon give him away. Unlike an eastern bear's, the grizzly's front legs were as long as her hind ones, as if for speed in pursuit, and the famously alarming grizzly hump bespoke the muscles contained inside. But though there were no trees to climb, Cecil, lying with his .44 propped across a rock, had calmed down. She was a bruiser yet fastidious in her motions as she examined the bones, which, combined with her increasingly prepossessing size as she wandered in his direction, pleased him. He wasn't hunting for a pet to beg in front of barbershops and he had worried that after venturing so far he might find the bears weren't direfully different from what he'd caught and sold back home.

She was too manlike to be wolfish but too bearish to be a man. In fact, the rings under her eyes gave her visage a theatrical tilt—that such a fabled and now quite immense brute, cracking hips and shoulderblades, looked to be about to weep. Watching this cunning, poignant-looking, curdled-cream-and-maple-sugar specter pummeling the buffalo bones like a pile of toys made Cecil think twice, as he was going to need to do if he ever hoped to perform with a grizzly. She was the master of more menace, he supposed, than any bear trainer had ever tamed, but he wished for a grand, imposing circus tent and tiers of people waiting on board benches to witness what he and the bear could do. He might need the help of the bear itself, as well as the inspiration of the moment of its capture—when his life might hang in the balance—to figure out what that would be. He wasn't going to quit his trip to catch the first specimen he saw, but would his foot snares manage to hold something so strong? Ever since he'd left the train at Cameron he'd felt the land and sky stretching his imagination, and apart from that, he suspected too that just as Sutton had told him, his friend's knack for showmanship was catching.

When she had tired of her bone games she slouched to the river beach and sprawled on her stomach, licking her paws, with her hind legs bent like a wishbone behind her, the way a puppy would have. She slapped and nibbled at bugs in the sand and observed the driftwood floating on the water. A cloud of carrion flies around her head didn't bother her, but she rolled on her back and playfully pawed at a flock of thirsty yellow butterflies flirting along the waterside.

Though Cecil had to sneeze, the river's sheet-metal racket prevented her from hearing him. She reclined on her side, stuck one claw in her ear, then rose on her elbows with an abrupt and grim attentiveness as a clot of brush shaped rather like some drowning animal floated by. He'd been about to pull out—she wasn't moving anywhere and he wanted to be away from her vicinity before dark—but now he hesitated, scared again. On purpose, at last he showed himself. The buffalo snorted at this, and the bear, swinging her bottle-shaped nose around to catch his scent, tossed her head repeatedly as though she were quaffing it. Her unbalanced coloring, silvery black and creamy brown, only emphasized what a mournful, bone-crunching, carrion-swallowing monster she was. Yet when she stood and ambled toward him she was as graceful as any circus bear, more fluid in her movements than a man.

Tall—on two legs with her forepaws held forward and loosely outspread—she examined him from an interval of twenty yards, weaving her nose to get a better purchase on the wind. He'd gripped his gun, but after a minute she dropped back down on all fours and stepped sideways. Groaning with relief because she hadn't rushed him, he stumbled out of the knot of rocks where he had taken shelter and gained some little willow trees, where for no real reason he felt safer. When she moved off, he moved on.

Across the braided sandbars and blackened channels of the Tongue the land rolled toward a late sunset like an ocean gathering height and force. The same tatter-coated trio of wolves began to trail him, along with a new male, blueberry-colored in the dusk, who pissed and ran ahead and pissed again, a courtesy to him which Cecil tried to return when he came to each spot. He was babbling happily to himself all the way to camp. Teal and redhead ducks took wing, while the river, still darkening, grew larger, much as the bear had seemed to do the longer he had watched her.

6

THE APPLEMAN

The night turned cold. An inch of snow was on the ground when Roy, screaming, woke everybody. He said he'd felt a hand choking his neck—his own hand, as it happened, which had gone to sleep under the weight of his head.

They warmed the horses' bits in a pan of water as an encouragement to them, loaded them all carefully, and swam them across the Tongue at dawn without delay or difficulty, holding onto the manes, though Roy looped himself to his saddlehorn for extra security, a procedure that Charley warned him was a dangerous one. As they were drying themselves and their gear on the far bank, Charley said that if he had known the swim was going to be so easy he would have gotten it over with the night before. Roy kept coughing nervously, however, shaking water out of his nose and ears.

"I sure do admire how those dogs swim. Like fluff. Easier than the horses. I'm just a desert rat." He said he was a mountain man from ever since the 1849 Rush, when his old man had brought him West in a caboose hooked to the saddle. He also told how he had lost his arm, working in a muley mill nine years ago. He'd dropped a stick. "God-blessed thing no fatter than a broomstick, but it was windy in there, six of us workin', and no walls, just a tarp on lodge-poles, and crowded with the logs and saw. The sawdust was flying off the saw—right in my eye this time. I couldn't see. I stepped side-wise and when I stepped sidewise I stepped on that goddam pine stick and it rolled under my foot and I threw this arm over here to grab ahold of the bench and it went right against the saw."

Charley, wriggling as peppily as a seal in front of the fire with his moose vest and fawn shirt off and his white-furred chest show-ing, ignored Roy's debilitations and explanations but didn't avert his eyes from Margaret's efforts to get dry. By way of making con-versation, he said he guessed half of the germs in him were dead by now. He felt them gradually croak whenever he left civilization and wouldn't meet up with any more until he went to town next year.

Margaret agreed with that. She'd been telling Cecil that silvertips could be practically any color, after he had described how his grizzly had been splashed as vividly as though with paint, and what a draw-ing card a coat like that baby's would make.

"They can charge at you or they don't charge. There are no rules for them," she said.

"A *winter bear* is what you want—except, in the city, he might just look like a regular old flea-bitten city bear," Charley remarked with a laugh. He had never acknowledged before that Cecil's rea-son for being here wasn't the same as Sutton's.

"A bear that's starving and can't go to sleep, he'll come out of his cave because he's too hungry to sleep," he explained. "When a bear dies of old age he dies in his den because he couldn't put on enough fat before he went in. He's emaciated like a very old person and he knows he's probably going to die, and if he accepts that idea, he'll go to sleep again anyhow. But some of them don't. They're fifteen or twenty years old and they're big fellows and they want to try to live to see another summer. They'll come out looking for a meal in January or February. That's the 'ice bear,' or the 'white bear'—the 'winter bear,' as the Indians call him. He's fallen through the ice somewhere or else he's swum a rapids and the water freezes on him and won't come off. It's like a coat, and if you shoot at him, your bullet hits the ice and glances off like it was armor; no better than an arrow. He knows if he can find just one big meal he'll live to see another summer, and you're the only meal there is for ten or twenty miles. That's what's terrifying. You won't often meet a bear track in the winter, but if you do, you make tracks fast the other way.

"But how could you present that in the city?" he said. "With the ice melted off him and a few meals in him, sitting quietly in his cage, nobody'd ever dream what he used to look like when he was covered with ice like armor up in the seven-foot snows in the Rockies, looking for a meal. That and a Bigfoot they wouldn't know."

"A what?" Cecil said. "A Bigfoot?"

"A Bigfoot. I don't think you'd make much money with him, either. City people wouldn't know what it was they were seeing, and yet an Indian, if you asked him, wouldn't know which one of them he's more afraid of. He's just glad there are no Bigfoots outside in the winter and that that winter bear's going to be a regular bear again in the summer with a bellyful of meadow grass inside him and no ice on him."

"Why are there no Bigfoots outside in the winter?"

"Because Bigfoots hibernate too, but they don't ever die, so they don't get hungry."

Margaret indicated her agreement with all this information, although she specified that you had to have forests for a Bigfoot. None inhabited the plains. Cecil—who was astounded to hear mention of this unknown other creature—tried to ask more questions. Shouldn't he want to catch a Bigfoot now? But neither was enthusiastic about answering.

They'd almost finished repacking when Margaret's soldier pony, who was a horny soul, began lunging in his hobbles back to the riverbank as if he'd scented a new mare to nuzzle. They had been itching for a showdown with anybody who might be following them, but for a moment they didn't understand that this event was at hand. Then the three men scrambled to find drift logs to duck behind, while Margaret hurried the horses out of sight.

"I'm going to shoot the socks off them," Charley said.

However, the figure that materialized was alone and on foot—a gangling, solitary, stick-legged white man leading a single horse with a thin blaze on its drooping nose. Cecil's dogs set up a clamor which was redoubled when they noticed that a stray brown mutt from New Horse Swim that had been with them but had disappeared a hundred miles back was pluckily keeping abreast of him on limping legs—as indeed it needed to do, because a wolf was tagging after the tiny party. The wolf was on their flank until, with its boneless, tireless gait, it purposely faded behind, as Sutton snapped a shot at it.

This strange newcomer seemed all bones, and didn't show a sign of having a gun. Though caked with mud above his knees, he had a bouncy, incongruously light, oblivious stride, as if the marks of whiteness in his hair were due to wear and tear and not real aging, and he had sufficient energy to spare that he could hardly stop his feet from walking when he reached the Tongue but continued up and down the bank opposite them. He was wearing canvas pants and a shirt of sacking and had a piercing-looking, unmalignant face that was small for his lanky body. He carried a walking staff tipped with iron, yet they still could see no rifle among the bundles strapped to his bald-necked mare—a lapse which, if deliberate, seemed suicidal for a white man rambling in this remote country.

Margaret's soldier pony and Cecil's sorrel studhorse Fred neighed a welcome to the mare, and Sutton waved to the man.

"Is he in trouble? Must have had an accident. He's local, isn't he? But I've never seen him. Have you, Charley?"

Charley, angry and suspicious, was the last to emerge from behind the breastwork of logs. What if this gentleman so meagerly outfitted was scouting them? he wanted to know. "You think he's really walking? You think he hasn't got two saddlehorses and three honchos or ten honchos hiding a day behind here? You've got nothing to lose."

"You think my heart wouldn't stop if somebody shot me?" said Sutton, smiling.

Because the fellow would need to recruit himself before plunging in to swim the river, Charley didn't want to wait for him to cross but to leave pronto. He even wanted to douse the fire on their side of the river to inconvenience him when he climbed out wet and cold. But no one else was willing to go off like that without more reason, and when their silence had grown strained, Sutton shouted to the stranger over the river's noise, "You ought to get another horse!"

"No, I just have bags for one!" the man yelled back.

Sutton drew a breath. "I mean so you could *ride* him!"

"No—I don't ride!"

"It's not hard tracking us, I guess!" Charley shouted, his voice rising and cracking with sarcasm.

All sounds took a while to cross the river, as though they had to fight their way through roar and foam, but after their visitor had digested this, he shouted back at Charley, "I guess if I was riding, it would be harder, huh?"

"And what do you want, you dirty shit?" Charley blustered, once he was certain that he hadn't misheard him.

The man leaned on his staff without replying and let his weary horse graze and watched Charley make ready to ride off.

"How about it? What do you want?" Sutton asked him more politely—had to repeat himself to be heard.

Nevertheless, the stranger only flourished his arms as if to say it was too hard to yell above the river, that he might talk to them if they lingered for a little while, or perhaps that it was a free country, or God's country, or simply a pretty country, and he was entitled to a slice of it. There was no knowing what he meant. His face, which had previously seemed friendly, insofar as they could read his expression at a distance, now looked as though he were jeering at them. But his horse was nibbling leaves from the same bushes their own horses had yanked at during the night, and the undersized brown dog was gulping scraps from the embers of their campfire.

They mounted speedily, more nervous than he was. The wolf had patrolled closer, yet—far from acting bereft—he smiled at their haste to get away. First he thumbed his nose and then he just rested his skinny, rangy frame on his large hands on the walking stick, letting out a sort of howl as a parting shot, which unexpectedly the wolf answered.

A long, long trot over the gumbo grass while the sun burned down. Each of the dogs managed to hit upon a squawking rabbit during the course of that day, and Sutton, who had been less perturbed by the advent of their peculiar visitor, said if he succeeded in catching up with them again, it would be like the story of the turtle that had licked the hare. He suggested he might be Cecil's kindred spirit, because of that strange howl. "If a man can talk to wolves like that, what do you suppose he could do with bears?"

Cecil was more concerned with how his dogs would do with bears, watching the extra ones for those who were clever and hardy, yet so comradely they would be ready to sacrifice themselves to save his life in a great crisis under the bulk of a bear. The key to winning love like that from a pack of dogs was to keep their life so quick and variable that they were willing to follow him anywhere to find out what would happen next.

But White Eye, the black-and-white-faced malemute who had been juggled among half a dozen masters, had had too much of that. Now, carrying a sack of baggage, working under concise, predictable instructions and watching his feet eat up the ground, he seemed to be much happier. He asked no favors except the satisfaction of Cecil's leadership, and in the evening would relax by slowly chewing on a stick and spitting out the pieces. But at unpredictable moments, he still appeared to anticipate a beating. He would squint, cringe and creep towards Cecil as if he'd learned at someone's hands that this was the best way to deflect the blows that otherwise were sure to fall. Sutton called him Black Eye because of this unsettling habit; and indeed it was hard to be certain whether he was creeping closer to soften a beating that he expected or to attack.

Moose, the other husky, was unremittingly loving, and Coffee, the airedale-collie cross, was worshipful as well as loyal, except when she was wringing a living from the villages of prairie dogs. When she got into the midst of a colony of them she was unusually brusque, caught more than she could possibly eat, and couldn't be called away. Her front end slunk; her rear end stalked. If she wasn't on the hunt, she trailed Cecil's horse from sheer adoration, willing to carry a pack or pull a travois or let his terrier jump on and off her back, ready to fetch his boots or coat at night but guarding his kit against even the approach of his friends—with those fast jaws, a very capable fighter.

Then there was Yallerbitch, as Roy called her—flamboyant, hound-sized, yellow, who lacked much coat for the winter but who had swum the Margaret to join them and was enjoying herself. Roy had adopted her as his pal, and Moose was her suitor. Moose would lie next to her and she'd lie next to Roy. When she wanted Roy to hug her she would bump his knee, always remembering which side his arm was on, and if she received encouragement, would try to climb into his lap. Though it was narrower than a proper hound's, she boasted a fine nose for tracking and was forever announcing olfactory finds. With sure, small feet, she seldom needed to swim the creeks. There would be a spar of dead timber lying across that she could tiptoe on, twisting like a tawny monkey between the blackened branches to the other side. And one time when they stumbled on a grizzly's dishpan-sized tracks angling catty-corner to their line of progress, it was this yellow lady who promptly grinned and began belling out a song for trailing it.

Smoky, the sixth dog in the party, was a coyote-mongrel mix, according to the Missouri cowboy who had traded him to Cecil for the box of lozenges. Slenderer than the huskies, he would go a mile in front and spring out at them from behind a rock, meanwhile eluding the wolves that sometimes lurked in such locations. On quiet nights he howled, along with Moose and White Eye, and could have lived quite independently in the wilderness—would vanish for a day or two for fun—except for his single pathetic failing, epilepsy. His attacks recurred with growing frequency, as if accentuated by the thrill of traveling, and yet he seemed so close to reverting to the personality of his wild ancestors that Cecil wondered whether only this infirmity held him back.

Smoky, without being as greatly fond of Cecil as some of the others, trusted him, so when he felt an episode approaching, he would interrupt an overnight adventure and dart from a coulee by moonlight to seek out Cecil's bedroll, lying down beside it even if Cecil wasn't inside. Soon he'd stiffen into a fit, ramming his rigid body around, his legs like ramrods, his back arched painfully, drooling fearfully through clenched teeth and whimpering. He'd fall repeatedly, but after lying on his side, would blunder up and stagger blindly toward the creek or toward the fire till Cecil grabbed him, lest he drown or burn himself. When the paroxysms let up on him, he would limp around, whining from the charley horses the fit had caused him, and carefully lick away the traces of his drool, like a wild animal covering the evidence of a desperate weakness which, if discovered, might set an enemy on his trail, and then would drop into a sleep until they got moving again.

Whenever this happened, Roy and Charley wanted to shoot him. They couldn't understand why Cecil wasn't afraid the other dogs would catch what he had. Besides, they argued for a more orderly outfit. But Sutton had a tender spot for freakishness of any kind, and Cecil himself developed a good deal of affection for Smoky from helping him and thought he might wind up with fewer dogs than he needed. Smoky, to prove the point, regained his aplomb as quickly as he could. He sprinted over and grabbed big Moose's pack or White Eye's tail, pulling in the opposite direction. Or he'd nip Coffee and outrace her, or might grip Yallerbitch's muzzle in his mouth and hold her still, the way wolves do to effect a conquest, until Moose growled.

They also had the heavy-furred, soft-mouthed, black mutt retriever named Sally, whose master had been the dead Swiss gentleman and whose virtues were that she could pull in the ducks they shot, living on the feet and chitterlings, and was a probable mamma—had mamma written all over her—and one more body for the wars to come, but mild. Though she had gone lame at first, she doggedly kept the pace until the regimen of overexercise began to build her up instead of wear her down. She was indiscriminately homey and would sit by Sutton as comfortably as by Cecil, and was so tractable that either one could use her for a pillow if he wanted to.

Margaret's rabbit dog lived like an elf among the others on a cat's diet of rodents, frogs, grasshoppers and minnows. She didn't comprehend English, only Margaret's Indian instructions, and padding deftly alongside the soldier pony, she kept her own counsel, contented-looking in the heat and cold, playing games with the cloud shadows and flying insects, separate from the rest of the pack.

The ninth dog that showed some promise of lasting was Kaiser, the serviceable gray shepherd who had belonged to the grocer in Horse Swim and who in the wilderness could about half feed himself. Otherwise he lived on Coffee's leavings. The two kept company, when she didn't outdash or outbite him. Like Sally, he wasn't a dog of the wilds but a man's dog, and was wiser or more accustomed to the foibles of people as well as older than the others. Though Cecil had stolen his affections, he seemed unsure now whether he hadn't made a mistake. Warily, perhaps even skeptically, he was employing his intelligence to keep fed, keep up, keep in the good graces of everybody, man and beast. He had a mashed toe that he had to favor, and a frosting of white hair around his lips. He was middle-sized, not huge, and was both brave and warmhearted but not scrappy or shaggy. He looked as if he had another few years in him—being more infantry for the wars—and Cecil liked him for his cautious savvy and his mistrustful and yet doggy love.

With the horses, a tiptoe but hard-handed order of fellowship was called for. Cecil had learned to duplicate the individual snuffles of each of the eleven animals they had brought along. Sometimes it did no good, because they hadn't the same canine hunger for affection, but he spent plenty of spare moments nose to nose alongside them, listening to the intake of their breath and their blood beat and their lungs work. He was looking for a "bear horse," a war-horse so steady or so crazy that it wouldn't throw him into the face of a grizzly's charge. His Kitty was loyal but small, and though endearing in her mincing gait when she was occupied within herself, she had too much of a mind of her own to be as dumb as he'd need for a job like that. Fred, the sorrel, was a shirker and a coward, though careful to dissemble when he did what he shouldn't. The red packhorse and the pig-colored packhorse were somewhat less easy to daunt but disliked being ridden. And he couldn't borrow Sutton's mule or one of Charley's darlings or Margaret's wheezing hero-horse for the task.

Their next obstacle was the Rabbitskin River, which Margaret said had an ugly reputation among the Indians for its undertow and rips. They finally hit it at a dogleg marked by a strip of box elders, and found it was indeed a slick and dubious river, glinting like oil in the slant of the sun. It had a queer whiff to it, like coal oil that had spilled, and although narrower, it appeared to pose more of a problem to swim than the Tongue, which they had been able to wade partway across.

Charley didn't know where the ford was here, either, but by poking around they found the black stubs of a cooking fire; also buffalo tracks—though no horse tracks—and killed two rattlesnakes. They figured the fire had been an Indian's, because the stubs were inconspicuously situated and sparse. Margaret turned up a broken Kluatantan-type pipe with a bird-bone stem to prove it, and being concerned about her son, she searched for other signs of who this individual might have been. If he'd been traveling alone and walking, it could mean that the band that he was with had had a fight and he'd escaped.

Roy looked quite gaunt and bleached-out and had a cough, so while he napped and Sutton fished and Margaret prowled the thickets for evidence, Charley rode downriver with Cecil, tossing twigs into the current and wading out to test the bottom whenever any buffalo had crossed. What they oughtn't to do, Charley had decided, was to be in such a hellish hurry. They should have pretended to leave that smart fool on the Tongue behind and circled around to see if he was marking his back trail.

"Crazy like a fox. There could be thirty men behind him—leading his goddamned cayuse. You think he *walked* here? I hope that redskin meets him. He'll kill him for his nag anyway, if he's got nothing else."

When Cecil asked how many Indian bands might be wandering around between the mountains and Horse Swim, he said six or seven or eight of them, getting shot at, shooting each other, "getting the wood put to them." He understood Margaret's distress but considered it inevitable that young Indians—or, for that matter, the old ones too—should be running around like chickens with their heads off and meeting sorry ends. He also thought it inevitable that an antiquated one-armed prospector from the Arizona Territory who had showed up too late in the game for this wet country was going to run into trouble and drown or die of an ague someplace along the line. As for himself, he told Cecil while they watched swallows grab bugs over the water, it was a question of making his getaway every summer from whatever town he'd ridden to. He was glad enough to get away with his good health. This wouldn't be the first time somebody had chased after him, and a pal of his had taken his furs over the Hump to sell for him on the Hainaino one time and really come a cropper.

"He met a nice young critter there on the big river, nice-looking young bloke off of the new steamboat that wanted to be his *pardner.* Now sure, that was all right. The fellow let Ben buy all of his grub and fixings and all my stuff that I had asked for, till the fur money was gone and there was nothing to kill him for, unless you were going into the mountains yourself. So they *went* into the mountains—nice old guy, and nice young chap just off a farm who wanted to learn the ropes from him. And he brought that critter right out to his stake on the Sixth Creek of the Eeejookgook River—might have been a four or five weeks' walk—where he'd been laboring like hell for fifteen years and had done just about all that you're liable to *get* done in fifteen years. He had his fifty acres cleared. He had two barns, two cabins, a root cellar you could have lived in, a hot spring and a springhouse and a tiled fish brook running past the door. And that's where that young gentleman killed him. He lives there now. He fishes out the door. He feeds the deer in the winter like they're pets, until he eats them. He grows a tolerable garden. He soaks in his hot spring," Charley said. "And I'm probably going to die sooner now because I can't."

Margaret had found smudged prints in the mud indicating that the Indian had swum the Rabbitskin from west to east, as a Kluatantan fleeing back toward the Margaret would have done. She was feeling and measuring these in a funk, but Sutton brought over a frying pan full of graylings he had caught and cooked lightly with salt and pepper to share with her, and afterwards sat nearby writing in his diary.

They noticed an otter that was suppering, too. It had caught a fish under the roots of a snag and was crunching bites off this while treading water, holding the fish in front of it. Then it slid up onto the log under which it had grabbed the fish, to nip off and chew more of its meal. For variety, it swam to the bank to eat, fearless in front of them despite the fact that Charley was wearing a fancy rain bonnet made of otter tails, which he had split and sewn together so that the tips joined at the top. Then it treaded water again until the dogs rushed it.

"Always nice to trap fresh country," Charley said. He had a beaver in the pond at his house that swam around just like a moose's nose rippling the water, whapping its tail just like the trout that jumped, but he'd never tried to kill that one, he said. Too much fun.

Sutton hadn't made a living catching beavers, as both Cecil and Charley had, but he hunkered down on the riverbank to demonstrate how in bayou country he'd called the gators out of their holes for half a dollar a skin. From his throat with his mouth closed he imitated the muffled clucking of a bunch of babies that had hatched from their eggs but were still sealed inside the mud of the nest their mother had constructed.

"She has to break it open, but any gator is going to come shoving straight out of his den when you do that. If it's the pappy, he wants to *eat* 'em. If it's another cow, *she* wants to eat 'em too, so they don't get in the way of her babies." And he showed how, when that slow snout jutted out from under the bank, he would seize the jaws in both hands, hold them closed, and yank upwards with his left hand while taking his knife from between his teeth with his right.

"How long did you used to stay out?" Charley asked.

"Oh, not like you, but I remember staying out till all my salt was gone and I was shaking gunpowder on my lunch. You can use your gunpowder for salt, but the trouble is you can't use your salt for gunpowder."

Cecil laughed at that. "Same as tea and tobacco. You can smoke tea if you have to, but you can't drink tobacco if you run out of tea."

"You've got wild teas, you've got wild leaves you can smoke, but you've got no wild gunpowder," Charley added. He remembered, though, and told Cecil there was a salt lick that went with the hot springs he wasn't allowed to visit anymore where he had used to be able to collect wild salt.

"Why don't you kill the guy?" Cecil asked, to see what he would say, but Charley only smiled and went to bed.

Roy's cough was better in the morning. Boiling the breakfast water, he told them he had thought about the river during the night while listening to it "hiss and clap," and that he wanted to tie himself to Sutton's mule for the swim.

Charley said that that was the foolishest notion he'd heard yet.

"He's going to slip and roll on you, Roy," Cecil agreed.

"You dern betcha," Charley said, drawling like a hillbilly to emphasize the point. "This is a worse swim than the Tongue. I never heard of shallows on the Rabbitskin. You need to be part otter in this country. You'll get a dunking—I'm in and out of the water any time of year the ice is off." Irritated, he reminded them that this was where they'd intended to wait for the Soak's Heaven outlaws, if any were after him, instead of playing musical chairs with the horse string because somebody couldn't swim.

Sutton didn't like the idea of trading, either, and it was his mule, but because of his soft spot for Roy he squinted at the river, looking at it through Roy's eyes. Even to Cecil the current appeared to run backwards or slip sideways. Its surface bulged.

Yawning, Sutton remarked at last that the mule probably did swim best. On these mornings he yawned a lot, which to Cecil under the circumstances—when he had just spent the night rolled up with Margaret in a blanket—was galling. Like Charley, Cecil didn't approve when Sutton told Roy to suit himself, but Roy, with an ingenious flip of the body, threw his saddle onto Laddie, Sutton's mule, and cinched it tight, gripping the strap in his teeth while fastening it, swung himself up, and snubbed a loop of rope under his armpits from the saddlehorn.

"No, I'm okay," he insisted, as Laddie, fidgeting beneath the awkward burden of a man who wasn't really sitting so much as lying across his back, moved to the edge of the swirling, pelt-slick water.

Sutton mounted Cecil's sorrel, after transferring its load to Roy's old plug—which acted a little miffed—and Charley hooted at the rest of the herd, pointing them at a trench the buffaloes' feet had chopped through the bank whenever they forded the Rabbitskin. He wanted them to enter in a bunch to reassure each other, though not so close they knocked each other off balance. Fierce as a bandit, he shed his years at moments like this, but now he had to swerve and sprint his pony because Roy's nag, loose and balky, had made a dash for safer pastures.

While Charley chased Roy's horse, Cecil whipped the rest with loads on their backs down the bank and into the river, where immediately they found themselves over their heads. The whorls on the surface had wrinkled and folded ominously, but the torrents underneath pounded and sucked at them. Cecil, inundated to his waist as he sat on Kitty, waiting for Charley, felt the suction on his own legs. Then, realizing that Charley wouldn't have any advice to give him, he stretched out alongside her as though preparing to sled across on his stomach, with one hand clutching the saddle, and spoke soothingly when her near eye fixed on him.

Soon he couldn't speak—too breathless. The water intended to sweep them straight down to the ocean, or, failing that, to grapple and drown them. From different directions, at different levels and rapidity, it seized them, as grim and quick as a wrestler working with hands and feet to upend them. The terrier gripped the saddle-horn in its teeth, but was washed away, swimming for its life. Kitty pushed ahead, however, paddling resolutely. In front, they saw that most of the other horses had floundered onto an underwater sandbar where they could get some footing. As their heads, their packs and then their rumps emerged they stood unhappily swaying and jostling, mud-colored, ratty-looking—even the white horse—with their coats flattened.

But the bar was too short for half a dozen horses. The weaker ones started spilling off again and either struck out for the far bank or back where they had come from. With the latter, it was imperative that Sutton and Margaret, who were closer, turn them. The pig-colored packhorse got by Sutton. Cecil, who after being frightened by the grip of the river had found it wasn't irresistibly powerful, began trying to raise himself out of the water enough to shout at The Pig. He was swimming with his free arm and shielding his body behind Kitty's—loving the confident cock of her ears, the hopeful, female persistence with which she pumped them both forward—but although he felt pretty good, he wasn't strong enough for any miracles. In fact, The Pig was washing toward a collision with him—and barely skidded by, teetering to keep itself upright.

Charley, in a temper, had pushed Roy's horse with the pack bags on it into the water, sticking right at its tail. (Roy, meanwhile, spraddled across the mule, was doing okay.) But Charley now had to stay by the bank to catch The Pig as well. Roy's horse had set off on its swim at a down-current slant, and the two errant creatures started to converge, and of course to panic as they did. Panicking seemed to ensure they would hit. About twenty yards from the near bank they did collide. The Pig, besides being bigger and more vigorous, had a better equilibrium, because its pack boxes provided a certain flotation, whereas Roy's horse was carrying sacks that, when wet, only grew much heavier—and The Pig, in climbing right across Roy's wretched beast, caught a foot in one of its bags and jerked it upside down. Cecil watched its four hooves bob out of the water and hop along like four fisherman's corks as the body traveled below the surface, slamming into logs or rocks, halting for an instant, spinning on. As Kitty struggled forward, he shouted at the horses huddled on the sandbar to move off, whenever he could get his mouth clear of the river's swirl to yell. Together he and Sutton finally drove them ahead, and Margaret and Roy led them to the far side. Sutton waited until The Pig and Charley—who was swimming as lightly as a ground squirrel beside his own pony—had also safely crossed the bar. Then he gave Cecil the reins of the sorrel, helped him get both Kitty and the sorrel started once again, and slid into the currents alone and—water animal that he was—swam in pursuit of the horse and baggage they had lost.

Cecil, after an interval of mindlessly extreme exertion, staggered out of the river as if he had been wading in quicksand and sat in the grass, rubbing one shin where Kitty had stepped on him in the shallows. Because they hadn't yet lost their buoyancy when it happened, he wasn't hurt. Yet the close call made him feel all the shakier, and the sensation of having been clenched by the river stuck with him as though he'd just escaped the clutches of a murderer. The horses stood flexing their charley horses, looking chastened and glum. The dogs were as bedraggled as wet chickens but were fine, except that the terrier was not among them. And the cat had survived, though it had left scratches on The Pig from clinging to him that appeared to have damaged their friendship.

When Cecil tried to spot Sutton he had quite a time. He was

deeply mid-river, cautiously sideslipping obstacles, moving more slowly than the water was and steering himself by catching hold of the snags he passed—like a gator or a hunter of gators, as Charley remarked. Charley, who was coughing, slicking back his sparse hair, and pale in the gills, said that The Pig *was* a pig, a goldarned pig horse, for certain. But it was really Roy and not The Pig that he was mad at.

"A sea horse," said Cecil, looking downriver for Roy's own animal. He hated to remember the specific items of gear, the food and other supplies that had been strapped to the poor creature. By following Sutton's progress, eventually he located it, tangled topsy-turvy in a drift pile, alive among the dead branches of uprooted trees because its head happened to be fixed in a position from which it was just able to breathe. The water was so swift and it was caught so relentlessly that all of them wrenching at once could hardly have pulled it free.

The spunky terrier had disappeared. Cecil expected to sight it clinging to a tree limb in the water, but didn't. While they built a fire, Sutton reached the horse and found some footing among the crisscrossed tree trunks. As wobbly as a keel-hauled sailor, bracing himself precariously, he worked at its bindings, with his knife in his teeth. When he glanced back towards his friends, he shrugged to show both that he knew nobody would swim out to help him but that he wouldn't be able to accomplish much of anything if they didn't. The horse may have been beyond saving, anyhow, and as he said later, he couldn't salvage their bags without pushing its head underwater, a measure the horse naturally resisted. He was afraid the cold water was going to immobilize him in the meantime, so he cut its throat "for mercy's sake," as he was to tell them. Perched in the branches of the drift pile like a man in a tree house, he waited for it to kick its last. Then he had another go-round at the pack sacks, while the river pummeled him. He swam ashore, shivering and aching, too soured at first by the failure to come and join the others.

Charley was cleaning a gash on his leg. "In the mountains, meat don't spoil," he said. He seemed cheerful, but it was one of many moments when he obviously regretted bringing them. Hearing that some of Cecil's traps were down deep in the water, he grew almost jubilant.

"That snow is going to fall and when it does you're going to lose the rest of your horses, because where we're going there ain't no hay or oats, and when you do, whatever you have left—those iron doodads, your pinch bars and your bear traps—are going to be a tribulation to you. You won't carry them far on your backs. My hammerheads don't need to eat oats."

Roy, feeling the weight of everybody's blame and after he had carefully fingered Sutton's mule for injuries, began to chatter about his best adventure in the Arizona Territory, when three Indians had stolen two mules off him and he had chased them three days in the snow. A fresh fluff at the end had made for silent crawling and he had cut the tethers and with a few well-tossed snowballs directed the creatures out of the thieves' camp.

"Those were sleepy Indians!" Margaret laughed.

Roy said that in retirement he had lived underneath a big old sunshine pine with a great round crown to it, as perfect a place as you could find. "I had deer and javelinas. Never had too far to hunt." But the tree fell on the house, so it became half a house. He'd lived in half the house and the other half was squashed. Waggling his stump and continuing to justify himself, he said he'd wanted more than half a house, and more than to rebuild—had wanted another shot. "Never say die."

"So you lay yourself on us," Sutton answered angrily, from behind.

"You're going to be walking. We're not going to be trading horses with you now. You've got nothing *to* trade and furthermore you got our horses that weren't scared, scared," Charley told him. "You're going to be like that scarecrow we saw that was pretending he was walking, only you're *really* going to be walking."

Indeed, Cecil's Kitty, after witnessing the disaster, had reverted to a former vice of hers of pawing, pawing, pawing. But he and Sutton looked away from Roy and Charley because they didn't intend for it to go as far as that.

Cecil with a lucky shot brought down a ring-necked goose, whose

cooked fat they all could use for a salve on their gashes and cuts.
Though he didn't want to have to swim again, Sutton persuaded
him to, and they did salvage some caked sugar, salt, flour and
garden seeds, a suit of oilskins, the stoneware demijohn of brandy,
which was miraculously unbroken, and a stake and winch designed
for pulling stumps out of the ground. Also a battered dartboard
Sutton wanted to tack on the wall of his cabin, his cobbler's lasts
and the precious Sunday gun, bent, with some of its inlay work
gouged out—which made him particularly mad. By the time they
were finished in the water, Margaret had the fat ready for two rub-
downs, which she administered with impartial goodwill, and had
filled their boots with goose feathers for the treat of how it felt to
push one's cold feet in. She'd also fashioned travoises from willow
poles so that Moose and White Eye could drag what was left of the
lost load.

Moose came over to assure himself that Cecil actually did wish
him to pull this makeshift contraption; and Cecil, petting him, felt
his ribs start to shake rhythmically. He realized he was sniffing
something. What he was sniffing was the strange stick-legged man
with the burdened horse who was following them and who by and
by hove into sight on the east bank of the Rabbitskin, walking at a
deliberate pace.

The mare was now halterless, not being led, but still had her nose
over his shoulder as if she were helping him to find his way. At her
heels wobbled a black foal with three white socks and its mother's
own thin blaze. The little brown dog was there, but no sign of the
wolf or of the outlaw horsemen Charley had anticipated.

"Is that your Bigfoot?" Cecil asked.

Charley, who was in a fury anyway because of what had happened, wasn't going to repeat his earlier mistake with the stranger
and ride off wondering what he might be after. "Get over here!"
he hollered as loud as he could across the water. He waved; he even
pointed his rifle at him, with only the concession to courtesy of not
grasping it in both hands.

The gentleman signaled that he would, although the first thing
he did was to sit down and rest. He fished a piece of bread from
under his shirt, and for a time they watched him chew on that. He

crossed one leg, then the other. The foal suckled. The mare grazed. Once Charley yelled at him to hurry up, but it was such an unreasonable suggestion under the circumstances that he ignored it, if in fact he could even hear the words. Busy with the processes of drying and repairing their own belongings, they nearly forgot about him. Charley himself was so sleepy that against his better judgment he took a nap. When in his sleep he rubbed his throat, he looked like Cecil felt, which was as if a case of the grippe inside him was trying to get the better of his resistance, weakened after the two swims. Without any more wrangling, they settled down to spend the night, as did the fellow opposite them.

In the morning, after watching him consume another couple of handfuls of hard bread and several cups of good cold coffee-colored water from the Rabbitskin, they saw him fasten his round black snap-brim hat around his chin, catch the colt around its middle, and holding the base of the mare's tail, embark with her into the currents, kicking to propel himself or bending his legs like a frog's to keep a steady keel. Though Cecil had been proud of the way Kitty swam, this mother mare looked still more picky and energetic in how she maneuvered across the channels and between the sandbars, if perhaps less touchingly hopeful in the personality and air she had.

"You didn't shoot me?" the man said, when he'd arrived at last. He laughed, exhausted, clambering up the bank coughing, spitting water out, while both the horse and the foal sneezed and sneezed again. "You thought I'd drown?"

Charley walked over and grabbed the horse's wet pack bags, unbuckled the flaps, and dug down to get a feel of whatever was there.

"Be my guest, my friend!" the visitor exclaimed.

"What do you have? Seeds?"

"Yep, that's what it is."

"You've got your kit bag and a grub bag and a lot of fruit seeds? No equalizer? No guns at all?"

"That's all, except I got your dog back for you. Somebody likes dogs, I guess." He rubbed the brown stray's head and Cecil's Coffee and Sally and the foal, squeezing the worst of the water out of its coat of baby wool as it nursed from the mare to comfort itself and wagged its curly-haired flat tail. Close up, he looked narrower in the chest and leaner in the face than he had from across the river, but his nose was bold and his eyes were intelligent.

"You dog me too far and I'm going to shoot you. I know just where I'm going to do it, too," said Charley, unappeased, staring at him. He kept reaching back into the bags, groping for evidence. "You play Johnny Appleseed with me, coming along so pitiful without a gun and a wolf follering you, and when you see that you are in the mountains—when you see mountains on all sides of you— that's where I'm going to kill you, and plant you right there, with all your blasted seeds on top of you."

Roy, as a brother Westerner, added, "Where it's *cold* ground." But Cecil, trying to deflect Charley's anger, suggested that the wolves might catch up with the man first.

"The wolves have plenty better to eat at his time of year than him. They'll maybe take that colt. But if a bear gets after him, as sure as shit he'll ride that horse of his or be sorry he didn't."

"I will," he agreed. He introduced himself as Millard Switzer from Allen County, Indiana.

"I don't need to wait till we get to the mountains," Charley pointed out rudely. "I got bullets with me here. Let me explain something to you. I don't want nobody trading with the Indians unless I know what they're bringing in."

"They don't have guns?" Roy asked.

"Sure they've got guns. But I know their guns," said Charley, and he asked Mr. Switzer if the actual truth wasn't that he was scouting for about twenty hombres riding along behind him with cannons on their belts.

"No, as a matter of fact it ain't."

"Who *are* you working for? I hate to break it to you, but we don't want you with us."

Reaching out again, this time Charley searched his clothing where his sack shirt met his woolen pants—though contemptuous that the clown would even allow it. However, Mr. Switzer reached back under his collar between his shoulder blades and produced a Bible that had been tightly wrapped in an oilskin tied to a string around his neck.

"I kept my powder dry, you see. A different kind of gun." He said he'd reached Horse Swim on the new railroad with his bran sacks of seeds and had bought himself this sorry-looking, kind-natured beast and for the glory of God had started on their trail because a well-mannered lady named Ellen Stephansson had recommended it to him as the best guide for going West. "It's funny your trail should be the Lord's trail, isn't it?" he told Charley with a grin.

Cecil wished he'd bought that horse, and studied her configurations to try to remember whether he had passed her up. The cowboy who Switzer said had sold her to him was the same one Cecil had enjoyed dickering with.

"Not the prettiest horse they had, sort of a dung color, don't you think, but she's got the heart. There's only a few things an old farm boy is going to know about this country, but horses is probably one of them," said Mr. Switzer.

"And you think the Lord sent you here?" Sutton interrupted, with a mixture of sympathy and exasperation.

"My stars, no. I'm a nit to God. He doesn't send people. I'm just doing the best I can."

To Cecil, he looked about forty-five or fifty years old, with a farmer's squint and meek forehead and sun-bit skin. And as if he was clever enough to know that Charley was the one he must convince, not the rest of them, he addressed him: "I knew Johnny Appleseed, yes. He was friends with my mother and my dad. He visited our home. I saw him, I sat on his lap when I was hardly old enough to sit, but naturally I remember him very, very well. He blessed me and he blessed them."

Margaret handed him a mug of tea, although the others remained standing inhospitably. The cup was so hot he sat down so he could set it beside him. He opened his book and in a passionate voice read them Verse 37 from Chapter 8 of the Gospel According to St. John: "'I know that ye are Abraham's seed; but ye seek to kill me, because my word hath no place in you.'"

Charley cleared his throat. "I'll be damned." He hunkered on his heels on the opposite side of the fire. "Haven't met a Christer for years." Turning his right hand judiciously, he warmed the joints, which he said always pained him the day after a dunking, ever since a beaver trap had snapped on him in March weather a dozen years ago.

"So the real Johnny Appleseed dandled you on his knee and you caught the bug from him, did you?" he drawled. "Well, I'll tell you something. I don't want to hinder the almighty march of progress, but if you don't turn off from my tracks before we get to the mountains, I don't care *who* gave you his blessing I'm going to shoot you just the same."

In the silence after he had said this—realizing that it sounded a bit strong to his companions—Charley added drily, and turning to Sutton in particular, "You may not be bowled over by my place when you see it, but at least it's mine and it's shipshape, and I want to keep it. I don't know if he *is* a Christer. Or if you're leagued up with him; or that lady that sent him—a lotta people told me she was a railroad spy. I'm sixty-seven and all bumps. My veins stand out bigger than my muscles do. But no cutthroat's going to take my place away from me."

"Can I give you some seeds? Have you got your trees in?" asked Mr. Switzer with that direct glance of his. "You can have an awful lot of fun training them with toothpicks when they're just little whips out of the green ground. You're welcome to take some home from me, without the Scripture. Apples are for everybody, and somebody else'll come along and get more seeds from you and maybe he'll be a Christer!" He laughed.

Charley was stumped for a minute. He liked to use a hillbilly accent in ridicule, or to ridicule his own ridicule, but he just spoke straight. "You heard what I said to you. I don't believe you're by yourself and I'm going to kill you and any bastards you've got tagging along behind you lookin' for gold. Don't you know what a damn fool thing you're doing? There's no shade here, no regular supply of water. You can't raise fruit."

"Can't raise fruit on the west side of the continent?"

"Anyone that wants to raise fruit would bring it in by ship."

Cecil asked what had happened to the wolf.

"Which wolf? I give them a howl. That's all they want to hear, that satisfies them," said Switzer. Boiling a pan of oatmeal with raisins in it, he said he had his pruning knife and walking stick and that his horse could kick to defend herself.

Margaret ate something, to keep him company, and Sutton flopped down with a sigh, yawning, tired of the job of repacking the horses. The oatmeal smelled like butternuts and Cecil accepted a taste of it, also a cup of apple seeds to stow in his luggage. Hearing him say he avoided eating flesh, he asked, "Are you a preacher too?"

"I *thought* I was a preacher, but when they took the voice of the congregation after about two years, the vote was to vote me out. I was humbled. I think if you look at history, there are three sorts of serving to be done. The Apostles, who are the Builders, build the Church up right from scratch. The Evangelists, or Preachers, preach to fill it; and the Shepherds, or Pastors, take care of the flock. And when I'd farmed my sixty acres, I did try the last two. Now I'm trying something new."

"But you must be lonesome?" said Margaret.

"You bet I am. An old farmer like me? My kids are grown. The good part I've discovered is that this isn't as hard as I expected it was going to be. It'll be interesting to see how the Lord leads."

"What do you do on Sundays?" Cecil asked.

But he was ready for that. Like a man who really knew his book, he opened to St. Paul's Letter to the Colossians. " 'Let no man therefore judge you in meat, or in drink, or in respect of an holy day, or of the new moon, or of the sabbath days: Which are a shadow of things to come; but the body is of Christ.' "

"You're going to make apple pie for the Indians?" said Margaret.

"I'm going to praise the Lord to them."

The mare was a frequent farter, punctuating her master's most solemn conversation incongruously, besides setting Kitty to pawing and the soldier pony to whinnying. Yet Switzer was amused when she did. "General *who?*" he said. There was a glint of fearlessness or humor in all of his comments and he seemed like comfortable company, except of course it wasn't possible to tell how his religious bent might twist him under future conditions.

But Charley, stubborn, insisted that they leave him psalm-reading, and that it was better to shake off the gloom of the place than to sit fussing over the loss of Cecil's little trick terrier and Roy's horse.

"If you're lonesome, then goodbye to you. We don't want to be with nobody lonesome. And we're going to be no protection to you, because if somebody kills you we'll never know about it."

7

THE SARSIS

The horses headed out happily, as if they knew that
toward the west the sweet grass grew. Sandhill prairies with buffalo
grass, tallgrass prairies with gama grass. Cecil let the cat ride on his
saddlehorn where the terrier had ridden, and after covering two
dozen miles, everybody felt more sanguine. They all rolled out of
their blankets the next morning by the light of the dawn, Margaret
by herself, as Cecil noted gladly.

Snowflakes were falling. Rim ice had formed at the edge of the
creek they'd camped next to. But twenty-six antelope were gazing
at them from a rise (the dogs having been roped). The goat had
joined these imps during the night, and by its imperturbability delayed their flight till Cecil had dropped a doe. He ran his hands over
the rump of the mouth-watering beast, riding with her across Kitty's
withers until lunchtime.

"Your lady?" Margaret said, catching him fondling her, which
was just true enough to embarrass not only him but all the other
men.

The antelope was like a feast of turkey meat. Charley, missing his
vegetables to go with it, said he wondered whether a moose had

gotten into his garden yet. He'd left his dogs behind to prevent that. The garden was round, planted in circles around a centerpiece of marigolds with paths like spokes leading into it. "You tinker; you do everything a little different when you're alone."

Eyeing White Eye, who was ruminatively chewing an antelope bone and spitting out the pieces, he said, "No, you can always sell a dog; you can't have too many of them. I don't care how good-for-nothing he is, some Indian's going to want to eat him. Or *him.*" He pointed at the goat. "He likes the same weeds I do. He eats so many wild onions I wouldn't need to season *his* stew."

But the billy goat, nibbling omnivorously, with its brisk, fastidious gait, cowlicky beard, bald knees, and deep-thinker's forelock, had gained a foothold in their hearts. Charley even confessed that he understood why Switzer avoided meat. As a young tiger, he had sometimes had too much meat hanging in the trees around his cabin— sheep and elk forced low for the winter. The snow up higher drove down so many bighorns you got the feeling you were a kind of tin-pot king; you shot more than you needed to and festooned the trees. Started shooting at the siskins, woodpeckers and chickadees.

"The woods get very still. You've got no friends there anymore. Even your magpies and your weasels quit robbing you. Meat everywhere. It keeps, but it's a bloody sight. You forget what you're doing until some chap comes visiting you and you see his eyes bug out at how many carcasses you've shot. So I don't kill meat in my backyard. You'll see bighorns pawing for grass under the snow with my horses. Or—*you* won't, because you're not going to stay around that long. But you'll be eating seals when you go on. Oysters, abalones, seals. You'll see the cougars come down on the beach and eat the birds and fish at tide line, and pick your teeth with sea-lion whiskers."

Cecil suggested he might have his hands full with his bears—leaving out the cougars entirely.

Roy said, "Now, where you going to find the strength to tame that bear?"

"From the bear," said Cecil. "The same as when you trip somebody, you use his own strength to put him on the ground."

They were all intrigued. "You mean catch him in a pit and tame him in the pit?" Margaret asked.

"I don't know yet," Cecil said; and he didn't. He guessed he would learn that from the bear.

"Catch him small," said Charley (though they had caught sight of a slate-gray bear that morning that didn't look as if it had ever been small). "You've got your grass grizzlies here. Mine are the groundhog grizzlies. They don't grow so big, because it's harder to dig groundhogs in the mountains than to eat a lot of grass down here. Mine are like six-foot silvery groundhogs when they stand up, but you want a small one that's still going to grow." And beyond the Hump, he said, on the west pitch of the Rockies along the rivers sloping toward the Pacific, were the salmon grizzlies.

"Grizzlies that smell just as rank as salmon, and they're bigger than these grass grizzlies, they get so many fish to eat. Besides that, they'll be closer to the ship when you get ready to take them out. These are red-legged grizzlies that are about nine feet tall and that stink too much from eating fish for you to eat. It's your grass grizzlies or your groundhog grizzlies you might want to eat, not those gorilla whoppers." But he laughed, because of course he knew that Cecil wasn't looking for a bear to eat and that a red and black monster grizzly—black like a gorilla, red like a salmon—was just exactly the ticket that Cecil wanted to bring East.

They met another river, slipping between sulphur-colored bluffs, with a shallow gravel ford to it. For this one Charley hadn't missed his turn, and pointed to the very hollow in the soil where he'd last slept. They were preparing to coast straight through, when the horses gave notice that they remembered the terrible brouhaha on the Rabbitskin. Balking, bridling, they started vigorously chewing the dwarf willows and buffalo berry bushes in this lovely spot, which, although not forested, hinted at forests roundabout. There were cat-birds in the brush and muskrats and crawdads in a creek that fed the river under the bluffs. A red-tailed hawk skimmed overhead as if it had a nesting tree somewhere close. And a moose made off— the first moose of the trip—with those wonderful web horns and the leggy, solemn trot, as regular as a metronome, that gave Cecil a homesick pang for the Maine woods. Six elk, like wild horse-deer, also went galloping out of rifle range—the first elk he had ever seen.

And the bushes were full of spider webs with a thousand bugs in them.

Casting around, they found the mineral springs, like a warm and dirty pool of ginger beer, which had made a zoo of the place. They let the horses rest and have a taste, while Roy and Sutton shook out a few panloads of sand from a creek bed, looking for color in it. Margaret said she thought this was probably the Kluakaz, a name that meant Last or Farthest River of the Kluatantans, whose name in turn meant Green Grass People—*tan* translating both as "grass" and "green," she said. But Charley claimed that their territory had ended at the Rabbitskin. Treating her with just the mixture of condescension and insinuation she liked least, he said he had once heard it called the Judy River, "by a trapper whose bimbo's name was Judy," and they could find the ruins of his cabin if they looked.

They noticed that the water in a deadwater of the river was still swirling, as though a largish occupant had been bathing and had scrambled out only a minute before their arrival, leaving black hairs in the water and claw marks in the mud. Some of the horses fought to shed their packs and shy clear of the area.

Crawdad Creek (as they dubbed the creek) entered below the ford but added noise to the river, and a bend above the ford caused the current to accelerate with a rush over the white and red and greenish gravel studded with round rocks as brown as startled eyes sticking out of the bottom. All this, too, inevitably combined to scare the horses. They took the opportunity to bury their long heads in grass so lush their eyes could barely see over the top, and Cecil, after having a go at communing with The Pig and Fred and Red and hollering at the rest of the herd, rode behind them threatening to sic the dogs on them, a tactic he had never employed for fear the dogs and horses would quit being friends. Charley and Sutton only watched, feeling they had done the biggest share last time, till finally in exasperation Charley mounted his shaggy pony and with a visible wrench, screwing about twenty years off his age, began to grunt "like a Bigfoot," he said, grunts so coldhearted and grim that the popping river itself looked yielding by comparison, and the tight clique of horses plunged in with snorts of relief—although the effort of scaring them left him still played out at sunset.

Cecil was saying how a new life like this was what he'd wanted, but Charley, looking peaked, muttered, "Yeah, and then you get a little sick of digging in the only round garden west of Ottawa." He said he'd been a spendthrift in Horse Swim and now was broke, though rich in goodies. "I've heard of people finding gold in stringers in the bedrock, if they get lucky, or gold like rice grains at the grass roots. But I never *have* found a valley like that."

Scouting through a morning fog and through sagebrush for Charley's old path between the Kluakaz and Ompompanoosuc rivers, they crossed a single set of fresh but lonely-looking horse tracks, the animal unshod but apparently with the weight of a rider on him. And soon after this bare warning, their small party bumped into a mounted gang of Indians. At first they couldn't even guess how many. Through the soup, four women, two men and a child, who rode seated behind her mother, materialized—but not before Cecil had had a chance to wonder if there might not be forty of them, or ninety. The elder of the men, wearing gum boots and a high bark bonnet, carried a Yellow Boy gun, the Winchester carbine with brass fittings made especially for the Indian trade. The younger buck, who could have been either the old one's youngest son or oldest grandson, had a bow and a quiver of iron-headed arrows, as well as a blunt, rusty, single-shot Hawken blunderbuss that would take a half-inch ball but had a crack in the stock under the barrel and was tied together with a length of gut. The women, though unarmed except for sticks and clubs and switches, wore black slouch hats and sat on their saddle pads with a certain bold beefy panache. One carried a buffalo horn with coals in it for their next fire.

The dogs yammered with their backs up like cats'. The horses shied, snorted and stamped. But both outfits stifled any further show of alarm and kept on moving forward slowly, exchanging silent nods, drawing away from each other while waiting to see whether a more numerous and ominous crowd of either whites or Indians suddenly emerged from the fog to change the odds. That Charley was as uneasy as they were frightened his friends. However, before they'd quite got out of earshot, Charley did gabble a salutation to the Indian band, using what he said was dirty talk and wouldn't translate, although the women laughed. He said that they were Sarsis, not some of his Thloadenni friends, and that the man carrying the Yellow Boy gun was called Shouts-at-night. He wasn't overly fond of the Sarsi tribe but said he knew a bunch of them from trading shindigs in the mountains.

"They're not your Indians who 'come to the fort,' " as he explained with a significant laugh. "But they're glad we're not Tlickitats. They're not supposed to be here. Where you see much sagebrush you see Tlickitats, and they would kill 'em."

No more Indians had showed up, and Shouts-at-night, apparently deciding that a handful of white travelers guided by Charley probably weren't dangerous, rode back to parley. When Margaret greeted him in Crow and in Kluatantan and Roy said hello in Apache and Charley added a Thloadenni howdy and he answered in Sarsi, it broke the ice. Everybody thought that was funny.

"He may have shot someone for those gum boots, but he's a curious old bird; he likes to see if he can learn something. I bet he likes running into a white man," said Charley.

Shouts-at-night, who was studying their armament and demeanor, had a big chin, a clipped-looking mouth, bushy eyebrows and a sparse, vagrant, lengthy mustache that curved down like a Chinese pirate's, but his watery eyes, the deep upside-down V of smile lines running from his nose to the corners of his mouth, his jaundiced coloring, and the way he squeezed his wrinkled shoulders inside a white and red and black and yellow Hudson's Bay Company blanket partly countered any wish he might have had to appear intimidating.

The four women, joining the group, responded so readily to Charley's jokes and sallies that Cecil rather believed his tales of being a ladies' man among the Thloadennis. Red-skinned, big-chested, they wore cloth shirts, leather skirts and bark vests, and they plaited their long hair from a center part under the swashbuckling hats. Derisively they stared at Margaret, who seemed muted and mild, or hybrid, by comparison. The eldest so much resembled Shouts-at-night—with her short upper lip, the smiling-lines around her mouth, and quizzical furrows above her bushy eyebrows—that they must have been an ancient couple together, Cecil thought. His hands were slick with sweat from this first encounter with wild Indians.

Shouts-at-night wasn't afraid now to begin kidding Charley for having shot a hole through his own skin boat once while he was chasing a moose across a lake. Margaret was able to translate the story because she said this was a blunder of Charley's that had become famous among the Indians all over—shooting his own boat out from under him. And when Shouts-at-night perceived that they knew what he was talking about, he mimicked how Charley's legs and lungs must have ached, how his deadened arms had floundered in the paralyzing water as he struggled for shore. The young Sarsi, and the women, who were equally uningratiating, lacking only proper weapons to face down the white men, laughed also. Margaret said they were reminding Charley that his trapping partner had drowned—had been a Sarsi, indeed—although they spoke not with the anger of relatives but more as if they had something on him. Shoots-his-boat, they called him.

"A bunch of boars and bitches," he muttered. Mad at Margaret for repeating everything, he said he had been young and foolish then. "Might be twenty years ago!" And no, these weren't all wives of Shouts-at-night. "Two are. Two already have their husbands dead."

Changing the subject and changing back to the Sarsi language, Charley told the Indians that Sutton could dive from way up high into a shallow pool of water—pointing at a puddle a foot deep that had toads' eggs floating in it. Of course they were dubious, and the young fellow, in hide leggings, naked from the waist up, gazed at Sutton with an unveiled, uncleverish expression that made Cecil think of Indian wars he'd read about. It was odd the way hair long enough to touch a man's shoulders could make him look tougher, not gentler.

Charley, introducing Cecil next, informed them that he was after bears.

"*Coats*," said Shouts-at-night, who maybe did know English after all. But Charley explained that Cecil wasn't a hideman; he was in search of a live bear to train for a show. They remarked on his crazy collection of dogs, and if Cecil had wanted the two younger women to look at him admiringly, they didn't. They flatly laughed. He had the unsettling feeling that they considered him doomed.

He asked Charley to ask what they thought would happen if he sicked his dogs on a Bigfoot instead of on a bear. "By mistake," he added, when he saw that Charley was amazed. "Is it something I shouldn't say? Would it matter to them?"

"No," said Charley, after hesitating. "They don't like the Bigfoot."

He went ahead and posed the question, although to piece together a word that meant Bigfoot in this pidgin conversation turned out to be difficult. *Nakina* was the Sarsi word, as he finally discovered, but *Nakina* had other meanings in Thloadenni and Kluatantan, and *Nakina* itself translated as "Brush Man," not literally as "Bigfoot," in Sarsi.

They were amused as well as amazed. "He'll run! He runs from a bear, so he'll run from your dogs, if you have enough of them," said Shouts-at-night, according to Charley.

"Would you do it?" Cecil asked directly.

"No," he answered, but wouldn't tell him why in English or Sarsi.

"Would you mind if I did it?"

After the purport of this question had been elaborated on by Charley, he said no again, rubbing at the pus of pinkeye at the corner of his eye, though with a smirk at the absurdity of the whole idea.

"They like bears better than the Bigfoot. He's like the black sheep in your family," Margaret explained. "Bears are a better relative, even if they're awful scary."

"But if nothing can kill him, why does he run away from a bear or from a pack of dogs?"

"Well, he don't want to be chewed! And he don't want people chasing after him and throwing firewood at him, either, so he don't come too close to people's camps."

"He can't kill a person?"

"Sure he can, but you could hurt him a little first!" she said, with a sort of jittery and emphatic awareness of conflicting loyalties that reminded Cecil of a particularly pensive evening when she had told him that although Charley had "joined up with the Indians," she herself had joined up with the whites. But as she attempted to mediate between the two groups here, that didn't seem so certain.

On the other hand, the Sarsi women watched them talk as if they might not agree with anything Margaret said. Their unexpected meeting with these visitors bizarrely ambitious to travel places where they didn't belong had brought a feminine animation to their faces, which otherwise must look a bit slab-sided, Cecil thought. Yet their eyes, in slits much punished by the sun, took him in and spat him out. He was dismayed to realize that they were probably prepared to laugh at him as cruelly as they had at the plight of a toad that Kitty, in shifting backwards, had stepped on. Only the small girl sitting behind her mother with her hood pulled up against the blowing mists and her black hair aslant on her forehead had a smile that was devoid of mockery. He wondered if the pang he felt was for his dead daughter Lindy and his living daughter Ottilie at home or the seventeen-year-old bed chum he hoped to acquire among the tribes in the mountains.

"You couldn't find a wife among these women, could you?" he asked Charley, speaking his mind.

"Oh, they'd sell you a slave. You might wind up with the same girl you could have got from her father up in my country. That bastard's killed a lot of Thloadennis in his day, but I'll bet you his price would be about the same."

Shouts-at-night was saying that if he had such good dogs to reckon with he'd be hunting buffaloes with them, not *Nakina*. But Cecil had Charley ask him where he'd go to catch a *Nakina*.

"We don't go that high up," he said in Sarsi, pointing toward the mountains, as Margaret slowly began translating again. "We got enough troubles." He pointed at Charley, presumably including the Indians Charley lived with. "And him for troubles"—gesturing at Sutton to denote the itinerant white man. "And him for troubles"—pointing at Margaret herself and meaning both the Kluatantans and all turncoat Indians.

"And you? *Nakina* will kill you in two flashes. He'll suck you dry, like sucking the juice out of a fish," he told Cecil through her.

Charley was disgusted with her for repeating this stuff, much as he'd begun to suspect that Sutton might be an agent for the outlaws in Horse Swim, for sympathizing with the character with the apple seeds who was following them.

Roy, too, said, "Heap big chief, heap big bullshit. You know what he'd do if he caught you out alone? He'd shoot you with your own rifle to see how it worked. That's what they used to do where I come from. Look at those turkeys. They haven't climbed outa the trees long enough to have learned how to fork a horse."

But Shouts-at-night, according to Margaret, suddenly mentioned something extraordinarily interesting. He said he'd heard that Brush Man used to trade with one particular white man—that he would leave his furs on a riverbank and this trader who took them left sugar for him. "He had a sweet tooth. He'd throw stones down on top of the Indians, but he would leave furs for this special white man."

Seeing that she was getting his sentiments across, he then announced as loud as a rooster crowing that he had watched lots of white men ride into the mountains—lots more white men than had ever seen *him*—and that half and more than half of them were dead. "More dead white men than dead Sarsis. Ain't that right, Shoots-at-himself?"

Old Charley Biskner, spitting contemptuously, jerked his rifle out of his scabbard and chambered a shell. They were all still mounted, and their nervous horses, heaving under them, seemed about to bolt.

"Yah, yah, yah!" shouted Shouts-at-night, flourishing his Yellow Boy as though the mountains beyond the fog were populated with Sarsis and Sarsi spirits armed with Yellow Boys and rarin' to ride out and avenge whatever harm Charley might try to inflict upon him.

Charley hollered back that he had fucked every wife and girl-friend Shouts-at-night had ever had; that every son he thought was his was really Charley's son.

The Sarsi women hooted at this. And Charley himself whooped. And Shouts-at-night yawped in response that Charley had no more bullets in his gun than an infant baby boy and was no great shakes at all as an "otter hunter," which Margaret said meant squaw man.

Nobody was friendly after the exchange, but the atmosphere

wasn't quite so tense. Everybody understood that the two had matched invective, that each man had scored a point and there was no need for gunfire. What rich guys these whites are, the young buck seemed to tell the others, why do they need this junk?—pointing at the filched roll of telegraph wire Charley was packing home to hang a bucket from for crossing his creek in and at the stake-and-wheel contraption for winching stumps out of the ground.

Shouts-at-night jeered at Charley again for having shot a hole in his own bullboat and said that horses loaded down like theirs would sink in the Ompompanoosuc River and die of a cramp, the same way his boat had in the lake after he had shot a hole in it. He imitated with his hands how powerfully buffaloes swam, and how effortlessly high in the water caribou rode. "An Indian pony is not like a caribou or a buffalo, but an Indian pony sure can make it across," Margaret said for him.

But then—according to Charley—he turned around and began taunting her for her dead husband's reputation for driving sleazy bargains with the Indians and her own notoriety as a woman who ate and slept with white men.

She grimaced when Cecil suggested she ask Shouts-at-night about her son.

"He'd kill that guy," she said—that is, her son would. She'd given him "an American rifle," she insisted, an 1880 bolt-action Remington Keene, not a gimcrack Indian gun like the Yellow Boy was.

"What's a Bigfoot like? A big Indian?" Cecil asked.

Charley was pleased to be able to repeat that notion to the Sarsis, knowing how it would offend them, and he expatiated on it. "No, he's not a bear or an Indian. He's not interested in bears and he won't breed with a sow bear, but he will breed with an Indian. Maybe he'll steal a girl and afterwards he lets her run home again—they used to say *his* father was a Bigfoot—but he'll run from a bear."

"Shouts-at-night's?"

"Well, they said that. He probably wanted them to say that. But I'm still telling you you'd make more money with just a plain old nasty yellow bear, or else a regular Indian chief. I don't mean an ugly-natured bastard like this one, I mean some of the nice old kind that they were saying in town this Buffalo Bill has signed up—so the people back east'll know exactly what they're looking at. I don't imagine you could stick a Bigfoot in a cage, anyway. He wouldn't stay. Some say they can vanish, some say they can't."

"I think it's white men that steal the Indian girls," said Margaret.

Cecil stared at the mordant young brave, who in his turn was staring not at Cecil but at his weaponry and horseflesh, and Cecil tried to imagine what he could have told him about this rolling country if they had become friends. Both Sarsi men, with their hair bluntly sheared across their foreheads, and the four women, wearing an aura of gay and hostile self-absorption, a confident, cross-eyed excitement, were unlike the disconsolate Kluatantans at Red Town. Yet would they have killed him, meeting him alone? Mightn't they have left him in peace? Other Indians had even adopted white men, and if he'd been offered the choice, would he have rather traveled with them instead of with Charley? If the lines of their faces were not merciful, at least they were playful, and it was adventure that he was looking for, not mercy.

The Sarsis sprinkled scorn on him with their glances, however. Deciding that the parley had ended, they swung their nickering mounts around and broke into a lope much in the same way a bunch of cowboys would have done, chuckling to one another that nobody had pulled the wool over their eyes.

The whole expedition had seemed simpler to Cecil half an hour ago. Did he want there to be such a beast as a Brush Man, or only to go on a bear hunt? Would the achievement now be spoiled for him if his plans were fulfilled and he brought back a grizzly bear? Beyond Charley's camp he'd hoped to meet Indians with necklaces of teeth and bone and queer forest-bird-feather headdresses above their ears, like Indians in books, who'd welcome him with countenances more primitive but less leery and more curious than the Sarsis' had been. But what was he after?

"Like I said, they don't come to the fort," Charley muttered.

"What do they eat?" Cecil asked, and Charley, watching him, understood.

"Nobody knows what Bigfoot eats."

"How many are there around?"

"Nobody knows that, either. And yet still, my friend Ben, that got himself killed by that young fella that wanted to be his partner in the bush, he knew, for instance, that Bigfoot ate, because he fed a family that was starving one time in the winter—and I never doubted anything he said in his life. He'd shot a moose and they showed up and they were looking pinched. That was a case of a Bigfoot that wasn't hibernating and that wasn't breeding with any human beings; so nothing's certain. They didn't threaten him or anything like that. They sat down in the snow at his fire, and when he offered them their fill, they ate an entire leg between them. They didn't talk—he said he didn't think talking was part of their life, and I've never heard anybody say that they do talk—but even so, he knew everything that they were thinking of without them talking. That was what was magic. I was kidding him a little because he couldn't tell me what they looked like except that they had hair instead of clothes and they were long in the foot and in the tooth and in the leg and back. I told him if they weren't Indians, maybe they were Eskimos who had walked a thousand miles looking for food—but he was perfectly serious. Nobody, he said, Indian or Eskimo or white man, could have made him know what they were thinking without speaking a single word."

"So, they do eat?"

"He's the only man I ever knew that's seen a Bigfoot eat. The Indians claim they'll steal food from a cache, or fish strips on a rack, and they don't like to draw them around a fish camp. But some of them don't think they do eat. The one I saw that might have been eating was on a river bench. Nice south-facing flat and slope with the sun shining. There was a bear there and there was me there and the Bigfoot was there and the salmon running by, but I don't know if he was there to eat the salmon or to enjoy the sunshine, because pretty soon he ran away from the bear. That answers you the question of who is more scared of a bear—a Bigfoot or a man. A Bigfoot don't have a gun, you know. Or who a Bigfoot is more scared of."

Sutton was still interested in the Sarsis. "What's going to happen when they find that guy with the apple seeds?"

"I couldn't predict. I hope they kill his ass. What is going to?"

Charley looked at Margaret. "As often as not it's the women who get to decide. Myself, I've always thought that women are more brutal. Not always—but over a lifetime."

Margaret laughed as loudly as if either he'd stumbled on a well-guarded and important secret or what he'd postulated was absurd.

Roy, speaking with the sort of pent-up disapproval he was master of, said he liked *white* women; that they were the real thing.

"There's no substitute. There's not a man on the Margaret who didn't leave a good woman somewhere behind him."

"Including you?" Sutton inquired tolerantly.

"Including an old bum like me, yes. I didn't spend the happiest part of my life bumping around the sticks on a rabbit-eared ground-hog like this one!"

Part 3

The Rivers

8

THE SWIM

They blundered onto the Ompompanoosuc in a chowdery fog, and Charley whooped it up because his guiding had kept them moving forward smartly in spite of the soup.

"That ain't no marsh, boys, that's a flood." He pointed at the slick of silt covering the grasses. Although the river's thunder had been muffled, they could hear it now, and noticed tussocks of an unfamiliar vegetation and the unusual shapes of juniper trees. They'd been riding between clusters of jack pine, but these mountain junipers had been seeded by the river itself and then bruised by the ice chunks of spring breakup. Big dead lodgepole pines and spruces had been carried down as well and were sprawled in gossipy clutches in the muddy meadows and on the mucky beaches. Like deadfalls after a forest fire, they were a struggle to get through.

Zigzagging across a series of sticky sloughs and former banks and beaches, they reached the river proper, though in the sloughs leeches fastened to the horses' legs and made them stop and bite themselves. The Ompompanoosuc was more voluminous than the Tongue or Kluakaz or Rabbitskin or even than the Margaret, and because of its many mud flats and wooded islands, they weren't sure where the far shore was when they peered westward. Unlike a prairie river, it had the push of the high-country runoff; the evidence of flooding had extended two miles back. Charley took some pains to indicate with his hand the general sequence of broad curves that it had traveled from the mountains, as far as he remembered them. He would have liked to pull away to avoid the drift logs that lay all over, but was afraid the river might bend off unexpectedly in the fog if they didn't ride close to it.

Their progress, although blind and picky, was exhilarating because of the roar. Logs hopped in the water like the heads of seals, catching and spinning at the ends of the mud bars. The water chilled the air, and beyond the nearest willow island, the currents multiplied, very fast and jammed with snags. They were scouting for what ought to be a beaten path to where he said the river spraddled out so wide that one of the last great populous herds of buffalo regularly crossed it. "An old lady leads them—an old mamma—and she knows where the calves can swim."

A pronghorn popped out of a patch of mist and skittered into another. A flock of cranes rose, blaring robustly, each bird in the shape of a cross, flapping just overhead because of the fog but straining, tilting, to avoid their party. Nobody had been ready for a shot at these, but Cecil noticed a porcupine hiding between rocks and skinned it across his saddle as he rode, feeding it in chunks to the cat and to Kaiser, the shepherd, and Sally, the retriever, who were the two dogs that hunted least well for themselves. Then all the pack fastened upon a desiccated, partially scavenged buffalo carcass, its head and shoulders buried in river sand.

They encountered nine buffaloes during the day, which were engaged in rubbing off their winter fur and looked as if they were wearing ripped and ragged buffalo robes on top of newer, lighter-colored pelts. The animal they got closest to was lying alone, shaking her head, in a swarm of flies. Her horns, pricked up like ears, looked to be the part of her that was the most alert, and she bounded away like a bulky jackrabbit when they attempted to hem her in. Under the circumstances, they didn't dare leave the pack string but chased her a short ways, dodging downed trees.

Finding Shouts-at-night's back trail, they followed it from the likelihood that it would lead to the ford, and eventually camped where the Sarsis had camped. Roy was fretting about this next swim, but Charley patted the several depressions in the ground where he figured that the squaws had slept. "Small pleasures," he said.

Sutton put out a salt block for the horses, and, not for the first time, produced a nifty snap-lid silver compass engraved with two cowboys chasing three Indians that he claimed to have won in a poker game in Memphis and that Charley, not for the first time, refused to look at. His compass was in his head. "That's how you goddamned well drown, going 'east' or 'north' in a soup like this."

"So you left a good woman behind?" Cecil asked Roy, to change the subject, because Roy's jitters at the edge of the Ompompanoosuc were jangling his own nerves.

"Didn't *you,* you lunk? I usually did the opposite, just the opposite, of what she wanted me to."

"Maybe me too," Cecil admitted a little sheepishly. "But I'm where I want to be and she wouldn't want to be here. That's the answer to it."

"Small pleasures," Charley repeated, hoarse in the throat. "You come home blowing blue smoke, all blistered up, and she cleans you up and rubs your neck like she's skinning a cat and pretty soon you're not tired anymore."

When Roy asked how many kids he had, Charley said several. "They know they can come round if they need me." He said if he was out, one or another of them, outbound on a hunting trip, would borrow a ration of whitefish from his smokehouse and replace it with a pair of ptarmigans when they came back.

They'd built a smudge fire against the mosquitoes, but he was coughing downwind of that as badly as Roy was and spoke of attacks on his "tubes" that had laid him low before—that's when he liked to have a ptarmigan to nibble on or make soup from. A chum of his who was now dead had been such a crack rifleman that right up until the end he could have provisioned a whole town like Horse Swim, but had suffered such pains in his stomach in his last years that he had had to reduce his moose meat to a scanty broth if he was to swallow it at all.

"Died in his bed. Nobody messed with him! He kept a field of fire clear of brush around his cabin, and if you were a friend of his—and nobody ever went near him that wasn't a friend of his—you still would need to fire off a bunch of shots and holler to identify yourself, and even so it was touch and go. That's how he was. So he believed I'd be dead way sooner than him: The Indians would kill me, awake or sleeping, or I'd catch the croup from their kids, or blood poisoning, or what he used to call prison fever. I told him it was us that brought in prison fever, because they didn't have prisons, but he thought we caught everything from them." Charley laughed.

But he did look sickly. Sutton put up what he said was a gator hunter's shelter of mud and brush around the place where Charley had chosen to sleep and kindled a separate alder fire for him, while Cecil, as the best shot, went out with Sally for the fixings for duck soup.

The ducks along the nearest slough had provided themselves with sentinels and got up snappily in front of him as he hunted, but he did break a widgeon's wing and Sally chased it through the badger brush. He also killed a mallard with coral-colored legs, sending the dog to camp with both birds in her mouth. Meanwhile, he managed to draw a large gray crane down to fly in low circles above him by lying on the ground in a cloud of mosquitoes, flapping his arm spasmodically like an injured wing. These red-capped, leggy, dancing fowl made as good eating as a duck and their *garroo, garroo* reverberating in the sky lent drama to the duller stretches of the trip. Like wild turkeys, they ran before they flew, but, taller than a turkey, could see over the grass, so that you had to trick them to shoot them.

Sutton had sent Sally back to Cecil, and Moose with her, and the three of them surprised another mud-caked, ear-sore buffalo trying to rub the bugs off her face—though she also seemed to be enjoying wriggling up on the rim of her hump, as a calf might do, and teetering there for as long as she could manage to before rolling over. First she dashed towards camp, then towards an oxbow, which turned her once again, and was chased by the dogs back towards Cecil, whom she quickly scented. He slowed her with a load of buckshot, however, and the dogs so hectored her as she dodged over the tangles of logs that she broke a leg and lay pinned and panting in her peeling coat of shag.

"Poor lady, you can rest," he said, although he was exultant. Calling the dogs away, he rested too, just out of sight, pleased to notice some marks of beaver-chewing on the trees around and a beaver canal leading into the slough. He hadn't seen beaver activity since he'd logged in Maine a year ago. Meat tasted better to him when the juices of panic had drained out of it, so when she had stopped gasping and swinging her head about and heaving ineffectually to try to stand up and was considering more calmly how she should get to her feet, he shot her dead.

In short order they had the crane trussed like a Christmas turkey and roasting and had hauled the buffalo over and had her tongue in the skillet and her hump roasting and her hide spread on four sticks like an upturned kite next to the fire so that the hair could be singed off. The dogs paraded the pluck—the heart and lungs and liver—and the aroma of all of this prosperity aroused Charley, whose color was coming back. His throat felt better, he said. He started on the duck broth, but switched to sliced breast of sandhill crane with some berries Margaret had ferreted out and stewed and sugared, a dish they all neglected the buffalo for—though Charley couldn't forbear boasting that his mountains' swans tasted the best.

"One scare a day, hey?" Sutton suggested, when the fog had cleared enough for them to notice that thunderheads were rising across the river. Cecil had never seen a river that was wider. Must be a mile wide. Grumpily Charley groaned that maybe it *was* his last trip; maybe as neighbors they could do him a service. Even the Thloadennis were widowing out. "They remember when the hunting worked good somewhere, so over they go, but now it *ain't* so good there and they get down-in-the-mouth, awfully sad and lonely at the old place. And every time they do that and then come home again, you see that at least one or two of them has gotten himself killed along the way."

He slept busily, twitching, talking in his sleep, while Cecil, couched comfortably on a bed of green branches, could hear Margaret murmuring to Sutton and Sutton's yawning answers, and enviously anticipated that land of mountain-Indian widows ahead of him, while the coals of the two fires collapsed into themselves. He dreamt, nevertheless, that he was flying east, gooselike, as low as the geese that Charley called snakeheads, and as if the entire spread of the continent he had covered from Massachusetts was neatly spooled in his mind.

When he awoke, Charley was cleaning his teeth with a split willow-twig and gazing about with that guileless expression of his. From the moment when he crawled out from between his blankets until nightfall he never quit staring about, so it was hard to imagine him burning up in a grass fire or freezing for want of a dry match or meeting any other bad end that watchfulness could have prevented. He said he too had dreamed that he was floating like a bird over their back trail—had seen not just the deceitful Mr. Appleseed toiling along in cracked boots but the tracks of thirty horses following him. Only the tracks, not the horses or who was riding them; but because the prints bore the marks of shoes, it must be white men, and he wanted someone to ride back and check whether his dream was true.

The rest of them did not respond. Cecil reminded him that he hadn't really seen such tracks any more than he, Cecil, had actually visited his kids last night. Roy of course was absorbed in whatever premonitions he was experiencing at the brink of this new swim, and Sutton indicated that he felt they'd all been rather nice and solicitous of Charley's health the evening before. It was a ride of fifteen or twenty miles being talked about. After running the risk of encountering Shouts-at-night alone, the person would have to come back and cross the Ompompanoosuc, too. Since Charley himself hadn't the energy for it, he sulked over breakfast, as they sulked also, watching a troupe of swift, dragony mists that snaked across the stretch of water confronting them and smoldered up in flattened spirals like steam, although the air was so chilly that all the bugs were lying low.

"Looks like she wants to eat somebody," Charley remarked cruelly. He said the Indians believed each river had a spirit inside it that gave it character or mood and got hungry and drowned a deer or something every once in a while. "Even on a hot day they'll keep their kids close to home when they see it like that. They won't let them swim."

"We haven't found out where the ford is yet," Roy reminded him, pushing his plate of food away.

"Well, anywhere in through here's not going to be too bad," he answered mildly, changing his tone. "We'll let the wind die down. The wind just makes it look worse than it is. Good bottom around here. It looks like muck, but it's black sand." Then, referring to his dream about the horse tracks again, he pointed out what a perfect spot this would be to hold out at if the horsemen were Indians. Flat ground with the river at their backs, all the water they could wish for and probably some fishing, their buffalo to live on for a month, their supplies all in hand, and plenty of driftwood for a breastworks if they needed it.

Sutton joked that although he had dodged the army recruiters in his dissolute youth, it sounded like the War Between the States. "My sins are catching up with me."

Cecil's dogs, like other dogs, got up every morning and nosed around for something to be happy about. Today it was a nest of muskrats they'd dug out. But in the west, rain clouds seemed to rub against the foothill mountains as though scrubbing them, and the Ompompanoosuc nibbled its bank so relentlessly that every minute a chunk beside the campsite would crumble off. Noisy, disguising its speed, concealing its currents in potholes, it carried the smell of the high mountains into this lower country, seeding a forest of high-country spruces and birches and firs which it promptly smashed down again with a spring spate of icebergs and boulders ripped from its islands and bends. It was a grander, sterner, much more guttural river than either the Margaret or the Rabbitskin—steely-colored on the surface except when, from the depths, long chocolate cords of mountain dirt were upchucked and boiled like giant balls of twine among the riffles and the waves and sank again.

"Oh, she'll drown you like a python sometimes," Charley sighed. Yet he didn't sound as harsh as before; just frank or fatalistic or perhaps ready to write Roy off if he had become so demoralized that he was going to destroy himself.

Like a python, Cecil thought as he dipped out a potful to wash with. The horses approached in a similarly gingerly fashion to stand and drink.

Roy chuckled. "You're going to be washed whether you want to or not. Maybe I'll ride back, huh?" Speaking of dreams, he told them that after he had lost his arm he had kept waking up in other people's houses, people he didn't know and who didn't know he was there. "I'd think I was dreaming, but I wasn't. I'd tiptoe getting out of there—and I quit drinkin', naturally—but the next night it'd happen all over again, maybe at some old fart's house who was in the habit of loading up his deer gun before he turned in. I was lookin' for trouble or I was lookin' for my goddam arm, the way it hurt so much." He squeezed his stump.

In Denver he had woken in the banquet hall of the Brown Palace Hotel underneath the serving table with hundreds of pairs of feet around him and only the skirts of the tablecloth hiding him from view. "Just the shoes I saw. Only it wasn't a nightmare, it was for real." His mind was going to pieces; it had busted up his marriage. Yet he had pulled himself together; and—pale and shaky though he was—you could still recognize the brawny pop-eyed horseman with a freshly stitched-up stump on his right side but a whinny for a laugh and high hopes once again who had ridden south from Denver into the desert and then into the Ruidoso country at Foley's Diggings in the Sierra Blanca. In fact, it occurred to Cecil that that green and hopeful embarkation of Roy's, gold hunting out of Denver, had corresponded to what Cecil was up to here, except that striking gold was a lot chancier than locating a mother bear and her family. By winter he expected to have a cabin built somewhere near the headwaters of the range of mountains this river drained, and his horses picketed in a beaver meadow below the house where they could paw for grass, and two or three or four half-tamed cubs stashed away asleep under the drifts like money in the bank till spring—no need even to bother to feed them while they hibernated—whereupon, in that special, muzzy state when the world seemed April-new to them and their instincts and memories were faint, they would be receptive to training. He was saving this buffalo hide to cut into muzzles and leashes for them.

"Boys, pick where you'd like to go in. Otherwise, we're at about as smooth a wade as any," Charley announced.

The wind had gentled and sunlight flickered from upper layers of the clouds. When Cecil signaled to the dogs, Smoky and the two huskies trundled into the water in a workmanlike manner and the others went in after them stoically, with the goat, so that the progress of their various heads marked the sequence of the currents. Margaret entered on her soldier pony, with Charley's shaggy mountain packing-pony and Cecil's red packhorse and extra paint and her own spare white bedroll pony behind her, while Cecil, Sutton and Charley whaled at the Pig Horse and the cat-hammed buckskin and the remainder of the herd.

"Nobody's meaner than an old man! Oh, these swims! This here's the worst. Good day to drown. Just imagine if you only needed to ride. Hooray for the railroad!" Charley yelled.

Roy had cut a pole to sound the bottom with. He was holding this against his chest with his good arm, gripping the reins in his teeth, having roped himself to the saddlehorn again, but because of his nervousness, the mule balked and bolted. Nobody would lead it in, so he was the last. By this time Kitty was shoulder deep in the greeny depths, picking her way among the underwater snags and rocks with a stylish bravery, though as the water wrapped around her Cecil felt her tremble and her muscles brace. With his pistol holstered behind his neck, he flattened himself along her back to distribute his weight as lightly as he could, ready to slide into the flow when she reached a drop-off point or tipped into a pothole. His own legs felt as though they extended the length of hers, probing with the same anxiety for each foothold, while the water stiff-armed her or curled around and wrenched at her like a giant's hands.

The horses in front had gathered their legs under them again on a sandbar when Kitty stepped into water deeper than she was tall. Cecil, swimming now, was glad he'd taken his boots off but sorry he had tied them around his neck, where they banged his shoulder blades and tugged against his windpipe. He kept one hand in her mane, paddled with the other, and kicked to keep his rear end high, singing to her and himself. Though drifting with the current's rip, she was pressing forward nonetheless.

With the bottom shifting from two to ten feet or deeper, they alternately waded and swam. There were logs riding the water about as fast as a bicyclist—you saw them upstream, thick as barrels, funneling toward you, and tried to guess whether they'd hit. It was everybody for himself, because the packhorses by now had despaired of turning back and without being driven were plugging for the far shore for dear life. Where the bottom lifted in a ridge between channels, the wading was often just as difficult as swimming. Waterlogged debris clogged the footing and stuck out in all directions, whole trees and splintered trunks and limbs. Between her whinnies to the red horse and to Cecil's sorrel and her snorts when the waves slapped into her nostrils, eyes and ears, Kitty was grunting quietly in desperate effort. Even when they walked, the two of them progressed unevenly, with Cecil either scrambling to keep up or attempting to haul her along at a pace which resisted the river's rush. If she stopped chest deep she couldn't rest, in any case; the water relentlessly shoved her around to face downstream and made it that much harder to get started again. From being with him, she sometimes let her guard down and waited for him to urge her on, as the packhorses, fighting the river independently, did not.

Laddie, the mule that Roy was on, kept waiting for instructions, too, lagging as it wouldn't have alone and becoming confused when Roy didn't react or else shouted for it to do things that were impossible. He had long since lost his sounding stick—as well as the droopy range hat that he loved—and wasn't balanced well enough on the animal's back to assist it, and wasn't looking ahead. They struggled abreast of and on the upstream side of a house-sized pile of trees, which for the longest while they couldn't get by. They were almost pinned. Roy's arm was thrashing like a bandmaster's to keep himself upright. He couldn't lean down lower across Laddie's side and still breathe, and yet the rope apparently had gotten an extra twist in it that was binding him tight to the saddlehorn with his face close to the torrent. He still looked desperately chipper, however—in the glimpses Cecil got when not engrossed in watery dilemmas himself—although he couldn't slip free and swim on his own and couldn't straighten up. Finally Laddie, from sheer steady-footed stubborn strength, pushed past the jam-up and into the next trench of fast water.

Roy waved. He was sufficiently clear to be able to breathe but was fastened weirdly sideways, as if the mule were a winged animal, grounded, sinking in the river with broken wings. Margaret had been shouting to him, but only the pitch of her voice carried. There was no single maelstrom, no surging and malignant horse trap to escape, just the constant corrugations in the bottom and the fluctuating velocity of the current, white-capped and rooster-combed, and so forceful that it sapped them, so cold that they ached. The wind put blue welts in the water, while logs high and cocky or low and hidden, logs like sharks' fins, rode the puckering, spinning currents as though they knew they were going to the ocean and were in a tremendous hurry to get there.

Charley and Margaret were with the pack string, encouraging them. Charley was as agile as a monkey as he rolled into the water and rolled out onto his pony again, according to conditions; and Cecil—marveling when he had a moment—remembered that this entire trip was just a backwards recap of what he had accomplished alone six weeks before. Cecil and Kitty talked to each other in the easier stretches, and moaned apprehensively in unison when the flooring fell away and spiky flotsam cascaded against their shoulders. The mouser cat, so tenacious of life, with claws like tenpenny nails, was swept away, abruptly, as the poor terrier had been. The water—pewter-colored, oak-colored—lapped up, ribbed and boiled across the root mass of a tree that had been upended, wiping her off that refuge as well, then curled sleekly back upon itself and rustled like taffeta, burying her.

On the far bank grew cottonwoods to fix on, and the gravel flat in front of them represented safety. Now the mule was doing fine. Self-reliant as a pack animal, it might outlive everybody. It was even beginning to catch up with the rest of them, when along came a floating birch tree with the new summer's leaves still on the branches, but traveling roots-end first. The birch wasn't a large specimen—the trunk extended for only a couple of dozen feet—but it was sailing fast along a curve that threatened Roy. The mule stopped dead in mid-channel, more alert than a horse might have been, and started trying to turn around. Unfortunately, that maneuver resulted in Roy, who was lying like a load of baggage askew across its back, having his head facing downstream instead of upstream when the tree sideswiped the mule and knocked its legs out from under it. Not seriously hurt, it skidded down-current on its side in the wake of the tree, with its head twisted up and around so it could breathe— quite calm, to all appearances. Cecil, happening to look back when the trouble happened, was reassured at first to see that nose up and working. But it was the mule and not the man who was able to breathe. Roy's head and rope-wrapped chest were underwater.

No cry from Roy had penetrated the Ompompanoosuc's tumultuous roar, and Cecil, who knew that he himself would drown if he cut loose from Kitty to try to do anything for him, didn't have the heart to holler to Sutton, who was a better swimmer but also must be dangerously tired. But he did call out an instant later when he stumbled up to his neck in a hole in the channel bottom and felt such a chill of terror that the sensations Roy was feeling in smothering were brought home to him. Sutton heard and turned and watched with equal helplessness. The others didn't hear; nor did the horses ahead swing around. The river in its second quarter-mile of width had toughened—cresting, humping, thickening, rumbling, the currents in a horde.

The mule recovered its feet for a second but was speared by a limb of the same tree, which was drifting alongside. It was whirled off its feet all over again, was spun completely around several times, scraping or bumping over logs or rocks on the riverbed, yet still didn't appear to panic, as its gaunt head succeeded in reaching the air. Roy had seemed alive—jerking to free himself from the infernal rope—when the mule had stood up briefly in mid-river. So now that he was speeding downriver again—though he and the mule were also floating horribly slowly—Cecil began counting the seconds that he stayed submerged. Forty seconds, sixty seconds . . . He gave up, it was so cold for him to stand still; and from deep water he could scarcely keep track of their progress anyway, except for when the mule, exerting itself to cross an obstruction, arched up and down like a carousel horse, with Roy plastered across its back like a dying

dragonfly. The animal would thresh and thrash to gain some footing, then lose it again, growing feebler, and give up struggling and
be rotated into a rapids as if into the headlong but involuntary in-
tricacy of a square dance, scudding round and round with its meek
head single-mindedly twisted up for air, and at last bob loose until
the next rapids or stoppage of snags. Finally it floated next to the
point of a needly little island and got on that, standing with its feet
tangled in a drift pile, too exhausted to move, and miniaturized by
the distance, still saddled and alive—but no Roy!

Kitty kept Cecil plunging forward to reach a sandbar where the
water was knee high and the current almost dimply. The sun came
out, glistering on the surface. They rested, though the cold would
have continued to wear them down if they had lagged for long.
They could see the leading horses lunging like an attenuated water
serpent across other bars and channels two hundred yards on. Wherever one found any perching spot, the others headed and shoved
against it until it made room for them. The gravel flats turned out
not to be particularly dry or flat, just a lazier and more braided section of the river. Cecil saw his dogs waiting individually for him on
moundy places there, before they swam two last deep eddies, waded
another quarter-mile, and climbed the western bank.

To know the shape of what was left was not necessarily to escape
turning blue and losing one's grip and drowning. Sutton had caught
up with Margaret, whose old cavalry horse possessed extraordinary
stamina, and the two of them lent courage to each other and could
learn from each other's missteps. Cecil just had Kitty and felt that
he might die of loneliness, or, anyhow, smother alone like Roy. He
kicked hard to catch up with everyone—the dogs, the horses, the
billy goat, and Charley and them. His strength was gone, but the
river had loosened its own fingers, too.

Charley, who was always the dry-match man of the party, kindled
a fire.

"Good day to drown," he repeated softly, lying down next to it.

Nobody moved except to shiver for the longest time. Not till well
past noon was anybody warm enough to consider hunting for Roy,
and Charley didn't go with them.

"I want to clean your guns. This is for real. This is Indian-land. This is no place to have a gun with mud in it." He said Margaret should collect the horses.

Cecil and Sutton, limping downriver, checked the pockets of dead water under the bank and talked about the properties of a body's gases and the folklore of when a body would rise from the bottom if silt had buried it. From seven to twenty days—the temperature and muddiness of different rivers made the difference.

The Ompompanoosuc was both cold and muddy; they even discovered shelf ice remaining where the sun hadn't had a chance to get. After slowly covering several miles, they walked back discouraged, and Sutton, grimacing painfully, took to the water above their crossing point. He intercepted a spar tree and wriggled onto it and traveled the closer currents to look again, although rocks caught and jarred and twirled him.

The mule on the spindly sand island stayed in sight. It had gained a grassy patch and was feeding fitfully in a woozy, shocked manner, favoring one leg. Sutton, after he had drifted around three lengthy river bends, swam ashore and caught his breath and ultimately walked back to where Cecil was waiting, deciding that before he gave up Roy to the water he ought to get out to that goddam island. The prospect was grueling, so he sat down companionably, although Cecil couldn't do much more than give him sympathy from the bank.

"Sorry you're here?" He grinned, because he was the one who most deserved to be sorry.

"No." Cecil laughed. "I guess if you're going to be crazy you might as well be *real* crazy."

"I think we're going to do okay. I'll make my million dollars and you're going to be famous. Now when we were kids, I wanted to be famous and you probably wanted to make a million." He said it was odd that after all the drownings he had witnessed on the Mississippi he minded leaving Roy in the river, but that he did. If Roy had been knocked loose when the mule hit the island, he might still be right there.

Indeed Roy was, caught by his clothes against the exposed roots of a leaning tree at a bulge of dirt that was fast eroding. But it required a miserable struggle before Sutton, swimming way offshore, reached mid-river and caught another ride on a big log, then left the log to connect with the island in a shallow rapids—curling through the riffles like a jumper, lifting first one arm and then the other, then his chest and belly, and finally his legs, to slide over the bars with the best flow of the water. He swam as tactfully as if he were in a Louisiana bayou full of alligators, and he actually spotted the body only while he was being carried past it at a double-walking-speed—just managing to land before he missed the downstream end of the island. He said he wouldn't have had enough strength to go back again.

He couldn't carry Roy; he simply pried him free and floated after him, holding the scrap of rope that was tied to his waist. Got him to a dry sandbar a mile farther down, rested for a while, steered him to a wet sandbar maybe another mile down, where the water ran inches deep, and waited beside him for Cecil to swim out and help. Margaret brought her soldier pony along the bank to pack him to the campfire, once they had laboriously wrestled him through more high water and a popping rapids to a pebble beach.

There was no blood on him—the river had seen to that—although the rope had cut red marks and though his head and body had been chewed at in collisions with the rocks. He looked aghast, his jaw lolling open, and he was deathly white, but so thin that he looked quite lifelike, because the toll of the hard weeks on the trail showed. Cecil, who was so much younger, had often forgotten how punishing the trip must be for Roy.

At camp, Margaret laid him on a loamy slope with his head downward so his lungs would drain. Feeling him, she did find breaks in his bones and gashes that began to ooze; yet, sprawled that way and seen from behind, he could have been a kid staring at a turtle or a trout under the lip of the bank. His hair was too tousled, his legs too limber, his arms too bent to be anything but a kid's. Without noticeable blood or any dents, it seemed that he might soon come to and sit up, spitting water out, with a frightened squall.

Cecil shied stones at the river and sat and chewed on a straw. Sutton hobbled off, rubbing his bruises, to "eat some grass," he said, the way a couple of the dogs, sick from the crossing, were doing. Charley, whose vision was not as sharp as theirs, had been asking whether the mule stranded on the island hadn't broken its leg and shouldn't be shot for its own sake. No, no, Cecil said.

"Is his kit gone?" Margaret asked.

"What does it matter if his kit's gone?" Cecil shouted, pointing at the nearly live figure of Roy, who might have been watching a fish-line popper jig.

"Lonely place for a grave. It surely is," Charley remarked disarmingly.

"There ain't no real nice places for graves," said Margaret. "But we have to dress the poor tyke. Not that he's going to feel the difference." She built up the fire and draped everybody's wet stuff over the alder bushes. The dog named Yallerbitch that Roy had adopted for his own, though scared to come and nuzzle him, was keening for him, cringing, circling, yapping, till suddenly its antics reminded Cecil that wolves would be scavenging this camp within a day of their leaving.

"Maybe we ought to put him up in a tree the way the Indians do."

"Suit yourself. I buried Mike," she said.

Morbidly Cecil wondered what would actually happen if Roy, bored with his "fishing," bounced back to life, broken spine and all. They couldn't linger here forever. Would they abandon him to his fate, or would they get cracking again in a few days and simply let the pounding finish him off?

He chose a grave site under a cottonwood, but after encountering an obdurate clump of roots, moved out into the open, licking his blisters, and started over. Sutton had returned at the sound of the shovel, still shaking with cold and hugging his bones after his immersion. He didn't lend a hand, and Charley, having cleaned and fixed the guns, looked as though he was absorbed in trying to figure out why he had saddled himself with this collection of lame ducks to begin with.

"The river'll have him anyway in two years, if the wolves don't," Cecil suggested—to excuse himself after completing a sloppy oval hole, which was all that his energies were up to. He'd dug his father's grave better. This was only his second—and what a change of scene, he thought. And how far out from under his father's shadow he'd got. People in Pittsfield had pegged him as a dullish son, a strong-backed logger with a taste for training animals who would sell his father's medicines off and never be heard from.

Margaret had unearthed Roy's spare bag of clothes. Cecil helped her tussle him out of his gritty garments into his best cotton shirt and pants, wet though they were, and wrap him in a blanket, and tie his poor jaw closed. The stump of his arm should have made these chores easier, but instead it flailed around, embarrassingly ornery. They went to sleep without burying the body, to give Roy one more night under the stars, "one more night to wake up and climb out of there," as Cecil expressed it.

No rain fell, so their scattered belongings were at least halfway dry by morning. Laddie had picked his way ashore and was grazing with the horses, with Roy's upside-down and stirrup-less saddle still cinched to him. Charley joked about the horses' charley horses, and they all indulged in a last gander at the corpse, which overnight had lost its sleeping-urchin vulnerability. The cold hours of death had hardened and discolored it with grayish, yellowish patches and changed the message in Roy's face from aghast innocence to resentful cynicism and disagreeable defiance. They shoveled in the dirt and piled driftwood on top of the grave—to hold him down as well as in order to stymie the wolves.

The dogs had been barking in dismay. But now they barked in quite another way. And here was Millard Switzer showing up dripping wet again, with the same aging mare that Cecil's horse Fred and Margaret's soldier pony liked, and her new capering roan-red foal, and the small brown bitch that had once followed them, and, surprisingly, a litter of black and tan puppies housed in a knapsack Switzer had strapped across his shoulder blades. These were sneezing. He set them by the fire, where their mother nursed them.

"You're a regular ghoul, aren't you," Charley announced, gazing over the river for any other figures who might appear.

"Your poor fella paid his debt to nature early? I'm sorry," Switzer said.

Yes, he'd run into the Sarsis, he told Sutton.

"I saw some Indians and had a good conversation with them. Had some problems explaining what an apple tree is, but we had a peach-leaf willow I could point to, so I told them the seeds were going to grow up into trees about like that, but they would have big fat berries on them to bite into if they planted what I was giving them next to a slow creek that already had some shade on it." He signaled eloquently with his hands.

Though Charley's suspicions were in everybody's mind, Charley merely went over and rubbed the mare's white blaze.

"You have a happy horse. There's nobody behind you except those Indians?"

"Nope. A lonely man would get lonesome. *I* get lonesome."

"You probably got your Bible, too. That's what we need."

Switzer nodded and took out the package wrapped in oilskins, which had been secured under the puppies' sack, drying the outside very carefully before he opened it. The book itself he didn't open, but recited in a clear, matter-of-fact tone: " 'God is our refuge and strength. Therefore will not we fear, though the earth be removed, and though the mountains be carried into the midst of the sea, though the waters thereof roar and be troubled, though the mountains shake with the swelling thereof. There is a river, the streams whereof shall make glad the city of God.' "

"Psalm what?" Cecil asked.

"Psalm Forty-six."

He thought again and went on: " 'And out of the depths have I cried unto thee, O Lord. Lord, hear my voice. For with the Lord there is mercy, and with Him is plenteous redemption.' "

"Psalm what?"

"That's from Psalm Hundred and thirty." He spat gently away from the grave and paused to squeeze a stream of water out of his shirttails and shirt-sleeves. Swaying wearily, ready to sit down, he offered a last prayer:

" 'I am the resurrection and the life. He that believeth in me, shall never die. Man hath but a short time to live. He cometh up and is cut down like a flower. In the midst of life we are in death. To Almighty God we commend the soul of our brother departed. We commit his body to the deep.' "

Charley hadn't heard a preacher for a number of years, he said. He did a kind of curtsy, as though just for a moment the boy in him wanted to kneel. Then, aggravated, he said he wanted to push on.

He didn't believe in hanging around a bad-luck place. "It's not going to help his soul. He's lonelier than we'll ever know until we're dead."

But his companions stayed put, and as Mr. Switzer enjoyed a bite to eat and a pot of tea, Cecil posed a question that his father had liked to stump a preacher with: "Where did Cain find his wife after he killed Abel, if Eve was the only woman alive? It says that Cain killed Abel and then it says he took a wife, but where did he *get* his wife?"

Switzer touched his book without opening it. "Well, it tells us Adam lived nine hundred and thirty years. So after Cain and Abel and Seth he had other children."

"She was his sister?"

"In a way she was. In a long life you're my brother."

"You'll go to Heaven when you die, but where do Indians go?" asked Cecil, pressing on.

"Indians go if they have led good lives."

"Indians go to Heaven?" Margaret asked.

"Of course they do."

"What if they don't want to go?"

"They want to go. It's like their heaven; it's not too different." He laughed along with her.

"I believe that, too. And I believe there's niggers in Heaven," said Sutton. "I'm about the only one I know that does."

Nobody agreed or disagreed with that proposition, and Charley's party lagged so long they began eating a reasonably friendly sort of funeral lunch, with their survivors' appetites doubly whetted because what was most likely their worst obstacle was behind them.

"Will you be happier in Heaven than me?" Cecil asked, being still in the stumping mood. The others laughed at the idea that he would be in Heaven, but Switzer answered with interest:

"I'll be as happy in Heaven as I am here and you'll be as happy in Heaven as you were here unless you were unhappy because of what you couldn't change but only God can change, if you get what I mean."

"Yes, but you've been scared, haven't you? Tired and scared?"

"Oh, I'm tired. I rested in Winnipeg. Then I rode from there to Horse Swim on the train. I'm tired now."

"I mean when you saw the Indians. Does He protect you?"

"I was afraid when I saw them, sure. Coming my way. Until I got a look at them. I wasn't scared of their faces, no, and they looked at what I had, like you did, and they told me that they didn't want it, just like you." He smiled, though he was wan and worn under his whitish head of hair and grayish beard and the terrific sunburn that he had.

"But does He protect you?" Cecil persisted.

Having eaten some of their meat today to give himself strength, Switzer was picking his teeth with precision, hugging a bony knee with gangling arms and smiling with a sharp, shy glance. "I don't know. It's not for me to know. Live or die, we're protected. Live or die. Whether He wants me to plant apple trees in the Rockies or for somebody else to plant them, somebody will."

But he was dozing off even as he spoke, which made his presence seem less weird and inexplicable. It grew practically commonplace to sit with him after he'd relaxed in the sunshine, had rubbed his bruises, dried his chest, stretched out his heels, and was threatening just to take a nap. Charley went through his pack bags once again, poking fun at what a meager show it was. "Slimy," he said, wiping a hundred wet seeds off his hands.

"It's good for them when they get wet. Every seed's a tree," Switzer reminded him cheerfully, scarcely bothering to open one eye.

"As wet as my daddy was," Sutton exclaimed. He started reminiscing in a stout man's mood of sociability that his daddy was an Englishman and his mamma was a Frenchwoman. "But he was a sailor and he crawled out of the sea to marry her—or that's what they used to tell me. His ship broke up in a storm a few miles out and he was drowning, but he kept on swimming. He grabbed hold of a slab of wood so he could keep on comin'. He was washed in and out and in and out and way down with the tide, but he slept on the beach. There was nothing there, just the crabs and him. Big grabby crabs waitin' for a dead man to eat. But he wasn't dead—and that's why he had me learn to swim so good. Then he had to wade across seven or eight miles of salt marsh, as the crow flies—which is about a dozen or fifteen miles, as a stranger that had never been in a Louisiana marsh that's five feet deep before would have had to walk it—

to get to the *chenier,* where it was dry enough that you could find a house. And this wadin' was worse than the swim. He thought he was barely alive.

"That's the ridgeline, where it might be two feet higher than the water, with some regular horse and cow grass growing on it and live oaks and hackberry trees. He saw a scratchy square of cotton and half a dozen fly-bit cows and a house that was hardly half built out of sweet-gum and oak timbers and oyster shell. A couple of niggers workin' and two white kids playing with a couple of dogs, and pretty spoonbills and redheaded woodpeckers flying around—a widow woman's house, four months widowed. That was my mother before she was my mother.

"Now, he needed her that day! He was like to die, all swole up from the bug bites, couldn't take another step. He'd brushed up against so many snakes he thought this was Hell. And she stepped outa the house, a little black-haired, blue-eyed Creole woman in a funny bleached-out frock that she'd brought with her from New Orleans. She could see she had nothing to be scared of from him—she had to raise him almost from the dead to start with. She had to feed him, dress the cuts he had, give him toothache bark to chew, and pull out all her husband's clothes to see what fit his needs. And she was complaining about the two niggers, because she had no near neighbors around where her husband had brought her to help keep them in line, so the first thing he did when he had caught his breath after a day or two was smack them for her. And she kept cookin' him good Creole messes of rice and fish and peppers to fatten on, so what reason did he have to leave? He had me and another boy and married her in a couple of years, although he already had kids in Baltimore that I've met since, but that's how it is in the marsh. Lotta people die off from the fevers, lot of new people show up from the Gulf. Not many people came in overland, because there's just as much marsh behind the ridges. Right out of the water!" he said, waving at the river. "Born again."

"Man is born of woman, not of water," Switzer said. "Except in the woman. Right?"

"I'm not gonna be born again. Once is enough," Margaret said.

Cecil had a story to tell about when he had herded turkeys to Bos-

ton afoot when he was a boy. Three thousand turkeys, four dogs and
eight herd boys. Two weeks, walking the roads. "The worst was
when we had to cross the covered bridges, because they'd roost;
they'd fly up in the rafters, thinking it was nighttime. Have to get
'em down."

"Gentlemen, we've got a piece to go," Charley interrupted, slapping his knee with a noise that roused the horses, too. Warily he
turned to Switzer. "You're on the trail to the head of the river and
it's like a paradise there, for the grass, for water to fish in and for
ice fishing, and plenty of Sarsi Indians you can preach to. Leave us
alone."

"Thank you, good folks," said Switzer, as the rest of them bowed
to Charley's wishes and prepared to leave. "I'd be dead like your
friend if I didn't have you to follow behind, only I wouldn't have no
grave to lie in by the riverside."

By the time they'd gotten organized, he was asleep and dry-looking
beside the fire, and less than ten sore-footed miles of bright daylight
were left before they camped again in a plush foothill side valley with
serviceberry bushes and chokecherry trees, whose last white blossoms
they appreciated for the few minutes they could stay awake.

Cecil dreamt that night that Ottilie, his daughter, was choking on
a chicken bone. Her face turned black. Clutching her, clapping her
back, he stumbled with her toward the fence behind the house, beg-
ging her to tell him she could breathe. She did catch several breaths,
but died.

It was too real to believe it was a dream. He wrenched himself up
and awake, squealing like a hog, his heart slamming. He realized he
had left home too early in her life, that she would never forgive him
when he went back East. He should have waited till she and Sammy
were older and better able to get along. They appeared in all their
frailty with open faces and thin arms. Between his own people and
his wife's family, he knew that they were eating well—they had
plenty of uncles—but he had lost them for himself. And if he hadn't
sneaked away in the night like a thief, he had probably done worse.
He'd left in a rage to make the procedure easier at the time, yanking
his wife out of Sammy's bed, where she usually slept, and telling her
to fuck herself, since she wouldn't fuck him. And now his children

were the width of the whole continent away. And if fucking was supposedly so important to him, how much even of that had he done?

So wretched that his chest felt as though his heart would quit on him, he stood up, lay down, and stood up to look at the shapes of the horses in the light of the moon. In the west the mists loomed larger than the mountains. Sally, Moose and Smoky came to his hand, along with the goat, always as quick as the dogs, but he bumbled over toward the lump on the ground that represented Margaret, who was sleeping alone. She woke and, hearing him groan, took his hands and drew him down. He was too miserable to stretch out next to her. He sat cross-legged.

"You dreamt about your friend in the river? No? You dreamt about your kids? If you want more kids you'll have more kids. I'll find you a girl. You're going to make brave Indians with her. And you're going to be rich, and that'll be good for them—the new ones and the old ones too."

But he didn't smile.

"You're not scared of drowning, after how you swam the Ompom?"

"No."

"You scared the Indians are going to kill you in the mountains?" She laughed and pulled him down where she could hug him. "I'll tell them not to kill you. I'll tell them you're a good white man."

She was sleepy and she drowsed, but first she murmured to him, "You got any Indians left in Massachusetts that you didn't kill?"

What he finally remembered that comforted him was two old men he knew who had been veterans from the original Pittsfield Gold Rush Company of 1849, as they had called it—Pittsfield's own. They hadn't second-guessed themselves. They'd picked up stakes and gone, leaving their families behind for several years, and even though they'd come back broke from California, nobody had held it against them for long, including their kids.

9

THE FOOTHILLS

The humming bees and flower flies, the nectar smells that drew them, the swallows flickering overhead to snatch them, and the mountain breezes slicing white swathes in the grass, which sprang up green again immediately, as well as the breakfast feast of buffalo meat spread with a beaten, sweetened foam of berries—these many pleasures helped to rouse the despondent party. A hundred ducks had taken to the sky when Margaret went to hunt for a few late eggs for a fancier breakfast for herself, but two duck hawks had been cruising higher still and plummeted like two rocks, each killing a bird in midair and catching it before it hit the ground, and all the rest gave a great disconsolate howl as they streaked off.

In following the valley of the Ompompanoosuc upriver, Charley's companions had plenty of chances to criticize his choice of a ford, but there were no easy sections. Whenever they dipped down alongside the water to get around a particular hill, the Ompom in its bulk and force kept twisting like an escape artist to climb over its bank and grab them. Yellow mud and chalky gravel boiled up from the bottom to scour the crumbling stretches as though rubbing a sore, undermining and upending trees along the bank which then became projectiles. The water snatched and whirled these—they'd pop half out, fall back, gyrate, roll over and over, and shoot ahead out of sight, with another set of logs storming around the bend, like a perpetual emergency. When it wasn't unnerving it was hypnotic.

Impatiently the land lunged into bluffs, cliffs and higher terrain, and the woods became real woods, not seeded by the river but extending to higher ground. The trees stiffened in height and complexity as new species joined the jack pines, white spruce, aspens and paper birch and red birch, like a crowd that collects—fascinating Cecil, as a lumberman. When they trooped across some of the tributaries, they encountered thickets of hawthorn and sometimes beaver glades that looped upstream, and occasionally through the breaks they could glimpse three startled-looking snowy peaks, where Charley said his Memphramagog ran.

There were peewees, nutcrackers, siskins and other woods birds, harebells and columbines, for flowers, and ferns. A kingfisher dashed out in pursuit of a fish hawk and actually rode on its neck for a hundred yards, sitting like a broncobuster, while underneath their conjoined, monstrous shadow a groundhog on the riverbank took such fright it bumped its head and stunned itself in diving for its den. White Eye grabbed the creature to lunch on.

A pair of yearling owls, overwhelmed with curiosity, fluttered in the wake of the passing parade, *pawk*ing like chickens, barking in falsetto, flapping between low branches to blink at the horses and dogs. The dogs leaped at them, but Cecil, imitating their peculiar cries, persuaded them to follow farther than they wished to, anyhow.

The Front Range now reared up like a thunderclap in intricate and awesome detail whenever a gap opened in the last line of foothills. You could spend the better part of your life climbing one of those massifs, it seemed. The enormous spectacle brought home to Cecil and Sutton how dependent upon Charley they remained. The mule that Roy had drowned on was following the packhorses, loose and burdenless while it recuperated, and Margaret claimed she personally was going to trade it for a wife for Cecil. But without Roy along to slow their pace for and condescend to, no amount of joking could stand between them and their various fears.

Charley, in a fawn-skin vest, with an antelope-hide sunshade affixed above him, and wearing bearskin boots which he said he'd stitched rough and then soaked in a brook with his feet inside them, so that they had dried to the shape of his feet as neatly as Sutton could have cut them, and which he'd laced with squirrel skin— Charley, the best horse trainer, beekeeper and squaw healer in this whole country, to hear him tell it—showed them buffalo fords and Indian fords, none of them easy. He said that he still hoped they'd be polite enough to head up the valley of the Ompom, however, "like Johnny Appleseed," instead of following him when he branched off.

"Make your own start, for goodness' sake. What did I have going for me? I had the grippe. I gave the grippe to that first batch of Tsimshians I met up with on the Hainaino, and then I nursed the chief until I had him thinking that he owed his life to me. And when the medicine man got a little disputatious with us, he borrowed some strychnine that I'd brought in for catching furs, so he could hold a fancy medicine contest with everybody that was turning against us. And it was awful simple going for him after that. He made a paste of it and got some awful sick Indians; and I didn't need no lame-legged mule to swap for a wife."

He mentioned the neighbor of his again who'd killed his friend Ben who owned the hot springs, and who nowadays hated people so much he swept their footprints off his paths. "Every footprint. I think he goes and hunts for them, he's getting so crazy. He comes out after you've gone by. First it was in his front yard, but I wouldn't be surprised if he isn't going five miles out now if he thinks there might be some footprints he can wipe away. He has a little hand brush." He mimicked how the man must stoop to do it. "Must take a lot of his time, checking all the trails like that."

This was a man who had shot every live thing in his valley, anything that moved. "Even the bloody nuthatches. And what a tomb he had to trap in after he finished doing that. His marten left him, naturally, because they had nothing there to eat. And he'd picked up a horse or two, but they got so lonesome living with him they ran off to live with the elk two valleys over. You know, if you think about it, he may be the man for you. He's real good in his garden, works around his place all the time. He has a water mill and some good diggings. I could show you a notch up in the rimrock where you could lie and get a nice clear shot at him. I've lain there, just to watch him."

"You wouldn't sic us on him, would you?" Sutton said, speaking lightly, because nobody knew how much of it he'd meant.

One day soon after, they noticed a vulture eating a snake—which disturbed Margaret as a bad sign. There were others wheeling lacka-daisically at a middle level in the sky, and more of them took off from trees along the ridgeline, like birds that felt replete. A raucous bunch of ravens materialized. Also two white-headed eagles, and crows enough to blacken the face of a cliff. A small cinnamon bear was hanging boredly in a tree, but it turned out to be stranded there, because a family of wolves was ensconced around the base in atti-tudes of satiety. Once the underbrush swayed tellingly, as though a beast heavier than a wolf or a cinnamon bear was leaving. They had their guns in hand, because if dead meat was ahead they might find live meat, too, and Indians watching it. Charley remembered hearing about a buffalo jump the Sarsis had operated somewhere through here.

Shortly they did come upon a tributary creek that was flowing be-tween broken bluffs and giving off a stench. Looked down at from above, it proved to be clogged with buffalo bodies. It was a sight as succinct as a dream and, like a dream, hardly to be believed—like the scene of a massacre. The drop that the buffaloes had gone over varied from seventy or eighty feet to only about half that, and the bodies had blocked the surface of the creek in the same way that a logjam would have, or were quietly revolving together like broken toys in the eddies that had been backed up. A fox was crouched on one of the floating carcasses, nibbling its lip. The smell downwind was stupefying, the place was an inferno of flies, and the animals lying on the beach whose abdomens had bloated scarcely resembled buffaloes anymore. Having lost their narrowish waists, they looked like dead, black, hairy cattle in a pasture that had been lightning-hit. Others, out in the cold current, hadn't blown up yet. A few had broken their legs but weren't yet dead.

A tatter-coated wolf was sunning itself among the bodies, not far from a turtle-backed chestnut grizzly that was snuffling and tooth-ing gobbets of suet from a buffalo's udder. But both gave up these peaceable pursuits and fled as soon as they scented Charley and his friends. To judge by the accumulated tracks, an entire "church supper," as Sutton put it, of wolves and bears had been mooching around—every sort of size. Also, a number of buffaloes had survived the jump intact, had managed to swim the creek and scramble up and out of the bloodbath, maybe as many as a quarter of the herd.

After they had put themselves behind the wind and ridden closer, they saw clusters of horse and moccasin tracks as well, coming and going across the sand, and many skinning jobs that had been done. A lot of animals had had their tongues and ribs and hams removed.

"Look. They wanted ten and they got ten times that. The meat's on the move and so are the damned Indians and both of them have been chased off their own territory, so neither one of them knows the setup here. They make a mistake and flap their blankets a little too hard and take all the meat out of the country," Charley complained.

Three buffaloes were still suffering, stinking of gangrene. They killed these, and Cecil as the axeman hacked at them to unearth some sweet meat. Margaret filleted whatever he cut, while Charley backtracked with Sutton to circle the bluffs, counting upon the dogs, as always, to protect them from a possible ambush. Margaret picked out the cow buffalo that, judging by her dimensions and bold momentum, had probably been the one that led the herd. Though she had broken her neck in landing, she had propelled herself well out from under the cliff, past the scrap of beach, into the shallows, where she lay sprawled on a mud bar, partly submerged but so lifelike that she seemed about to plunge forward, except for the fact that her head was twisted around as if to nose at the blowflies on her hump before she got started again.

They worked quickly because of the smells, and when Charley appeared above them shaking his rifle, they threw the meat into sacks and rode out of the low box they were in, seeing when they were on top of the north bluff a thin pillar of smoke where he pointed, and a couple of figures emerging from behind it.

"Just a meat fire. I don't know how many there are."

Four additional Indians joined the two, all men, with what looked at that distance to be rifles and not bows.

"Gentlemen, we are going to go around you," Sutton murmured. But Margaret stopped him, rode closer and stood in her stirrups and gave a keening shout for her son, on the chance that he was among them. No one answered.

"Are they Sarsis, Meg? I don't know them," said Charley, with a more sympathetic tone than he had ever shown her.

The six men on foot and naked in the noonday heat had been reinforced by half a dozen others and a dozen or two dozen women and youngsters, some with lances or bows and some holding guns.

"This is trouble," Sutton muttered nervously. He believed in his own sixth sense for danger, as Cecil would have too if he hadn't found himself preoccupied with this opportunity to ask more about the possibility of catching a Bigfoot. The leerier a bunch of Indians looked, the more he had decided he ought to talk to them, and these individuals were squat and spiky, primitive-looking mountain dwellers, to Cecil's hopeful eye.

"What do you think?" Charley asked Margaret again. "Maybe they're Sarsis or maybe they're Tlickitats from the south, where the railroad's going to push 'em out?" When he hollered in Sarsi, a flat-sounding voice like a hammer on an anvil replied in a different dialect. "No, I don't know that bloke."

"There's a lady that has skunk bear skin on her. You don't see much skunk-bear skin except on people from the mountains. I used to wear it myself," she said, turning to Cecil.

"That's a husky bastard, that guy is. Ugly customers. No, they're Sikinks or Sarsis, a benighted bunch. Old Minie-ball rifles—wouldn't do 'em much good. I don't think they have horses," Charley said. "Maybe Sikinks." But then two men moved into sight on dappled, stringy ponies, dismaying him.

"I think the railroad's doing it, and I think they've got more rifles with them than they ought to have—wherever they got 'em from— and I think that when the people that were working this buffalo jump killed so many buffalo, they sent for all these extra Indians. And I also think we ought to scoot on out of here pretty quick."

He shouted inquiringly in Thloadenni to see if he knew anybody or anybody's relatives and friends.

"They're Sikinks. They're not Sarsis. But that girl there is a Sarsi and they're telling her what to tell me," he concluded, indicating a young woman with a broken Roman nose who was wearing a leather shawl with what appeared to be glass bits and ermine tails attached to it. He said it was a good thing he wasn't alone but that he wouldn't have stopped, either, if he had been alone, and that his barefoot pair of ponies would have left tracks like an Indian's ponies, except for their loads.

The Indians had moved nearer, though still not into dead-shot range. Sutton sighed as if he were staring across that belt of scrub at his own death—a premonition powerful enough that Cecil caught the chill of it. Yet he realized—as with the smaller band that had been led by Shouts-at-night—that eventually he was going to have to put himself into the hands of people like these if he wanted to accomplish anything. He even rode a little nearer, spotting an elderly savage with a face that between the braids framing it looked as though he knew whatever Cecil needed to know. His friends didn't stop him, assuming that Cecil was craning to get a view of the Sarsi woman. And of course he did look at her—he wondered whether he could live for a winter with that nose of hers; maybe he'd come to like it—but he was fascinated in particular by this old bird, who appeared in turn to be straining toward *him*.

Head down in the manner of a butting ram, and oaring with his arms, the fellow stepped forward, peering intently as though his eyes were bad—as though, too, he didn't believe that the usual diplomatic distancing between such armed and dangerous parties applied anymore to an old man like him. He came up to within only a few yards of Kitty before he stopped. The words he spoke, although forceful enough, were not intelligible to either Margaret or Charley, and Cecil guessed that his reason for approaching might just be that, encouraged by Cecil's own curiosity, he wanted to see these three white men for himself. His eyes were a milky, cloudy color, so the way he was glowering out from under his brows might be simply that he was trying to see over the rims of a set of cataracts.

Cecil, as it happened, had learned years ago from his father how

to dislodge cataracts from the eyes of dogs and push them harm-
lessly into the liquid of the inner eye, and had done the job as many
as a dozen times for householders with pets, using the most delicate
instrument he had, which was his thumbnail. He slid off Kitty,
offering to shake hands, while turning over the riskier idea of volun-
teering to give this old man a new lease on life, or at least a new
pair of eyes.

But the guy didn't know about shaking hands, and he had a bush
knife in one hand, which further complicated their greeting. Was it
for protection or did he harbor some savage notion of taking a white
man with him, since he was going to die soon anyway? He smelled
as wild as that first buffalo Cecil had killed, just west of the Margaret, and his three-foot-long braids seemed maler than any clipped
head of hair. Besides his language being incomprehensible, so did he
himself appear to be, like some battered skate out of the sea. Yet
nevertheless he communicated to Cecil, who had never killed anyone,
a jolt of recognition that he had killed a good many people, and
how natural a procedure it was in fact, how thoroughly and at your
leisure you would examine your enemy once he lay there, stripping
him thoughtfully but totally of whatever he had. It was what he
would want to do if for a kind of warrior's swan song he killed
Cecil now; or what Cecil would do to him.

"They're the wrong batch, these Ompom Sarsis and Front Range
Sikinks. We don't want to be here," Charley announced, after the
Sarsi lady had translated her piece of bombast from the loud-voiced,
long-winded Sikink to him. "And I do miss that gun," he added,
meaning Roy's. "A man like me can only live where he lives because
a batch like this can't get to him. I'm in Thloadenni country, and
they hate these suckers."

"So we'll call it a day, will we?" Sutton suggested restively. But
Charley was yelling again, temporizing through several exchanges,
because, as Margaret explained, they wanted the white men to stop
and smoke with them and were asking payment for the sacks of
meat that she and Cecil had cut. The loud Indian had a barrel body
to go with his ringing voice, as if he ate a lot of meat, but when
Charley said he could take back what was in the sacks, he refused;
he wanted the three pickaxes tied to Charley's spare horse instead.

His name was No Water, which caused a lengthy confusion, because water was plentiful hereabouts and they couldn't understand
why when they asked his name he asked for some.

Raucous but slow, the bargaining continued in this twangy, chesty,
expostulatory combination of tongues. The true subject was whether
they would get a safe-conduct, not the price of meat, and yet they
didn't know if they even needed a safe-conduct from them, if their
firepower wasn't more than sufficient to scare this ragged band. The
trouble was they still couldn't tell how many Indians there were, or at
a distance of fifty yards, exactly what rifles they had—ancient Henrys
and Spencers from the Confederate War and before, or a more
formidable gun. Margaret laughed, because the Sarsi woman who
was translating had remembered who Charley was and had called
him "the Thloadennis' titty sucker," but Charley, instead of feeling
insulted, remarked that there were worse things for an old man to
be called.

The horses were exceedingly apprehensive, both because their
riders were and because of the stink of the buffalo jump, which had
been such a massacre that even the awed dogs slunk about. Cecil
wondered how important among the Sikinks this Indian codger
within an arm's reach was. He was indulged by them, but did he
make any decisions? Bare except for a brown breechcloth, with his
legs gone spindly, his chest wrinkled, his nipples drooping, and a
calculating, brutal grin, he gripped his knife like a club held at his
hip, and stared as if he'd barely left the woods to join his more
sophisticated kin but acknowledged no diminution in his powers
because of old age. He was fierce and made no bones about it, yet
Cecil, looking at his blindish squint, was fascinated by the possibility that he could clear those cloudy eyes, as he had done with a good
many Massachusetts poodles and Maine sheep dogs.

By sign language Cecil conveyed to him that he thought he could
improve his vision, a message which took a while to get across.
First he had to be convinced that Cecil thought there was something
wrong with his eyes—a most untactful observation to have broached—
that Cecil wasn't, rather, asking whether he had noticed some particular noteworthy sight, or wasn't rudely communicating to him
that he had pus next to his nose. This wasn't what he'd come to

inspect the white men for, to be examined medically and treated by them. He was huffy and at a loss.

But Cecil was certain he could do it. Having watched his friend Sutton go into a kind of crescendo of showmanship for his leap in Horse Swim had lent him confidence that when the time came for him to try some comparable feat, he could, too. He was suggestible, as he knew—his father's raffish example being much behind this trip—and lately the sight of Johnny Appleseed trudging with assurance through such chancy territory had affected him also.

The old man, after considering what to do, grabbed him to bring him over to the Indian side.

"Now you've fucked yourself," said Charley, low and serious. But Sutton, who had been alarmed before, said nothing; only told him he had better bring his horse. Cecil, in collecting Kitty's reins, sneaked a look at his thumbnails to remind himself that he hadn't bit them lately. He cleaned one with the other.

No Water, with a torso like a beer keg, a flat, quite joyful face, an energetic style about him, was consulting closely with the black-haired woman with the broken Roman nose. Though they had a nondescript assortment of guns, there were ten or twelve individuals who ought to be capable of shooting them, as primitive in appearance as he could possibly have wanted, so much so that it would have been hard to make fun of them. Their caribou and wolverine and red-fox and groundhog fur pieces, their mottled hawk feathers and snail-shell necklaces enhanced their naked dignity; and they were as busy as a heron rookery, conferring—talking all the faster because he couldn't understand them. Yet he wasn't afraid of them. He moved still tighter into their midst because he was now at their mercy to begin with, a tactic among strangers that his father had taught him. He pretended they were Quebecers, that this was a summer jaunt to visit the French woodsmen across the border from New England.

They did want those three pickaxes and probably wouldn't have minded killing all three white men to get everything else on the horses, but may have wanted to spend the afternoon in pleasant trading conversation, as well. Cecil's proposal was another matter, and Margaret—keeping her distance—had to be brought into the palaver, shouting the gist of what he said to them and what they an-swered and what he replied in return. It was her childhood lan-guage, Crow—not Kluatantan—that Sikink was related to, and she told him that Sikink was easier for her to understand than the Sarsi woman's translations into Sarsi, which was a bit like Kluatantan.

"You want to make his eyes right, is that right? He's the grand-father-uncle. You're dead if you do it wrong," she said.

But he felt like his father spieling snake oil or Sutton on the wa-ter tower, and without having received a definite yes or no, he moved toe to toe with the old man, who gazed straight at him stalwartly.

"Put your knife down. This is going to hurt you. Put the knife down," he repeated, pointing at it. He decided that the cataract on the right eye hadn't ripened enough to deal with, but the left one was delineated almost like a little fingernail.

The kids had stopped giggling at Cecil and teasing his dogs. One of them had rickety knees. He was the boy the old man gave his weapon to and hugged and held next to him with the same knotty arm. No Water bristled like a boar with disapproval and anxiety but didn't interfere. Still, he was remonstrating; and none of the words the others uttered sounded encouraging. *This faker may be playing with you* they could be telling him; and Cecil kind of agreed. But he felt as though he'd charmed a ledge hawk off a cliff and didn't dare even to take the time to ask him to lie down. In one slow seamless series of motions, as if he had accomplished a hundred of these op-erations, he held his patient's left eye open with his left hand and laid the fingers of his right hand on his forehead and the heel of that hand on the man's cheek and deftly inserted his right thumb-nail against the edge of the cataract in the pupil and punched it loose and through into the interior of the eye so that light and im-ages could pass more freely inside and be seen.

His patient grunted in pain and covered both eyes.

"Tell him to bandage it. Tell him to take it easy and keep it cov-ered for three days," Cecil yelled to Margaret, which, with some dif-ficulty at finding the words and hollering them back, she did. Everybody waited for the man to react further, but it became evi-dent that there would be no blood and that his pain was diminishing, not increasing.

"Tell them he'll see better. Tell them now I've paid for the meat," Cecil said, which got a laugh after translation.

This was a point of decision for him—whether to gather his gear and stay with them. What was most attractive about the Sikinks was also the most intimidating. They were as full of life and energy as white men in a city. Where would he sleep and what would he eat? How would he keep up with them after the novelty of having him along had worn off and they lost interest and patience? The new ritual of shaking hands amused the young men, and after Cecil had done so all around, they continued doing it among themselves in vigorous slapstick style, gobbling their regular goose and turkey talk, and he discovered that he really couldn't guess whether they were grateful and reasonably friendly or whether they were making fun of him.

Cecil fixed an eye patch from moss wrapped in a rag for the old man to wear until the moon was new, as he instructed him. Expansively, he wanted to tell No Water to bring him all the Sikinks' furs to sell, but Margaret was as worried as Charley about venturing any nearer to help him out, even after Sutton did.

"I guess if they'll talk to you maybe they will to me," his friend said. But without a language in common or an interpreter negotiating with them it began to seem impossible.

"Tough as hickory, ain't they?" yelled Sutton back to Charley.

"I've seen 'em split a man's head open like an egg while they were talking to him. Sikinks visiting some of my chaps up at the top of the Ompom. They had a rock strapped to a club and banged him one," Charley yelled.

"Not this minute they won't," muttered Cecil, remembering being so mad that time when he had just shot his buffalo and Charley was trying to upstage him with tales about the seals and porpoises he had encountered across the Rocky Mountains from here.

Three kids were wrestling with Coffee, Moose and Sally, and two young women in groundhog G-strings but with no tops on were bent over them, refereeing so excitedly that their breasts bobbed.

A man in a shirt of fur Cecil wished that he could identify handed him a bark bowl containing a paste made out of roots so tasty he would have liked to hear how to find more. No Water had stowed his old Spencer .46 away and was running his fingers through Kitty's mane, praising her sensible behavior and examining the way her shoes were nailed. Speaking with his hands, he said he'd seen prints of horseshoes in the dirt but never shoes right on the horse before. Meanwhile the grandfather was affirming good news about his eye, and the woman wearing the skunk-bear sash that Margaret had admired offered Cecil an empty bark dish and bowl, which he naturally thought he was supposed to trade something for—but no, they were a gift. Unceremoniously, he pointed to her sash instead, and she promptly proffered it, laughing at his directness and baring her breasts in the process.

" 'Stinkers' is what we call them," Charley shouted.

Again, because the moment of his triumph felt so brittle, Cecil didn't dare take time to walk back to his more prudent and experienced friends and argue with them. Indeed, their prudence might still be what was preventing him from getting killed. He sensed, as Sutton immediately had, that these flat-faced Sikinks were potentially as dangerous as Cochise, Chief Joseph and Crazy Horse had been, and for that reason didn't try to help poor Switzer's prospects by mentioning him. But in this moment of truce he remembered too how his father liked to say he'd never blundered in amongst any hillbilly clan in a hole in the hills still speaking Czechoslovak, or any Shakers, Doukhobors or Holy Rollers, or a family of feebleheads with half a dozen fingers on each hand, that he couldn't make friends with with a cup of sweet syrup or by juggling pears to make them laugh or rubbing hedgehog oil on some gentleman's bellyache or building the children a toy hay-wagon or dabbing wood alcohol on their mother's neckbone to make her headache go away. He'd even made friends with a waterhead. "Sittin' in an easy chair with the candles on, head like a pumpkin, couldn't get up. Couldn't cure him but sure could make friends with him before he died."

So why couldn't Cecil befriend some gabbling, rawboned, befeathered savages like these for a month or two, or even a Bigfoot?

10

THE BEAVER HOUSE

Trailing the packhorses was eerily placid as long as daylight lasted after that. The animals were stunned after smelling what must have seemed like a maniacal slaughter to them, and often tripped on sticks and stones along the river benches and rocky flats. The dogs had drooled and started gorging on a buffalo but then had lost their appetites. Now Smoky underwent two epileptic fits.

Charley admitted that the "Stinkers" would probably remain pacified for a couple of nights and word of Cecil's peculiar talent would be gabbed about. "I wish they'd seen Sutton jump, while you were at it. That's going to travel too."

Taking no chances, they stayed awake in four-hour watches. The very trees turned into hostile Indians under the slivery moon. Charley, who was Cecil's partner in their first watch (or "dogwatch," as Charley called it), ruminated about why his beloved mountains were becoming more hazardous for a white man than when he'd arrived.

"It ought to be the opposite. But nobody knows where they're supposed to be. The animals don't, the Indians don't."

Cecil cheerfully told him to go to sleep. Coffee knocked her wagging tail against his legs and leaned her shoulder against his chest, as he sat up keeping watch. Sally wagged so hard her hind end shook, and rounded her ears ingratiatingly and lolled her tongue, and Smoky bumped against him, sniffing his forehead, licking his hair. The increasing incidence of Smoky's fits had made him more dependent and less exuberant and wild, as though he sadly despaired of ever being able to survive on his own. But Cecil, in a mood to tease them all, leaped across a brook, tiptoed over rocks and hid, when they had dashed off in pursuit of a rabbit that Margaret's rabbit dog put up, to see who scented him first.

The Ompompanoosuc skirled through a sequence of close-hedged passages with blowdowns everywhere and huge rock heaps in the channel that the water pounded into and next to which the horses had to slide and hop and skid, as Charley's party continued pushing upriver. When the pitch of the ridges permitted it, they stayed above these difficulties, and Cecil lagged behind with the dog pack in case anybody was following. Periodically also the river spread out on its best behavior with a spear-point glitter, a fish-scale glisten, wriggles by the frantic millions glistering in the sunlight—its high-key rattling sibilance louder than a rustle but softer than a roar.

The dogs howled at night, and Cecil's elderly gray shepherd Kaiser got bite marks on his muzzle from unrealistic sexual aspirations. Nevertheless, he'd spring into a pool, spring out, jump in again with a splash, facing the other way around, and playfully chew on underwater sticks, when Coffee was palling with him.

"Are we going all the way to China?" Sutton joked, riding in his tireless fat-man's slouch, and ever more contented to be where he was.

Charley silently knitted up the miles like yarn; old men so often looked like old women anyhow. Though daily they were in the mountains, when they forded tributary rivers or creeks they could catch a glimpse of a grander topography behind these preliminary peaks which had such an extra dimension that Cecil remembered the story of Jack-and-the-beanstalk—mountains which carried the shock of the first grizzly tracks he'd seen, with the indentations of the claws extending out beyond the outline of the toes as a black bear's would never have; mountains large the way a shaggy-throated Western raven was bigger than an Eastern crow.

In the forestland, they'd started encountering black-bear tracks, but whenever the country opened into grassy parks and rockslide areas where the sun hit hard again, the bear marks had been left by grizzlies. "Wherever you can't climb a tree," as Charley explained it, because if they could catch them the grizzlies ate the blacks, but a grizzly couldn't climb trees like a black.

Though Sally hadn't the best nose in the pack, more than any of the rest of them she now understood that bears were what most interested Cecil, and focused upon puzzling out bear signs for him. One fine day she turned up a set of prints with each hind paw as big as both of Cecil's boots, each forepaw the size of his two hands, and claw tips that registered like five dimples in the dirt a finger's length in front of the toes as a kind of last word and a shock even to look at. The bear had strolled about, scuffing its sandy feet across bare rocks but then walking in wet places as if for the pleasure of feeling soft mud on its toes.

They'd camped early because Charley wished once more to get rid of his nagging premonition that somebody—white outlaws or a Sikink raiding band—was trailing him. With Sutton he rode back a few miles to lie in wait beside the path, while Margaret worked at housekeeping repairs and Cecil lingered over the bear's progress, wondering if he couldn't insert himself into its mentality—whether besides following its tracks he wasn't able to pause at the same places and peer in the same directions toward which the bear had pointed its ingenious nose.

At first the creature's meanderings seemed rather muzzy as he painstakingly followed it around. Then the chronology of where she'd gone and what she'd munched on seemed not muzzy at all, but personal. He almost forgot she was a grizzly; she was a fellow citizen of the valley of the Ompompanoosuc, enjoying its complexities like him, and he tasted several of the plants that she had sampled or feasted upon and smelled the traces of herself she'd left. He was startled when, after a mile or two, her tracks abruptly swung across a short red beach, straight into a deep stream just where it entered the river, and vanished into a purling current which was only ankle deep before it shelved into the thicker water. The current was still chipping away at her last print as if she were right beyond there, under the black surface.

Cecil explored this tributary, with its tea-dark water and red beaches, for another mile, until her tracks reemerged in a marshy patch—she'd probably traveled on the other side—where the dogs sent up an explosion of birds, and frogs plopped desperately for cover. Two beavers which had been dragging a birch bough out of the woods rocked back on their heels, clattering their teeth, as the dogs raced at them. Then they tumbled into the nearest of their stick-hauling canals, which was so full of water the dogs didn't dare to try to grab them.

All the trees at the spot were beaver-bit. White chips lay all over, and unfinished business, stumps with topknot twirls of sappy wood, tree trunks that had split in falling, and loose branches everywhere. Beavers, deer and bear that were nocturnal back east were out and busy in broad daylight in this new country. A marten, too, hung spellbound in plain sight, watching Cecil from a spruce. There was lots of beaver feed, aspens and birches so dense that he was wiping spider webs off his face. He stumbled, the dogs tangling his feet—how silly it was to have so many of them with him, scrapping and tussling with each other.

The bear had nipped off fireweed shoots and nibbled biscuit-root, parsley and cow parsnip; had consumed several frogs, to judge from the prints and scraps left in the mud, and parts of half a dozen rotting fish and clusters of salamanders that had been eating the fish. But when he noticed that these tracks appeared smaller than the earlier ones, it occurred to Cecil that this might be a second bear. He was suddenly glad all the dogs were along, and if they were nonplussed a bit by the bear's activities, they were bolstered by him—their magic man, as he liked to describe his position among them when he felt smug.

Red-rock sidehills rose prettily three hundred feet in the sunshine to ledges that supported junipers and pines. The little canyon had no end as yet. Modest waterfalls twined down and you could see a game trail descending from higher terrain. The floor widened into slough-grass meadows, as Cecil dawdled past beaver dams and ponds at a deliberate pace, the water gradually dwindling till he could observe the opposite beach so clearly he saw tracks emerge from, reenter and reappear at the edge of blackwater there.

He sat down awhile to soak his feet, rest his butt, and check his rifle. The gray shepherd had not been enjoying himself even at this easy pace, and Cecil was reminded of a dog in Maine whose master had brought it into a bar one night, intending to get drunk and pick a fight with some of the other loggers, and you could see that the dog knew very well that in about half an hour its master would be on the floor, that it would have to jump into the fight and try to save him, and would feel the spiked boots in the room, the fists and axe handles on its ribs. He realized that Kaiser, who a hundred miles out of Horse Swim had already regretted leaving his German master, was gearing up regardless to face the charge of a bear in order to save Cecil if he had to.

Smoky was also fearful, but Smoky was afraid of his own inner deterioration even when there were no bears nearby. Roy's hound Yallerbitch, like Sally, was hardly bothering to trail the scent, it was so strong—perhaps was trying to ignore it—and the two huskies, as tall on their feet as Cecil's hips, clung close to him, as did the goat. The goat had grown a veritable mane up to the top of its head from all of its adventures, and devil-may-care, was scratching its hip with the tip of one horn. But why had he brought the goat?

Tracks had materialized from another direction. Again he was puzzled, because although he wasn't seeing two sets together, his impression was that they weren't the tracks of a single bear. He knew that adults didn't travel together, yet the difference in size wasn't so disparate that it could be a sow with her yearling cub. The tracks were alarmingly large—but with his gun and his dogs, what had he come for except to trail bears?

He was sneaking slowly along like a deer hunter, but pulled up short at a ring of sparkling drops of water fifteen feet wide on the bank, where the bear must have climbed out after a swim and shaken herself. Thereupon—realizing he'd just been staring at other tracks— he remembered that since this was June it was the courtship season, a brief, uncharacteristically sociable period for bears. Twice in Maine he'd crept up close to mating black bears to watch them play and paw and nuzzle one another, and belatedly he recognized that the wayward footprints crisscrossing the creek had not been made by a lone animal foraging but by two creatures courting. That was why it had been so simple to see what they had been eating: they hadn't finished anything.

Of course he wanted to drop back for at least a mile. There were never cubs near mating bears, and cubs were what he was after. What was he doing? What foolishness, to track this bear of bears so carelessly; and with the dogs, a surreptitious withdrawal was now impossible. He was in a brushy stretch, no trees to climb. The hound and the duck dog were ahead, Coffee, Smoky and the huskies behind them, and the goat and shepherd next to him. The creek had been dammed into a two-acre pond in front of him on his left side, and he could see the impressive dome of a beaver house across a diffuse swirl of currents; also a smaller one. On his right side, he had a few dozen yards of meadow grass to operate in, then dense alder bushes that would provide better cover for a bear than for him, and finally the steep sidehill with occasional trees spaced about on ledges above that he could never reach if he was being chased. A game trail descending from unknown territory seemed only to add to the sinister possibilities of whatever awaited him.

He heard his dogs already breaking sticks, scrimmaging with a mystery beast around a bend in the path, and hoped that maybe it was just another beaver. Moving sideways, he held his rifle against his chest, but stopped dead when he caught a reflection in a clear puddle ahead of him which seemed to be that of a grizzly sitting dog fashion in the brush with a head like a stump, plain brown and stationary as though neutral, head-on to him, not facing the yelps of the pack. In contrast, the commotion in the alders grew to an uproar as a second grizzly, as purple-colored as a plum, plunged around a boulder in pursuit of Sally and the huskies. Bits of flowers were stuck to her lips from the vegetation she'd been feeding on, but the enormousness of her front legs at such close range astounded Cecil. Under the bulk of her hump, they were undiminished from her shoulders all the way down to her paws—paws which promptly veered toward him, as lithe as a cat's. But she paused and waved the right one as if a dog had bitten it, half upright on her haunches and fulminating as if her privacy had been outraged, as well as the sanctity of her foot.

He didn't fire, because he thought he'd be killed for sure if he did; and despite all of her violent manifestations, her elbows as thick as a ship's timbers, she had a prissy and fastidious air which delayed her slightly. Sniffing for information, she was uncertain where to rush or who to charge. He couldn't guess whether she had met a human being before, but in spite of her air of fussing, there was a pell-mell daring about her, a freedom such as he'd not seen in many animals. The dogs had run straight to him for protection, had then scattered when they sensed how frail a reed he was, but now were circling tightly—Moose on three legs—in order not to abandon him, while the shepherd, his hackles up, his muzzle high, although his hind legs were cringing, backed into Cecil's knees, preparing to die defending him, just as he would have died for the German grocer in Horse Swim in front of a holdup man, or if a drunk had owned him, under the hobnailed boots of bullies in a bar.

The male bear broke from a standstill into a lope, bigger, calmer, bluffer than the female but scarcely looking at Cecil—looking at the goat instead, which was still hanging next to him. Cecil fired a shot into the sky, not because his friends would ever hear him, but to try doing something to save himself, and yet afraid of wounding either bear.

That loud report decided the female. She bounded at Cecil like a round-backed cat going for a mouse. He was so scared he dropped his rifle and snatched at it wrong-side-to. He would have been a goner if she hadn't been blocked for a moment because the male, intent upon the goat, collided with her. Cecil sprinted out of the way, but the billy did the one thing he had learned to do when chased by the dogs. Instead of running as quick as he could, he stopped so as not to be mistaken for an antelope or deer and swung his little horns around. The bear didn't even pause to swat him, simply lifted him in his mouth, puncturing the ribs on both sides of his backbone, and carried him horizontally and alive like that toward the same thicket of brush, till with a last twist he died.

Cecil ran for some poplars by the pond, though they were not substantial enough to climb. He had no other place to run, and had been so close to the goat he'd heard the bear's teeth in its back. He heard the female start after him again and noticed the shepherd dog still braced to die for him at the old spot—knew therefore that the dog would be spared. Though he was running for his life, he could barely subdue the impulse, formed when he was a child being chased by older kids, of falling to the ground, rolling into a ball, and surrendering, to be let off with a few slaps. The dogs couldn't save him, at best could give him a few extra instants of life, but as she closed the gap, he glimpsed Coffee and Smoky darting with the utmost agility from either side to bite her thighs—noticed, too, with preternatural clarity, Smoky's lips beginning to twitch and drool as if a fit was overtaking him. Cecil had dropped his rifle once and for all in wriggling through a brushy tangle, and found that he was unexpectedly next to the male, which was already chewing at the goat like a lion on a hunk of meat and rose bristling and roaring. Shedding his hat and jacket for the grizzlies to examine, Cecil turned into the water, hearing Smoky grunt as if more than just his breath had been smashed out of him. He was splashing knee high in the pond when he remembered a cruel series of rotogravures in the Pittsfield *Register* of a grizzly wading after salmon and biting them in two. Either of the bears could chase him like a groundhog on the land and like a fish in the water.

He had nowhere to swim except away, and could see the dogs arrayed about the meadow in positions of collapse or stupefaction. Smoky was writhing in a fit while the she-bear rocked over him, waiting until she understood what ailed him before she finished him off. That gave Cecil another delay. He was belt deep by the time she came after him. Spotting the big beaver house, he resurrected from his trapping days the memory of the nesting chamber that would be above the water level inside, if he could somehow reach that. He floundered forward into the deepest water he could find and ducked under, pulling himself down by grabbing lily and bullrush stems. Making up for his clumsiness with the gun, which had nearly cost him his life, he swam and crawled along the bottom among a welter of branches the beavers had stored for food, grasping them to keep below the surface except when he had to gulp a breath. He could hear the dogs barking from the shoreline and the bear searching for him, thrashing across the pond with what sounded like explosive noises underwater, snuffing and sneezing as she tried to nose him out.

He knew beavers and beaver houses from Maine, and pawed

through the murk from snag to snag, past cached piles of succulents, to locate the main igloo of sticks without revealing himself. It was conical and four to five times the length of his body across its base. After he had groped for much of the way around the structure, he felt the lip of the underwater porch and finally the precious gap that was the entrance hole. A beaver swam out past him hastily like an underwater muff brushing against his arm when he began wriggling inside. He punched and ripped his way up through the claustrophobic L-bend of the passage, terrified that he would become jammed and drown before he reached the air. Would there *be* air? Or would he feel the grizzly grip his legs and be wedged inside that stick tomb with only his head safe in the nesting chamber while she gnawed on the rest of him? One of his arms did get pinned at his side, but he kicked and pulled himself up to where he could finally breathe, his free hand seizing the grown-up flabbergasted beaver that was cornered there, while he wrenched his other hand loose to strangle it, although he suffered a serious and bloody bite. Feeling badly scraped along his hips, he lay exhausted with just his head and chest in the chamber for a considerable while before he thought to congratulate himself.

It was too low for him to sit up, but by jackknifing his knees he could lie wholly dry inside. The flooring was of shredded wood and moss and grass, lighted faintly from the area of the smoke hole, where in the winter the beavers' body heat would show outside as steam. Though he was shivering and rubbing the wounds in his hand, he found the supply of air sufficient. He moved the four whining kits from where they had huddled to the edge of the exit, and sure enough, the live parent's wet and chattering head appeared after an interval and removed each, and also the dead beaver afterwards.

He was lucky. *Well, you poor sap, you're all right for now,* he told himself, fingering the ceiling a foot or two above. His impulse was to push, *push* and try to make more room, but he resisted doing that lest he turn frantic, resisted thinking about the fearfully narrow passageway from which he would have to swim out of this cell—he wouldn't have been strong enough to break through the roof, even if the grizzlies hadn't been waiting for him.

Exploring the weave of sticks, his fingers found a blunt-headed arrow of the type that Indians shot at ducks. The beavers must have pulled it from the bottom and treated it like any other useful piece of wood. He was so awed and so scared and wrung out that he soon fell asleep, waking horribly as the house shook. Something had stepped on it; and he heard a snuffle. Were his dogs looking for him? The whole intricate basket-weave of the edifice shook like a bird's nest in the wind but resiliently absorbed the weight of whatever was walking on it. Figuring out whether the beasty voice he heard was bearish or only doggish ought to have been a simple matter, but he was not in good shape to decide. The creature felt like an elephant, the way his mind was running, and yet the lodge was springy under its tread as though ready to give and give if necessary but never be clawed open. Ultimately the animal did depart. He heard marsh birds flying over, which he thought a peaceful omen. Later two small birds hopped about picking at seeds or bugs over his head, perhaps a pair of wrens: *tsuk-tsuk*.

Still jackknifed in this inner sanctum, he calmed down enough to nap some more, and fitfully imagined what was happening outside—the forlorn, bewildered dogs waiting about, the purplish, pussy-bodied grizzly wading after him, venting her spleen on bushes and trees in the meantime, before she climbed with her mate out of the canyon on the game trail to higher country. His mind drifted high and wide above the little creek and the Ompompanoosuc's main valley, wondering if he had ever had three better friends than Sutton and the others. Yet he could have died so painfully and quickly. And once he'd shot his mamma bear and trained and harnessed her cubs and built his raft to float with them to the coast, he'd never see his friends again, except perhaps for Sutton, who on the other hand might never go back East. Margaret would latch on somewhere with another white trader or trapper, not with Sutton permanently, he thought—at least his jealousy made him hope not. Charley would die snugly of heart failure while hilling potatoes on his homestead. And *he* would return with many stories for his children, with maybe a Thloadenni wife, and a sensational bear act, for which he'd sport a green frock coat and red silk hat and wow the crowds. But the gypsy in Sutton was more powerful than the gypsy in Cecil, and Sutton's grin as he stared at the mountains they were entering wasn't that of a settler like Charley; it was a traveler's pleasure at moving along, whether he ever found any gold or not. Cecil would wind up in Massachusetts, but Sutton might end up in China.

A sow bear bred once every couple of years, and once every couple of years she wanted her privacy, thought Cecil, managing a smile at what had happened. With the return of his common sense came claustrophobia, however. He dreaded reentering the passage and becoming wedged underwater. He remembered his father's death of cancer, scrunched up in the maple-sugar tub on the wood stove. Sucking his beaver bites, fighting his panic, he debated for a long time whether to go out head first or feet first—which would be the worst way to drown? Or if he panicked lying here, he would never get out; could rave till doomsday in this tomb, securely enchambered by the same basketry that had stymied the bear.

He lowered his legs into the tunnel, kicking carefully to learn how far he could maneuver like that and keep his head out of the water. A bend or bottleneck stopped him, and he hoisted himself laboriously up again and turned around, under the two-foot ceiling, remembering a stillbirth he had witnessed when the child—a nephew, his sister's son—had died in the birth canal. Putting his head and shoulders into the icy water, he thrust his body halfway down head first, but was unable to reach the sticking point and quite quickly pulled back for breath. He was so much bigger than a beaver. But the more he hesitated, the grimmer the outlook for him seemed, so without thinking any further he committed himself, remembering that the tunnel was only ten or twelve feet long and if he went into it deep enough he'd soon be out.

The worst moment of his life occurred after he had pushed past where his legs, crooked at the knee at the top of the passage, might still have extricated him backwards. He was completely underwater and inside, his legs immobilized, his arms struggling, but was stalled belly down at the L angle that led outward, whereas he should have been positioned belly up in order to bend and maneuver. He had to rotate himself in the corridor, inching slowly, unhooking his clothing as it caught on spiky sticks, with no chance at a breath of air if he failed. Then his right calf cramped on the last stretch when he thought he'd already twisted free. He wriggled his whole body, desperate as a hooked fish.

Once he was breathing again, his head well out of the water, underneath an azure sky, the pond without a ripple in it, and no bears rampaging on the bank, he was sure he'd live to be ninety—he would make sure that he did. He heard a dog yelp, and another one, from where they had been waiting for his body to float up. His legs and back cramped as severely as if they would stay cramped for at least a week, the way they had one time when he had fallen into the Androscoggin River during a log drive and nearly drowned. As then, he scrabbled sideways like a crab to shore.

Poor Smoky wasn't dead, but his spine was broken. Nevertheless, he dragged his hind end towards Cecil, his foreparts moving as stiff as crutches, apparently in full faith that some magic touch would be able to heal him. Cecil, after retrieving his rifle, simply sank down next to the dog under a tree that he could climb if the grizzlies returned. He cleaned the gun and stroked Smoky, while preventing the others from bumping against him as they competed apologetically for recognition, and watched the hope die in his eyes.

Moose's left hind leg would need to be dressed and splinted. And Sally, who he hadn't known was pregnant, was lying in a daze with a bloody litter of puppy fetuses that she had miscarried strewn around her tail. Cecil himself was dizzy and sick, and vomited. In much pain from his back, he lost his temper when White Eye started licking the stuff up, but quit shouting at him when Smoky woke up whimpering from his slide into a coma and flinched. He had to shoot him, finally, as the rest of them slunk about and crouched. Glancing at Smoky's body afterwards, he saw that the colors of his coat were not really as much like smoke as like the marvelous salt-and-peppering of intersecting light and shadow that disguised a wolf or coyote in the brush. A beautiful dog; and of course it hadn't been the coloring of his fur or even his epilepsy that had betrayed him to the grizzly but Cecil's foolishness. He hated leaving him unburied for the bears to come back to.

•

"No goat and no Smoke, huh? Yes, we figured we might have to slit open somebody's gut to find ya!" said Charley, when Cecil and his sorry canines straggled into camp after nightfall.

Margaret hugged him. Moose was injured the worst, and Sally was bleary, but Sutton pointed out that the old shepherd's face appeared to have whitened clear back to his ears and throat. "He got two years older all of a sudden."

Shivering, coughing, Cecil lurched around to find a bearable attitude in which to prop his bones while telling his story of hiding in the beaver house. His hearing was sharper than usual, and when he listened to the horses munching grass, it didn't sound peaceful; it was a violent sort of crunching, like the noise a bear would have produced if it were munching on him. When he wasn't giddy with the tale he had to tell, he fell silent and glum, though he ate hungrily.

"You figured you were safe, huh? A skunk bear could have dug you out—that's how they eat all winter, tearing beaver lodges up. So if a skunk bear could have got to you, what makes you think a grizzly couldn't have?" said Charley.

A "skunk bear" was a wolverine, a beast Cecil hadn't yet encountered. He wondered whether or not the skunk bear's proficiency meant he might at last have extricated himself from inside if his life had depended upon it.

Charley, who softened in response to his silence, remarked a bit sympathetically that when he recalled anything he wished he hadn't done, "It ain't what you did to a person—because there was always reasons there. Maybe the reason wasn't good enough, maybe I'd do it differently now, but there was *some* good reason. No, it's generally what you did to a dog. Do you know?"

He was obviously reluctant to go ahead and tell them what may have troubled him. "How about you?" he asked Sutton, who laughed.

"Oh, I guess I've done some dirtier things to people in my time than to doggies. I guess if you rub shoulders with thousands of people you've got more opportunity to do somebody in, and most of us are different when we're young—that's when you bash somebody."

Charley said his friend Ben with the hot springs, who had been murdered, had come up here from Nevada along the coast on the freight boat, starting from San Francisco, and had walked in on the

Hainaino River trail, like him. He was a prospector; he didn't mind a two-month walk, looking at all those pretty creeks and meeting Haidas, Tsimshians, Hainainos, Tlickitats and what all else. In Nevada he'd had a wonderful big dog that had been with him everywhere and understood English and Spanish and Injun or whatever was on the menu and still had a lot of life in him. He loved that dog, but all he'd heard about was how cold it was going to be up in British America.

"He was making preparations, fussing like you do when you're planning the best trip of your life, worrying about things you don't need to worry about. He got so concerned about this dog not being a 'winter dog' or a 'snow dog' because its fur only went as deep as his first knuckle that he had a man take him out and shoot him. Couldn't do it himself, and the bloke that did it for him came back and said, 'You shouldn't have shot that dog; I've never seen a dog as intelligent as that, that knew what was going to happen to him and why.' And when he got up here, of course he had plenty of dogs, he trained a dog team, because he liked tinkering with dogs, and he learned they could either grow a coat or else get by without a coat, if they had the heart for it. He never did find a dog so bright and loyal as that dog that he'd destroyed."

Cecil, who'd expected from the beginning to lose most of his dogs in fracases and pursuits, asked what Charley regretted doing himself, but Charley had said all he would.

Sutton responded with his story of letting his circus's hippo go into the Mississippi. "He was swimming upside down, he was having such fun, eatin' duckweed. You could argue that he froze in the winter; probably he did. But if he got far enough downriver I don't think so. If he swam to Baton Rouge he could have got into the Atchafalaya swamp and lived forever. He was letting that current catch him and take him down and he was about the fattest fish you could imagine."

11

CHARLEY'S PLACE

Cecil got up twice during the night to reassure himself that the creatures he heard stamping the ground and cropping grass were horses and not polar bears or Chinese tigers, as he was dreaming. He patted them, under the slender moon. Skinny and undersized, they had stovewood heads and poignantly rounded ass ends and a dip in the profile in back of the withers that was a weak spot, considering all the work they did. Several were short-winded, night-blind or sore-footed, weaknesses which Cecil had missed when he'd bought them and which the trip had both exposed and aggravated, and he was eager to trade at least half of them at the first Thloadenni village on the Memphramagog. But three or four had turned into real friends.

After traveling hard the following day, their little party swam an elbow of the Cold Water River, a stream that swarmed out of the mountains to join the Ompompanoosuc from the west, its currents like a herd of swordfish. They camped in a sprucey meadow between the two rivers in a defile with a sharp skyline of palisades on the northeast side and a moribund cabin where Charley said he had occasionally enjoyed the hospitality of a Negro trapper two decades before. "I think he was a runaway. He'd helped us explore this country, but I don't know where he came from. He was afraid to say. Chunky guy. Used to sing to himself. Used to make marten hats for the Indians—three skins apiece, and he left the tails up on top for a decoration to wave in the wind. Didn't buy nothing from me regularly but ammunition—I picked that up for him. He named this the Cold Water River, but I don't think he was very cold. A 'skookum' guy, we say—tough—but still he disappeared the same as if he wasn't skookum."

Charley, who'd been welcoming many landmarks of the junction of his beloved Memphramagog with the Ompom, went wading in the meadow pond for duck potatoes, digging with his bare feet in the muck below where the arrowhead-shaped leaves floated on the surface for the tubers, which drifted up when his toes freed them. He boiled these to celebrate, with his hat propped on a stick to lure the flies away from his head.

Sutton trimmed his beard for him, and then his own beard, using a gold pan for a mirror. He told Margaret she should dress in her best calico to meet the Memphramagog, and, clowning, did a backbend such as he claimed to have done on the riverboats when a pretty show girl named Delilah had danced in stockinged feet on his chest.

Charley said that one time near here he'd come to a creek that looked too skimpy to wet his boots for, so he had knotted them to toss across. "Except the blessed water caught them. I threw short. I had to walk about fifty miles before I killed a deer to sew some shoes from and I lost my toenails before I was through with that."

He said this was also the country where he had trapped with his Sarsi friend. "He was a washout on the water animals. I don't think he liked to wet his hands. He couldn't trap a blanket beaver to save his soul. I don't think he understood the critters. He was a lynx man, or he could catch a string of marten. He was a good tracker and he could set a snare, but he never got the hang of the iron traps."

"But what was he *like?*" insisted Cecil, still reaching for a sense of the sort of Indian who might bring him to his Bigfoot.

"Oh, he was a quizzical fellow, always trying to decide what the difference was between him and me. Sometimes that's why they'll kill a white man, to try to figure that out. I used to tell him he never would. That was two dozen years ago, when he drowned. I never learned that language very well. Never had a long-haired dictionary; and it was only a year we ran that line together. That's all. You sure don't expect to have so many partners. One year, two or three years, and they die or they clear out."

After plodding on in a twelve-hour drizzle, they fetched up at a gravel spit where they could either gaze up the ample expanse of the valley of the Ompompanoosuc, which curved toward its sources in the mountains in the northwest through a row of loaflike hills that were neatly severed near the water's edge, or up the slim chute of Charley's precious Memphramagog, which led directly west. Charley showed them a clutter of moldering bark hutments and rotting skin huts representing what was left of the settlement where his drowned Sarsi companion had lived.

The Memphramagog had been their destination for many weeks—perhaps Cecil's since he'd left Massachusetts—and so to see its debouchment blocked by wild piles of rubble and smashed trees was disheartening. But once they'd trudged past this arduous exit chute, with its congestion of rock, sand heaps, and downed or drunken forests and escarpments, the river ran between its banks like an arm in a sleeve. It was a comfortable, clear-water river, not muddy, as he had somehow expected, with a spinning-wheel fullness but easy gradations of terracing, no unruly-looking evidence of recent flooding or peeling cutbanks, and a thorough feeling of abundance within its modest valley's winding course.

"A three-man river," Charley called it, meaning that any more than three trappers might clean all the fur out.

When the dogs chased two black bear cubs across the grass and up a tree and drove off the mother, Cecil climbed after them. One cub lost its grip, fell, and was killed, but he secured the other—the size of a spaniel—lowering it to Sutton on the end of a rope, while it squawled like a bird. They lunched on its brother cub and on new venison also, which at first it refused to eat but did gobble bites of at supper while the brother's paws were roasting, blistering savory juices into the coals—what Sutton called "an internationally known delicacy" because his people ate bear paws in Louisiana along with helpings of alligator tail.

Cecil fed the living cub whitefish, which she liked better than deer meat, and gently tugged her fur, soon needing no muzzle on her, and he duplicated the ticking-crooning noises bear cubs converse with and got her responding to the taste of the fish and through the fish to him. He bent close, confident she was too cowed to snap, though he could feel dismay wash through her whole body in waves like seasickness. After each siege of this malaise she would consent to browse again on sprigs of goosefoot plants and pigweed and fish live from the net—then would shudder, wrenching her head away again, her purple lips turning inside out in a grimace, as her stomach rebelled at the smell of his fingers on the food. He persisted, burbling to her while he rubbed pet areas of her belly that soothed her. Hocus-pocus, Sutton called it. "It's like cooking," Cecil said, "taming an animal down."

They'd camped under an ospreys' nesting tree, so the parent birds slanted and wheeled overhead, mewing, even though the babies had already fledged and were posted about on other trees. Two foxes with cubs had denned underneath this eyrie to scavenge what fell, so the ground was clean. In the body of the nest, sparrows, wrens and a pair of night herons had nested as well. And there was a neighborhood weasel underfoot, raising friendly inquiries whenever the dogs permitted it to. Margaret and Cecil bathed in a warm-water creek and Sutton fooled at panning for gold a little while. Then they all worked at searing and drying their fresh meat—the weasel bobbing between their feet, dragging scraps toward its lair—while Charley napped. There were Angels' Ladders in the sky, as Cecil's mother had used to call the rays and streaks extending from the sun by which she said angels slid down and by which, he now believed, the sun drew water into the clouds. The sky reddened, before gradually fading to a kelly green in front of a black buildup that developed into an all-night storm.

The Ompompanoosuc had narrowed from a width of nine hundred or a thousand busy yards where they had joined it, and where Roy had lost his life, to an even faster two hundred yards where they had left it at the fork in the mountains where the Memphra-magog came in. And the Memphramagog had gradually dwindled in a gentler fashion from a width of one hundred fifty or two hundred feet to perhaps a third as much as that as they rode along, although its valley remained at least a half-mile wide.

They saw another cabin, collapsed upon itself, before the Mem-phramagog mounted to a short plateau with snowy, blunt-fronted mountains arrayed around, and orange tiger lilies and brilliant pink-flowered bushes growing to stirrup level next to the path, as well as "Indian turnips" that Charley pointed to as good eating, in the ground. Just the general plenitude—a bull elk; and a trio of caribou on the move, the first caribou Cecil had ever seen—made that day particularly fine. The elk dashed away with a breezy clockwork gait when the dogs took after him, as though he recognized that they were wolves but as if he had never ascertained that he might have anything to fear from human beings. The caribou were smaller, heavier-set and chocolate-colored except for the handsome white mantle across their necks. When Charley clacked two stones to-gether they stopped running, looked back and listened curiously, po-sitioned for a shot, the way a hunter would want.

"They think it's horns they heard," he said.

"Now, what in Hades would you do with *that* dreamboat?" Sut-ton yelled when Cecil's Kitty, aghast and staggering, gathered her feet under her to bolt because a silver-backed bear with nostrils which together were as big as its mouth stood up on its hind legs in front of her in dense scrub, with its paws folded like an alder-man's on its midriff. It charged for several steps to clear a space for itself but then backed off, choosing not to tip its hand. The bank here was pitted with bushel-sized holes where it had been digging for bulbs.

"I'd wear his coat," said Charley—whom they kept kidding for trying to shunt them away from this snicketing, snappy, cheerful lit-tle river, with a lovely bottom of cherry-colored pebbles now, which had cut such a ripe spread of land for a man to settle on. It was a "three-man river" only if you considered that each man ought to have thirty miles of the main valley and four or five tributaries of a similar length to dabble with. The gophers, ground squirrels, rabbits and red squirrels everywhere gave evidence that one just needed to snatch from this rolling abundance some few dozen lynx and fisher and mink and marten that you wanted to bale and carry to the trading post to exchange for supplies, without ever denting the populace of next year's fur, and devote yourself mostly to prospecting.

They met a mountain lion, which was a certain harbinger of the presence of bigger game because of all the meat it ate. With a body as sizable as Cecil's but legs built for leaping and a streamlined flat-nosed head, it was crouching facing him at the mouth of the gulch of a creek that dropped twenty feet over hard blue rock onto the river's grassy bench, switching its tail. It was such an unexpected apparition that he absorbed it without speaking, like a snatch of a daydream. Of course he'd never seen these creatures before, either, and almost faster than his eyes could register the spring, it reversed its direction and sprang up twenty feet to the slot the water fell from, looking back at him. And then it wasn't there at all.

The dogs had missed it, but Margaret and Charley had not. Tracks as round as soup bowls on the beach corroborated what they'd seen.

"This used to be a regular hang-out for a Bigfoot too," Charley said, pointing up the gulch. "They probably like the taste of that creek. It's minerally, kind of like milk of magnesia. Good for the bowels. And they're not afraid of lions."

"Do they have bowels?" Cecil asked. "They're that real?"

"Well, I don't know! I never saw the scat."

"And why aren't they afraid of lions, if they're afraid of bears?"

"Because I doubt that lions attack them. Maybe they're friends."

"He didn't have much of an expression, did he—that lion? It's all in the tail," Margaret observed.

"Bears don't change their expression and gators don't have much change of expression, but monkeys have expressions," said Sutton. "I had a monkey once. Dogs do. Parrots don't. Parrots, bears, gators, lions have it all built into their faces to start with, and they're interesting expressions, except that it don't change."

Cecil asked if he shouldn't camp here for a week or so and keep his eyes open and catch up with them at Charley's.

"You've gotta be very quiet for a Bigfoot. They're the first critter to leave if somebody starts banging an axe. They say you'll see one once on a river but not after that, because he don't want to see you. You can't homestead somewhere in order to associate with a Bigfoot; you're better off just taking your chances traveling through."

"But you say they'd like a woman?" Cecil asked.

"Yes sometimes, but I've seen a woman run off with a white man and her husband didn't want to know about it or else her relatives didn't want him to know about it, so they claimed it's a Bigfoot who grabbed her," Charley said.

"How about before the white man?" Cecil asked.

"How in hell would I know about before the white man?" Charley laughed.

The pitch of the Memphramagog steepened and the sidehills stiffened into slab-sided mountains, pathless and scree-strewn, which shut off a view of what Charley said were much higher mountains lying beyond. Corkscrew draws choked with water twisted back toward these, wicked to cross and permitting no peek at the country they drained. The meadowy intervals became few and far between. The river where it stretched away from the sun was gray, but bright silver heading into it, or fig-colored or lead-colored under a cover of clouds. It would crash through a city of rocks; then burble and purl for a while; practically seem to stand still; then ripple deceptively as if it were flowing backwards over the forest floor; but then war some more with its riverbed for a bend or two.

Charley, to his companions' astonishment, let out a full-throated half-minute holler, "a two-mile holler," he called it, on their fourth morning on the Memphramagog. Really a yodel, it began in his throat, skidded down to a deeper tone emitted from his chest, and went up and down between throat and chest.

"Just happy," he explained. "I sound like a sick moose now. You oughta've heard me ten years ago. Morning and night. Me and Ben—Ben with the hot springs—we couldn't hear each other two hundred miles off, but we'd sure try twice a day. Wake up the sun, warn off the Indians." He smiled because he was indicating that he was so close to home he wasn't afraid of the Indians anymore.

"That's one difference between an Indian and a white man," he added. "Couldn't get 'em to holler. Just like using a knife and spoon. They didn't mind if *I* did, if I was camping with them, because I wouldn't do it if we were hunting or out of the valley somewhere that was bad. I might even get an answer, but if it was a Thloadenni, he'd give me a crow's call or sound like a wolf pup or scream like a lynx or a jaybird. He wouldn't scream like a human being."

"Maybe he didn't think *you* were a human being," Margaret said.

He laughed. "How do they call each other? They sure don't yell—it's all crows and jaybirds."

"Maybe they don't think human beings yell."

"Or use forks and spoons," he answered her, but didn't go into a sulk as he would have done after an argument with Cecil or Sutton.

Soon everybody saw reason to whoop, when they had climbed wearily past a thunderous, white, cake-frosting waterfall and topped a laborious rise which in gradual fashion opened into an entire basin a dozen miles wide and fifteen or twenty miles long that appeared to be completely encircled by incisive yet intimate, comely-looking mountains, snowy on top but grassy on the sides, that proclaimed that good hunting was here. Such abrupt spaciousness with the height of the mountains backing it up—after they had traveled the shallow river valley, which, lovely though it had been, now seemed only like a corridor leading them to this grand sanctum—made them stop and stand and gape.

"You'd like to live here, huh? You're on probation," he warned, proud that they were grinning ear to ear.

Way back, way high, lofty rock gullies cut out a series of dark demarcations thousands of feet above them in the otherwise boundless expanse of snow, which was itself a startling sight after the weeks of brown and green prairie—spring snow they might perhaps have climbed to in a hard day's scrambling. They simply feasted their eyes while Charley chuckled and, sitting on his horse, hollered his earsplitting yodel again, his seamed old face an odd-looking source for it. The silence was too great for echoes and absorbed the sound, yet to Cecil it was a sort of birth yell as well as a yawp of triumph, in this utterly peaceful wild scene.

He tried one. Sutton tried one.

"Tooth Mountain. And that one's Goon Mountain. And that's

Bootjack Peak," said Charley, pointing and coughing, having exhausted all the hoots in him. "My names," he whispered, when Cecil asked.

Goon was neckless, big-skulled, slope-shouldered, like the back view of some kind of a goon. Another mountain, runneled with avalanche scars, looked like a magnified molar, but was glittery up on top where the wind was blowing snow plumes that were diamond bright. Among the birches and willows along the river were moose trails—the calves' tracks next to their mothers'—moose prints of all sizes.

"You could feed an army," Margaret said. But Sutton noticed with some apprehension four sets of wicket-shaped hoofprints on the path.

"Oh, that's my James and my Mildred and my Melbourne and my Joan. I retired them," Charley remarked, pleased at every discovery. "That's when you know you have good neighbors—when they don't kill your horses when you go away for a spell."

He pointed to a speck on a vast grass slope above the chaparral and just under the snow line a mile or two up and away as a bird would fly from their clearing. It was a grazing grizzly that he believed he'd known for as long as he had had his place. "Must be twenty years old, and I'll tell you, you go up there and you'll have no beaver houses to hide in from him."

Cecil asked, "Now, why isn't that a Bigfoot? How do you know?"

"You really want one, don't you? In this country you're liable to get whatever you want. Up close a Bigfoot would look about like the hunchback of Notre Dame, if you remember him. A Bigfoot is a lower order. A bear's a good deal prettier, if you ask me."

They rested, basking in the sun and the opulent sweep and slant of the terrain, with the sound of tons of water cascading in the distance from the mountainsides, and let the horses eat.

"I guess you can fit more growing grass and trees into a given mile if you put them on the bias," said Sutton. He teased Margaret that the Kluatantans in Red Town wouldn't have much to say for themselves here.

"I'm not a Red Town woman. I came from mountain country. Are you a Hungarian because you're white?"

"But would they be afraid if they saw this?" Cecil asked.

"They would feel closed in. It's a good place to starve in the winter, I think. They don't like it being so close." She waved her fingers vaguely at the slopes of earth and snow towering up nearly to the height of the clouds.

"And how about you?"

She laughed the way she did whenever they looked at her a bit like an animal in a zoo. "I think there's worse things to be afraid of."

"I never went up the Missouri—never saw the Rockies before. But you know, they used to claim the Indians aren't as smart in the mountains as they are on the flat," Sutton said.

"They're more primitive. It's a feast or famine for them," Charley agreed, though Margaret sniffed.

Cecil was not tempted to scramble up the endless-looking inclines, but they immensely gladdened his eyes. Charley went on about that wise bear nobody had killed in twenty years.

"Not me or him, neither one. He winters-over in the rocks and he spends the summers up there too, so he only comes down here once a year to eat the aspen buds in the spring. He drinks and he digs roots. He rips up the last of the ice to grab the fish that got froze in it and digs into the snowslides if he can smell a sheep that got caught underneath and died. And then before he gets his ass in any trouble he goes up where it's bare and high along the snow line again, where only a fool would follow him, and looks down at us the rest of the year."

They crossed and left the river where Charley's creek, Coldfoot Creek, joined the Memphramagog, and watched the moose path turn into a horse path with blazes spotting the trees wherever Charley had thought he might need help in finding his way home after dark. Then they reached a clearing filled with raspberry hoops and brambles and old swallowed-up stumps which made for stumbly riding, that looked like a hay pasture he'd maybe given up on. But ahead they rode into another one that was about ready to mow—the seed heads tickling Cecil's bare feet as the prairie tallgrass near the Margaret had done—and soon into what he called his winter pasture, which included a tidy parcel of swamp and some low, fertile dry land. Then they found themselves at the edge of a fat but weedy round garden, its spinach having bolted and its broccoli having flowered, yet which the wildlife hadn't contrived to destroy because Charley's two pooches had stayed behind to defend it. He said they would have holed up under the house if a pack of wolves had happened by—as one dog did now, faced with this pack, though it was also yipping for joy.

Charley's house looked so nondescript and hunchy at first that Cecil assumed it was a shed. Except for two shuttered windows in front and a rockwork chimney rising above what would be the tide-mark of the winter snow, it looked more like a trapper's overnight cabin, a hole-in-the-ground eighty miles out on a trapline, than the very fine setup he had imagined.

Sutton, however, was ignoring the house. "This guy's a miner!" he whispered, staring up and off at a complicated trestlework of attenuated, skinny flumes carrying water for hundreds of yards from scattered springs in the walls of this side valley to scattered pockets that had been laboriously picked out of the strata at a lower level, where sluices had been constructed for washing the ore.

"You're a carpenter," he told Charley ironically, just controlling his anger. Cecil's quick reaction too was that they'd been hood-winked, after all of Charley's talk of not really being a prospector and his Trapper's Oath of truthfulness. But maybe he was preparing to share and share alike with them—which could be a bonanza.

Charley had been watching for bear tracks as they approached his place and had been relieved to see none. But now he let out a bellow and rushed inside his house. Though he had laid a crosscut saw blade across the doorframe to foil a bear that might try to break in, apparently a bear had torn the shutter off the window on the west side, had crashed through there, and afterwards had burst out through the window on the east wall of the house. In fact, the sec-ond dog was stretched in a rotted condition in front of this second window and everything inside the two rooms had been heaved around.

"Some bear! Son of a bitch. A bear with a bowie knife," he said after a minute. Indoors, he showed them the punctures in his stew-pot and bean sacks, suspiciously bladelike. His best kettle was gone. "He pretends he's a bear, but a bear don't haul away your horse hoe on his back. A bear don't carry away your adze and pulley blocks and choker cable." And the dog had been shot, not pawed by a bear.

"Ah, it's mean country," he said. "He understands lunatic better than he understands bear, so even though he's trying to pretend he's a bear, you can see it was a lunatic that got loose in here."

His distress was palpable, and they pitched in, opened the rest of the windows to light the rooms and make the house less sinister, and helped him carry out his damaged and undamaged stuff to inventory and examine it. Many of the floorboards had been jimmied up. From the condition of the dead dog and of the dry foods he had stored but which were now wet and strewn about and spoiled, they concluded that the robbery had occurred soon after he'd left. "He saw my tracks."

"At least the bastard didn't burn you out," said Margaret.

As they poked around, Charley was consoled to learn that his root houses, fur house, horse shed, utility shack and outhouse—each equipped with an eccentric but efficient-looking steep snow roof—had not been ransacked. Nor had the robber searched the cabin methodically. He seemed to have been nearly as random in his actions as a bear.

Margaret was the one who discovered the skull which had been tossed on Charley's bed. It rattled when she tugged the blanket to straighten the coverings, and she shouted in fright. Sutton too jumped away, thinking he had heard one of his Louisiana rattlesnakes. But it had rattled because there was a glass eye inside it.

"That was a white man. No Indian I ever saw ever got hold of a glass eye to wear," she said, when she had caught her breath. "Look. Blue."

"I wonder, did he find the head and throw it in here for a joke, or did he kill him and cook it to get the skull?" suggested Sutton rather brutally, because like Cecil he felt none too happy to have been pulled unawares into Charley's mysterious feuds. And after Charley's fuss about truth and loyalty back in Horse Swim, his protestations that he prospected for gold only at odd, not very profitable moments in a life spent gardening or trapping, to gawk up at the walls of this box canyon—which was a half-mile wide and a couple of miles deep—and see a dozen precariously situated, rickety flumes delivering springwater to twice as many pickaxe workings along a strip of whitish, probably quartziferous rock that was squeezed between thicker layers of ordinary brownish stone, was to feel both recklessly elated and betrayed.

Cecil went off and unpacked, hobbled and released the horses, buried the dog carcass, staked his own pack of dogs on their gang line so Charley's surviving dog could crawl out from its refuge under the house, and kindled a cooking fire at the wide spot in Coldfoot Creek where, sure enough, Charley's pet beaver was swimming around looking like a moose's nose protruding from the water. When the kettle whistled, he persuaded Charley to come sit down and calm himself, though the rest of them continued to eye the rimrock all about above them on the chance that a bushwhacker was posted with a rifle somewhere up there. Charley didn't act as if that was a possibility, but they were also watching him for behavior that would show he was a man whose pay dirt had been buried and now dug up and stolen—or maybe *hadn't* been.

"Why did he quit throwing your stuff around? Did he get what he was after?" Sutton asked.

"He was after mischief. Otherwise I don't think he knew what he was after."

"Who was he? You claimed the Thloadennis protect you from that," Cecil said.

"I said they wouldn't let the Sarsis in. They don't care what a white man does to me if they already know him and if he doesn't do the same to them."

Charley cheered up nonetheless. He could set everything right, apart from the broken window glass, and would use moose parchment for that—"moose glass"—as he had for years. "The real article spoiled me."

Trickling peaceably, the little creek reflected gray and golden ripples on a barkless footlog he had laid across. White clouds had given way to black clouds which were supplanted by much more mountainous, muscular white clouds, except for a part of the sky that was turning pink. High on Tooth Mountain the wind had stopped blowing snow plumes and the snowfields the cloud shadows traveled over changed from a glistening white to a blood blue. They heard a rockslide thudding down, too far away to see, but also the gentle sound of water leaking at a hundred points from the flumes on trestles now decrepit which he'd installed to transport water where he'd needed it while chipping at his canyon walls.

"You can see just what a fool's paradise this was. You can see how hard I picked and hauled. But it's falling down. What'd he steal? The adze, my hoe, my otter traps, a few doodads. And my floor had a frost heave in it where the rain seeps under it in the fall, so he figured he had to dig that up. Then he figured out it was a frost heave. And he left me my friend's head because that's what he'd wanted to do in the first place when he heard I was gone."

"It's the hot-springs man?" Sutton said.

"The hot-springs man. Wanted to aggravate me. Yes, he could have burned me down, but that wouldn't have been as much fun, because I might have left. I never did know where he buried Ben. I thought he'd put him under the ice." He waved as if beyond the Memphramagog.

"You have your gold mine and he has his hot springs," said Sutton mildly. He hugged Margaret, and Cecil felt a pang, being alone, distanced from Charley, distanced from her and him, and from his home. Charley grimaced.

Nobody said anything else that evening. Margaret and Sutton wandered off to pick a spot for their tent. Cecil tended to his black bear cub and bedded down in the midst of his dogs.

Sutton, when he had slept on it all, emerged sounding companionable and even ebullient, irritated only that Cecil was already baking cat's-head biscuits for breakfast, so he couldn't do it. He took the skillet away from him and fried the venison cutlets, announcing that the biscuits looked more like owls' heads than cats' heads and ought to be done over. He greeted Charley by extolling the winding creek, the granddaddy beaver and the sea-blue, concave cliff of Bootjack Peak, which was scalloped like a seashell and which Charley said he'd named because he admired it when he flopped down tired late in the afternoon outside his door to pull his boots off.

They were waiting somewhat uneasily for him to give them their marching orders. In the silence, after eating, as the sun heated up, Cecil, meaning to make a joke of it, asked Margaret, "So could you spend the rest of your life here?"

"She couldn't and you couldn't. Don't crowd me. This is private land. Why don't you get your feet wet?" Charley said, motioning toward the wilderness beyond Tooth and Goon. "You haven't been two miles from another white man since you left the state of Maine."

It was a startling reminder, after all of their adventures together. Charley had carefully packaged the skull of his friend for burial, and he went off with a shovel by himself. Then he established Rules of the House, which he wrote down. Margaret was to cook. Cecil and Sutton were to cut a cord for the woodpile every day that they stuck around. But the habits of the trip soon overturned those uncomradely formalities, and they went to work with him in the garden or at scrubbing his cabin clean and dusting off his numerous curios—old scrimshawed powderhorns, albino muskrat hides, a stuffed wood frog, various home-rigged household oddments and one-of-a-kind fox or wolf traps that he had inherited from trappers who had died or given up and left, a posthole digger, a carpenter's slick, chisels, vises and pincers, several spruce roots he had carefully carved into the likenesses of whole people or just faces, and the frayed, blue-gray, dense-furred, white-spotted sealskin parka he had worn on his original hike from the coast.

"Suppose my heart had crumped out on me on the Ompom. You'd never have found this property. You would have wound up in some other fool's paradise but you wouldn't have liked it so well." He spoke of how amazed his neighbor would be to know that "the barbarity" he had committed had been witnessed by three disgusted newcomers. But he still told them, "If you kill me you'll get nothing and if you don't kill me you'll get nothing." He hinted at wealth, and yet the plump garden he had painstakingly laid out and improved upon season by season, as well as his obsessively comprehensive assortment of traps—most of them whittled at with a file to deepen the teeth—his drags and chains and setting clamps and clevises and bolts, his wire stretchers and wooden stretchers for curing furs indicated that his "badger work," as he called his digging, hadn't been his main occupation lately. Indeed, he said he sometimes wondered if he didn't work more on his traps than actually trapping.

Although the house was cramped and humpbacked, he'd dug twin storage cellars outside which were timbered as skillfully as the opening to a mine. Sutton teased him about how well he could buttress a hole in the ground, for a man who didn't know how to find gold. He was showing them his boxes for whole-wheat and white flour, for rolled oats and kernel corn, his sand-filled bins for beets and carrots, others for potatoes, and his crocks of moose meat in salt, saltpeter and sugary brine. His beets had grown as corky as the inside of a cow's horn, so he had started trying to cross them with squashes to invent a better vegetable. Last year's onions were still stored in his house, braided in chains by their dried tops, the chains looped across the low ceiling beams, along with split string beans, which were strung up by the many hundreds like tiny two-legged dried-leather britches in walking postures all around.

They unearthed a soured pot of birch syrup and boiled and skimmed the liquid until it became sweet. Lying by the brook, they could watch a thicket of trout coursing above the buff-colored bottom, chasing Charley's hook so zealously that when one grabbed his worm the others followed it almost out of the water to the pan. Meanwhile the horses rolled in the grass or rubbed their sore backs on the trees, browsing farther up the valley, where Charley would not allow Cecil and Sutton themselves to go. They built a bonfire every night, as if to let the wildlife and any other life for many miles around know Charley was home.

Cecil kept his dogs chained at Charley's request. When they'd yank and plunge to get loose, he said it was good practice for pulling a sled. His own shaggy, sloe-eyed mutt, called Shy Boy, had a peculiar way of rocking his head back and forth and looking upwards and backwards when talked to or petted, like a dog trained to the traces and accustomed to watching for praise or instructions that came from behind. He said his dead dog Jill had been his leader, between the two of them, and that she had started lifting her leg to pee almost as soon as he'd made her the leader. "It's a wonder Shy Boy didn't start to squat."

"What *did* you do that you regret so much?" Cecil asked, reminding him that he had once said it had to do with dogs.

"Oh, that was a hundred years ago." He didn't want to talk about it. He told instead about a friend of his who'd built a cabin close to a buffalo lick in the foothills, for a good meat source, but while he was gone the buffaloes came and rubbed their itches against his walls—like the horses were doing against these trees—until the walls fell down.

He wouldn't discuss his dynamite and pickaxe workings and his trestles and sluices, but agreed that tomorrow they could go look at the lion trap he kept permanently set next to an animal trail under the rimrock so as to catch any lion from another valley that might be heading for his horses. Irritatingly too, he wouldn't chime in with their attempts to relive the epic events of their trip—on the contrary, almost pooh-poohed what they'd seen and done, interrupting with tales of the first hut he had lived in beside the Pacific at the mouth of the Hainaino River, which the Haida Indians had built with a beached whale's ribs. There, he said, the bears had so many salmon to choose from they ate only the fish with eggs. "They'll catch 'em, smell 'em, and if it's a male, they throw him back."

"But what *was* it you did?" Cecil repeated, teasing him.

He told how once he'd snapped a beaver trap on his right hand in the shallows of the Memphramagog and had lost his footing in three feet of ice and water and couldn't reach the trap with his free hand because then his left foot went into another trap and kicked that one shut on him as well.

"The most I could do was try to pull the stake out and I had no purchase, lying the way I was. I'd driven it into the ground with the axehead, and the ice overnight had done a double good job of fixing it. I tell you, it would be as bad as choking on a fish rib to die like that, spread eagled in a yard of water. I pulled like Satan to get out—couldn't now!"

"But what is it you're sorry about?"

"The *worst* thing I ever did?" he said ruefully. Maybe the effect of the firelight made him more accommodating, after all the meals they'd shared.

"I had a little dog. He was my smartest dog. You'd say he was too small for here, but any track you pointed to he'd trail. You didn't have to train him on any particular animal or explain it, just point to a track in the snow and away he'd go for twenty miles. He had short hair, but if he shivered he'd work harder. We traveled all over and he slept next to my head to make sure nothing got after me during the night. We saw a lot of country together nobody's been into since. Up near the glaciers sometimes for fun and up into head-less valleys that went on and on—we traveled for years. And then one night when we were both of us wet clear through and played out and siwashing it in the sleet with no cabin to snuggle into, I was having trouble getting wood that would catch to a match. I had a couple of rabbits laid out for supper, tied together, and he snatched those and ran with them. He was so hungry and so done in that he couldn't wait another minute, and I couldn't wait a minute for him to come right back. I just shot him, I was so hungry and cold. I was sorry the instant I did it. That infernal temper I had. The bullet hit him. He curled up, shuddering and shaking, and looked at me and died. Died in my lap.

"Get this guy out of here. Get him screwed. Get him a squaw. Makin' me talk!" Charley shouted to Margaret exasperatedly. "And this other one, he's like a fox in a chicken coop. He drools, looking at that badger work all ready-done for him. Tomorrow, out!"

Suspicious, sick of shepherding them, and glad to be secure at home, he meant it, too.

"Go up-valley. You'll see smoke," Charley told them in the morn-ing after they had hiked to the lion trap, only to find that pack rats had consumed the bait. He was adamant about not allowing them near his veins of quartz. When Sutton asked whether it didn't re-appear elsewhere off the valley of the Memphramagog in canyons where nobody was working it, he said if so it was either under-ground or had "gone to the Ompom." They could store some valu-ables with him and leave half of the horses for the summer and, for Cecil's convenience, the bear cub.

"I never found the lode," he insisted in response to Sutton's search-ing look. "That's why I dug so much. I got my dust from Coldfoot Creek. I've never found where it came from."

Sutton laughed. "I think you're a millionaire."

Charley made a motion that embraced his humpy cabin, his round garden and hammerheaded runty ponies, the leaking flumes, the mutt Shy Boy. "A millionaire? You'd shoot me if you stayed a month, wouldn't you? Out! Out!" He picked up his gun and made a good-natured show of shooing them off.

When they'd packed, Cecil asked how to tell a Thloadenni from one of the Sikinks or Sarsis, since the first thing they were going to be looking for when they got to the top of the valley was Indians.

"If you see a Sikink he'll be a dead one," Charley said. "What in particular? Oh, they sew with a different sinew and a different root. They have a blue dirt they find up on Weather Mountain that they paint up with, and they'll wear an owl's feather, not a hawk's. I think their noses are a little thicker up close to their eyes, and I don't think they're as dirty, but I'm used to the smell. You'll see a sort of duck-tailed haircut on a young fellow where he's sawn it off for his scalp lock, but mine don't shave the sides of their heads as close because it's too cold."

"Anybody to ask for?"

He hadn't laid his gun down. "Out! Out!" he said. "They won't hurt you. We haven't had too many horse's asses shooting at them. And don't *you*."

He wanted to keep the honey-colored dog Coffee to replace his dead dog Jill, and Cecil gave her up, quick and loving though she was.

"No, they'll be friendly," he said. "Still and all . . ." He walked over to his saddle sitting on a sawhorse and pointed out a bullethole in the heel of it. "You can think you've made all the friends in the world, and you run across somebody you haven't had a chance to make friends with yet.

"*Out!*" he said, waving his Winchester just as he had with Johnny Appleseed. He pointed straight up at the sun to indicate it was already noon.

"You may run into a trader—a half-breed. He works east from Hainaino Village all the way to the Eeejookgook, where Ben lived. He's one that traded with the Bigfoot that Shouts-at-night told you about, leaving sugar out for him. He'll have you a pissing match. He whips it out, goes right into a pissing contest when he meets another white man. So save up for that."

Part 4

The
Mountains

12

THE THLOADENNIS

Longloaf Mountain, miles long.

Shipshape Peak, with a jib and topgallant sails.

Belly Mountain, good for game.

Weather Mountain, cowled in clouds.

Arab Mountain, also cowled.

American Mountain, where Charley had said an American named Helmut had once mined.

Halfway Mountain, halfway from Charley's place to the headwaters of the Memphramagog.

Ice Mountain, with bluish crenellated ice formations high on top.

Drowning Mountain, misty and watery, lavishly forested.

Hat Mountain, rock-capped.

Snowmass Mountain.

Muckaboo Mountain, mysterious to the Indians.

Mother Mountain, mysterious differently, according to Charley.

Four days' leisurely and nervous trekking through the steep scenery of the Memphramagog Range, which Charley had named, described and even jotted down for them beforehand but which appeared less beautiful and more formidable and claustrophobic now that they were on their own, finally brought them to the smell of smoke in a tangled gully opening northwest off the valley of the Memphramagog between Muckaboo and Mother mountains, at a point where they couldn't see ahead more than a hundred yards.

They stopped and tried to analyze the smell and took some time to ponder what to do. The smoke, from a sweet-scented wood, was laden with the luscious odor of roasting meat, but nothing in these desirable aromas told them whether they would be killed if they let their presence become known.

"We're only three," Margaret warned, but Cecil, eager to hear news of a Bigfoot, said that he felt bold.

Sutton suggested shooting off a shot to allow the Indians to decide whether to welcome them or hide. However, a sledge dog or "rag dog," as Charley would have called any Indian dog, alerted the Thloadenni camp. The dog was with a young girl who was carrying two gophers and a killing stick and who bravely tried to conceal her surprise before she dashed for home.

Margaret hollered in slightly jittery Kluatantan that their approach was innocent, and Cecil and Sutton raised their hands to show that their weapons were holstered, and Cecil jumped down and leashed his dogs. Haltingly, they walked ahead, seeing boughs tremble and bushes shake as people ran and crept to get a look at them.

They saw five hide wickiups set beside a fishing pool, and ten or a dozen women and kids, lightly clothed to the waist and not unduly underfed or scared. There was no air of dissolution or destitution like Red Town's to this camp, just the utter isolation of the place. Cecil had shot a moose the day before and presented the skin and head to a woman about Margaret's age who seemed to be in charge—the brain of which she could tan the hide with; the broad curved nose would be everybody's treat. She accepted these without fuss, along with fifty pounds of meat, though the ground already smelled rancid from the meat they had.

Margaret, who had now relaxed, winked at Cecil because he hadn't met many women in his life who as a matter of course did not wear shirts on a warm day and he was trying not to gawk. She murmured to him and Sutton that real, wild Indians were not as dangerous as half-wild Indians.

An age-bowed man with thin, mud-caked braids, no teeth but a skeptical-looking mouth, one functioning eye and one eye like a child's yellow marble, and a scalp knot which was bound into the shape of a thick horn pointing forward from the crown of his head, emerged to examine them.

"Charley?" he said.

"Charley, yes. We're from Charley." Cecil hesitated about offering to shake hands in case he wouldn't know how.

"Kobuk," he announced decidedly, yet had no further words he could exchange with them. Rubbing his cheeks with his fingertips, he looked away politely to where the woman had split the moose's head open with a hatchet and was spooning out the brains. When she put the rest of the head on a spit over the fire and the hair began to singe and spark, everybody watched that.

Cecil realized after a while that Kobuk could be either a greeting or the man's name. The girl and the other children were too shy to take a red pocket handkerchief he was holding out to them. "Should we wait?" he asked Margaret, frustrated by the difficulties.

"Sure. They're waiting."

It seemed safe enough; he hadn't actually thought of leaving. The wealth implied by his and Sutton's horses' bulky packs, his numerous dogs, and the alien tribeswoman who could speak English with the two white men but not Thloadenni did not seem to excite an avariciousness among these Indians, and the campsite was permanent enough for Cecil to recognize bits of bone scattered about as belonging to marten, otter and other trapline animals from the winter months. He was squatting, handling a fragmentary skeleton, when a boy brought him a whole handful of marten penis bones, thinking that might be what he was after. He was startled; the women laughed. He pointed to himself to try to tell the boy he'd once collected raccoon penis bones. Unable to convey that, he gave him the red handkerchief, and gave out more.

It felt natural to wait by the fire, coveting nothing yet full of questions to ask eventually, with the Indians presuming him to be as amiable or as reliable as Charley. Two of the women had attractive breasts, which they covered with a piece of hide or their long hair if Cecil stared. But the covering would slip away again, reveal-

ing these dear globes reclining on their ribs much as they themselves
were reclining against a mossy log while sewing the seams of a pair
of leggings and taking turns smoking a short pipe containing the
leaves of a small creeping plant which Cecil knew as bearberry in
the East and they called *kinnikinnick*.

They all tried it. And Kobuk imitated Cecil stalking and drawing
a bead on the moose, as a respectful kind of joke that they could
share, saying in sign language that he, Kobuk, would not have
missed the shot either. Sutton studied the walls of the gully specula-
tively, not as though he were looking for Charley's vein of quartz
but as if he were considering a jump. Kobuk—for that did turn out
to be his name—disappeared to lie down, and Margaret had her
friends teach the other Thloadennis how to play tic-tac-toe, scratching squares in the dirt. After an hour or two, a breathless youngster
ran from the woods to Kobuk's hut and Kobuk reemerged at the same
time as four younger men arrived, well armed, out of breath, and
bristling with offended curiosity, though one of them held out a
fine fluffy lynx robe that he was willing to trade.

"What you want, you guys? Who are you guys? Charley get
back? How many did he bring?" said this one. He said he was
called Blizzard, and he ignored Margaret and scanted Cecil, talking
directly to Sutton, as the senior man. "Are you with the choo-
choo?"—which was a surprising word to hear him use, as if he'd
worked a stint on the railroad crew and could afford to be sarcastic.

"No, we left there. We don't work for that. Do you?" Sutton
asked him.

Blizzard, a long-jawed individual in pants of pale caribou skin,
no shirt, but with a yellow ribbon around his forehead with an owl's
wing-feather stuck in it and a bone ring on his middle finger, said
no. The left side of his chest was scarred from what had probably
been a gunshot puncture wound and he'd been nicked by frostbite
on his hands, which had white spots and patches on them. Wary,
although not unfriendly, he was near Cecil's age. They'd all come
on the run, prepared for trouble, and needed a chance to calm down,
despite the fact that Kobuk and the women had no complaints to
raise.

Blizzard wanted tobacco and received some. He asked for ammunition for his gun, which was a .44-40 like Charley's, and Sutton told him Charley had brought back a supply. He circled the stack of pack bags and boxes appraisingly but didn't lay a hand on anything.

The two whites and five Indian men sat down and enjoyed a smoke together and a pot of English tea and divided the moose's nose, while Margaret and the Thloadenni women ate and drank likewise but separately. The new language, which even Margaret couldn't penetrate, sounded like Gypsy to Cecil and like Chinese to Sutton, except that when the Thloadennis spoke to each other they were brief and might laugh after only a couple of words, like people speaking English among friends. None of them showed the tints of skin which Charley or an earlier prospector might have left behind. They were dark-reddish, fist-cheeked, black-eyed. So where were Charley's kids? Cecil wondered.

"What are you selling? What are you buying?" Blizzard asked, although the others didn't seem so inquisitive along that line.

Sutton explained that they had traveled from very far away, from the ocean—the farthest ocean—as he already knew Charley had done originally.

"What are you selling, what are you buying?" He was not to be euchred out of anything.

"To tell you the truth, we're looking to settle down someplace where it's okay with you for us to be."

"Hey, you can't move in on me! Are you crazy? What are you gonna grab away? You white men skin the Indian. You let the Indian do your trapping for you, and after he gets through, you skin him," Blizzard exclaimed, repeating Sutton's statement to the others, though with a tired frown, as if he really meant that too many people had crowded in on him. He didn't seem to be the leader of the band, only the one who spoke English, and was watching for Kobuk's reaction.

Cecil tried to argue that in such a great lone land nobody could crowd anybody.

"So why didn't you guys stop before you got here?"

Sutton, attempting a different tack, asked whether they had heard yet from the Sikinks about the cure that Cecil had performed on the blind man. This information Blizzard stopped and translated carefully for the others, afterwards making no answer except that he would like to have seen that. In the silence, Sutton waded shin deep into the brook that fed the pool in front of the camp and told the Indians through Blizzard that if they found a spot where he could leap from a rock seven times as tall as his own height into water as shallow as that, he would accomplish the feat for them and walk away without a single cut or bruise.

Blizzard translated his words again, and at Kobuk's request, slowly checked the points of what to both of them was obviously an outlandish offer. At the end, they scarcely let on that they had heard at all.

After a minute Cecil asked Blizzard where he'd learned his English and where he'd seen the railroad.

He hadn't seen the railroad but had met the team of scouts for the railroad in the Valley of the Tlickitats while trapping for a white man who "treated me bum," he said. "I don't know why. I carried a lot of packs for him."

"Where do Charley's kids live?" Margaret asked.

"Charley don't have no kids."

"Why not?"

"I don't know why not. We like Charley, but he don't have no kids."

A man whose mouth appeared a little blunter and whose face and forehead were a trifle bleaker than Blizzard's spoke up to the effect that they had no gold to give Sutton if he did that stunt—no payment, as Blizzard specified for him again. They had brought Charley and another fellow, who was dead now, to the places they knew about that had had gold.

Sutton smiled and thought for a while before he replied. This being the very conversation he'd been aiming for from the beginning, he didn't want to spoil it. Later he teased Cecil that he would have asked for the youngest woman with the roundest breasts to become Cecil's "mountain wife" except that "the aura of mystery" would have been dispelled. Instead he asked them for a Bigfoot.

"My friend has come to catch a Bigfoot and bring it back to show the world."

Blizzard didn't know that word, or "Brush Man" either. He and

Margaret needed to explore the several dialects they were familiar with until they hit upon *Nakina,* learned earlier from Shouts-at-night. He did know *Nakina,* and when he understood he was astounded. He, Kobuk, the other men, and the woman Cecil had given the moose meat to tossed the notion around in considerable detail, with Blizzard occasionally reporting how it went.

"Why should we pay you for doing that? What good does it do us?"

And another time: "Charley has Bigfoots. Why didn't you ask him?"

And finally: "If you can do that, maybe *you're* a Bigfoot."

At this last remark the Indians, to their visitors' astonishment, suddenly began striking camp. It was late in the afternoon, but they packed abruptly, as though unhappy at the prospect of spending the night at close quarters with anybody who was asking for a Bigfoot or who claimed he could achieve such a stunt as that. Yet they also made it plain they wanted Sutton and his friends to accompany them; and they traveled throughout that night, leading the white men and their pack animals blindly along a series of invisible trails under a clouded moon. Wet to the waist, they all arrived in daylight but before sunrise at an encampment which was triple the size of the first one, on a larger and more sinuous creek that constituted the Memphramagog's headmost fork—the whites too worn out by the pace to be properly scared. Their guides promptly tumbled into other people's huts and went to sleep, even as the occupants were roused to come outside and stare.

Without Charley's guiding presence, Margaret was their best judge of how to behave and what the dangers were. "It's the same bunch," she said reassuringly. She built a tidy fire, baked some hoecake of cornmeal for the three of them, watched the village of perhaps fifty souls wake up, and fell asleep herself.

Cecil dreamt of mobs of Indians, and of his pal Sutton staked across a low fire to burn, and him the next captive in line, as in the illustrated stories of Indian captivity in the newspapers back East. But when the hot sun on his eyelids woke him up, he saw that Blizzard and Margaret were drinking coffee with the woman he'd given the hunks of meat to—Blizzard's mother's sister, whose name was

Fox Belly, Blizzard said—as well as old Kobuk, with the strange
horn of hair pointing forward from his head and one good eye and
one yellow eye that Cecil realized he might be asked to cure. His
dogs, who had surrounded him while he slept, guarded him still,
but there was no confrontation building here, as with the Sikinks at
the buffalo jump and the band of Sarsis before them.

A new Indian, husky, with an enlightened, vigorous sort of face,
approached Moose and, after nodding to Cecil to obtain permission,
peered at the roof of the dog's mouth and palpated the knob on the
back of his skull, commenting approvingly to Cecil in Thloadenni.

"He says must be a smart dog. He's got a black mouth, all black
inside, and a good bump on top of his head. That's how you tell a
smart dog. He's Lost Axe," Blizzard explained.

Cecil, mishearing, thinking the man had lost his axe and would
want to be given another, was not very responsive, but Margaret
perceived the misunderstanding and saw an opening for Cecil to in-
troduce himself. She handed him their camp axe.

"Show Lost Axe how you throw."

Everybody laughed at the wit of that, and Cecil, who was nicely
loose from having been asleep, was more accurate at flinging it into
a tree than if he had prepared beforehand to put on a show. Then
he had his dogs display their training and obedience. The audience
of Thloadennis, who had seemed as ready to mock him as applaud,
were much pleased, in particular because they'd heard by now that
it was Sutton who claimed to have the magic powers. Cecil's down-
to-earth talents were a relief.

Lost Axe, much friendlier than Blizzard, told Cecil through Blizzard that he was Kobuk's son and that Blizzard was his daughter's
husband.

"We used to have a horse, but it died. We took care of it, but it
died in the snow up in the pass coming back from the Chickamin.
Five foot of early snow that year, and it didn't have no snowshoes
on like we did." His family hunted on the Chickamin, Lost Axe
said, and to Blizzard's evident surprise, he invited Cecil to come
and visit. He crouched and mapped accommodatingly in the mud
how four rivers had their headwaters in these mountains: the Mem-

phramagog, in springs and a lake near here; the main stem of the Ompompanoosuc, over a pass to the north and east; the Eeejook-gook, over a lengthy pass toward the southwest; and his own Chick-amin, over a pass that crossed a shoulder of Muckaboo and of Snow-mass Mountain, northwestward.

"Do you like moose?" Lost Axe asked, and in his enthusiasm, kept Blizzard translating. "Moose are here, plenty of moose. But you like caribou meat?"

For caribou hunting, the best valley was his Chickamin; and even in Thloadenni he waxed practically wordless while trying to con-vey his delight when he returned to that tasty diet after spending the summer eating mostly moose and whitefish in these environs over here. Yet he loved moose too, he wanted it understood. With his smiles and his more serious squints and the fluttery motions of his hands he tried to communicate all this—the way caribou trav-eled the high tundra at a joggly, flustery trot, and the fun he had in stalking them up there on the bare slopes; but also the way that moose tramped solemnly in thick willow woods, moody, secre-tive and statuesque, and the joy of trailing and tracking *them,* down on the valley floor here. With his face turning anxious and drawn at the memory now, he admitted you could starve in the caribou hills if you couldn't discover where the herd was wintering, because they would be all together, whereas moose in the winter were to be found scattered singly and more dependably about. But if you did locate the caribou herd you could kill fifteen in deep snow at a pop. Fif-teen if you had fifteen bullets, or nearly as many with your knife in deep drifts—you running on top of the snow while they floundered—and sit back all winter eating them.

"One hunt!" he declaimed, and jeered in comradely fashion at the moose hunters like his father Kobuk from the Memphramagog here, who would have to keep on hunting once they'd eaten each lone moose they shot.

Kobuk, although past his hunting days, saw that Cecil had caught the gist of what Lost Axe was talking about. He said emphatically that a moose was so much bigger than a caribou and each piece was such a heavier, bloodier meat, what difference did it make? Furthermore—gesturing at his stomach—no caribou tasted as good as a cow moose did in the early spring with a baby in her. You cut the unborn calf out and ate it. *Hey!*

"The calf, not the moose. You're talking about the calf," Lost Axe argued, smiling as Blizzard translated. But Kobuk warmed to his theme—how after the bitter winter, when you had been eating too many skinny rabbits and no greens, you cut her stomach open and stewed a wealth of sweet and sour green things along with the calf, still in its caul. No caribou ate greens that were as interesting as a moose's greens. And though there might be better meals in the duck-come-back season or the find-birds'-eggs season or in berry season, you never enjoyed one more.

Blizzard interrupted his own translation to say that nothing was better than a nine-month-old bear cub dug out of his den in the late fall, and everybody laughed and several agreed. But he was tired of talking. He reminded Lost Axe that Cecil was not after caribou; he was after a Bigfoot, a *Nakina*.

That put a damper on the party. Lost Axe said something to the effect that his Chickamin had caribou, not Bigfoot. The Eeejookgook River had Bigfoot. He faced away.

"So you cleaned up that man's eyes?" Blizzard asked with revived curiosity, neither hostile nor hospitable but staring closely at Cecil. "Yes, I believe you did. That old bastard, you should have left him blind." He pointed at Kobuk. "They used to get behind two rocks and throw spears at each other."

Kobuk listened impassively when Blizzard told him Cecil had healed the Sikink's eye, but Lost Axe called for a boy to be brought over who was crying and holding his ear. Cecil dabbed a little castor oil inside, hoping that might help an earache. There was a sweat-house by the creek, a lean-to built of bark, and he suggested the boy should spend a while inside.

"He's from the Eeejookgook. He's a Sikink that we caught and Lost Axe is gonna take him to the Chickamin to live for the rest of his life," Blizzard said.

In the buttery sun some of the women were shrugging off their capes or shirts again. One was suckling her new baby; another was chewing on a strip of hide; and a third was suckling a baby and also chewing on a strip of hide. Cecil tried to imagine wearing leather clothes his wife had chewed for hours like that and made pliant and soft. It was both unsettling and arousing. But the Bigfoot—wasn't it maybe just a type of Indian, like these?

Blizzard spoke of having met "the Major" and his "flying squadron" of surveyors in the Valley of the Tlickitats—the advance party Elmer Mcccham, the survey chief, had mentioned when he was passing through Horse Swim. They had shocked poor Blizzard, though he wouldn't admit that. It must have been plain to him from their blunt manner that everything was canceled and wiped out for that valley and all the people there. He said even the trapper he'd worked for had told him nothing was ever going to be the same again.

"And you'd just as soon you never see another white man? But there are bad Indians too," Sutton said.

"A bad Indian, you can put him under the ice and that's the end of him. You can follow him—he's got nowhere to run—he lives in the woods."

They offered to share their breakfast meat and oatmeal, but Blizzard was wrought up now. "I think my old lady's got some kind of slop cooking for me. No beaver here, you know. The beaver's gone, the gold is gone. And you're lookin' at us in the summer, so you see the game, you see us move. In the winter you wouldn't see no game. You'd see the hunter go out lookin' for an animal, but nobody else would move."

Cecil, who was feeling scratchy, got up and washed and soaked in the creek, putting his head underwater and blowing bubbles. The bottom was greeny yellow, hatch-marked by the moving shadows of the wind's ripples and by the waving stalks of water rushes. Three ravens sailing overhead croaked and cocked their wings to lift and drop. The mountain to his left slanted toward a peak he couldn't get a view of, but as he bathed he rather enjoyed the sensation of being watched by probably fifty of the wildest Indians left in North America in 1887.

Margaret—figuring that Blizzard was too grudging and suspicious to be a useful spokesman for them, and guessing that one of Charley's woman friends might still be around—managed to flush this personage out by watching the women of the village who were observing

Cecil dunk himself. Though this particular lady was trying to be as poker-faced as some of the others, she wore a reminiscent smile.

"Sure I was Charley's girl," she admitted, but wouldn't tell them whether anybody else knew English and was pretending not to. Short, stocky, a bit wizened but planted solidly on her feet, with a flat, competent gaze, and gripping her forearms with her wrists crossed, she probably harbored an exaggerated idea of how well she knew the many wiles of white men passing by. She grinned as if whatever they said to her might be so much malarkey and as though no answer she gave should be considered reliable, either.

"Why aren't you with him?" Sutton asked.

"Oh, he don't want me there. He's too old to be horny now. I could go to him if I had to."

"How horny was he?"

"He was horny."

"You worked with him on his mine?"

"He's a good guy, Charley is."

"And you used to work with him?" Sutton asked.

"I don't talk to guys like you about where Charley digs. You rode with him from where the Kluatantans live and you have to ask me that?"

Sutton agreed she had a point. What they wanted was somebody to help them, he explained. "Who was it that first helped Charley when he showed up?"

"Oh, my father was a sucker for the white men. 'Here come the white men,' he said when he seen Charley the first time. He wanted them to come—he'd heard about it, he'd been looking forward to it."

"So he helped Charley?"

"They made a lot of changes around here. They did all right. And one day Charley said that he was looking for a calving ground, and my father brought him home and brought me to him."

"And you didn't mind that?" Cecil said.

Glancing at Margaret, she laughed. "No, I didn't mind that. I liked the white men. We thought it was going to be the best white men that came to us."

"And Charley wasn't?"

"Yes, yes, yes." Impatiently but eagerly she went to a lean-to and

returned to display a fine old cloth robe and sash that she had decorated with numerous straight-hanging little white ermine skins with
black tail-tips and Canadian, American and British coins with holes
punched through their middles.

"Help you with what? Help you make a fish trap or catch the caribou? Sure, anybody can help you," continued Charley's Woman, as
her own relations called her, she said. "But if you want to catch a
Bigfoot, nobody can."

Her sudden chattiness brought several individuals over with a cartridge pouch stitched out of squirrel or groundhog skin, or a bulky
pair of bear-fur mittens to sell, a fancy fluffy cape that had been
sewn exclusively of lynx's paws and would have brought a thousand
dollars in Boston, or a handful of agates like cats' eyes. Unlike the
volatile and hostile Sikinks, they gave their two white visitors no
sense that they would just as soon knock both of them over the head;
but Cecil, wondering whether some of the families didn't winter
three hundred miles away from here, thought that what Blizzard
claimed about the gold being gone might not hold true.

"Oh-oh," said Charley's Woman as an elderly Indian stepped out
of a wickiup which was as domed as a mushroom. He wore only a
dried eagle's head, which shaded his penis, and a necklace strung
with songbirds' beaks. His face was striped with blue, his hair was
oiled and dusted with what appeared to be a goose's snowy down,
and he flourished two rattles, one fashioned from a fawn's hooves,
the other out of bears' dew claws.

"He's Coomsinah. Tell him your story," Blizzard suggested.

He translated while Sutton provided a short account of their journey, dignified by many pauses.

"Yes, we know Charley brought you. We saw the tracks," the
chief answered through Blizzard. "And you want to fix Kobuk's
eye?"

"No, I can't cure Kobuk's eye," Cecil said.

"But you want to catch *Nakina*? How can you catch *Nakina* if
you can't cure Kobuk's eye? It ain't going to be any easier."

Blizzard laughed in saying this, as though they ought to have another translator, but when Cecil glanced at Charley's Woman to see
if she was going to help them out, she was stifling a smile. The man

in costume must not be of the same faction that her father—the chief who had first welcomed Charley—had been in.

Blizzard motioned derisively at the horse packs piled on the ground stuffed with trading goods. "We can show you lotta copper—what Charley says is lotta copper. A green cliff full of it. But that's not what you're after—you run after the gold?"

Sutton answered by saying he wanted to do for them what nobody else on earth could do. If they had flying squirrels, they would see that although he couldn't fly quite like a bird, he could fly like a flying squirrel. "I want to show you that."

The Thloadennis had been netting yard-long jack pike in the creek's spawning pools, and Margaret sat with Charley's Woman at the fire to scale and split a few of these, partly to slow the pace of things. Cecil tried to persuade Coomsinah in his solemn regalia to sit down too.

They heard a clacking sound, like two boards hitting together at a great distance, and couldn't figure out what it was. Then Margaret remembered the sound from years and years ago as probably being two rams banging their horns together high on the mountainside out of sight. The Indians were gazing up. A couple of men grabbed bows and guns, waded the creek, and began climbing quickly, but before they had got out of earshot, the mischief-maker Blizzard, deciding on his own that Cecil must be in need of a wife, shouted in Indian and English, "Hey, I'll tell you what! I'll sell you my sister!" He pointed at a long-haired, comely lady with puffy lips and cheeks and an amused and noncommittal frown. Both hunters swung around and one of them drew a bead on him and then on Cecil, while everybody laughed.

Two new Indians arrived, which worried Cecil and Sutton for a moment because they were afraid that reinforcements were being called in. Margaret said no. She thought it was funny that Sutton had the Thloadennis imagining that he would suddenly turn himself into a flying squirrel before their eyes and that they had him scared they might gang up on him and kill him at nightfall. She did acknowledge, though, that she had never seen an odder combination of young savvy Indians like Blizzard and old ones such as Coomsinah, "very primitive, like forty years ago."

Charley's Woman brought around the newcomers. One was a non-descript-looking teenager named Tom Ben, with somewhat sharper features than the rest of his tribesmen and skin the color of fried dough, who gradually because of his lighter skin and lengthier nose and unusual name they realized must be the son of Charley's murdered friend Ben. He was leery of them like the rest and spoke very little English but at the same time seemed so fascinated that he couldn't move away.

"He don't know many white men," Charley's Woman explained. "He's going to shoot Ouddo someday if he can, but I tell him Ouddo will be a skookum guy to kill. Tough."

Mr. Ouddo turned out to be the white wanderer who had killed Ben and taken over his place and had "put the fear of God into Charley too," she said. Ben had roamed this big territory with Charley and had fathered this boy, Tom Ben, on one of his visits to the Memphramagog. But because Ben lived on the Eeejookgook in the Sikinks' home country, Tom Ben's mother had never been able to bring him over to visit Ben while Ben was still alive.

Nevertheless, it was only right a son try to avenge the murder of his father. "He goes over that way lots. Maybe he's practicing up. He catched that girl last time he was over there," she added, pointing to a young woman Cecil hadn't picked out as particularly distinctive before. "She's Sikink. And her boy." She indicated the child of five or six with the earache whom Lost Axe was adopting.

The woman Tom Ben had captured was standing with a stone knife in her hand, fleshing a caribou skin he and his hunting partner had just brought back, which she had secured by slits cut at the corners to an upright log. Her expression was grimly self-contained and hardly changed even when the Thloadenni woman closest to her noticed Cecil's look and dealt her a box on the ear.

Charley's Woman chuckled at that, but Margaret stared at the Sikink and walked over to her and came back. "Isn't that funny," she told Cecil. "Most everybody here, you know what they look like under their clothes because they take their clothes off when it's hot, but *her,* that you'd want to see because you could probably trade that mule for her if you wanted to, you can't because she covers up."

Cecil didn't dare to look again for fear she'd get another sock in the ear. He rubbed his own. Sutton was napping, as a sensible way to pass the tense hours remaining before he planned to do his jump, so Cecil lay down too. By now they were able to fall asleep immediately anywhere the ground was level and the skies were dry, and the six dogs that were left formed a watchful perimeter around them and their supplies.

They ate a large meal when they woke up, inviting Charley's Woman, Tom Ben, Blizzard, Lost Axe, Kobuk, Fox Belly and the alert and cautious Coomsinah, dressed up with the eagle's beak shading his penis and a woodpecker's headdress, to join them. And Cecil contrived to include the boy with the earache also, using the excuse of dabbing more oil on it—pretending to want to please his new father, Lost Axe, but aiming instead to attract the attention of and please the Sikink woman, who although separated from her son, watched him constantly.

"Do people ever become a Bigfoot when they die? Are people related to them?" he asked, turning to Kobuk. "Or are *bears* related to men? Does a man die and maybe become a grizzly bear?"

"I like to see how your guys operate," Blizzard remarked, deliberately delaying translating. "It's the 'winning of the West.' That's what the one I worked for used to say. You can't wait a week. You can't wait a day." With his lantern jaw, ice-punished hands and the puckery gunshot scar at the side of his chest, he interjected such a disparaging note that Charley's Woman took over the honors of interpreting this time.

Cecil's question didn't offend old Kobuk, however. It quite excited him. He hooted.

"Why not a mouse?" she said he said. A gush of palaver started that she quit trying to keep up with in order to join in with her own ideas. Cecil leaned back, petted his dogs, watched for clues to what was being suggested, and unobtrusively eyed the Sikink woman, whose rounder, somewhat Chinese face was growing on him. She wore a torn hide jacket and a hat with a broken visor—the visor being a beaver's tail—under which she promptly stuffed her hank of hair, which she had been throwing first over one shoulder and then the other, as she noticed Cecil's gaze.

Although she couldn't hug her son, he could. The boy was wearing a kind of inch-sized leather cube on a cord around his neck, and Cecil signaled to her, asking what it was. She was surprised but signaled back that a bit of his umbilical cord was contained inside.

"So what are they saying?" Cecil asked Blizzard.

"You can't control what happens to you after you die."

"But do people sometimes become a Bigfoot?"

"They don't want that. It happens, but nobody wants it," he replied.

"They'd rather be a bear?"

He winced at Cecil's oversimplification, and Charley's Woman wiggled her hand in the direction of the creek in imitation of perhaps a running mink, and lifted it to include the birds.

Sutton—being requested to describe again what he was prepared to do—repeated through Blizzard what the feat consisted of. Lost Axe, who was friendlier than Blizzard but ignorant of English, told him that within an easy walk the creek narrowed to an ideal gulch. "But he wants to know if you could die," Blizzard finished.

"Sure I could."

"He wants to know why you would do this if you could die."

"I'll do it because it's what I want to show you. It's what I do that's different from anybody else in the world."

"Will you die when you get old? Kobuk asks you that," Blizzard reported, disassociating himself from the question.

"Sure I will, just like you and my friend here, but nobody else can do this in the meantime."

Though a fairly simple proposition after all, it seemed to be subject to numerous interpretations, the way the Thloadennis kept discussing it. Cecil began to wonder if one of the questions they were putting to each other wasn't whether Sutton would stay dead if they should ever decide to kill him—or, under the circumstances, how dead he would stay. Watching Charley's Woman helped to allay his suspicions, because her straight and generous-looking mouth as she listened remained benign. Nor was Margaret nervous. She took the opportunity to go and talk in pidgin Indian with the Sikink woman and came back to Cecil.

"She says her husband was killed but her daughter got away. She says they will keep her son if they let her go with us. But she says she would go with you to be with her people again if they let her."

Cecil shrugged in perplexity. Although the possibility of bargaining to bring her along aroused an intense longing in him, how could he know that she was the right person to bring along—a stranger, miserable and primitive, impossible to speak to even if he were permitted to, whose face was frozen into resentful stoicism and whose tribe supposedly was the most dangerous tribe?

Blizzard, who was pleased by the complexity of the debate between the older Thloadennis, now demanded of Cecil: "What would you *do* with this Bigfoot?"

They all stopped to hear him answer.

"Make friends with him."

"Why?" said Blizzard.

"I want to travel with him. I want to take him East. I don't think I could if I wasn't friends with him, do you? I couldn't do it even with these guys." He won a laugh by gesturing at his dogs. "Have you seen one?"

"No, I never seen 'em. I heard 'em sing sometimes," said Blizzard.

"What do they sound like?" Cecil asked.

Blizzard considered. "I guess they sound like what the northern lights would sound like if the northern lights could make a noise."

After all of this was translated and enlarged upon, the Indians—who had nothing going for them if not imagination—started another round of argument and speculation, though there were also giggles at the expense of the two hunters who had climbed off after the bighorn rams that morning, because the same thwacking had resumed from high above the village on the mountainside, which meant they'd failed and must be hiking home.

Coomsinah asked if Cecil had Bigfoot where he came from.

"No."

"Who told you about him?" Blizzard responded.

"Charley did. And the Sarsi whose name is Shouts-at-night. And the Sikink named No Water. Has Coomsinah seen one?" Cecil asked.

Coomsinah muttered at the boldness of the question, though he was staring at Cecil much in the spirit that Cecil had stared at those two earlier Indian men to try to penetrate their thinking.

The boy with the earache cried again and somehow struck exactly the pitch of Cecil's own dead daughter on the nights when she had suffered from quinsy and nothing could be done for her. Because the ear was hot and inflamed, he persuaded the boy to open his mouth—his throat wasn't as red as Cecil had feared. Hugging him of course put Cecil also in mind of his two kids who were alive and well. He stirred a powder he had for treating fevers into a cup of water and gave him that. Lost Axe, for his part, produced the dried second stomach of a caribou, whose intricate contents, as he explained through the good offices of Charley's Woman, could be medicinal for everything from black piss to lumbago. Cecil told him he agreed with that, from having used deer stomachs.

Coomsinah, speaking to Blizzard, caused the whole crowd, old and young, to collect.

"You understand we can't give you a Bigfoot?" Blizzard announced.

Kobuk spoke too, so he added on behalf of Kobuk: "Only a Bigfoot can give you a Bigfoot."

Both talked, and he translated: "We can give you moose meat or you can give us moose meat, but we can't give you a moose, in the first place, for you to kill. Only the moose can give himself to you for you to kill."

Cecil said he understood that. Indeed, he did, as his father would have before him; it was a notion that seemed natural, not strange or primitive. Hearing the vaguely rhythmic clack of the bighorns fighting at an upper level of the mountain, he waved his hand to remind the Thloadennis that their own hunters had been unsuccessful.

"You're doin' fine," Sutton murmured, having recognized like Cecil how much the Indians liked matching words or wits.

Lost Axe, deep-featured, dark-skinned and gentler than Blizzard, with small eyes that were slightly recessed as if from decades of snow glare, elaborated:

"We can tell you it's okay with us for you to live here. We can tell you we won't bother you if you move in. But we can't give you this valley. Or you couldn't kill us and take away this valley," Blizzard explained, interpreting for him. "Do you know what he means?"

"Yes," Cecil said "Sure."

But they were waiting for more. "I can see that no rock has fallen on Charley's head where he's lived for twenty years, and no rock has fallen out from under his feet when he was working on the wall where his mine is."

The silence persisted after Blizzard repeated this.

"You can see my friend is not a man with enemies in the woods from how the animals mind him without him hardly needing to tell them what he's after," Sutton pointed out. "And I'm the same. The water won't let me die when I jump. No matter how far it is, only a very little water will save me," he said.

Lost Axe, Blizzard, Tom Ben and many of the others wanted the jump to happen now, but the older counselors continued to wish to postpone it, as though even witnessing it might be an act that would become irrevocable.

"Hey, I'll sell you my sister," Blizzard repeated, coughing, bored. He had noticed Cecil's glances at the Sikink woman, who, having finished with the skin, had been given a willow-withe fishnet to mend.

Two of Blizzard's female kin ran over and cuffed her, made her stand up and come to him. But Tom Ben and his mother, wife and sisters and his hunting partner loudly objected that she wasn't Blizzard's to dispose of. Blizzard, joking, proposed asking two horses for her, one for them and one for him.

Cecil was both embarrassed and awfully sorry for the beating she was getting. He said he had business to settle with them, referring to the heap of trade goods he had brought.

"If you want a Bigfoot, you can stick her out one night and if the Bigfoot comes for her you'll see the Bigfoot," Blizzard said.

"Let's look at where I'm going to do this jump," Sutton suggested. He summoned his full panoply of showman's gravity and swagger to turn the focus on himself. Most of the village went along.

The site, two miles upstream, was a stretch of mossy seeps and shining, hooped, diminutive waterfalls that corded down two red bluffs of crumbly rock that hemmed the creek fifty or a hundred feet high— a spot the Thloadennis were obviously fond of for its watery rustle and its ferny foam. The kids began to demonstrate where they liked to climb and where they dove into the deepest pools, but Sutton after admiring their bravery set them instead to finding him the shallowest pools.

He rather lost himself, wading slowly, enjoying the lacy current, the feel of peaceful water again, and looking up at different knobs of rock he could leap from. The place was perfect for his purpose, with perches at every feasible level and space for an audience to watch, because each bluff formed an amphitheater facing the other. A pair of kingfishers on the creek got into an awful huff at the disturbance, and when they swooped from the clifftop to the water, he said he'd fly like them.

Dawdling brought the holdouts, including eventually Coomsinah, wearing a cape of cedar bark rubbed in goose down so that it was buffy white, with a fringe of clicking bird beaks. The sky had gradually dimmed to dusk as Sutton explained that he was going to perform his jump at the next high noon—pointing straight up to represent the sun—and showed the chief the shin-deep pearly pool of sliding water that he had chosen to leap into from almost the top of the bluff.

Cecil joined him in checking the bottom for hidden rocks. All the kids waded with them, helping clear these away. He was allowing himself sixteen inches of water to land in for forty feet of height; or, if he shifted his perch, an extra inch of water for every four or five inches above forty feet. He climbed several times to measure prospective cyries he could launch himself from, and with the darkening light, the mysteries of perspective were enhanced. He winked at Cecil as he scrambled one last time to the particular perch he had picked out over a braided waterfall that spiraled beautifully into the now black-and-silver pool. He had the kids stand under him to emphasize how shallow it was and how high on the bluff he'd climbed.

"Good," he said, confirming that this would do. He didn't depend on Blizzard to interpret for him anymore but simply clambered about like a circus performer able to entertain a crowd of any nationality or size by letting his actions speak for themselves.

"The water saves me. And I want to meet my brother Bigfoot," he said, knowing that his words would be reported and recalled.

He had spread his arms a couple of times as though practicing for tomorrow. But just as part of the crowd started to turn away—when they all still had at least a side view of him, however—he arched his back again and stretched his arms like wings and sprang, kite-shaped but dropping like a stone, and hit the water with a smack like a tree falling, in a wide, fanlike plume that rose back upward half the height he had jumped from and reached out in a sheet and drenched every soul who was watching or, in turning away, had just missed watching. They seemed to be wetter than he was, because immediately he stood up and strode out of the pool, rubbing his belly, nearly before his splash had finished landing on everybody, as swift and matter-of-fact as if the spectacle were like the kingfisher's dive after a fish—fish stunned by the impact floated on the surface—although the water didn't come up to his knees.

He said nothing to Cecil or anybody else. He only quickened his step to camp in order to leave the Indians wondering what they'd seen. Many of them were wading out to test the depth he'd plummeted into for themselves, or they climbed the bluff, and Cecil heard the word for "flying squirrel" invoked, as well as *Nakina*." Even those who hadn't quite witnessed the jump were compelled to wring the water off themselves, sorting through the various disputatious accounts of what exactly Sutton had done, apart from getting to the ground terrifically fast.

Margaret wore a look that was almost smug. Nobody would be sneering at her for a while for casting her lot with these white men. And Charley's Woman and Tom Ben both behaved as if they felt their status had improved, though they didn't know any more than anyone else among the Thloadennis what Sutton was building his suspense to.

"Was good!" Tom Ben kept assuring him, frustrated by more than the language difficulty. He was trying to talk about his father but couldn't muster either enough words or memories to do so. He knew, for example, that the white man Ben had come from a place called Lake Erie, but didn't know where Lake Erie was.

Sutton told him with Charley's Woman's assistance that although he and Cecil hadn't been there, they had certainly heard of Lake Erie and the fishing was good and he would like it if he ever went and it was an excellent place for his father to have come from—that Cecil lived not very far away and would be going back with the Bigfoot.

"You can come back with us if you want," Cecil mentioned casually—though the boy of course was flabbergasted. "But I want a Bigfoot too."

Charley's Woman assured Tom Ben at some length that if the white men said that, it was probably true. The idea that he could go East apparently had never occurred to him, and she laughed, although she was nearly as startled when Cecil suggested she could go along and see Charley's home in New Brunswick if she wanted to.

Tom Ben told her in Indian in a serious tone that he doubted there was such a thing as a Bigfoot.

"He's never seen one?" Cecil asked.

"He saw one that was running away," Charley's Woman explained.

"So why doesn't he think there is one, then?"

"He thinks the Bigfoot is a wolverine."

"How?" said Sutton.

"He says Wolverine turns himself into Bigfoot when he sees you're going to shoot at him so you won't shoot him and kill him. He blows himself up big, big, big—twice as big, five times as big as Wolverine was—and gets up on his back legs and runs away from you like a man and leaves big tracks like a hairy man so you won't shoot at him."

"But he's a wolverine? Well that's all right, we want one of those. Get him home and scare the shit out of him before every performance so he turns into a Bigfoot just for the show, but he'll be a regular ole skunk bear sittin' in his cage the rest of the time," Sutton said. He was smiling placidly, more than content with the jump he'd staged—he had never underplayed one better, he whispered to Cecil.

Cecil asked whether, then, a Bigfoot *could* be killed.

"Maybe he don't like the aggravation of getting shot," said Margaret.

Charley's Woman stiffened in astonishment at Margaret's irreverence, although generally she seemed more free and easy than Margaret had been when they'd first discovered her in Red Town.

Charley's Woman, having spent her whole life in her home valley, had none of that Red Town glumness which saw the writing on
the wall. Standing solid and savvy on her too-short legs, she crossed
her arms with a foxy air, as if as well as living with white men she
knew all about them, the bad along with the good—though undoubtedly it was Margaret who knew a great deal more.

"Me and Charley believed in most of them," she said. "But Tom
Ben's mother still figured they were Eskimos. Maybe Ben told her
that. He was a kidder. That's why they're so hairy, he said, coming
from that cold country; maybe there was a war that drove them out.
They sure can take the cold. You see them up in the snow so high
they're almost out of sight—a black speck up above where any bear
would be. A bear'll stay in the green. He wants to eat."

A number of Thloadennis packed up and moved a hundred yards
away to spend the night, in fright or excitement at the powers that
Sutton might be presumed to possess. They were singing and rap-
ping single-headed drums the shape of tambourines. Cecil roved a
bit, visiting campfires where he was offered a portion of pike's liver
or moose's nose, though as soon as he appeared the singing stopped.
He inspected the eye of a boy who'd run into a stick, and felt an elderly woman's sore stomach and a hunter's hurt shoulder, which
had been twice out of its socket, the man said. Afraid he had been
stingy, he distributed a bunch of bandanas he'd brought from Horse
Swim for a moment like this. After Sutton's jump, each family appeared doubly attentive but also eager for him to move on, as a man
perhaps not entirely made of flesh.

Charley's Woman ate supper with Sutton and him for the sake of
indulging her taste for oatmeal, which she called "Charley food."
But if Sutton had hoped that by risking his life he could learn more
about Charley's mining from her, he was wrong; she was impene-
trably loyal.

She called the Sikink woman, who was still drudging at camp
chores for Tom Ben's family by firelight, to come over so Cecil
could get a closer look at her. "She limps kind of bad. Somebody hit
her with a stone and it was a hard walk before that. They call her

'Fish-smell' here. She's 'Young Basket' at home. She's maybe never seen a white man before, and now they're thinking about giving her to you."

Despite the element of sympathy with which she spoke, she shouted venomously when Fish-smell didn't obey her, blaming the lady herself, although Tom Ben's mother, wife and sisters had surrounded her, brandishing sticks to keep her where she was.

Cecil suddenly got angry. He was confident Tom Ben wouldn't oppose him, and walked over and told them to back off. He'd thought the Sikink woman's face had appeared somewhat unformed, as well as simply foreign, because it was so often expressionless, but he realized now that she had only been submerging the fearful misery of her position. She looked exhausted, persecuted and pained, with liverish marks of beatings on her neck and head and arms and legs. She hadn't been permitted to watch Sutton's jump—which, he guessed, might be for the best—and met his glance and squinted at him as though at least expecting no worse treatment from him, holding his eyes long enough that he could see she didn't find him overly scary. To his nose she smelled no different from the Thloadennis—a sort of mixture of pikefish, smoke, charcoal and tamaracks. He had Charley's Woman tell Tom Ben's family he was bringing her to his fire, and there had Margaret ask her in the language of the Crows, which she found much more understandable than Thloadenni, whether she wanted to try some oatmeal and sugar.

She was hungry and said she liked it. He asked where she lived and she said the Eecjookgook.

"What does 'Eeejookgook' mean, the Bigfoots' River?"

"No, no. Gravel River Where the Redfish Lay Their Eggs," said Margaret after talking to her for a while. He asked if she lived near Mr. Ouddo, and she said no, nobody was near him. He asked if she knew No Water and the band of Sikinks No Water traveled with. She said she knew about them but they lived on their own rivers, which were the Sizi-kah and the Sweetin—that the Sikinks were a big tribe. When Cecil asked if she had ever seen a Bigfoot, she answered with the same readiness as she had every other question, telling Margaret that once when her husband had been very hungry and was hunting, a Bigfoot, which she called *Sasquatch,* had led him to a pond so thick with moose, who were eating water lilies, that he thought at first the pond was full of floating logs.

Sutton took Tom Ben to where the horses were staked and indicated that the mule Roy had drowned on was up for trade. The boy was not a judge of horseflesh or at all sure of what he wanted. Charley's Woman told Cecil there might be a Thloadenni girl who would be willing to accompany him instead of the Sikink, but, amused at her own objectivity, she agreed with Margaret that Fish-smell would be more useful on the Eeejookgook. "Ugly Indians over there." They would have killed her if she'd gone with Charley to soak in the hot springs.

Margaret, just as amused, reminded her that Cecil must pick somebody who wasn't going to run away. "I was supposed to run home after we got eighty or a hundred miles away so my father could sell me again, but I didn't do it."

Charley's Woman laughed and said she'd never seen one run away for good, not from a white man.

Cecil, irritated at the turn of the talk, might have felt like walking away from the whole proposition, but Coomsinah interrupted with the worried and vociferous argument to his tribesmen that to sell the daughter of an enemy to two such formidable newcomers as Cecil and Sutton was stupid. They could become the Sikinks' allies because of her. Several young Thloadennis, however, after examining the tethered mule, had dug out a set of pony bells that Cecil supposed Charley had given them to tie to the saddle of that horse of theirs which had perished in the snows of the mountain pass, as well as a ceremonial horse necklace woven of colored straw threaded through clusters of caribou hooves. They boasted to Blizzard that if they took this mule they could go over the mountain range and grab two or three girls like Fish-smell any time they wanted to.

Blizzard sided with Coomsinah. Sarcastically he suggested that from now on their job could be catching and selling "Fish-smells" to all the white men on the railroad.

Cecil asked her if she could ride. Through Margaret's halting translation she said she would not be afraid to learn, but then became uncomfortable because Lost Axe had joined them and it was

Lost Axe who had appropriated her son as his own. Unable to look at him or ignore him, she inserted her toes under a stone, looking at the ground.

"Is she ugly? Is she mean?" Sutton asked Blizzard, who was coughing but made a gesture of dismissal to say she would have been killed if she had proven "mean."

Coomsinah had cast his eye around the circle of his band and concluded that all the women were spoken for. Charley's Woman stopped translating when he jerked his thumb at the Sikink with a caustic outburst that seemed to tell Tom Ben she should have been killed along with her husband, or else right now—with whites riding through, it was too risky to still take prisoners like in the old days.

Sutton, who was tying his shoe, rolled to his feet weaponless but pointing a warning, as strangely catlike as he had looked on the cliff when he was on the verge of jumping, or the day when he had gone into the Ompompanoosuc to locate Roy.

"Hey, hey, hey!" Cecil said, to calm the rest, as if he and Sutton were working as a team. "White men and Thloadennis don't fight, Charley says. It's the Sikinks that fight everybody."

Blizzard, although he was prepared to speak as acidly as Coomsinah, was by no means inclined to threaten any harm to Fish-smell or to these white visitors. He simply withdrew from the scene without ever putting into words exactly what he thought. Indian bands were democratic in their organization; nobody would support the notions of the chief only because he advocated them, and the young men fooling with the mule were nettled, if not angry at him. They all retired for the night, including Tom Ben, who was both at a loss for words—Charley's Woman wouldn't help him—and undecided what to do.

The Sikink woman stayed where she was, not having been told to follow him. Her real name, Young Basket, was *Xingu* in her language, according to Margaret. She was rubbing her mosquito bites with alder leaves, a trick Cecil didn't know, which furnished them with something to laugh about when they wound up alone at the fire—also how much more sugar he was spooning into her tea than he had given Blizzard and the other Thloadennis.

She touched his mustache tentatively but quite as Margaret had done that day when he'd shot his first buffalo. The Thloadennis hadn't just been menacing her, they had been beating her, yet she didn't look at him to save her; she looked at him more as though to figure out what kind of tribe his was. He found he didn't care that she was as tall as him and her arms nearly as muscular. He liked her quizzing eyes and the planes of her face, which were less hefty than the Thloadennis' crowded cheeks, and the bulge of her hank of hair under her hat, and her strong hips. He opened a jar of liniment for her to rub on her bruises, and played for her on his mouth organ. Having no spare blanket roll, he gave her the saddle blankets for warmth, signaling that she could crawl inside his tent with him or stay outside, as she chose, but that she shouldn't sit by the fire after he had gone to bed or she might be highlighted as a target for Coomsinah's friends; then even the dogs couldn't protect her.

She went to sleep on the dark side of his tent, with just the canvas separating them. Later he woke up dreaming that the dogs were clambering in on top of him and discovered it was her. He didn't know whether her reason was loneliness or that she was afraid of being murdered or that rain had begun tapping the tent. She didn't dare resist his hands too actively, but by blocking them she expressed her feelings enough that he didn't keep after her. He slept late, with one arm around her.

When they woke up they could hear Sutton telling Margaret how when he was a kid the only use his father had for a bearskin was to stop up the holes in their pig fence.

"That's the only thing they wouldn't dig through. Oh, they're scared of bears! That's the cruelest sound I ever heard when I was a kid—when a bear caught a hog and that hog begged for his life."

She didn't know what a pig looked like.

"Well it's just like a bear except its ears come over its eyes and it has hooves instead of claws. So the one with the hooves was beggin' and squealin' not to be killed and the one with the claws was growlin' and holdin' onto him."

"Maybe a Bigfoot's a bear's pig," suggested Cecil, holding Lizzie's hand as they emerged. He'd decided to call her Lizzie in the middle of the night because it sounded like *Xingu* and in honor of a girl he had grown up with in Pittsfield, had always liked, and maybe should have married, and who could have withstood the gaze of all these Thloadennis as her namesake was doing.

Coomsinah and Blizzard had a new concern. A white man had been spotted coming up the valley of the Memphramagog. Who was he?

Cecil and Sutton, thinking quickly, described Millard Switzer as accurately as they could to show they knew him and his harmlessness—a skinny stray with a long staff but no other defenses leading a lone lean horse loaded with two pack bags, and a small brown dog.

"He's a holy man. He plants trees," Sutton explained further.

"We have too many white men who are shamans," Blizzard remarked. In fact he would have been less uneasy with Sutton himself if the jump had been a fake. Here he'd trudged so far to get acquainted with the practical skills of the white men clear over in the Tlickitats' valley and, for his pains, along came this mysterious white with talents nobody could fathom—closer to what the old men of the village might understand than him.

Cecil helped Tom Ben examine the mule and piled up other goods to enhance the swap he was offering. The horses munched the meadow grass, and Moose and Sally licked each other's lips and mouthed each other's mouths, standing woolgathering, until Moose yawned so heavily he actually staggered and they both lay down. Sutton was doing lazy exercises, meanwhile, and sunning his tummy, pointing at the sun, which wasn't yet at its zenith, whenever the Thloadennis' kids approached him impatiently.

Cecil asked Blizzard if a white man like Ben or Charley could become a Bigfoot when they died. Blizzard repeated the question so everyone could laugh.

"Whites don't know this country so good. They go home then." He made motions like a flustered, fluttery bird.

Sutton fetched the dented, greenish Civil War bugle, which they had packed for all these miles on the chance that it would come in handy, and licked the mouthpiece and pressed his mouth to the metal without blowing. Even Blizzard didn't know what such an instrument was for.

The bighorns were banging their heads together again, so Cecil asked Tom Ben if Bigfoot ever changed places with a bighorn ram

instead of with a wolverine. He didn't know. Cecil then asked
Lizzie. Through Margaret she said the Sikinks believed that Bigfoot, *Sasquatch,* was people who had drowned or the snow killed.

"They froze?"

No. With her hands she illustrated graphically a snowslide—a
towering mountain, a huge cornice of snow on the ridge top, and a
man walking on snowshoes underneath. The snow broke off, fell,
and crushed him. She showed his soul's natural trajectory through
life interrupted, not reaching its natural resting place.

"Nobody wants that," Margaret added. And because the Sikink
woman executed an extra finger twirl at the end which Cecil didn't
understand, she said, "Oh, and when they become a *Sasquatch* their
feet get twisted around."

"How twisted around?"

"Backwards—their feet are on backwards. That's how you tell a
Sasquatch."

"Backwards? You go backwards on his trail?"

Margaret laughed to hear his astonishment. "Eskimos or wolverines or dead people or whatever they are, you track 'em backwards.
Didn't anybody tell you that? You're going to be in trouble, going
after him all wrong."

"How do you know whether it's a person's foot or a Bigfoot's foot
that made the track, so you know which way to go?"

"Well you don't know! That's why he put his foot on backwards!" She laughed.

Sutton rescued Cecil from the position of ignorance he'd stumbled
into by bouncing a bright ribbon of music off the mountain, tonguing
soldier calls and fluent and staccato versions of "Dixie" and "The
Battle Hymn of the Republic," or as many notes of each as he could
lip into the bugle. Rally calls and wake-up calls—his gaiety made
them sound better, as did the flourishes with which he wielded and
blew spit out of and polished the bell of the instrument. The sheep
quit clacking their foreheads together. The horses stopped munching wild flowers and cocking and stamping their hooves. He trum-
peted elephant calls and elk calls.

"Even our brother Bigfoot's going to march to this. I haven't had this kind of fun in twenty years. Tell me, what was Charley like when he first got here?" He turned to Charley's Woman.

"He wasn't in too good shape. You can't hunt with a cough like he had. You can starve to death with a white man's cough like that because the animals hear you," she said, glancing at Blizzard, who, coughing, seemed to have brought one back from the Valley of the Tlickitats.

"But it didn't stop him prospecting?"

"Yes it did. He didn't find nothing. My father brought him where he is." She was grinning because Sutton had finally wormed out of her what he wanted to know.

"So how did *he* find it?"

"He was walking up the little creek there when the ice was on it. He was hunting, but he broke through and wet his feet. He built a fire—nobody lived up there then—and when the fire had melted the snow, the ground looked funny to him. It had a funny shine to it, so he thought if he ever met a white man that he especially liked he'd bring him over there."

"And how long did that take?" Sutton asked.

She laughed. "A few years."

He stretched in silence, did backbends, examined the grass elaborately to see whether his shadow had disappeared, and set off for the walled amphitheater where he was going to do his leap again—blowing his horn biblically—while the whole village fell in behind him. The bugle's bell tones rang down from the rocks above, clashing like cymbals, chiming like church bells, strutting giddily like a trumpet, marching like a tuba, clowning like a trombone.

He lowered it for a moment. "You understand what we're here for? I'm not here to swim. I'm here to meet *Nakina* with my friend and bring him home to our country. And I'm going to do the jump for him and see if he can do it."

The Thloadennis, though they were delighted by the bugle's clanging and the suspense, seemed to evince a muted fatalism, as if knowing that he would succeed again and that the feat, besides remaining inexplicable, would be out of character for any other white man they had known. The other whites who'd drifted through had been jacks-of-all-trades—indeed, could not have survived otherwise—and they expected to be baffled and not entirely happy at watching this. Cecil sensed that there was even a kind of overkill in doing it twice.

"Show us where one lives and I'll blow for him," Sutton repeated.

He gave the bugle and his gun belt to Margaret. Trout fled in front of his feet as he checked that nobody had thrown any rocks into the pool overnight. Knee deep in the lacy foam, he pointed to the roost he'd leaped from yesterday, but slipped on the slime underfoot and skinned his shin.

"Ouch! Okay, let's bite this bullet," he said.

He climbed so nimbly there was a wizardry to it—now-you-see-him, now-you-don't—chinning himself weightlessly wherever he could get a handhold, swinging a leg up, waiting for the rock to finish crumbling, and wriggling onto the next rib of the bluff. The sting of where he'd skinned himself appeared to throw his timing off a little, but when it did he hesitated for an instant and focused harder. Instead of white man's brag he used his nimbleness to build expectancy, and when he'd hooked his toes over the particular knob that he proposed to leap from, he had below him not a horse trough but a living creek.

He paused to attune himself to its rustling rhythms and coiling currents, amber shadows and light spindrift. Waiting for the breeze to die, he only seemed to grow more certain, which may have been what Cecil most respected him for.

"You think *Nakina*'ll watch when I do it for him?" he said.

This was an official all-eyes jump, not playful, just a test of daring. He sprang out, kited his arms and legs and plummeted—astoundingly heavy in that second—but landed like a wild goose on his chest and belly, fountaining water, and stood up before the splash had finished hitting everyone, unimpeded by whatever pain he felt or any difficulty in seeing straight, moving, breathing. Glittering, streaming water, he hollered like a steamboat whistle on the Mississippi.

"Eeejookgook," said the old chief, bravely swallowing his alarm. Many of the Indians had whooped and hollered, but they too gradually summoned a reserved and offish dignity, as if realizing these were not magical powers they wanted exercised by anybody regularly. Sutton rubbed his stomach and dried himself when the wind from the mountain made him sneeze.

"You'll go to the Eeejookgook. There's a lotta Bigfoots over there. You'll hear them yell," Blizzard told Cecil, speaking for the older men after a while. "We're going to send those young guys to set you onto it where they caught your friend that smells." He motioned at Tom Ben and his hunting pal. "No gold here now. Ouddo has some. Or you can go on to the Obo River from there and run onto some more."

"And will it sound like a wolf pack?" Cecil said.

"Not a wolf pack. I told you, like the northern lights." He pumped and pulsated his hands.

13

MANY BERRIES

Each night the moon waxed like an omen of good fortune over them, as the party, guided by Tom Ben and his friend Dogan Kish-koosh—a warp-shouldered but peppy boy who was overgrown for his middle teens—climbed out of the drainage of the Memphramagog to the topmost trickle of its headwaters creek and over to a series of naked rivulets and bare brooks that flowed south, west and north. It was rough going. They had to walk as often as they rode, so the fact that the Sikink woman knew nothing of horses didn't prove a significant handicap.

Lizzie was a vigorous walker despite her stone-bruised leg, and though she preferred not to get up behind Cecil on Kitty, she soon mastered the knack of leading a pack animal across the talus patches that interspersed the tundra heath. She pitched in agreeably enough with the camp chores she saw Margaret engaged in, including washing herself in the evening with an amused exactitude until her skin became as russet as a jug Cecil's mother had kept milk in and her hair grew glossy black. He could outfit her with a decent change of clothes because she was almost his own size.

He and Sutton rode his two painty horses, and Margaret her soldier pony, and Tom Ben and Dogan Kish-koosh shared the mule Roy had drowned on, which now belonged to them. There were also three pack horses—the pig-colored, short-necked freighting horse, and Red, the red one, and Fred, the versatile sorrel who could be ridden as well as led. They'd left three others at Charley's, with some winter's supplies, which provided an excuse for them to go back to the Memphramagog by and by. Sutton in his mordant moods said that inheriting Charley's claim when he died was their best chance for finding a pay streak of gold. Cecil's dog pack still comprised Moose and White Eye, Sally the retriever, Kaiser the old gray shepherd, and Roy's Yallerbitch, which had taken a shine to Lizzie and tagged after her, as Margaret's rabbit hound dogged Margaret. According to Tom Ben, the Thloadennis *had* had dogs, but during a famine the dogs had had to be consumed.

Tom Ben assumed the manner of the white men, which at the moment was collected, cosmopolitan and cool, whereas Dogan Kish-koosh (who insisted upon possessing a double name too) treated them much more as exotic visitors to be studied or furtively peered at and hastily catered to. Expecting surprises, he was more tolerant, and strangely, it was Cecil who most intrigued him. He tried to anticipate what Cecil might want to learn, drawing his attention to songbirds, potherbs, spoor of many kinds. He even woke him up after the moon had set to watch the northern lights, a spectacle of such splendor Cecil didn't mind. Lavender and reddish and greenish organ pipes vibrated against the backdrop of the wall of the sky; then vanished rapidly as though sucked upwards; but reappeared, flickering eerily; and metamorphosed into streamers and coronas that pulsated across three fourths of the dome—so much vaster than the displays he had admired in Maine—and turned lime green. Cecil, impersonating Coomsinah, lay on his back. Coomsinah and Blizzard had never seen an organ's pipes, so what sort of howl or cry or other sound could be called up in their heads by gazing at night colors and configurations such as these?

It would have been a pleasanter climb if the hatred between Lizzie and the Thloadenni boys hadn't turned murderous now that they were living on equal terms. They had shot her husband with the very rifle Tom Ben carried, and though he hadn't slept with her in front of his wife and relatives, she implied that they both had raped her at some of these same camping places when they had crossed from the Eeejookgook to the Memphramagog. She made no bones about hoping both would get themselves killed by the Sikinks on this trip even if she and Margaret and the two whites had to be caught in the crossfire. She taught the yellow dog to growl at them, and when Tom Ben mentioned his vow to kill Mr. Ouddo, trying to enlist Cecil and Sutton in the idea, she jeered in his direction that she hoped Ouddo killed him. Her one grievance too painful to speak of was of course having had to leave her son behind.

This change in her, throwing him on the defensive all the time, was bewildering to Tom Ben, who, besides sparing her life, undoubtedly had treated her no worse than a Sikink would have treated any captured woman of his tribe. He was exasperated that she was permitted to rave at him under Cecil's protection—it was not behavior befitting an ally—and perhaps might have deserted them if Sutton hadn't taken him under his wing, growing avuncular and giving him one-armed hugs. He was caught anyway by a nearly helpless fascination with them as representing probably what his father had been like, but without Charley's Woman to interpret for him, was thrown on the abilities of Margaret, who spoke Lizzie's language much more readily.

Sutton told Tom Ben that he wouldn't shoot any man he'd never met before, but that he would be interested in going through Mr. Ouddo's effects with him, or through his father's belongings, if they could be identified. He unpacked luggage to show him white men's odds and ends and explain the use of everything, and confided how he'd done his leap-for-life, so there would be no mystery to it, and freely allowed him to observe that white men got as gray and shaky after a hard climb as anybody else, that they weren't magical and should be as easy to befriend (or, in the case of Mr. Ouddo, to kill) as anybody else. Coaching him, Sutton listened to his efforts to speak English, as apparently Charley and Charley's Woman had never done. Yet Tom Ben, deciphering the smudged and scrabbly trails that crossed the Hump, and hunkering around a twig fire on a mountain headland in the evening struggling with pidgin English under Margaret's condescending glance and Lizzie's baleful glare, still felt how deep a gulf cut him off from what Sutton knew of his father's world.

Lizzie, meanwhile, poking through Cecil's pack bags and finding him "very rich," according to Margaret, was only entertained. She also enjoyed the growling-nickering the horses indulged in and would boldly plunge into the melee of a dogfight to haul the culprits out for punishment even before the dogs quite recognized who she was. Cecil hadn't yet lent her a gun, but once she realized the knife he'd given her was hers to keep, she gripped it purposefully a dozen times a day without saying why. Margaret talked persuasively to her about all of the Indian women she had known who'd wanted to have a salt-and-pepper baby and after they had had one had looked for another white man to give them another paleface to keep the first one company, but Lizzie shook off that suggestion. When Dogan Kish-koosh and Tom Ben walked ahead and Margaret was with Sutton, she was alone with Cecil, however, and less and less resistant to him. She hid her face when he kissed her, as if the practice were unfamiliar, but clasped him encouragingly when he rubbed against her—and he was more moved than he'd expected when she let him put his hand between her legs at night and he felt her come to a climax, so well versed in the subtleties of masturbation that he asked Margaret how Indian girls first learned about making love.

"With boys or with old men. How else?" Different tribes had different customs, and she reminded him that in his sympathy for Lizzie as a widow, he should remember that if she'd been in No Water's Sikink band and they had killed him, she would have pawed over his body afterwards and cut his prick off for a toy.

"They're cruel if they catchya. Sometimes I don't know but what they're meaner than the whites."

The mountains mobbed into a jumble of slopes and pitches, gunmetal heights and gunstock-colored gorges which didn't separate into isolated cones but ran together in multiple masses connected by short, cloud-stuffed plateaus as cold as the snow in the saddles not far above or the blade-edged crestlines that were an icy blue. During foggy spells they couldn't see the mountaintops, till abruptly the sky would blow clear for an hour or two, deafeningly deep and radiant—the *heavens,* as Cecil thought of it then. Or sometimes a large peak blocked the morning sun and made its own weather, a sopping cloud that might be irradiated by beautiful umber and ondine yellows by noon.

Often socked in, they could travel only terribly slowly, sticking within shouting distance of one another, with the panicky sense that they couldn't hunt here if they had to or find their way out if Tom Ben should abandon them. They would need to squat down blindly in a fireless sinkhole—the dogs were fasting already—and live on their sacks of store food. The grass was too skimpy for the horses to forage a proper meal, no matter how early they gave up their search for the trail and camped. Clouds sailing by eight feet overhead brushed them and wet their faces teasingly in this chaos of hogbacks overtopped by broken black and gray pyramids three thousand feet higher, of which they would obtain a glimpse, before the glimpse was snatched away—this famished no-man's land across which, Tom Ben said, the Tlickitats also hunted or raided occasionally.

The horses, goose-rumped as they struggled downhill, or stick-necked as they scrabbled up, threw themselves into the trek just to get it over with. They seemed to rejoice, emerging from the forest onto the tundra, to break free of the windfalls, but like everyone else, got out of breath in the thin air and found it no fun to stagger and reel across a boulder-blocked avalanche chute in a chill wind funneled between two ridgelines. Cecil wondered if they didn't sometimes share his foreboding that their route would tempt them all into a box of cliffs or precipices with no way out ahead or back and a smothering shroud of fog. In several precarious places, he noticed white objects moldering between the rocks, the skull of a sheep or a wolf that had lost its footing or been trapped in a snowslide and that was unnerving to approach because he visualized it as the relic of a human being.

Although the country was too bare for game to concentrate, they saw both sheep and caribou in little batches when the clouds split at the seams and revealed this gullied arch of the world—animals on the move between better feeding grounds. The ewes grazed with their lambs, chatting in *blaats,* and distinctly apart from the bachelor parties of helmeted rams, blockier than the ewes and phlegmatic-looking, which from a mile off could resemble a colony of sullen, staring gnomes, until they uttered warning snorts and scattered upward, bounding from rock to rock with dauntless precision when the dogs went after them.

The caribou, by contrast, paced elegantly like high-strung trotting horses to clear out, their ankles clicking rhythmically and oddly, their noses horizontal. Though their new sets of antlers were partly grown, they were losing their coats and appeared to be quilted with patches of molting shag and shedding skin. As gracefully as they moved, whenever one of the horses whinnied at them they answered with disreputable grunts, like hogs.

Three times Tom Ben brought his white men past a sagging or a caved-in cabin that was decomposing to moss and lichen in the high timber, where a lonesome prospector had labored for a few summers during the era of the beaver men thirty or forty years before. The beaver men had been the same people as the prospectors, because a beaver man prospected for gold during the summer when beaver-pelts weren't marketable and a prospector trapped beavers during the winter after his creeks and sluices froze. So the same man whose meager living arrangements they casually autopsied had probably lived from November to May in a winter-thick bunkerlike cabin somewhere down in the welter of willow and softwood valleys thousands of feet below. To guess at his individual talents and preferences, you would have had to locate his trapping cabin too and compare how homey it was and how elaborate his trapline had been with his setup and diggings here.

Decades of rain had washed away all but the most determined shoveling these men had done and given their huts the look of abandoned animal dens, but it was still spooky to thrust one's head inside, anticipating the specter of a skeleton wrapped in mouse-chewed hides lying on the log bunk. Neither Lizzie nor Dogan Kish-koosh nor Tom Ben remembered hearing any conclusive histories of them, not even whether they had managed to find gold, survive the mountains and head for home.

"They didn't trust the Indians. They didn't want us to kill 'em, you know?" said Lizzie, hunching meekly to mimic a timid white man watching Indians go by his house, as Margaret translated; and a groundhog whistled and darted for cover, sounding like a human being.

To Dogan Kish-koosh, Cecil's solicitude for her was simply more grist for his curiosity. Unlike Tom Ben, he wasn't offended by it, and he kept searching for the tracks of a Bigfoot to show him— once said he had just seen *Nakina* run across a gap, staring almost as though Cecil was *his* Bigfoot.

Cecil had heard or read long ago that Indians disliked climbing to the tops of mountains, so he asked Margaret how high was too high for them, and if Bigfoot was the reason why.

The sky was clear, and she waved at a row of sun-rinsed spires behind a snowy peak that itself looked like the brink of the end of the world. "Spirits," she said. "Bigfoot is not a spirit."

"What could a spirit do to you, for instance?"

"He could make you jump. You'd be holding on tight when you climbed, but he might make you turn around and jump." After thinking for a moment, she gave another example: "Maybe you'd be sleeping in your tent up there, and you wake up in the morning but you don't get up. You don't get yourself up the next day either or the next day. You feel like you can't get up and finally you stay there in your tent so long you die with a pain in your chest."

"But that's not the Bigfoot?" Cecil said.

"No."

Lizzie, being brought into the discussion, contributed a Bigfoot type of story, however. A Sikink on the Eeejookgook who had killed somebody ran away to Bigfoot territory to escape the dead person's relatives, she said. "But they didn't want him there—*Sasquatch* didn't. When he went to sleep, *Sasquatch* would come and tap on his feet so he couldn't sleep. Finally he had to come back," Margaret added.

"And what happened to him?"

"Oh he had to pay a lotta skins."

Cecil remembered having heard nevertheless that although Indians were afraid to climb to mountaintops, they went into the mountains seeking visions. He asked both women how they did that.

Margaret laughed. "She says she don't get visions. Her brother gets visions."

"How?"

Lizzie wouldn't respond for a while. When she did, she searched about for a cartwheel-sized stone and when she found one, sat down in front of it and put her forefinger at the center and began to rub with a circular motion, doing nothing else for several minutes until the bizarreness of the business evaporated and it became rather hypnotic for Cecil as well.

The mountains of the Hump Range didn't give an inch, squeezing the couloirs they looked down on, descending into auger twists pinched between slab cliffs that were tinted metallically and from which lynxes and owls screamed, a country so frigid at night and so unremitting all day that Sutton spoke of passing through "on borrowed time." He had acquired a wheeze—"too high for living," he said—and slouched on his paint horse humbly, but swore at the sight of the mile-long belts of minerally greens and metallurgic aquamarines above and below him which might well contain exactly the mother rock he would be picking up itty-bitty flecks of in the river gravels weeks and leagues to the west of here, wondering where it had originated.

He pounded at it with his miner's hammer when he had a chance, smiling a despairing smile. "You know, I really don't know what I'm lookin' for looks like?" When they discovered a prospect pit that somebody had dug, they could only speculate about what he'd found. If he'd filled a whole bean sack with gold to drag away, would they even know it now? Or had the Sikinks maybe intercepted him before he reached a river to float down and burned him, as Tom Ben maliciously suggested they would have?

Sutton wheezed and sighed but was enjoying himself, hollering to produce echoes and cause the dogs to howl and the eagles to cry. They spent a night in a col with a feathery forest of aspens around, gray simple poles with giddy gray leaves, set in such a tricky placement in relation to the sky that when they woke up they didn't know which way to turn. Wherever they went they seemed to be riding out into the clouds, with unearthly consequences, riding across a bottomless sky. But then the dogs attacked a badger family, the down-to-earth mamma digging a desperate hole in four seconds flat—spinning in it, lunging, snarling, hissing, fending off the pack but unable to save her babies. Sutton salvaged a tuft of fur for a shaving brush.

When would they see the Eeejookgook? they kept asking Tom Ben. Surely every mountain had a river at the foot of it? In this dribbling, trickling, spouting, spurting, gushing, gurgling, topmost terrain that seemed to spill water in all directions they should be able to see the seedling creeks of all the rivers in the world, and they pestered Tom Ben until Margaret protested that her head was woolly from translating. Charley had boasted that his valley was a year's walk east of the Pacific, but had he meant a summer's season or actually a year-round effort? Had he meant by way of a shortcut or following the rivers? Had he meant that only a fool would walk instead of raft it, or that you couldn't raft it? The Thloadennis were increasingly distracted, because this was the territory of their enemies.

Lizzie and Cecil, when they were alone, bandied wrestling holds, linked arms, or tripped each other to help surmount their difficulties in talking, though when she twisted him off-balance and the dogs charged in to join the fun, she yanked him out from under them, not trusting their intentions. By not raping her or forcing her he had won her friendly affection, but couldn't keep his hands off her—he was starved—and gradually, as they walked, she came to let him do much as he wished; would stand with one leg stiffened for him to press against, and hold and support him as he groaned. At night he could make love more conventionally, though she preferred to sleep outside his tent in good weather, under a blowdown, where one could slip away in the event of a raid by enemy Indians, and she might tease him by crawling into a dense tangle of bushes, but then would move again, picking a space for two. Holding her, handling the familiar and yet exotic parts of her body that reminded him of the half of his life he hadn't spent in the woods, he couldn't get enough of stroking her, but at the back of his mind, felt guilty too and missed his wife, whose body was more delicately proportioned—

more wifely, he thought—though Lizzie soon kneed and elbowed him if he grew absentminded in her arms.

To keep their almost wordless love-play lively he revived some of the games he and his daughter had invented, like pretending that his index finger spiraling above her was a buzzing bee in search of a place to sting; that all his fingers had become a spider; that his hand was a bat skittering or a fox biting. She entered into the spirit of it, squirming, thrashing, and by new rules of the game, declared her nest of hair a spider's web that once his hands got in they could not leave—that he was hers for life.

Her moccasins were wearing out; he gave her moose hide that she cut and sewed. He let her fire off his weapons and boss his dogs so she would know how to if he were incapacitated. She thought the whistling teakettle a fine addition to a meat fire, and sitting shoulder to shoulder with him like a friend, was herself a great addition for him. She'd started eating with a knife and spoon instead of with her hands, and he thought he observed a contest going on in her between the lady who might want to turn into a squaw man's woman like Margaret and the Sikink who didn't.

Realizing he was watching for unusual tracks, she brought to his attention anything the Thloadennis didn't, such as a fisher that had been trailing a marten, which had itself been hard upon a squirrel's prints, or a small cougar whose footmarks showed it had been heeling over on one forepaw because of an injury. He was interested that the particulars of what she liked to try or do were not so different from what a stump-farm girl in the backwoods of Maine would have enjoyed. But she was also bitter, chuckling angrily, muttering memories to herself which may not have had to do only with her captivity. They were both jittery and their chumming had an edge to it that didn't always prove they were fond of each other.

He remembered with some surprise how his father, C. R. Roop, on his later and more eccentric peddling trips, had picked up a waif woman if he could—a widow who had lost her home or a girl with a belly—whom he made a point of dropping off somewhere better than wherever he had found her, such as at one of the church safehouses he'd learned about while traveling. It had been part of his outlawry after the age of forty that he might leave his wife and kids at home for six months or a year, roaming by wagon with his bee-hives and his nostrums, the poultices he mixed himself from roots he believed in, as well as "Dr. True's Elixir" and "Dr. Pearce's Favorite Prescription," which he bought wholesale through the mails. With his goaty, sidewise way of walking, he made his living "by the back door," he liked to say, collecting valuable medicinals on other peo-ple's woodlots that the landowners didn't know about, and setting his bees loose on cutover forestland the lumbering outfits were fin-ished with, and it had been plain enough—at least to Cecil—which cordials and pharmaceuticals he'd made himself and which he'd bought. But then it wasn't so clear anymore. And he stopped both-ering to explain what he was up to in the cow pastures and sugar-bushes where farmers might encounter him. Or he would settle in for a lengthy period like a patriarch with another family, whose sick mother or father he was treating for cancer; and though some people swore by him, others claimed he'd bilked them. He hadn't really, but he had drifted away from the ordinary person's aware-ness of what other people frown on. He used to say he'd saved maybe two dozen lives and been "a law unto himself," and shrewd and fearless, he would have loved this trip. He'd always kicked him-self for not getting in on the California gold rush.

They picked their way lower, into thorny devil's club, brushwood, alder, rhododendron and bracken, with tick bites that swelled up, and much pulling and hauling to force the horses' pack sacks through. It became such a mess they were glad to climb again onto a scree slope that caused the horses different sorts of trouble and tilted them northeasterly of where they had intended to aim.

They woke up to three inches of new-fallen snow and the cold cotton of a fog whose dynamics were such that even the rock face behind it appeared to turn and swirl. They got above the rainbows and the clouds and watched the fog unfold and separate and stream below them like a narrative being dramatized. Yet there were cliffs that stretched taller than where they stood and a mountain to be seen above these. A mob of farther mountains spread like islands from which they were isolated, archipelagoes of land that emerged and enlarged from the steaming soup of fog, held still for a while, then swiftly shrank and vanished.

"Makes you say your prayers. No place for a family man," said Sutton.

There were yolk-yellow fogs and milky fogs and brown fogs. Chalky brooks trickled alongside violets and orange avalanche lilies, and the endless stubby passes looked out across a chaos of choppy peaks, an epoch of summits. At timberline at night they had the pleasure of a bonfire, and Cecil gave himself over to envisioning the triumph of rafting down one of the great trunk rivers of the Pacific next year, without a penny to his name but with a troupe of red and golden bears and black Bigfoots already trained, like nothing else the world had seen, performing on the steamship to pay his fare.

They scrambled onto a broader, more cohesive mountain pennanted with meadows covered with white blossoms which Lizzie said the Sikinks called Many Berries. In a month you'd see the bushes nodding as creatures of many sizes half hidden in the foliage tugged off the fruit—such a crop of berries, she said, that all the birds and bears and foxes and Indians couldn't eat them up. Now the mountainside of flower fields swarmed with butterflies after the nectar, and swallows in ping-pong pursuit of these.

Following a draw that angled to a lower level, they stumbled on a pair of yearling bighorns that in midsummer blithesomeness had unwisely wandered off the precipices and put themselves in an uncommonly exposed position. They were rams, three-quarters grown, and skittered out of bowshot range as if at one point they had been hunted by Indians, but must have also had experience with wolves, because they didn't venture to run up the walls of the draw to escape into the flowery brushland where a wolf pack would have made short work of them. Gnomelike, they bobbed among the housesized rocks confusingly, as though there might be three or four, their helmet heads as gray as fedoras.

The men, spreading out to cover any route the animals could have taken through the debris of scrub and boulders, lost sight of each other. Cecil, being a good deer hunter, was trying to figure where a deer would have hidden. He didn't want to shoot one of his friends, and carefully held his fire at twitches of movement in the six-foot brush—again when a creature that appeared to be two-legged raced between the helter-skelter boulders at breakneck speed. Implausibly high-haunched and bulky-shouldered, it was canted forward, dashing at the pace of a madman, but blanketed with hair.

Lifting his rifle, he crept ahead, neither afraid nor hurrying, though he recognized that what he'd seen might conceivably be a Bigfoot. He was concerned that nobody shoot it and didn't yell for the others. He didn't know if it was running from him or one of them, and replayed the image of it in his mind, considering whether he had mistaken some animal for the caveman-Indian he wanted. He needed a better look, but what should he do then to stop it from escaping? Should he shoot to lame it?

When he got to where it had been, he saw a couple of spider-light but platter-sized tracks, more toed than heel-and-sole. He spotted too the stationary white rump of one of the rams, which was facing but concealed from another hunter, probably Sutton, who by the sound of things was progressing at a stalker's pace in the opposite direction. Cecil, who wanted to be certain both that the rump patch wasn't attached to a Bigfoot and that the Bigfoot itself wasn't close by, observing him, waited. He knew the silence wouldn't last, however. Finally he shot straight into the center of the white splotch of fur and watched the sheep jerk, shudder and founder, the earth-brown coat of the rest of its body emerging from camouflage to sink to the ground, while its eye cast back in its large, severe head to find him.

He waited again in case the Bigfoot made a break from hiding after witnessing this; then went to the ram, which was lying in a puddle of blood, too stricken to get up—and was unmistakably what it was, nothing more, nothing less—and cut its throat. In the meantime there were shouts from farther down the draw, because his shot had frightened the second one and it had betrayed itself and had been taken.

Deliberately, he didn't mention the Bigfoot until Dogan Kish-koosh made churning, running motions with his hands and pointed at him. Though nobody else had seen it, they searched for tracks, finding pebbles that had been kicked out of line but no succinct im-

prints. Lizzie set off an uproar once by whispering "Sikink!" with a
sharp intake of breath and a glance overhead. The two Thloadennis
assumed somebody had got a bead on them from the top of the
draw and threw themselves into sheltered positions, but Sutton was
nearly as mad at her, because he wanted to hold onto their services
for as long as he could and because he was scared of meeting the
Sikinks too.

The draw led down from the spongy footing of the tundra to
a gorge which dumped them into the much worse morass of a forest which recently had been burned over. Charred, acrid-smelling
poles lay everywhere or leaned akimbo, clogging many miles. It
was too tough for the horses, so they camped, worked on their sheep
meat, and the next day climbed back up to the muskeg and meadows to try another tack to get themselves lower, sighting several
bears along the way.

The first was an impetuous blondie streaked with cream, who
couldn't stomach intruders. Custard yellow, with a corn-colored cub
and a tobacco-colored cub, she was lifting a boulder to reach after a
rock rabbit, but let the rock rabbit go to rush at the dogs, who all
fled riotously and yet afterwards went back to piss or defecate defer-
entially on her tracks. The second was sprawled in a fagged-out,
overheated posture under a spruce in a notch that they crossed. He
was black and gaunt—a black grizzly, almost indigo where the sun
struck him, as if other pigments were glinting underneath. Being
inclined to pretend he hadn't scented them rather than raise a
storm, he looked so placid and oblivious it was a start to notice a
moose calf's head between his paws. He bent and wiped the grease
off of his lips onto the grass.

Bears must be what horses were invented for, Lizzie told Margaret when she vaulted onto Kitty behind Cecil as they rode past.
But all four Indians watched him with the grave, whole-focused interest people devote to the phenomenon of death.

The Thloadennis went off scouting, taking their meager kit with
them as though they might never come back. Sutton's paternal approach to Tom Ben had worn thin because of the laborious problem
of translating, and Sutton was sometimes a bit sulky anyhow because of becoming convinced that in this trackless topography they

were never going to return to Charley's place to reclaim their stuff and hang around tactfully waiting to inherit the gold Charley must have been hoarding all these years. He felt, according to Margaret, that he had given up his own best opportunity in order to help Cecil along.

The horses needed a rest, but to loll about the dispirited camp in a rocky glen under a nameless promontory was disheartening. Cecil and Lizzie took two of the dogs and sallied up a side valley which had no visible top to it, Cecil hoping it would continue on forever into basins nobody knew of, where Bigfoot lived. They walked till they were tired, still encountering no headwall, and watching for a beast that bobbled as it shambled, not a fat-footed bear but a Brush Man, a creature with queerly elongated, toe-strong feet, as Lizzie sketched them in the sand. She was alarmed nonetheless to be seeking one out, and especially after the omen of an eagle that flew up in front of them with meat in its talons; then by a knot of ravens feeding on carrion that were so unaccustomed to the presence of people they wheeled at head level to investigate. The stream bouncing along the steep floor of the valley was pitted with potholes, and she and Cecil bathed in one of these when the sun shone hot for a spell.

Wandering sleepily on, they met with a more severe omen. Another figure was bathing in a sunny scoop in the streambed—gray-muzzled in the white-flecked water, and apparently the size of a Jersey cow, although its shape was hidden in the bathing hole. When they crawled cautiously closer, it turned out to be an elderly bear so comfortable and preoccupied she only sipped the thin breezes blowing from their direction to her as if she were smoking a hookah. Her cub sniffed them first, somersaulting sideways into a thicket at the unknown smell. The mother, wrenching around, didn't know what or where the danger was. Lying on her back like a fat old party in a bathtub, she whipped her nose to and fro, raised her paws so high that Cecil saw her rusty teats swing, but slipped repeatedly and comically on the wet stone margins in trying to right herself and scramble out. Then she stopped trying to stand up and locate or identify them. With a strange, frozen dignity she stiffened in her tub like a matron in a mineral bath wishing to be rubbed, and expired with the semblance of total aplomb, her hind legs up, her fore-paws stretched straight to the left of her, dead of a heart attack.

Lizzie thought a magic event had occurred and by sign language warned Cecil that the bear might have another face underneath her regular face and was going to wake up and peel back the skin of her bear mask and speak angrily to them from this other face if they attempted to catch her cub. The ravens had followed and their excited behavior frightened her too. Ravens had helped make the dry land of the world and put man on it, as Charley had told him many Indians believed. When Cecil asked her if this was *Sasquatch,* the Brush Man, the Man-that-flees, she shook her head, however. He approached to examine the bear, then didn't—stood queasily, feel-ing pains in his chest and the fragility of his own heartbeat, much as he would have done beside a person in the same circumstances and unknown to him, and left willingly. Nor did the dogs need to be called away.

The Thloadennis showed up at moonrise the next night with an air of having outgrown their companions. They'd looked down from another slope of Many Berries at Mr. Ouddo's chimney smoke on the Eeejookgook, and if Sutton and Cecil weren't prepared to help them kill him, they would quit this trip and walk back here another time, they said.

Sutton—who after a life of saying goodbye to many towns and all the people in them was easy come, easy go—got avuncular, ex-plaining again that his "one rule" was that he wouldn't kill a man he'd never met. Margaret smiled as she put this sentiment into Crow and Kluatantan for the Thloadennis, because she was fond enough of him by now to know that he had plenty of other rules for de-cency.

When she passed along Tom Ben's rejoinder that Mr. Ouddo might kill *him,* Sutton squatted and drew a map of North America in the dirt. He noted with care and diligence where the three oceans and the Gulf of Mexico were; where in this northern portion of the Rocky Mountains Tom Ben, Dogan Kish-koosh and Lizzie lived; where on the faraway East Coast Tom Ben's father and Cecil had come from; where Winnipeg, St. Paul, Chicago and St. Louis were; approximately where in the American Rockies Margaret had been

born and had ridden from with her white husband; where on the
faraway Gulf he, Sutton, had been born; and about where he and
Cecil hoped to emerge on the shore of the Pacific with their bears
or Bigfoots to find a boat for San Francisco. All of that was gripping if not intimidating in itself to the Indians, but he next delineated
his own meanderings from New Orleans to Florida, St. Louis to
Baltimore and New York, and on and on, showing not a summary of
his travels but each trip separately, including his shuttles up and down
the Mississippi, on a map three feet high and five feet wide in the
moonlight.

"I've met lots of murderers. A murderer ain't going to kill me,"
he said.

He gave them smoking and chewing tobacco, knives, combs, a
magnifying glass, a hatchet, and complimented them as good and
honest guides who could go and make their fortune on the railroad.
Of course what Tom Ben had longed for was not so much to learn
the tricks of the white man's trade as to find part of himself in them
and make them his friends, but they'd both been too absorbed in
their tent life to bestow special attention on him.

Sutton, seeing his distress, suggested that they meet in the Valley
of the Tlickitats in the falltime, where so many white men would
be working. But how could Tom Ben imagine accompanying them
to see Lake Erie, as they'd invited him to do, when he couldn't explore even the Eeejookgook with them? Cecil, surveying the pale,
lumpy ambiguities of his nose and cheeks—too skinny for a Thloadenni's, too chunky for a white man's—tried to reconstruct what his
father had looked like. What had most astonished Tom Ben was
watching Cecil make a chum of Lizzie instead of using her as his
people had used her, lavishing the afternoons on her that he might
otherwise have given over to befriending Tom Ben. In the personal and tribal vituperation between them, she now had that advantage, but he could devastate her by reminding her of how he'd
split her husband's head open after shooting him, and yesterday had
gone back to the site to spit upon his bones.

Dogan Kish-koosh had bundled the pelt, meat and back fat of
the sheep he'd shot, along with Sutton's presents, agreeably onto the
mule, which when it fathomed that it was being separated from the

rest of the herd began to kick and buck forlornly. Lizzie was gloat-
ing, and Sutton, who believed Tom Ben represented more of a loss
as a guide than she could compensate for, shouted at her until she
left the firelight. He coaxed both boys to sit down for a cup of
brandy and to draw a parting map, beside his map, showing the
Eeejookgook's course before it ran into the Obo River, and then the
route of the Obo before it debouched into the Hainaino—the great
river, bigger than the Ompompanoosuc, like a bear next to a groundhog. Only the salmon knew how long the Hainaino was, they said,
before they got too raucously drunk. Dogan Kish-koosh made pro-
nouncements on the nature of *Nakina* to Cecil, while gesturing at
both maps, but they were lost for want of a translator; Margaret
was also drunk. Because Lizzie had remained out of sight, Cecil at
Sutton's urging stayed awake till daybreak to be sure she didn't
materialize knife in hand and slice up the Thloadennis.

They got off safely, though with hangovers, and left the white
men to contemplate the lower complications, accordioned with
waterfalls and watercourses, of the enormous dome of Many Berries
Mountain, whose actual top Cecil and Sutton had still not seen.

With Lizzie, with Yallerbitch at her heels, they moved another
day's march southwest (Sutton blowing bugle calls occasionally to
invigorate himself and warn away the mountain's demons) to a
high mesa of grass where the six horses could stuff their bellies but
which, although it didn't seem to tilt, had boundaries on two sides
that fell directly for a thousand feet or more. Below that, a green
shelf of earth prevented them from glimpsing what lay farther
down, until way out beyond this drop the opposite mountain rose
muscularly from the trench's hidden floor, enfolding hundreds of
clefts and slivers of summer ice and snow in whole jagged geogra-
phies of rock. It had a gigantism you could stare and stare at and
never turn away as if you'd had your fill.

Clouds started to cross the face, but stalled and split into streamers, evaporated, dissipated, or hugged a shoulder or an arm, smothering a dozen miles of brutal mountainside, while the curve of the
next dozen glistered in a diamondlike radiance at the same time.
Clouds swam up its cliffs and sledded down its contours, concealing,

then revealing shark's-fin upthrusts and gentler ridges that went out
on a limb and ended nowhere. Slender cataracts of meltwater tumbled from precariously situated, pewter-colored ponds and corru-
gated, crusty, gray-blue glaciers. Cecil, just in gazing, wondered
whether even finding gold or successfully netting a Bigfoot in one
of those myriad crevices wouldn't be like picking up a seashell at
the beach—a pleasant matter that in this giant setting lost its
meaning.

"You know, I bet I should have gone back with them," said Sutton, who perhaps was thinking the same thing.

"And wait for poor old Charley to die?"

He nodded.

"Hey!" Margaret exclaimed.

"No, I'd have took you."

"I'm going to St. Louie," she said.

Both men laughed. "If you think this place is closer to St. Louie
than Charley's is you're crazier than I thought," Sutton told her.

She shook her head. "As long as we're moving we're getting
closer. If we stop we're not."

"That's true," Sutton agreed. "But you're the one that didn't want
to go into Horse Swim, ain't you?"

"Maybe I'll do better in St. Louie," she said; and they had to grant
her that possibility.

Lizzie shrugged off St. Louie, whatever she pictured St. Louie as
being. Instead she twirled her finger to show how they would need
to wriggle down this precipice to get to where all the gold was, after
probably having to shoot the horses halfway, and wouldn't promise
at all to guide them—just grinned, eating a biscuit. Cecil, who was
finally free of the censorious Thloadennis, seized her, put her on
her back, and pretended to throttle her, while she hooted. Below
them, she told Margaret, under the coercion of his tickling, lay the
Straight River, flowing into the Eeejookgook, which headed nearby,
up in the twists of this mountain they were facing.

He let her go but asked why the Straight wasn't straight, and she
answered through Margaret that it was straight farther up. It was
fed by three forks. The East Fork, she said, headed at a pass from
which her people would be able to reach the Chickamin and kill

Lost Axe and take her son back. The Middle Fork and the West Fork led to the territory of different Indians whom no white man had ever approached, not the beaver men and not the gold men, because they'd hunt down a horse like it was a moose and fill it full of arrows whether it had a man sitting on top of it or not, and put enough arrows into the man that he looked like a walking porcupine.

She spoke with the flash of vehemence that shocked Cecil when it surfaced occasionally, and made Margaret smile noncommittally. Why didn't those Indians on the upper forks of the Straight come and kill Ouddo, or get Charley? he asked her. Because we'd kill them, or the Thloadennis would kill them, she answered through Margaret. "Ouddo is their pet. They like to watch him," Margaret explained, amused to observe his surprise.

Cecil was offended but less so than Sutton, who liked Lizzie less and besides felt some strain rung in him going back to his childhood spent with the slaves his father had peddled. From the beginning he had acted homier than Cecil with most of the Indians, but there was a kind of spring in him too that at a certain point snapped. Even with the Thloadennis gone, he wasn't in favor of entrusting Lizzie with a gun. Yet, on the other hand, when Cecil had once mentioned to him how the only bad thing about her was the way she always chewed her meals with her mouth open, he'd practically guffawed.

"They do that," he had said. He'd pointed to Margaret, who was scratching her left breast and the ribs under it in such a manner that the breast became a wad of flesh instead of a breast. "Don't let it bother you."

Sutton killed a caribou as fat as a frog that ran the wrong way from the dogs, and was cheered up by that. They rode to another promontory, where they could peer directly into the valley of the Straight, which wasn't straight but braided in numerous lens-shaped, egg-shaped, snow-colored loops and figure eights along a narrow, mushy-looking, treeless floor hemmed in by roof-pitched forested walls incised with cuts that let the mountains' meltwater pour down—walls that would have afforded scant living space on the bottom for an Indian family or a homesteader, or even for a Bigfoot, as Margaret remarked.

No, that's right, you seldom heard a *Sasquatch* sing on the Straight, Lizzie told her. There were no redfish to catch and dry for winter, either.

"Maybe that's why the Indians on the Straight are so nasty," Margaret added. "They're hungry! And awful cold down there. You couldn't stretch your legs, you couldn't take a dry step, the sun would set on you before it rose most of the year."

Sutton wanted to pan the sands of the Straight nevertheless. If whites had avoided it, so much the better, and he muttered that maybe Margaret didn't translate right if it didn't suit her. Margaret overheard him and startled both men by imitating with uncanny realism a hacking cough she claimed had emanated from a lonely prospector who had rambled into Crow country when she was a girl and had chosen just such a sunless, tight, wet, airless situation for his sluice.

"We watched that guy die."

Although the horses couldn't negotiate the sheep trails, of which there were several going down, Lizzie found them a caribou trail to give Sutton his chance. A fog bellied through the valley then, however, turning scarlet from the sunset when it ballooned to their level, so they took to their tents—but not before a squawking goose, lost in the fog and lifting itself frantically, flapped into their vicinity and Lizzie grabbed Cecil's Winchester. Cecil, who hadn't seen the goose, got such a scare from the explosion next to his ear that he smacked her. She managed to dodge enough that he only hit her shoulder, and, laughing, hit him back.

"You better watch your rifle. She may be signaling somebody," Sutton suggested quietly. But she was chewing a piece of sheepskin to sew Cecil some winter gloves, and he had progressed from teaching her the English words for her own eyes and ears and knees and hair to "bridge," for the bridge of her nose, and "small," for the small of her back, and he didn't believe she'd want to get him killed.

Part 5

The Bigfoot

14

AT OUDDO'S

They descended by switchbacks to the valley's broken bottom, changing every perspective within a few hours, and began to think of ambushes again. Mosquitoes swarmed into the windless air as thick as whining hail, and the boggy grass was stumblingly tufty, though sometimes crowded to the riverbank by invasions of drunken-trunked spruce trees. The Straight itself from close up was slate-colored with a chestnut under-tinting and churning concentrations of glacial milk. Amounting to some thirty yards of water, it skidded rather than flowed, banging raw spots on the bank in its quicker stretches, rubbing the clay away and unstringing the roots of the trees. Unlike a flatland river, it had no pride of pace or place, just wanted to hurry by, building wigwams of debris and dividing around these but undermining them, improvising a new bed of loops and straightaways.

Sutton, after having complained that he was being hustled along without a chance to prospect anywhere, never got off his paint horse once they had reached the floor. The valley had no trail, and irregular rock formations interrupted the river's braided incoherence with rapids, barricades and waterfalls. The mountains on either side, although they couldn't see much of them now, were fresh and awesome in his mind's eye, so the idea of stopping to search the mud for evidence of gold-bearing gravels or sands was easily postponed.

Their long-sought Eeejookgook River—though no more voluminous—came brawling into the Straight from the west side the next morning in two white boiling prongs, with a black spiky island in the middle, out of a V-shaped valley which was all snake-wiggles upstream as far as they could guess or see.

"Charley's *walks*," Cecil said to Sutton, thinking of the distances Charley had covered and the risks he'd run to visit his friend Ben and soak in the hot springs. Or—what was weirder—Ouddo's trip in the reverse direction, clear to Charley's cabin, carrying Ben's skull.

The horses were happier with the taste of this grass. There was turf underfoot alongside the Eeejookgook, and many moose tracks were in evidence. In fact a seat had been rigged in the crotch of a tree for still-hunting. Fish racks, a cache on stilts, some charcoal picture-writing on birches and stones that told where one or another hunter had gone, and the shiny jet-black stubs of dead campfires all marked the junction of the rivers as habitable yet probably dangerous. Lizzie insisted he wasn't going to get killed when he asked her in sign language what those hunters would do to him if they caught him. The nearest Sikink settlement, she said, was five days' walk down-current from here.

Cecil kept visualizing Bigfoot faces, not Indian ones, at the edge of the trees. The rockfall blocking salmon from entering the Straight extended from a bluff that was fronted with mica and therefore dimly luminescent with the sky's own dove-blue illumination and the forest's greens. The dogs, who had been engrossed in piecing out a dozen scented tales, discovered a white man's grave, one end of which had collapsed and created a cavity in which, to judge by the feathers left behind, a pair of merganser ducks had nested this spring. Lizzie said he had been an unknown traveler (curled up now like a bird in his rotted rags) and had been buried by a companion, but nobody ever saw the companion. He must have floated out, leaving no prints.

Smiling more than she talked, she refrained from guiding or ad-

vising them except to call attention to a few curiosities, such as a man of the mountains whose face had been chiseled by the elements along the fringe of a cliff, and a purple lip of stone protruding from the riverbed at the head of a fishing hole. In an eddy they spotted their first chicken-headed, particolored salmon, red and blue and white creatures with their noses grown into strange beaks for the spawning season and many bruises from the journey.

"That ain't a fish!" said Cecil.

"Looks like a garfish," said Sutton, who on the Mississippi had seen worse.

There was living space for man and beast on the Eeejookgook, and the side valleys that joined every five or ten miles from the west were rich in willow woods that moose could thrive on, under the lavish tiers of crenelated, misty mountains juxtaposed above them and above each other so complexly that any number of canyons might be hidden among the twists. Riding behind Cecil and chewing sheepskin for him, Lizzie gave a hoot and holler when he reached back and rubbed his fist between her legs. She slid off Kitty and mounted the sorrel, and showed them all a salt lick of chalky, puddled soil about the area of the base of a barn which was stippled with the first deer prints they had met with in a long time, looking prim and pear-shaped compared to the moose and caribou tracks also plentiful that they were used to pausing beside. A hunter's blind had been constructed of brush close by, and other mineral springs trickled into the busy river inconspicuously, yet left their whiff of ginger and their greenish and vermilion stains in the water for half a mile, twining with the glacial flour contributed by several bigger streams.

That night a howling like the wind woke Cecil and Lizzie. Yet the tent wall wasn't flapping. In pitch dark but without moving his hand to her face he felt her mouth break into a grin.

"*Sasquatch,*" she whispered, tapping his ear to make him lie still. From her lack of fear he understood that the noise did not really pertain to their presence and she was glad he could finally hear it. It was a zipping sort of howl, more flexible than the wind, yodeling up and down from an undeterminable distance. He wondered what occurrence had started it, and whether it didn't ring more different

notes than a mouth organ—if not a church organ. Creeping out to his baggage, he extracted the harmonica he had bought in Horse · Swim and softly tried to duplicate or at least analyze the sounds, a cacophony of more notes than he could produce at once with only one instrument and one mouth. He lay listening as fearlessly as to a great migration of geese.

Both men were eager to lay over. Cecil helped Sutton get going with his gold pan in the morning, wading with him to find boulders under which the current had worn a depression where the heavier mineral particles floating down the river would have collected. Then it was a process of putting a likely shovelful of dirt into the pan, submerging the pan to its rim in quiet water, and rotating the contents so that the lightest silts and sands washed out. They weeded out the tiny sticks and bits of roots, nubbins of gravel and blades of grass, dipping in new water over the edge while gradually working the residue of granules down to a cupful and at last a spoonful of the heaviest, blackish, reddish grains. These were the magnetites and hematites, but also yielded a flakelet of gold.

Even glimpsing it, they hardly celebrated. Gold like half a hangnail in the panload; gold so sliverish they had to wet one fingertip to dab it up and bring it close enough to look at. But it *was* the precious metal; Sutton, who had wondered if it would be recognizable, relaxed and beamed. The next panful produced two flakes, and the third none, after they'd devoted altogether maybe an hour to dipping and swirling river-bottom sands and muds. "Gotta find where this came from if we're gonna make money."

Cecil crossed the river on a wind-thrown tree with Moose and Sally to do some prospecting of his own, after trying to persuade Lizzie to explore with him. When she refused he asked her through Margaret if she knew anyone who had been stolen away by a Bigfoot. Sure, she said, but that woman had luckily got away before the winter, when the *Sasquatch* would have taken her to sleep with him till springtime under the snow.

"She was afraid to go up to any high place after that. I think he picked her up and carried her up high. And she was afraid of big dogs or big skins like bearskins and afraid to be left alone and afraid of what she dreamed, but if she went to sleep she slept for a long

time." But Lizzie repeated that a *Sasquatch* had helped her husband hunt when he was starving once, and led him to a pond where all the moose on the Eeejookgook were eating water lilies.

The weather was warm and clear, though woolly clouds blew fast against a mountainside a dozen miles away that a fork of the young Eeejookgook drained. Cecil went up this, discovering an unexpected lake filling a valley wider than the main one they were camped in. The hard walking through buckbrush that tangled into chest-high mats was relieved by the sweep of open space above him, with birds gaily scudding, and by the novelty of being alone—though he saw a wolf go coiling up a ridge slope like a puff of smoke, her hair bouncing on her back, and picked out her pups on the knoll, standing in a ruff of snow. The lake was fed by any number of streams that clucked as peaceably as chickens as he moseyed along, checking the banks of each for unfamiliar tracks. It was such a simple and absorbing task that the time didn't drag, while the sun shifted around. His dogs were trained to stick next to him and stay mum, and it was like a meat hunt, except that he ignored meat tracks.

At the head of the lake he found what he'd been searching for. Six impressions of feet which were like human feet although proportionately narrower and longer, with the little outer toe canted out to balance the effect of the narrowness. For a moment he reacted with the pleasure of a hunter, but then he jerked his head about, chilled and fearful, remembering that a Bigfoot was supposedly a supernatural beast that walked with its feet screwed on backwards. Hunching to keep out of sight, he tried to recall how long ago a rain had fallen—these marks hadn't been rained on.

Couldn't it be a lunky-footed Indian? No, too large; and the tracks, squirrelly or muskratty or raccoonlike in their attenuations, were somehow *animal* in human form. Did it have a sense of smell, this quarry he was after? He'd never asked, yet now his life might depend on that. He studied the brush slopes going up toward the castellations that crowned the mountainside, but high or low, nothing moved. What a crazy errand—to hope to grab and transport such an apparition East.

Listening to the howling—unmusical but sonorous—in his mind again, he stayed put until windy clouds brought rain that swiftly smudged the prints, and the thousands of scrub bushes and aspen limbs up and down the valley bobbed, rattled and shook as if the Bigfoot might be coming for him from all directions. He could have subdued the terror of that notion except that one spruce in particular was vibrating with real vehemence, a bear-sized commotion, as though its roots were stamping their feet. The mountain went up to sheared-off places where no rescuer could retrieve him (even had there been a possibility of a rescue party in such a region), and the spruce shook with such an animating personality he didn't want to know the reason. But what else was he here for?

A moose turned out to be the culprit, encapsuled in the foliage, rubbing its back against the trunk. Tame as a horse, it slouched away from him as if it considered him just another Bigfoot.

He spent the night on a sandbar in the shelter of a cutbank at the head of the lake, after gazing up the short course of the sinuous creek that fed it from the waters of a higher basin whose mouth he could just see and where by moonrise he imagined the Bigfoot lived. The howling didn't start till late and then was like a hundred thousand toads emitting their snoring trill around a lake at home in Massachusetts, with harmonica harmonics too and churchy chords. He lit no fire. He kept his dogs beside him and, lying tautly in his blanket, watched the moon throw cloud shadows that were like replications of a magnified Bigfoot both monstrous and benign against the rising ground—the stars like pointy teeth strewn across the sky.

Continuing down the west bank of the Eeejookgook again, Lizzie sat behind Cecil on Kitty, hugging him proprietarily but choking him whenever he put one hand behind him between her legs.

They started to encounter the skeletons of butchered deer hanging in the trees, as well as a few corpses of bears that appeared to have been pulleyed up and were tacked by the heels. This was a strange practice, for a man to leave such relics strung up about his neighborhood when wolves would almost certainly be drawn to chase whatever game was left and kill his horses or eat his sled dogs off their chains, and the remains could as easily have been slipped into the river to fatten the fishes instead. A man who put up with the grisly stink and inconvenience of outlandish trophies of this kind must be awfully proud of his marksmanship.

They saw three wolves hung up, indeed, and four more partially butchered deer, gone ratty in the rains.

"A rifleman! It's a marvel he don't have no Indians nailed up," Margaret remarked. Sutton and Cecil strapped on their gun belts and spaced themselves so as not to become sitting ducks for this individual, whom they assumed to be Mr. Ouddo.

A wire tram-rail spanned the river with a moose-skin bucket suspended from it in which a man could sit and pull himself across by hand. Lizzie said that Ouddo used it to reach his diggings on the other side; and in a snug boathouse a flat-bowed johnboat was stored. Soon she pointed out the path on their side of the river that led to where he lived. They heard the strokes of a pickaxe or sledgehammer at work from still a third direction—interrupted now by a dog's bark—and so they hurried straight along his trail, at her prompting, to beat him home.

His house was astonishing. Three stories tall, with gingerbread fretting pieced about the small, moose-parchment windows, and the logs squared off so neatly with an axe in front that they resembled boards, it boasted a queerly citified aspect for these far woods. If somebody had applied a coat of paint, it could have been taken for a frame house. However, a sort of pillbox-shaped turret had been constructed on top, which made them glad to have hurried when they saw that it had slits cut for a gun.

Much passionate consideration had gone into the embellishments of the dooryard too, with its revolving windmill, its smoking smokehouse, its dragsleds and dogsleds, sawhorses and shaving horses, wooden washtubs, four-legged and three-legged stools, a candlemaking apparatus for processing tallow, and two scarecrows for the garden, one stuffed in the shape of a female. The windmill was twenty feet high and geared to a waterwheel immersed in a brook—the gears and other parts of both mechanisms having been whittled of wood—by means of which two little buckets attached to the blades of the waterwheel continually delivered water to a flume raised five feet high that by its incline cleverly carried it into the house when the wind blew. Bells on the windmill's vanes clanged and donged to announce what was going on.

A spyglass stood on a tripod aimed at the sky for stargazing; and a peppy fawn was tethered to a log, though this, like the gun turret, seemed a rather sinister talisman to any visitor who had passed by the skeletons spread-eagled in the forest. Perhaps it served to remind this isolated man of all the meals he had wrung out of the wilderness. But he did like vegetables too. Cecil recognized rhubarb, horseradish, parsnips, carrots, onions, spinach, crookneck squash and other good cold-weather stuff, as well as a patch of melon plants that must have been started earlier in a forcing bed, all nourished by a loamy soil that looked as though it had been cultivated not with iron tools but by being sifted for days through the man's hands.

The house's owner emerged from the underbrush. He was a strapping, burned and deafish-looking figure, cradling a rifle but missing a thumb, and his face, which was mostly concealed in his brown beard and gray sideburns, displayed a harsh and yet confiding smile. The black dog yammering behind his legs seemed to act as his ears, because he didn't hear Sutton's howdy.

"What have you got? I thought you was a bunch of Mountain Chinamen," he said slowly in a discordant, creaky voice that sounded like a door that hadn't been opened lately. "You didn't have the wit to bring in a pair of pigs, did you? I like pork. I don't see many white men up here. I'm Isaac Ouddo. I'm pleased to meet you." He squinted not as if to examine their goods but as though he were preparing to read their lips.

"What do you need? We're just ridin' through," Sutton told him. For safety's sake he didn't dismount, but offered to shake Ouddo's hand.

"Are those your scarecrows? IS THAT YOUR SCARECROW?" Cecil asked.

"She does keep the blackbirds off." He laughed. "That's just potatoes I grow for the dog."

"I admire *that*," said Sutton, louder than before, and pointed to the turret on top of the house. "But I still think they could burn you out."

"I don't know why he built that," Ouddo said, disowning it. "I need flour. I miss my bread. Oats I got. I grow oats. Most people eat to live, but sometimes I think I live to eat."

There were few heights close by, unlike the view at Charley's place which had disclosed his diggings immediately. They kept glancing about for a clue to how well he was doing. The flume carrying water to the house was a miner's flume, but otherwise he could have been any settler who was ingenious with his hands. He showed them a lathe he hoped to hitch to his windmill to make table legs "if it ever blows like cyclone." But he disowned the ginger-bread fretwork also. "I didn't build this. The man was dead when I got here."

Lizzie hissed at Cecil, waving at what he perceived was a snare rigged across the opening of a trail at the head of the clearing. "For *Sasquatch*."

"That's Meat Mountain," said Ouddo, who directed their attention to a corner of Many Berries that loomed above his stretch of the Eeejookgook. "That's quite a meat tree, that one. And that one over there is Mad Me Mountain, I call it," he added, rusty voiced, naming the other peak they could see.

Cecil, on the ground now, told him they had flour.

"What can you spare? What do you want for it—fur?"

"No, gold'd be better," said Sutton. "We're going to get rid of these horses. We want to float out of this country. We'll sell you some of them too."

Ouddo absorbed this statement, after appearing to have lip-read it. "You got some gold?"

"No, we're *lookin'* for gold. We don't want to buy no furs," Sutton explained politely.

"Well I need flour. So there you are," Ouddo answered, too loud for the heedful expression he wore. He cleared his throat. The crisping air had put ribs in the clouds. "Cuttlefish clouds," he called them. "Come in the house. We'll see what we can swap. But I don't allow any Mountain Chinamen in there, even the women."

The trees around the edge of the clearing had been girdled to dry for firewood as they died and were in various stages of doing that. They stepped through a litter of dogsled rails and runners, a wind-lass he'd been working on, a whiskey keg he'd been recaulking, and

assorted mummified animal paws chopped off in the skinning that
he did and that his dog had got tired of gnawing on. Slanting under
the eaves of the house was one of those funny tilted windows known
in New England as lazy windows, but when Cecil mentioned it,
Ouddo said, "That's the crazy window. I didn't build this house. I
can't vouch for how sane *he* was."

"Your dog loves you," Cecil said.

"She's like me. She does everything either for love or for spite."

Ouddo had a persnickety walk, like a fellow who prided himself
on being a character. But Lizzie, who was holding Cecil's extra rifle
and Kitty at the fringe of the woods, shouted in Sikink.

"Keep out of the house!" Margaret, who was with her, yelled.

Cecil noticed a smile play over Ouddo's mouth, as if he wasn't
really so deaf. Because Sutton had joined them, however, and because he was in one of his sieges of perfect confidence, he decided
to ignore her. As they reached the door, Sutton seemed to stumble,
and knelt on one knee to tie his shoelace, leaning against the wall
under the ground-floor window. Ouddo executed a kind of hop just
as he crossed his doorsill, and pointed casually behind him after he
had done so. Cecil, who was anticipating what might be inside,
wasn't paying much attention, but he did stop for a second, wondering what Ouddo had pointed at. It was a trip wire at ankle level.
He turned, warned Sutton, told his dogs to stay outside, and stepped
gingerly over it, while Ouddo grinned as though to share the joke
and gestured at a shotgun in the shadows that was set to fire through
the door at about chest height if a wire rigged from the trip wire
was tugged.

"Three rooms down here," he said. "I shut the upstairs off during
the winter. It didn't make much sense to build three floors in this
climate, do you think?"

Cecil touched his pistol holster for reassurance and chambered a
bullet in his rifle, but short of shooting him, couldn't decide what to
do. Sutton entered, cat-footed, and they both looked for guns on the
walls or tables that Ouddo might grab for. The house logs had been
peeled as clean and yellow as bananas on the inside, and a few dili-
gently whittled items of furniture were situated cozily about a sand-

pit fireplace which had a funnel over it to catch the smoke. An inventive arrangement of mirrors at the windows threw light into the darker crannies of the place throughout the day as the sun moved, their host said.

With an old hatchet blade in a frame, he'd fixed himself a toothpick-manufacturing machine. He showed them that and a new rocking chair, some shapely hardwood canes, his wall candle-holders, his rabbitskin pillows stuffed with moss, and his flour bin.

"Empty. What do we swap? I wasn't always deaf as a post," he added, keeping his eyes fixed on Sutton's mouth. "Although I could feel that it was coming on. I had to get settled pretty fast, and I still don't fancy getting taken by surprise."

Cecil, remembering Charley's Trapper's Oath, wondered whether it could ever register with any deep effect on such a truncated soul as this. He wanted raisins and a bow saw and store salt, he said—he was using hot-springs salt—but had saved a little hyson tea for a special occasion, and brewed a pot for them.

"The bells are company, huh?" Sutton said. But apparently Ouddo misunderstood.

"I think there's other values in the ground. I know there's iron and coal that people will come in after when we're dead and gone."

He showed them a leather flyswatter and a little pile of snail shells that memorialized a meal he'd had and a tuft of fur he said he'd clipped from a grizzly's back in trying to "nip the cord." His own dog had hopped over the trip wire and followed him inside and Cecil's dogs had stayed outside, but Margaret's rabbit dog, who had never accepted Cecil's efforts to train her, impulsively dashed in and triggered a shotgun blast that all but busted everybody's eardrums. Cecil staggered to the floor, sure that Ouddo must have shot him, and the women screamed from the clearing. Sutton fell into a chair, holding his heart with one hand and his pistol with the other. But the rabbit dog herself, being small, had not been hit, and Ouddo's cur leaped at her.

"You've got some work to do with that one, don't you?" Ouddo laughed, as though he couldn't see how mad they were. Charley had referred to him as young—had his solitude aged him, or had Charley lost his sense of the passage of time? A discernible path had been worn in the wood floor by Ouddo's pacing.

"Let me show you my thunder mug, my pride and joy," he said. It was an indoor toilet. Another curiosity was a rifle that his horse had rolled on. The horse had died from eating locoweed.

With a sigh as the pretext to shoot him passed, Sutton said, "Who built your house?"

"Never met him. Never had that pleasure. The Indians didn't want it, so I moved in. He was quite the cocksman. He had kids with this tribe"—pointing downriver—"and a kid with that tribe"—pointing toward the mountains across which the Thloadennis lived—"that would just as soon kill each other." He smiled, because it showed the folly of dipping your wick in tipi country.

Cecil, trying to compare Ouddo with the Texan back in Horse Swim who had shot the Swiss gentleman simply for snoring, at first could sense no similarity. Ouddo was frenetic and ingratiating, not punctilious and prickly. But the cowboy had not only taken responsibility for the murder; he had insisted that the logic of his act must be accepted by everyone, like Ouddo in the matter of the shotgun.

They climbed the abbreviated staircase which his predecessor had installed and carved with daisies—Cecil groping for a sense from it of the personality of the dead man—to look at Ouddo's furs, which had been skinned and scraped expertly and gave a solid and un-squishy *thunk* when he banged them against the wall the way a fur buyer would have done. Baled hides were pegged from the ceiling, and he had a shelf arrayed with boiled skulls of many sizes—shrew, lynx, porcupine.

"No Bigfoot?" Cecil asked.

"A Bigfoot?" Ouddo whooped as loud as if he were alone. "I don't shoot Bigfoots and I don't shoot Mountain Chinamen. There's too many more where they came from."

"Do you know Charley Biskner?" Sutton inquired.

"I've heard of him. He's a miner, a dynamiter. Dynamite I don't like. It can blow back on you."

"He's your closest neighbor?"

"I guess so. Him and Groundhog Morris, except they say his tunnel fell in on him. Them and the Mountain Chinamen."

"You've probably got your own ideas about how a fellow should dig for gold?"

"I wish I did," Ouddo said. He kept eyeing the two women through the blurry window, which had a crack in it, while fingering his softest, darkest, finest furs, marten and mink with no tears in them that the animal itself hadn't acquired in fights and hunts. They were skins he'd killed, like a fastidious trapper, by crushing their hearts with his fingers or getting them under his heel.

"It's funny to think who's going to wear these—here in the mud and blood," he said, rubbing his bare wrist over the most luxurious specimens, as a woman purchasing a marten stole might do, and thrust his whole arm up inside the hollow bales erotically and groaned.

"Tell me this. Is it a bar to prospecting—these Bigfoots? Do you run into them?" Cecil asked.

"Seen 'em and heard 'em. But I don't dig or dynamite or pan. I told you that. Come," he said, showing them the elbows in his cellar hole for storing food, and then pulling a dozen each of carrots, parsnips and turnips outside to exchange for some flour.

"Getting sticky over there." He pointed at a cloud bank over Mad Me Mountain, swinging his arms and hugging his chest. "Plenty of hill-climbing there. You could climb till you coughed blood and still not stand on top."

That brought him to the subject of his hot springs. Smiling like a man who enjoys living dangerously, because he perceived that they had already heard about them, he rubbed his forehead as though from the strain of all this stimulation. "If your ladies would like a bath, it's about like body temperature. It tastes like beer, but you can't get drunk on it." He fetched a fishline from the house—"I'm going to show you a trick"—with Cecil accompanying him back inside lest he grab a pistol and conceal it.

The hot springs were a series of scalding, spongy seeps that had eaten shallow orange and vermilion trenches in the varicolored earth, a minute's walk away. "Good fire clay. You could make a chimney with it," he said. Trickling relentlessly, these seeps converged into a soapy-looking pool lipped with layered mineral deposits, scarlet and prune-colored. "You get in there you die," he said. But almost alongside ran a cold stream whose source was an artesian pond which he said had been lifeless until he'd put fish in it.

"Let me show you my trick." He threw a worm on a hook into the stream, and a cluster of six-inchers bit at it. When he pulled one out, the others fled. "They're scared, but you wait and see how they forget." He carried the line with the fish on it to the boiling pool and dangled it there till the flesh came loose. "That's the trick. You cook your fish without a fire and it tastes like beer at the end." He tossed the hook back in the stream. "Remember how scared they were? But look at 'em come."

After catching another couple, he asked if the girls didn't want a bath. The bathing pool was a separate shoveled-out timbered pit seven feet square and five feet deep, crusted with minerals as vivid as coral but as smooth as talc, into which two wooden runnels led. He opened the stopcocks, diverting a faucetlike flow from the hot springs and another of cold water from the stream. Though he was clean of weapons so far as they knew, Cecil and Sutton called the women closer in case they were wrong. Cecil, kneeling in the velvety cistern, whose sides felt lined with mushroom skins, wanted his turn to last all day. He shut his eyes and positively groaned. In such deliciously heated water he was suddenly sorry for himself for all the hardships of the trip. Was this guy really so deranged—because if he *wasn't,* couldn't they settle here for a while?

When Sutton asked about pay streaks of gold, Ouddo would only talk about coal mines, iron mines, copper mines. "Well, we'll put in a word with the railroad for you," Sutton responded sarcastically. "Maybe they'll run a spur up."

When he got into the hot silken waters and Cecil stood guard next to Ouddo, Cecil asked the man about his trap lines. He said he had overnight cabins in three directions and ran one line five nights long.

And how about the dead body curled up like the bones of a crow in the grave they had found? Cecil asked.

"I don't know about him. He was lucky he got buried, wasn't he? It means he was with somebody and it means it wasn't a Mountain Chinaman. Most of us ain't going to have a friend around when we cash in." Smiling thinly, he nodded toward the wall of high mountains to the east of him, then cast his bitter, lively eye toward Lizzie. "You ladies want a bath?"

Of course the temptation was simply to shoot him—as doubtless he'd shot Ben—and have the place as their own, but Cecil realized with a touch of amusement that murderers murdered; it would be hard for a beginner to do.

"You still cutting hay, even without the horse?" he said.

"Sure I do, and I still build fence." Ouddo pointed to some newly peeled snake-fencing enclosing his meadow along the faintly discernible line of the original beaver dam that had created a site for it. He patted both corners of his mouth with a swatch of cloth as if he were worried that spit was collecting there.

Cecil asked about the snare set for the Bigfoot. Had he ever caught one? Did he want to?

"No, that's to scare him."

"What would happen if I shot one?"

"Why? You want a monkey skin?"

"You saw one dead?"

"No, but if you shot him he wouldn't look the same. It's like a bird flying. You'd only have a monkey skin to show for it. Or are you gonna play cards with him?" Ouddo hollowed his cheeks as if he were sucking a piece of candy, and scrutinized Cecil. "Well you can try. You should go to Fourth Creek. This is the Sixth Creek of the Eeejookgook. Groundhog Morris worked on the Fourth Creek and he got pretty thick with them. Mountain Chinamen and Bigfoot— he wasn't afraid of any of them. He was an old country boy and he'd treat the moose like a milk cow and the Bigfoot like a milk cow, and you know, nothing hurt him. He was just like a groundhog, always underground. He'd come out blinking in the sunshine to eat his lunch and nobody bothered him, not the bear, not the Bigfoot— only that his tunnel fell in on him. He wasn't here but about two and a half years. Came in during the winter."

After Sutton dressed, they moved to the house to give the women privacy and counted out a few pounds of precious white flour in exchange for Ouddo's root vegetables, which were "proof against the scurf," he said. He claimed that if a market ever developed he could grow a hundred twenty-five pounds of oats to an acre here, yet had what appeared to be more like a miner's calluses on his hands—the same as Charley's—as they still watched him like a prisoner.

"So did you get Charley's gold when you dug his floor up?" Sutton asked abruptly.

"I don't know what you mean," said Ouddo, with a smiling, quirky defiance.

Sutton tried another tack: "My friend, we're lookin' for a stake and trying to stay out from under a rockslide. We're not on anybody's side. We're lookin' out for ourselves."

Ouddo was silent.

"You could help us with that."

They waited, saying nothing else, while he fidgeted and sought to draw their attention to more of his handiwork in the yard.

"I had a kind of cold that settled in back of my ears and spread from left to right," he told them at last. "That was one hell of a winter. But I know as long as I can read a track I'll never starve. You just set your number fours or number fives for deer instead of for beaver and skunk bears. A guy like Groundhog couldn't shoot to win a prize, but he did shoot whatever he saw and he could trap plenty of food while he was underground—just do his regular work and let his traps hunt for him. A guy like him," Ouddo went on, "I don't know how much yellow rock he wanted to dig up before he left. He might have just kept digging it up and burying it again. But *I'd* be in London, *I'd* sail to Paris if I hit the lode. I don't know about you, but if you see me here at all you know I haven't."

He stared at Lizzie intently when she strolled over with her hair wet, but it was impossible to tell whether his look meant he coveted her or only thought he recognized her—just as, when he stared at Cecil, he could have been sizing him up as a prospective neighbor to sound him out and get to know him, or as a prospective dead body he hoped to dismember and toy with. He was an awkward man, and the jaunty nut-brown house with its extravagant third story and gingerbread fretting and lazy window produced a stridor in the conversation as though it were an interrupting voice attempting to speak for poor Ben. But neither Cecil nor Sutton could puzzle out the history and true story, or wanted to spend time trying.

15

THE FOURTH CREEK OF
THE EEEJOOKGOOK

After their call on Mr. Ouddo, they moved about forty miles down the west bank of the Eeejookgook, picking their way along animal paths through cold, dense fir forests to the river's junction with two middle-sized streams and one large one, which Lizzie said was the Fourth Creek Ouddo had spoken of. It was the fourth creek on the west side, counting up from the river's mouth, where the Eeejookgook met the Obo River, and only creeks that a walking man still had to swim at low water in the fall were counted, she said.

Luckily, although perpendicular slopes abounded on the Eeejookgook, the valley floor provided some level ground in front of the notch through which Fourth Creek emptied its water, and spring floods had cleared considerable acreage for swamp grass and willows. When they turned the horses loose to enjoy all of this forage after what had been grim going, the little herd immediately swam the river to put as much distance as possible between themselves and the hard labor and discipline of the past weeks. Soon a curious moose, with his brown bell swinging and two upside-down chairs on top of his head, emerged from the woods to join the group, but in order not to scare them Cecil didn't shoot him.

While cutting firewood, laying a net for salmon, setting their tent on a rise where Lizzie said her own people camped on occasion, spreading a mattress of sweet-smelling grass, and lolling with her on it inside until their hunger drove them out after dark, he ignored his fears and premonitions of what might be about to happen— meeting not only a Bigfoot but maybe the Sikinks, who could be much more dangerous. Or Ouddo might decide to follow and stalk them.

Lizzie cupped her ear to tease him when a belt of northern lights dashed in sudden streaks and zebra bars and picket patterns over Mad Me Mountain. These were as pink in the night sky as the salmon she was splitting open by firelight, and glowed like antler tines, vibrated like a dozen tuning forks, fanned high into an arch of organ-pipe columns, and blanketed the sky with orange sheets that turned to a diaphanous white chiffon before sweeping upward into instant oblivion. They heard no Bigfoot sirening a song that night, but again after a little while a shimmering light, now lavender, ascended from tree line and pulsed serenely across hundreds of miles, fading gradually into a coal-red incandescence as if reflecting the blaze of a forest fire beyond the horizon, except that during the period they took to eat, the glow became lime green.

Instead of a Bigfoot, a pack of wolves ranged close and started to interrogate the dogs—an event that triggered an apoplectic hullabaloo of blubbering and barking, because Cecil had fastened them at isolated points outside camp to give warning if either Ouddo or the Sikinks came sneaking around, and till he freed them, the dogs felt doomed to be devoured there on their chains. The horses, thinking better of their wish for independence under the re-echo of these drawn-out howls, stampeded back across the river, kicking Sutton's tent pegs loose in their haste to claim protection, and even brought the moose with them, which Margaret shot when the northern lights, burning in immense, elongated, yellow S's, flared bright once again.

Lots of howling and hysterical barking, whinnying, stamping and galloping about continued through the night, but Lizzie and Cecil stayed entwined in a giggling though tenacious hug—she partly to make up for all she'd lost, and he for what he'd left behind—until the rising sun began to bake them. Sometimes as he watched or made love to her, he suspected that she already knew what was going to befall him and Sutton if they fell afoul of her own people—whether, for instance, she would be able to intercede for them and shield them. This busy night he thought she might.

They were sucking knuckly salmon bits from a fish's spine, bumping shoulders companionably, sharing a log, and enjoying the happy antics of the horses, who at daybreak had swum the river to revel in the liberty of the other side, when it was jarring to see a bulky rushing figure vault into the midst of the herd and, going up on two legs, start them bucking as frantically as a merry-go-round. At fifty or a hundred yards, the drama was somewhat miniaturized. It didn't quite seem serious until Cecil saw his Kitty drop like a wooden horse knocked from its pole. He had carried his rifle to breakfast and got off a couple of shots. Still fearing Ouddo, he wondered irrationally if this *was* Ouddo, lunging on two legs all over the place after the horses like that. Then he realized that it must finally be his fabled Bigfoot and held his fire, almost forgetting his upwelling rage at what was happening, until Lizzie shouted "*Nahukwa!*"—the Sikink word for bear.

The rest of the horses scattered from it like pigeons to save their lives and splashed into the Eeejookgook and swam toward Cecil, except for Margaret's soldier pony, who paused to try to defend Kitty's twitching body for a moment with his teeth and hooves and only barely escaped, with two raw swathes of red flesh showing and half of his mane gone. Margaret and Sutton chased him to clean the dirt out before it poisoned his blood, while Cecil—with the picture of the creature rearing up on two legs with a lunatic rapidity to kill Kitty repeating in back of his eyes—shot into the trees and brush to hit it if he could, still not believing he knew what kind of being it was.

Though Kitty's front end had been pulled under the foliage, her hind end jerked as if she were alive. Did it have her? Had he hit it? Had it fled? Margaret's injured soldier pony and his own sorrel studhorse and the spare paint nickered to her, but her movements were so mechanical he decided she was merely being gnawed on. He shot at the area until the jerking stopped. Lizzie rubbed his neck.

"Not a very homey spot, is it?" Sutton said. He measured out enough of their slim stock of tobacco to help them quiet their nerves.

None of them was in a hurry to cross the water and look at the horse's body when the beast that had mangled her might still be there. Dolefully they butchered Margaret's moose instead. Then Lizzie led Cecil on an excursion afoot up Fourth Creek to distract him, bringing her Yallerhound along and White Eye.

The creek was river-sized by Massachusetts standards but mounted unceremoniously to broken breaks and tablelands facing Ouddo's Mad Me Mountain, a name Cecil disliked but couldn't shut out of his mind. It was indeed a mountain with pitches that a man could die on, sharp in several profiles and dingy gray, and had a head-on-shoulders on top like that of Charley's Goon Mountain. Meat Mountain, on the other hand—which was the Indians' "Many Berries"—although as high, was draped with comely passes at several levels where game could cross to further feeding territory and graze or browse along the way.

Green gravel underlay Fourth Creek. Other stretches were cocoa brown, and the surface, sparkling, crinkling in the sun, lent the afternoon a hopeful air. Kitty's stark death seemed more natural after an interval had passed, but Cecil could feel her nostrils snuffling and plastering their wetness on his ears and cheeks. He remembered her tripping trot and idiosyncratic amble, her chesty grunts and stomach grumbles, her whooshing sneezes and the phony stumbles she indulged in just to startle him, though she was sure-footed; her hooves click-clacked. Ahead, he recognized the obstacle of a muskeg bog by slender-spired black spruces that were massed like those in Maine. But Lizzie and he climbed indefatigably, sighting a new mountain marked with a green transverse stripe of rock in vast cocoa-colored formations and snowy tundra ridges above them that connected it with small massifs on either side—all confronting Mad Me and Meat Mountain across the Eeejookgook's valley. Fourth Creek appeared to stem from the striped mountain, and it made an inviting-looking destination. By their accelerated and telepathic sign language she told him she had never met the white man who'd shared this creek with Bigfoot, but he had lived in what by her hand sweeps she described as a pit house and had been called *Itene,* or Groundhog, by the Indians also.

They spent the night back at camp, rafting to examine Kitty's carcass before the wolves got hold of her. The bear's trail as it had retreated was unbloodied—a bear scarcely out of its adolescence, to judge by its feet, which might account for how fast it had moved, though Cecil still couldn't reconcile his fearsome glimpse of Kitty's killer with these quite ordinary tracks. The biggest toes were the outer ones, like a bear's, not the inner toes, as they would have been on a human foot—or presumably a Bigfoot's—and the hind feet had swung forward to hit the ground just in front of the forefeet as it loped, which Lizzie said a Bigfoot's didn't do.

Before sunup the wolves that had been drawn to Kitty's body caught Margaret's rabbit dog, cutting her off and chasing her between them like a bounding ball that escaped from one mouth only toward another; and they were circling the remaining horses and dogs like waving scarves you could just glimpse between the trees. As when they howled, they seemed to be more numerous than they probably were; their very tracks multiplied as if spontaneously. Sally, the soft-mouthed retriever, and Kaiser, the old German shepherd who'd acted from the beginning as if he regretted coming along, glued themselves to Cecil for safety.

Despite Lizzie's impatience to reach the first band of Sikinks and learn whether perhaps her daughter had gotten home after surviving the raid when Tom Ben and Dogan Kish-koosh had killed her husband and captured her, they all agreed to ride up Fourth Creek to where she and Cecil had left off. Margaret barbequed a good-luck banquet of well-peppered fish with watercress on top and baked a strawberry pie. But looking at the subdued, diminished clump of dogs and horses, she remarked that Bigfoot might end up making them too feel the same as that. It was too bad their friend Mr. Switzer, the appleman, wasn't with them, because of his fearlessness and gentle air of mystery. "A man like that—it wouldn't hurt him."

Sutton took up the suggestion and wrote with charcoal in big lettering on the side of a rock near riverside, "SWITZER TURN UP THIS CREEK HERE," in case he did wander by.

By noon they were wet to the thighs in the muskeg bog, shivering in a rainstorm, losing their bearings when they couldn't see "Stripe Mountain" over the trees, driving the long-suffering horses ahead of them. Drier ground put them in a poplar forest and, higher on, the creek, studded with elephantine stones but decorated with frilly wild flowers on both banks, pushed through a bushy, steplike terrain where they saw a bear submerged to its very ears, waiting for salmon, its head a scarcely decipherable wedge in the current's ruffles. The vast jadelike stripe on the mountain was alluring, and the creek, much reduced, acquired two stripes of its own that revolved around each other in a stately fashion, red and gray, like the stripes on a barber's pole, signaling that there must be a fork in it soon.

They camped on a sand flat in the shelter of the stump of an uprooted cottonwood, deliberately kindling a smoky fire so their presence would be advertised. Owls howled and foxes barked and the creek rustled past from origins Cecil intended to explore. Listening for more, he tantalized himself with the notion that in its bubbling sounds was the answer to everything. The bear in the stream twice superimposed its prints on top of his party's during the night.

The red and gray waters revolving together in stripes had signaled a fork; and it turned out to be so. Up early, he was peering into the aperture of a canyon between walls of gray rock when his friend Moose, who had not been hunting but was sticking uncommonly close, touched his nose to Cecil's hand in the way that he had of inquiring what they should do. They were next to a clawless but distinctly toed imprint, attenuated yet still much more than bear-sized, with the large toe on the inside and the little toe canted out to correct any imbalance caused by the foot's preternatural length. Although he had brought a coil of capture rope, Cecil felt silly holding it after putting both hands into the track to measure it and finding he had space to spare.

When he sniffed it he caught an oily whiff which mystified him until he followed the path into the gray-cliffed canyon and crossed a side brook with a black slick on it that smelled like oil which the tracks also had crossed. The canyon looked to be limestone and was miles long, timbered wherever it wasn't choked with avalanche rubble and buggy wherever the water ran. Being buggy, it was hog heaven to the swallows, of which thousands were diving and climbing the sky. Did the bugs bite the Bigfoot? he wondered. His rifle seemed useless in such tight topography. Just walking was strenuous in the alder thickets, whose split trunks formed hoops and nooses to be wriggled through. But a limestone canyon should be full of caves and therefore a fitting home for a master of fissures, such as Cecil supposed a Bigfoot would be. An eagle flew past, yelping in exasperation at being chased by three croaking ravens, and he envied it the overview it had. He didn't dare go far or even look upwards very often on this first day. He kept imagining that he might meet his Maker right here and now by a blow from behind or a stone from above, or else would catch sight of some horrific ungodly creature materializing at the corner of his eye.

The other fork of Fourth Creek was walled with red sandstone layered with a few gaudy whitish strata as well. A hatch of sulphur-colored butterflies fluttered prettily over grassy swales, lending the floor of its little valley a genial atmosphere. Swallows were ferrying bugs and butterflies from both canyons to late batches of nestlings tucked into a honeycomb of holes that the birds had dug in a sand-bank over the stream. The volume of water going by indicated that this was the shorter of the forks, but Cecil recalled that a spur of Stripe Mountain must slope down to coincide with its head and offer him a route upward if he wished to climb.

Sutton, who was mainly interested in finding Groundhog Morris's old place, had discovered a faded trail in the red valley but no tracks yet to identify it. The trail veered away from the grassy streamside and butterfly meadow into a birch woods and towards a conspicuous rockfall, where finally, to their uneasy astonishment and delight, they encountered a tiny stump-clearing with a pit house in the middle of it, and beyond the pit house, the crumpled mouth of a tunnel that had been pickaxed into a seam of white pudding stone partway up the valley's low wall.

They yelled to let off steam, and hearing nothing, ventured to scramble up to the pile of rocks and to a pair of disintegrating boots and a thatch of human leg and hip bones protruding from them. Though Mr. Ouddo (or whoever it was) hadn't bothered to bury these, apparently he had taken a good deal of trouble to dig up rather thoroughly the earthen underpinnings of the pit house—which in any case was simply a rectangular hole in the ground about six feet deep, with log walls on the surface extending three feet higher than that, and a turf roof rising to a peak not much above eye level for somebody standing outside. The single moose-gut window had been chewed away in the time since and meat and fish racks had fallen over in what had been the dooryard. A stack of moose horns had been gnawed by pack rats or porcupines. It was the humblest dwelling, probably warm in the winter but uncomfortably chilly in the summer, suited to an obsessed or dedicated digger, yet giving the sense of a man living under siege.

And had he dreamed of going out to San Francisco for the winter, after he made his stake, and finding a friendly woman, feasting on oysters, attending the opera, and drinking champagne? They salvaged his bones and laid them under the flowery soil where the sun shone best—"Old Groundhog, you're under the ground now"—then sat back for a while, wondering what had sent the rockfall down, sufficiently nervous that Sutton, seeing a dark, energetic figure clambering up the slope, whispered, "That's one of your Bigfoots!" But it was a woodchuck—a groundhog—which made them laugh. Sutton was appropriating the whole property in his mind and wanted to start cleaning up before he even explored the rest of the valley.

Lizzie and Margaret, left to their own devices, had fixed the camp at the forks into an Indian camp, with the dogs closely tethered to tree roots, the two tents almost invisible in the vegetation, and sliced moose meat drying over a small squaw-wood fire. Both had pistols and subjected their men to a careful examination before admitting them to the fireside.

Sutton took a couple of horses back to Groundhog's to clear the tunnel of rock and broken spars, while Cecil and Lizzie, bareback on the sorrel, rode on from there to the head of the red canyon, which opened into a basin where Groundhog appeared to have dug a number of prospect pits and to have sluiced lots of gravel. It boasted a handsomely detailed view of Stripe Mountain, as well as of a peak to the left that was gaily serrated on top like a rooster's comb, which he named Rooster Peak. When he tripped as they were walking about, she grabbed him and threw his arm over her shoulder as though he needed help and made him shut his eyes so she could lead him around helplessly and make him stumble plenty more. The rudimentary communication between them left him studying not only her expressions but the structure of her face, which he realized resembled that of a Russian woman with cheeks just as wide who had worked in a saloon he'd drunk in in Bangor. Nevertheless, he was worried people back home might think she was a Negro, and if they did, he would have trouble living with her—as he'd begun to hope to do. Nor would she be such an addition in that case, appearing in a circus ring with him and a bear or Bigfoot. The Indians New Englanders were used to seeing were half- or quarter-breeds, whereas she was a full-blood, redder and darker, as hadn't been present in Massachusetts for a century—also different in subtle, ineradicable misproportions that, plumpish and healthy though she now was, stamped her as somebody who had starved during not a few winters until no fat she could ever put on would cover her frame quite evenly, a hunger more brutal than any New Englander, whether white or half-breed, suffered these days.

Fourth Creek at the forks chug-chugged like a train with the extra water of a rain squall whose clouds they had seen on Stripe Mountain while riding in sunshine themselves. This fast water made the gray canyon noisier than Groundhog's red-walled canyon was, but Cecil had Sutton blow bugle calls at its mouth to tempt the Bigfoot to respond. When it didn't, he got his mouth organ, sidestepping Lizzie, who was convinced he would be foolhardy when confronted with what he was after, and angry at him about it. He scarcely heard the three of them say goodbye, the trees swallowed him and Moose so quickly. Swifts and swallows still swooped like pendulums to gobble the bugs that enveloped his head, but clouds blowing from nowhere threw unnerving shadows over the jagged-walled valley.

Half an hour inside he stopped to sleep, silent and fireless. Then he walked for half the next morning, almost forgetting his mission, until, hearing stones rolling down on him, he was utterly scared. Moose rushed toward the sound, however, which reassured him. A ewe had descended for a drink at the creek and now was leaping up successive ledges to get away. He hurried to check her tracks, remembering that the Bigfoot he thought he'd seen on Many Berries Mountain had been in the vicinity of two bighorns. They seemed like true sheep tracks, but noticing several spawning salmon wearily rubbing against each other in the creek bed, he remembered Charley's story of meeting his Bigfoot on a salmon river too.

The ewe, bounding beyond where Moose could climb, had passed out of sight, so Cecil was startled when a spatter of pebbles hit the ground next to him. He dodged, supposing at first that the swallows were diving nearer than ever. Instead, looking overhead—appalled and then jubilant—he saw two brown elbows waggling at him and a kind of shaggy-ruffed, ruddy-colored, baboon-nosed yet vaguely human physiognomy directing its attention straight down at where he was. When it had captured his regard, this giddy apparition stopped tossing stones and promptly scrutinized him—as, bending his head back, he did it—neither of them very fearful of the other for the moment.

Its hands were like a man's or a monkey's, not pawlike, and so Cecil's wire foot snares, which had proven so effective at catching black bears in Maine, would be of no help; if he tried to use them the creature could merely peel them off. In fact he was lulled into feeling he was looking at an unarmed man, till he observed that those tremendous fingers were twice as big as his, its close-set eyes were black and beady, and its boxy muzzle bore no resemblance to a man's nose. Because Moose was also watching it he knew he wasn't hallucinating. Moose's nostrils worked busily, but Cecil noticed the creature's weren't. Intriguingly, its eyes moved more. And Moose cringed in the manner he might have assumed in front of a threatening man, not before a bear. A bear he would have been prepared to run from, but any dog knew that a man could hit him at a distance with a bullet or a stone.

When Cecil tried to smell what Moose could smell, he thought of a mustardy piquancy or the vanilla scent of joe-pye weed. At least the Bigfoot didn't smell like carrion or a garbage dump, the way so many bears in his experience had. It mimicked his efforts to smell it. Its breasts were larger than a young man's but not than an old man's might have been, and though he couldn't see below its chest because of his angle, he had already concluded that the story about its feet being on backwards was nonsense, it balanced so nicely.

"Let me see between your legs," he said, feeling stupid not to have insisted on asking every Indian they had met about Bigfoot all along. This Brush Man, or Man-that-flees, or Woods Man, this *Nakina,* or *Sasquatch*—were they sexless creatures, or could it possibly have a child to defend? How many might inhabit a hideaway area like this, just one *Sasquatch* or a bunch of them? Would they recognize a rifle as dangerous and thus a protection for him?

It hadn't yowled or spoken in reply, and since he and it seemed to be reaching a preliminary understanding, he scouted for its footprints among the bighorn tracks at the drinking pool for evidence that, like other living beasts, it needed water. There had been visits by three or four individual ewes and a couple of lambs, but no recent ram-sized hoof prints, and no bear, wolf, or round cat prints. The idling, exhausted, blue-backed salmon didn't even stir to avoid him.

Gazing at the fat-elbowed, hairy-headed Bigfoot two dozen yards up the side of the bluff, he shouted, "Hey, don't you eat or drink, my friend?" He had gained confidence, but a shriek like a locomotive's steel wheels on a curve sent him and Moose both sprawling into the water. His ears hurt as if they had been shattered. Overwhelmed, he lay in the school of salmon, recuperating, and looking up, saw the two bald spots on the Bigfoot's buttocks disappearing.

When he climbed to where it had been, he found plenty of canted-toe pugs, heronlike or spidery in character and yet bigger than a bear's or a man's. Moose refused to remain beside him, but the grade was not forbiddingly steep, so he crawled and scrabbled on into a maze of scree-strewn washes, sighting the heights of Stripe Mountain occasionally, finding the tracks again with a tickle of terror, and losing them. Partly, he hoped his mind was playing tricks on him, converting an ordinary mountain sheep into this phantom. But it wasn't a ram or a phantom. Across a narrow chasm he spotted an animal ambling with a gait more human than apish or ursine, which halted after a time at the opening of a cave that was shaped like a band shell. It seemed taller and more stooped than the one before, with thinner, longer, reddish hair and shoulders less imposing than the other's, though much stronger than his own shoulders. It had a reserved, somewhat haggard face, as he studied it, boxy like a baboon's that he had once seen in a circus but without the baboon's fierce expression, and he agreed with what Charley and Ouddo had said—that if he shot and skinned it, the skin would do him little good. A showman back East would pay no more for it than for the skin of an orangutan from Java that a sailor might carry in.

Was the cave its den? Did they *have* dens? If they were indeed the ghosts of people who were dead, were they ageless, or did they start young as a Bigfoot and get older all over again? Though he was glad that the short chasm with a pond at the bottom of it separated the Bigfoot from him, he dangled his rope like a fishing line to see whether he could coax the beast to come over and investigate—but quit doing that when he felt, or imagined he'd felt, a tug at the nether end.

It stayed where it was, gave a mild peacocky scream, and chattered like a pygmy, touching its knuckles to the ground and shifting across the width of the entrance to the cave with the swinging motion of a man to whom the gift of locomotion with the aid of long arms had become second nature now, and shot glances at Cecil when it turned back and forth. It was immensely formidable. Nevertheless, he didn't believe his luck would have been so extraordinary as to deliver him here if the purpose was for him to die.

"Hey, my friend, I'm here to get acquainted with you. I'm not afraid of you and Groundhog wasn't afraid of you. He didn't hurt you and I don't believe you hurt him," he told it in nearly his normal voice to test its hearing. It chattered briefly as if it had heard him, and screamed a banshee scream. In the quiet afterwards he counted how many seconds the sound had lasted—five seconds—to distract himself and preserve his nerve. He also blew on his mouth organ.

It did a popping variety of holler, *wow, wow, wow, wow,* and another, much lengthier ululation. Was it talking, or was it attempting to frighten him? He tried to picture Groundhog Morris working and eating and sleeping for months on end within earshot of such a menagerie of wails, each of which could coil into the potential for splitting your eardrums. When Cecil sounded a minor chord on his harmonica, back echoed an infinitely huger, more complex variation, but mercifully keyed not to damage his hearing. As if playing a risky game—though only he, not the Bigfoot, was standing there

with an apple on his head—they batted these minor and major po-
lyphonies about, while the canyon's surfaces threw in further and
simpler repetitions that amassed with the Bigfoot's music into more
than his ears could comprehend. Altogether, he forgot the risks for
the fun. The Bigfoot, however, was both casual and distempered in
its movements, as if of two minds.

A scream of a different timbre answered from higher on the
mountain, surprising it. The note was like that of a woman who
had been terribly injured, but because there wouldn't be an injured
woman on Stripe Mountain, Cecil guessed that it must be a mountain lion, whose regular caterwauls, Charley had said, were apt to
sound like a woman being murdered. The Bigfoot, whatever its relation might be to human beings, didn't look as human as that
shriek seemed. More softly, as though not wishing to be overheard,
it emitted an eeric, unearthly wail, like a bagpipe without a melody.
Cecil tried to duplicate this on his instrument but couldn't begin to.

The Bigfoot whistled like a hurricane wind, and his boldness
drained out of him as if he hadn't been breathing enough air. He re-
trieved his rope, becoming alarmed as it snagged on an outcropping
below that he couldn't see but that felt like the grip of a hand. Then
when he looked back at the band-shell cave, the Bigfoot was gone.
For his own future reference, he figured out how to climb down to
the green pond and up to the ledge where the cave was, and memo-
rized his route when he returned to where he'd first seen the ewe.
Building a fire, he scrunched close to it with Moose, wishing he had
Lizzie there and a mug of beer and a pound of cheese. Most prospectors didn't run out of energy or time, he decided; they went deep
into a crisscross of canyons and got stupefied.

Rain fell all night. In the heavy drifting mists of the morning he
encountered a grizzly as white as a polar bear which held two fish
in its mouth and had a hump like a camel's. He waited for it to pass
by, but since it was waiting for him, neither of them went anywhere
for a while.

The second incident that enlivened his hike down the gray fork
of Fourth Creek was sighting a man, naked, of middling age, without any adornment even in his long hair, who carried a bow and a
quiver of arrows yet seemed to know well what a rifle was, because

he stood warily in the line of trees, ready to dive for cover. He didn't reply to Cecil's clumsy salutations but was so utterly human in his posture, his countenance and his nakedness as to emphasize that the Bigfoot had not been a human being.

Cecil, who'd been limping from a blister where his sock had worn through, noticed a rabbit in front of him and shot it, after carefully pantomiming for the Indian that he intended to. Like skinning a grouse, he pulled off the supple little hide in one piece inside-out and put that on for a sock, as he'd used to do in the woods at home, and flourished his foot for the Indian to admire, and left the meat of the rabbit for him.

Lizzie had heard bad news of her daughter. There had been a series of sandpiper calls from a patch of forest. Dashing out, she had talked with a person who otherwise kept himself hidden, and learned from him that the rest of the Sikinks had never found out what happened to any of her family, herself included. Her daughter must be dead.

These tidings both soured her and made her more clinging. She wasn't so impatient to hurry on, but still associated Cecil a bit with Tom Ben and all the Thloadennis. For him the news meant a grievous reminder of the enormous scroll of rolled-up geography already stuffing his memory, the country he'd traveled over since he'd left home and would have to cover again before he found out how his own kids were.

"Gold in the gravel. Gold like walnuts. Gold like rice grains. Gold at the grass roots!" Sutton said to cheer him up, shaking his head at the same time, because he suspected now that Groundhog had wrung out of the tunnel whatever of value may have been inside and he was going to have to make his living by digging new prospect pits and tunnels or from the creek margins. "I'm forty-eight years old and I've worked this hard before, but I never wanted to work this hard again," he said happily.

He'd jury-rigged harnessing for the pig-colored horse and the paint that was left, dragged in logs for a decent cabin, and was scraping the soil off the gravel on the creek bank and building a sluice box beside it, with Margaret laboring the same white-man's hours, to Lizzie's amused incredulity. She couldn't believe that any self-respecting Indian would sweat over pails of dirt for a dozen hours a day like that. Though Cecil joined in the work for a week, at night she put him through their whole private theater of spiders that nipped, foxes that bit, bats that skittered, bees that buzzed— lodging his hands in her hair forever and ever—as if to force a choice upon him between how he spent his nights and days.

The skin of Stripe Mountain looked as wrinkly as an elephant's hide in strong sunshine but turned to black satin at dusk, and later the moonlight glazed it white and made the snow streaks high up silvery and the streams chaining from them fluffy. Cecil dreamed of his Bigfoot, waking up chilled by the notion that the image he had seen across the gulch had really been a mirror reflection of a creature standing on his own side just underneath him, twitching his rope. Sutton accepted his reports of the Bigfoot as scarcely more remarkable than that his own dream of striking gold had come true, and he promised to do one of his jumps for it eventually into a suitable pool.

Lizzie, riding the sorrel—with him on the red packhorse and a couple of watchdogs along—consented with some bravado to have a peek at this *Sasquatch,* if he could show her the band-shell cave by an easier route. No Bigfoot was on view when they got there, but he played his mouth organ and dangled his capture rope over the fissures where he thought he'd elicited the tug before. As in deepwater fishing, this time too he wasn't sure whether he felt a nibble or only a gust of wind down in the canyon or the friction of a knob on the face of the rock. The stream at the bottom sent up noises as of pebbles sliding under the pressure of a foot and produced black and white reflections as though a creature was moving against the pale walls.

This fork of Fourth Creek was a sweet-water stream loud in birdsong, and by staying on the tableland on top of its canyons he hoped they could ride to its source. Galloping elk barked a good-humored warning to each other ahead of them and vanished into a passage of pines. Stripe Mountain gradually lost its stripe, becoming a lopsided monumental brown pyramid, as they circled a section of it, but the creek elbowed itself with foaming fast tributaries that poured out of an intriguing labyrinth extending like a starfish's arms from the broken-faced south flank of another mountain. In yard-high crests of jostling white water, these fed fields of flowers but flowed out of ice fields sky-high.

Cornering a family of muskrats, Lizzie spitted them ducklike over a flame like a saw blade, and with Cecil, lay on her back, watching a family of golden eagles learning to fly. The fledglings bumped between crosswinds, rose precariously on a thermal, lost their balance, and fell off it. Besides the delicious morsels that the muskrats made, she had with her such a collection of meats she and Margaret had snared—beaver tails, lynx steaks—that Cecil took pains to remind himself what an ice-swept hungry country the Eeejookgook would be in a few months. And where would *she* be? Would she have vanished like a fox?

Though not farther-sighted than him, she always spotted the movements of game or the still outlines of single animals in concealment before he did. She pointed at a miniaturized but thick-torsoed, shaggy figure with bent stance traversing a pocket of ice which just as they watched missed a step and glissaded down, miles away and out of control yet holding a certain element of its dignity intact, till it met a shark's fin of stone rising out of the ice and scrambled up that, hunkering into a squat afterwards to preen its mussed coat. Cecil wondered why she was murmuring something about a *Wasichu*, or White Man, her hand fluttering almost as a Roman Catholic's would in crossing himself, until he realized she meant that only a white man would come here. Indeed, the plentiful wildlife acted unhunted. Several caribou bulls with their antlers in velvet pawed one another playfully till the dogs got close, and a moose—its gangly legs trotting out of rhythm with the rest of its body, in the special manner of moose—never did galvanize itself to run away very seriously.

After heading into a slot-mouthed gorge between two arms of the starfish, they left the horses behind and walked under ash-colored convex configurations of stone that focused the wind like a tunnel— the soil too scant and the light too dim for trees to grow—wind that felt like wind that had fallen from the zones of the snow. Cecil promised to name the entire mountain Lizzie Mountain so that white men would always call it that, as she knew Margaret's husband had named a big river Margaret's River, but it was difficult to explain and she was unhappy and kept her eyes peeled.

The site seemed too uncomfortable for a Bigfoot to choose, but she said she saw a face—didn't know what—above them. They pretended to have noticed nothing, walking on, and at a signal, raised their heads. The face, though it quickly pulled back, was as round as a plate and as tan as buckskin except for the white lips and black whisker patches, and must belong to a lion or else something masquerading as a lion. The ravine had tightened to a twenty-foot slit between bulging overhangs, when its tawny, tail-heavy body leaped across above them and a squirt of piss dropped on them, as if to convey a pungent message—which was more than Lizzie could bear. Not the squirt, not the glimpse of the lion, but being toyed with in a style that proved it wasn't really a lion. His gift of her pistol had given her confidence for the outing, but there was no safety or fun in confronting a spirit with a pistol. The thing yowled at their leaving as though disappointed, and at Cecil's parting shot with his harmonica.

They camped on the tableland and watched an arrowhead form in the clouds, plus other florid signs, shapes and portents in a brilliant sky. Cecil remembered one of Charley's stories of the seacoast where the waters of the Eeejookgook and the bigger Obo and the bigger Hainaino and all the other streams that fed it flowed. Charley had lived on the beach for a period of weeks while catching his breath and packing supplies, and on most of those days a lion would arrive at about high tide to sample the dead fish and seabirds that had washed in. Once, he said, a shark was profiled lengthwise in the blade of a series of waves just before they broke and thumped on the sand. And repeatedly the shark had eyed the lion and the lion the shark.

After dark the northern horizon glowed as if a city lay beyond it, a city that now began to move. Curtains of shimmering salmon light rose and spread out in front of it, hovering in blowing folds across much of the crown of the sky. On top, flames danced like the miniflames that pulsate at the top of a fire, but after an hour or two these were transformed into shooting streaks of apricot which fueled a long, lazy, vibrating S that stretched over the whole starless sky. Then green and peach and white and lemon shafts ran from the mountains to the heights of the arch, shaking furiously and rolling like gears that meshed into and dizzily gobbled one another, jerking toward a vanishing point, until the heavens were blacker than if there had never been any light.

Stripe Mountain possessed a straightforward bulky magnificence, but the starfish mountain was more intricate. They spent the day exploring its base, peering into a dozen snub-nosed ravines and short-headed valleys, finally tying the two horses and entering the greenest of these, where robust trees lifted full canopies to catch the sun. A brook fell in stair-steps of splashed rock into a pool with bulrushes growing in it and cattails waving hospitably in the breeze on the bank and water striders dashing on the surface and long-soled Bigfoot tracks ennobling the mud alongside as naturally as the humbler prints of the rock rabbits that had come down to drink.

Though the canyon wound around another turn, Cecil took in the presence of the beast itself, hunkered attentively in the sunshine about half as high up the shelving wall as the trees reached. It was bigger than a man, as dark as a black man, but balanced weightlessly on its fists and the balls of its feet. Its pupils filled its eyes, which were set closer together than a man's, and its muzzle, instead of being bearded or mustached, was the least furry part of its head and body. Yet its concentrated gaze was manlike, intelligent and quite serene.

Lizzie uttered a low sound of revulsion and dread, squeezing Cecil's hand. She retreated to a crack underneath an overhang where the Bigfoot, besides facing her pistol, would need to pry her loose if he went after her. But it idly flexed its fingers and pinched its toes, not pursuing her or staring at her because of her sex. It pitched a pine cone at Cecil's belly instead, licking its baboon nose with a purplish tongue and turning to avoid his look. He stooped after the cone to reassure himself that everything he was experiencing was real, and sipped the water falling from the shelves and ledges to find out whether it would object to that, also trying to catch its scent— which again reminded him of joe-pye weed in Maine and of the mustard plasters of his baby's death from quinsy, as well as of the ginger in his mother's kitchen and of the gingerbread she'd baked. He searched for any dung lying around that might provide a clue to what it ate.

"Hello, sir!" he called upwards, as, nearly motionless, it sucked a twig. When he blew on his mouth organ, it imitated the chord, so he tossed the end of his rope for it to grab. At first it refused him that chummy favor, but when it did snatch the rope it yanked so hard it burned his hands.

"Ow!" he hollered, to see if it would holler back. It did yowl absently, and jigged the rope like a fisherman to wheedle him into taking hold, before throwing the rope away, bored.

"I can see he has a prick," he told Lizzie. Otherwise he couldn't pick out differences from what he'd seen of the Bigfoot at the bandshell cave in the limestone valley, unless this one was older and browner and more dome-headed. Did every valley between here and the Pacific have a Bigfoot, or Brush Man—a "Man-who-flees" (though this fellow wasn't fleeing)—self-absorbed and grooming itself like this specimen? Would he and his friends be seeing them on the shores of every tributary for a thousand miles of river twists, along with all the Indian settlements and tribes, if they rafted clear down the Eeejookgook, Obo and Hainaino to the Pacific?

When it shifted to a higher post half concealed in brush, Cecil took advantage of the Bigfoot's quiescence to go to the next bend of the canyon, hoping maybe to surprise a family of them, but saw a small, empty meadow and sunny greenery with another blind curve leading on toward the core of this fifteen-armed starfish.

He heard the faintest screams, far too faint to be Lizzie's, though he raced back to be certain—screams that reminded him of a rabbit's in a fox's jaws. Lizzie was all right and the screams subsided; but in a hurry now, as if his time was short, he edged nearer to the Bigfoot, which had descended almost to ground level.

"My friend, I wouldn't hurt you even if I could. I'm just trying to get to know you," he said in a whisper, and the ginger and joe-pye-weed-smelling creature wheezed and snorted mildly. Its beady gaze ranged over him, however, while the heat of its presence made him start to sweat and the activity inside its head somehow agitated and yet seemed to stall or blur whatever was going on in his own mind. He realized he needn't try to talk to it, because—either being indifferent to his sentiments or unable to understand him—it wasn't listening. But he wanted a sense of precisely how smart and how strong it was, and once and for all, whether he should harbor any hopes of capturing or taming it.

The shrieking had resumed, awfully animate, not eerie like a Bigfoot's, and too voluminous to be a rabbit's. Glancing over to see what Lizzie might have made of it, he remembered simultaneously that he had heard the same sound when the brakes had failed on a sledload of logs going down a hill on the Androscoggin and the two-horse team hitched in front of it had lost their footing and the sled had run over them and crushed them and they lay dying and screaming. His horses were being killed. But as he recognized this, he was knocked reeling and cartwheeling backwards into the pool, where he struggled against the pain in his ribs to breathe. Lizzie yelled her anger and exasperation and sympathy for him and he was finally scared, but laughing too. In that saloon in Bangor where the Russian lady had worked, he'd fought with a kangaroo a showman had brought in one time—a kangaroo that you paid fifty cents to fight for a ten-dollar prize—and had got knocked head over heels like this. It wasn't the little forepaws that took the swing at you, as he'd expected, but the hind clodhoppers.

When he stood up, holding his chest with one arm and shielding his head with the other, he saw not a Bigfoot at all, only a bighorn sheep at the fringe of the cattails and underbrush, facing him as though it had just charged and butted him. Now it swung around and bounded up the footholds of the canyon wall before he could reach his rifle and avenge himself.

A deeper-to-higher killer scream interrupted and engulfed the horses' shrieks, so he knew it was a mountain lion that had them; knew too that Lizzie believed the *Sasquatch* had changed into the bighorn to bowl him over and was also mangling the horses, although the language barrier between them prevented her from telling him how mad at him she was. Because of his cracked rib he couldn't keep up with her as they rushed back to the canyon's mouth, but both of them arrived to find the red horse moribund and the lion lying on it turned in the reverse direction, with its head buried inside the flesh between the horse's hind legs and its black tail-tip twitching across the horse's stark head.

He crippled the cat with a quick shot as it leaped off—infuriating and alarming Lizzie still more, because she believed the lion might be the Bigfoot. The sorrel, much bloodied, had broken his rope and stumbled beyond reach; even if they caught him they were going to have to walk. He shot the downed horse and the lion—both of whom were so badly wounded they seemed to acquiesce to being shot—and cut meat from both and enough of the lion's skin to wrap the meat in, while Moose and White Eye, although abashed and frightened, fed on the horse, and ravens flocked overhead to feed as soon as they were through. Lizzie, believing that the ravens also might be a supernatural manifestation, shouted at him in Sikink to throw away the meat. She strode off as if never to look at him again.

With Kitty and the red horse dead and the sorrel and the soldier pony out of commission, their party would not be able to ride anywhere anymore. Yet Cecil, walking after her, shaking off his gloom after half a dozen miles, cherished a gambler's wish to go for broke, considering that if Lizzie didn't like how a white man's mind worked here in the wilds, she wouldn't in Massachusetts, either. They walked for three days together in returning to Groundhog's diggings, often holding hands, after she had bound his chest with wet strips of willow bark, while he clarified for himself the fact that he did want to take her East whether or not she could be useful to him in show business.

Sutton was giving Groundhog's side brook hell, digging up and sluicing the bed. But the surprise was that Millard Switzer, the appleman, had shown up. His travels to the Eeejookgook, so much tougher and farther from the railhead at Horse Swim than the riverbank on the Ompompanoosuc where they had last met him, had glazed and aged him. He looked not only peeled by the sun but peeled underneath. From his heels to his neck, his walk had stiffened; he was grayer and stumbly. He craved a rest, and although no less interested in planting apple trees—smiling wearily, he said he "still believed in the Rapture" and was "a soldier for the Lord"—he seemed less interested in practically everything else.

No, Charley hadn't shot him and the Indians hadn't. "I planted a grove for them," he said. The little roan foal had died, as well as the puppies his bitch had had, and the Thloadennis had taken away his mare, but they had guided him to the Hump of the Great Divide in what they claimed was a fair exchange for his mare, and had left him the services of his dog, who had managed to follow Cecil's and Sutton's cold trail over the Hump and down into the trench of the Eeejookgook, where the lucky occurrence of salmon had saved him. They hadn't stolen his remaining seeds, and he'd strapped these sacks to a packboard. But the load was so heavy as he crossed the mountains that he had eaten seeds by the handful to allay his hunger and had fed the birds. "I made some friends."

He planted what would become another grove for Sutton and told Lizzie he'd do the same for her tribesmen when he met them. He didn't know who Mr. Ouddo was but said he had stopped at Ouddo's place, where nobody was home, and had planted seeds for him, grateful to find bees on this side of the Main Range, because without bees to fertilize them there was no sense in planting apple trees.

"And you ain't afraid to die? You won't miss this?" Sutton teased him, waving at the lovely green willows, the red sandstone, the birches, the bright quilt of flowers and grass dappled with sulphur-colored butterflies all around.

Switzer laughed. "I don't think Heaven won't be just as pretty, do you?"

He proved to be ungrudging with respect to Sutton's gold fever. He didn't quote them speeches about God and Mammon as they shoveled gravel or pickaxed pudding stone, pounded and hauled the ore on a sledge drawn by the pig-colored horse to the sluice and dumped water on it to wash out the silt, and picked and pored over the fine points of what was left like small print in a Bible. He asked about the two jumps the Thloadennis told him Sutton had done, and Sutton got to talking about how he hadn't used to do it in the same way. Wobbling his froggy belly, he mimicked how scared he'd looked in a clown's costume on a platform above the crowd, huddling, creeping off into space like a man on the ledge of a burning building aiming for the firemen's net. Hitting the water feet-first in those days, he had received an involuntary enema, but had been proud that he could jump with his hat on and not get the hat wet.

Golden specks, flakes and peppercorns were turning up in the paybox at the end of the sluice, caught in the black hairs of a piece of moose hide Sutton had laid there. When he stopped pouring water through, they could lick their fingers and dab the golden midges up, or employ the mercury he had brought to collect it more slowly and thoroughly—a dollar or two a day apiece, as he calculated, though he had neglected to outfit himself with a set of scales.

Lizzie was Margaret's friend but was nevertheless contemptuous, seeing her continually washing dirt with the tedious, head-down concentration of the white men for as long as the sun shone, then doing the cruder chopping and digging and shoveling until dark. Margaret, who was seldom entirely serious, explained that all this work was going to pay for them to cross the ocean to meet the Queen. The Queen loved for Indians to come to London to visit her—she gave them tea. Though Lizzie laughed, even Lizzie had vaguely heard accounts of Indians doing that.

Groundhog's door had been a thick, valorous bearskin, but Switzer cut and trimmed a wooden one with leather hinges for the new cabin. As the regular meals restored him and his eyes lit up again, Sutton called him Hawkeye. But Cecil was eager to learn what he would make of a Bigfoot and what Bigfoot might think of him, and borrowed him from Sutton's various projects to hike up the gray-walled canyon for a couple of days.

The glory of the mountaintops early and late when the sun hit them excited Switzer, as it did Cecil, but Cecil to tease him asked if it "really did any good," compared to planting trees.

"I guess it *does*," said Switzer.

"How so?"

"Because we're looking at it!"

"Supposing we weren't?"

"Then it'll still be waiting when somebody else comes along," he said. "God is in the light."

"God is?"

"Sure, all kinds of light."

"Is He in the northern lights?" Cecil asked, very curious.

Switzer smiled. "I don't know if the northern lights can grow wheat and corn and potatoes."

Cecil asked him why he never wanted to stop anywhere and enjoy himself for a while.

"I got so much to do," Switzer answered. Later, in the evening, drinking a cup of water to settle his stomach, he spoke of all the hundreds of brooks that could have apple trees fruiting beside them when the settlers arrived. "That'll be beautiful too." His errand in life was that, and no man had long, he said.

They saw a black four-legged creature crossing a gap, but when Cecil suggested he catch up with it to give it some seeds, he was suitably wary. "That's not a person."

"Is it a bear?"

"I don't know if it's a bear, but it isn't a person."

They heard night sounds like a vast fiddle's strings being scraped, saw fanlike displays of blood-red and goldfinch-colored northern lights shimmering, and ate ptarmigan and ground squirrels. The next day, when Cecil, ranging the limestone canyons in search of a genuine Bigfoot to show him, eventually brought Switzer back to the neighborhood of the band-shell cave on a repeat visit—there the beast was. Simio-ursine but also quite like a Brush Man, it sat on the sandy floor of the little chasm, catching and crushing deerflies in its fingers or dipping up water from the edge of the pond and delicately sucking the fins off a shiner, when it happened to catch one.

"Is that a bear?" Cecil asked.

"No, it's not a bear."

The questions which logically now ought to follow seemed too important to ask. They approached with deliberation and care, though several finches and wrens were hopping close to the Bigfoot, or Brush Man, without fear. It opened its mouth soundlessly when Cecil called out "Bigfoot," but watched its two interlocutors draw nearer without wrinkling its muzzle or bristling its fur. It was shoulderless and neckless—stern in the tilt of its brows but mountainously shapeless—when sitting. Very much as before, though it wasn't threatening him, his hopes for inventing a strategy for capturing it simply evaporated as he gazed at it.

" 'But they that wait upon the Lord,' " Switzer quoted softly, fortifying his resolve. In his unrushed but businesslike and singleminded manner he stared from a stone's-throw off. Then, despite having heard about Cecil's cracked rib in the previous encounter, he walked right toward it.

"That's not an Indian. I don't know what he is." He stopped within ten yards of it. "He's kind of beady, but I think he'd like to have his say."

"Is it an ape?" Cecil asked.

"I've never seen an ape. But no, not an ape. He'd be too quick for an ape, and he's stronger than that. Bless your soul!" he told the Bigfoot.

"Has he got a soul?"

"I think he's God's," said Switzer decidedly, walking back to where Cecil waited. "I'm glad I saw him. I don't know what he is."

The Bigfoot kept catching flies or sipping water and casually grabbing at shiners. The wrens cried *tee-tew*, and water percolated through the jumbled rocks so musically that Cecil was reminded to blow his mouth organ. Two bighorn rams out of sight on the heights were clacking their horns together, and the little branch of the creek clicked over wet canyon ledges that glinted with snaky colors. The sky was dove blue, and a toad next to Cecil was eating beetles.

The echo produced by his playing started to sound louder than the harmonica's own notes did—almost like a steam calliope—and the Bigfoot's head inclined rhythmically to the beat. Again Cecil felt his own brain somehow being numbed or scrambled or blurred or made sleepy or interfered with. Partly to wake himself up, and in another attempt to persuade the Bigfoot to react directly to him, he stood on his head. It didn't imitate him, but its willingness to witness his antics might mean it would be content to pay real attention to a much grander stunt, such as Sutton's.

When he threw out the end of his rope, which extended for sixty feet, it picked it up, tasted it, and tugged in response to his own tugs in a seesaw, gentle, heartbeat rhythm. Lizzie had told him after their last adventure that no, these weren't all the same *Sasquatch* in different guises, but that the Sikinks believed they did travel and visit one another. Some Indians said they went underwater; some said they went over the mountains through the deepest snow. But even if its mind was of human calibration—which might account for its fitful, preoccupied character that disrupted the processes of his own thinking—the Bigfoot's was surely an Indian's mind, and furthermore, according to many Indians, a mind that had *died*. So how could he understand it?

It yanked the rope. Having suffered rope burns the last time, Cecil was on his guard and dropped his end immediately. But he was astonished to see the beast now materialize as a hooded and parkaed Eskimo—the parka white but the face black from the sun—stepping into the pond and striding straight for him.

He went rigid with fright. Fortunately Switzer didn't. Switzer stepped forward and stopped the apparition, putting his hands on its chest—which had substance to it, as he said afterwards. Then, just as a Brush Man or Woods Man or Man-that-flees would have done, the Bigfoot raced in a zigzag path up the rock wall and bounded along the ledge where the band-shell cave was and rapidly higher to the scarf of forest up on top.

"Fur, flesh and bone. He's God's too," Switzer said. But he'd seen no parka on him, and no Eskimo's blackened face.

16

FLOATING OUT

Ouddo had turned up at Groundhog's diggings, and was of course the object of general concern. He said he'd been checking his trap-line cabins, had come across the lion-clawed sorrel dead and worried that something had happened to them.

He admired Sutton's brand-new cabin. "Now, that's a house put where it oughta be. I've seen so many goddam prospectors build their house first, and when they strike a streak it's someplace else."

He pitched in agreeably with Switzer on the fireplace, which he claimed was his specialty, and at chinking the walls—"*Cold* here"—amused to hear that Switzer had passed by while he was away from home and planted an orchard for him.

Cecil, shouting over his deafness, asked what Groundhog had been like.

"He was a chunky-looking geezer, kind of a sad old fart," Ouddo said. "But he kept himself fed and I think maybe he'd had enough misery wherever he was that he was pleased to be here. He grew a big bushy beard to make himself feel a little bit better. Very quiet. See no evil, hear no evil."

"We buried him, anyhow," Margaret said.

"Well good for you." Ouddo grinned as if she weren't calling him a bastard for not having bothered to do so. He tapped the corner of his mouth with a rag where what appeared to be a slight paralysis on the left side of his face caused him to drool now and then. When he realized that this frailty had been noted, he pulled up his pant legs to show how the skin had frozen so badly last winter it had split and suppurated, leaving scars like stretch marks. Besides trusting that they wouldn't shoot him, he seemed to assume rather cheerfully—though his face could be read to contain two expressions, one he wanted you to see and one he didn't—that these improvements being worked on the property would someday redound to his benefit; that he would inherit them. He confessed, however, to experiencing a change in his ears. They were getting worse, as if a waterfall was inside. He asked Cecil to give him a second dog to help him to hear, a favor Cecil refused.

"A deaf guy can trap as good as anybody else and eat what he traps. You said yourself he don't need ears."

"He can trap, but he can't hear the ice crack under him on the river. He needs ears to hear a storm brew up, or where the wolves are," said Ouddo.

"You know what I'm afraid of?" Sutton remarked to him loudly. "After my cabin's finished and my garden's in and my mine is working like a clock, with a horse tram for hauling, and everything else I want? Somebody could come along and shoot me for it."

"I'll tell you what," Ouddo said with a grin. "If it ever comes to that, I'll set a number-eight trap for him right here in his own dooryard."

This was such an unsettling suggestion they stopped talking to him, and he left when his restlessness got the better of him. Switzer, who was already eager to get back to his principal work, had to be dissuaded from accompanying him out, believing that though, as they said, he might have murdered somebody, it was only "the gold bug" and he wouldn't be dangerous to anybody who had no gold and no other possessions on him.

Besides disagreeing with him, Cecil and Sutton—joking but semiserious—told him he ought to wait for the "command performance" for the Bigfoot, a jump that would also be a "dress rehearsal" for the special gala jump Margaret wanted done for Queen Victoria in London. After all, the idea wasn't impossible, and he'd heard the awe in the voices of the Thloadenni Indians.

Cecil kept exploring in the meantime, obsessed by being so close to what he had wandered so far to see. On the north shoulder of Rooster Peak, a rangier specimen blocked his way, as if trying to get a handle on what he might be. Did it know he was different from the Sikinks? Cecil kept looking up at the mountain's stiff rooster comb for relief, expecting that the Bigfoot wouldn't be there when he looked back.

"Am I dreaming you? Are you real?"

Remembering Lizzie's story of how young Sikink shamans induced some of their visions by rubbing their fingers or a pebble slowly in a circle against a rock for hours, he picked one up. But instead of rubbing the pebble, he suddenly tossed it to see whether it would pass through the Bigfoot as though through a shadow, or bounce off flesh and bone, like Switzer had said. He missed, so he never learned the answer to that. And it replied with a sudden ear-ringing hammering almost loud enough to blind as well as deafen him, and in its grimace he glimpsed its pointy canines and flat front teeth. He was knocked into a swoon and didn't shoot, but from his squatting position, lit a fire in the grass, as Charley had once told him to do if a grizzly bear ever cornered him.

The grass was wet and the fire went out, but the Bigfoot got over its tantrum and gave a macaw's jungle scream, cupping its domed head in one hand pensively and reverting to a language of nickel-odeon cries and shrieks.

How *smart* was it? *How smart was it?* He wished he'd visited more zoos, or had paid better attention one time in Boston when he'd happened upon an itinerant organ-grinder with a monkey that climbed the wagon pole and danced for coins. In fact, on that trip a sailor just in from Africa with a monkey chained to his wrist had offered him the monkey for twenty-five dollars. He'd been afraid it would die in the woods in Maine, but he should have bought it anyhow, studied it, trained and worked with it the same way as he had with his bears.

After allowing Cecil to recover his courage, it lost patience with him and went loping up into the ramparts of the notch above, swinging its arms like a person running but kicking heavy boulders loose that rolled down at him and he had to dodge. He built a dead-wood fire and lay in his blanket watching the sunset tincture the cliffs of the Rooster's comb. "Brush Man," "Woods Man," "Wild Man"—how should he bill the new beast in an animal show? His father, a man who had believed in as well as excelled at magical effects, could have helped choose a billing. Only new country begets strange beasts, he'd believed, and hearing that huge lizard bones or a sword-toothed tiger or a woolly elephant had been discovered preserved in mud somewhere, he'd known they had died when the first settlers came swarming in.

An agile, unearthly, drawn-out cry slid up-scale and down-scale like a fiddle magnified hundreds of times and doubling itself against the mountainsides. Homebound at dawn, Cecil backtracked the Bigfoot past drinking holes and bluffs that were cheesy with crevices and caves, on the alert for flocks of long-tailed magpies, gray jays or black ravens that, being scavengers, might betray where it lived and what it ate. He found the pugs of a lion which had confronted it and the marks of the waltz they had performed around each other, avoiding a tussle. He saw a hawk plummet and devour a snow-shoe hare.

Sutton—who felt ready to take a day's break anyway—joked that he was going to have to make the jump for the Bigfoot pretty soon if Cecil was ever to do a lick of work at the sluice box again. Because he hadn't taken time to explore the region at all, he laid himself in Cecil's hands.

"Where to? What a show you're going to have! I'm going to make you rich as Buffalo Bill."

And Switzer came along, and the two women, tucking their pistols into the folds of their skirts in case the Bigfoot rushed at them, because as Margaret said, although she was too old to have a man's child, she might not be too old to misconceive a Bigfoot's baby.

She had picked up Lizzie's caution and fear. "Maybe we should leave the thing alone. You'll be the death of me yet," she said, wearily pushing on her knees with her hands to climb the steeper grades of the gray canyon, while Sutton scrambled up cattishly.

Cecil hoped the Bigfoot would be at the band-shell cave with the pond underneath. The other sites where he'd encountered it or its brothers were so far away he might lose the patience of his party in the meantime—five people with only two able-bodied horses left and no safe place to stake them.

But when they reached the rim of the little chasm, a mustardy, gingery, joe-pye-weedlike smell did announce the presence of *Sasquatch*. They heard its peacock or parroty scream, saw its baboon muzzle and bearish set of teeth, its body haired all over like a shaggy pony's, its hands like a giant man's or an ominous ape's, its forehead and face more spiritual than intelligent but more human than animal. Its body, although dark and strange, looked wholly palpable as it bounded out of the cave, using its fists as forefeet, and Cecil felt at first dizzy, as he sometimes did after standing up suddenly. He sensed no imminent physical danger but rather the possibility that he might drown in a swoon.

"Holy Christ, you'll never bring that sumbitch home," Sutton muttered. No pitfall, no foot snare or leg-hold bear trap was going to capture it alive, he said.

Margaret, like Sutton, had never faced one before. Aghast at the reality of what they'd been chasing, she was glad to sit down cross-legged with Lizzie at a distance of a couple of hundred yards with her pistol in her lap. Switzer lingered with them, uncharacteristically uncertain, holding the lead ropes of the pig-colored horse and the paint horse.

Often during stretches of their long trip West Cecil had found Sutton's reactions to be so inexpressive as to be impenetrable, but now he realized that it was partly that he was a professional showman. At the same time as he didn't believe they could catch the creature, Sutton was intrigued to imagine how they could stage its debut under a big top. Though he was not optimistic, nevertheless, seeing Cecil stand on his head, he laughed and did a handstand and walked on his hands, changing again from a potbellied, middle-aged, blunt-minded individual into an acrobat.

"I wonder, could we train him? Monkey see, monkey do?" he called to the Bigfoot. But it wouldn't oblige.

"So, you have a flea? So do I," he called, watching it scratch itself. "Well, it'll just be a free show then. Bringin' culture to the Eeejookgook." He rubbed his stomach. "Oh, I hate the sting nowadays. Where do you have me scheduled to do the deed?"

He liked the pond, which they descended to and which, though rock-rimmed, was deeper than both the horse trough in Horse Swim and the Thloadennis' bathing pool had been. He waded in it for a while, examining the bottom with his eyes and his hands, not just for hidden boulders but for the possibility that there might be a nugget of gold. Bigfoot tracks had been incised around the margins and several bushes had been uprooted as if for landscaping, although so recently that earthworms were still clinging to the clods of dirt that were exposed.

"Wouldn't it be a corker if he tried to do what I do? Maybe he will. Well, I'll put it in my book of memories anyhow, whatever he does." Sutton beamed, unafraid of the creature on the ledge above and to the left of them, as if, like him, it was already a circus personage. But he was almost equally curious to prospect this new little stream that fed the valley. At the inlet and outlet of the pond he turned over rocks and jiggled handfuls of silt and sand scooped out from under them in his palm. Anywhere in this country you might strike evidence of gold, he said, or real eight-sided crystals in a lump of quartz, or leaf-veined "picture rock" fallen from a cliff.

The sky was a dark shale-blue and the pond was sea gray, sea green or sea blue, according to where you stood on the bank gazing at it. The stream sang its soothing song, and they discovered a daisy-like disk of brittle fool's-gold on the bottom to pocket and laugh about. The creature meanwhile sprawled at its ease like a monkey that had got loose from a cage and onto a rooftop overlooking all this confabulation, leading Sutton to speculate that if a similar one was ever caught near the railroad, after the line had gone through, maybe it *could* be transported East and eventually trained. Dig a pitfall, cover it, bait it with food, envelop the Bigfoot in nets when he fell in, build a cage around him, hoist him onto the train with a crane, and gradually find out what he liked and responded to.

"But I think that'll be for our kids to do," he said.

"You've got a kid?"

"Who doesn't?" he said.

Once Sutton started to climb, the Bigfoot lunged upright, peering around to be sure the others weren't trying to surround it as well, but then raised and scratched its long right foot in an easy manner as if remembering that it had the entire mountain range to escape into. Its muzzly face distorted the intensity of its expressions until they became almost the same. It appeared amused or bemused by how slow his progress was, and lolled watching, inoffensive enough and unchallenging-looking except for the humanlike focus of its beady, close-set eyes.

Sutton shrank in the scope of the canyon, small not because he climbed very high but because the walls immediately asserted their scale and he seemed to have left the here and now. Cecil shouted to him to take his time, meaning that he should take care of himself, also not to frighten the Bigfoot into running away, and not to stint on the showmanship, in case it could be entertained, or might even learn something about showmanship. But Sutton grew too tiny for a stylish, suspenseful buildup. The niche he clung to was probably as secure as any of his jumping-off points had been, but he looked as if he'd been glued there at random, not as though he had chosen the spot.

The sky had evolved to the blue of a jewel and the pond was blue green. The Bigfoot—whom Cecil kept staring up at—occasionally resembled another prospector who might have come hunting gold but had paused here to witness this leap. Then it turned into a lanky bear feathered with fur on its legs like a setter, and next and quite separately it looked like a shoe-brown, observant, noncommittal gorilla. The swoonlike sensation that overtook Cecil had become familiar now.

Sutton, apparently recognizing how trivial a figure he made on his perch on the bluff, went ahead and did his brief little heartbreaking stunt. He leaped like a cliff swallow swooping, but the noise of his impact was as if a small tree had fallen, and there was no splash. The Bigfoot, all arms, sprang from its ledge and swung down the bluff to a lower level to stare more closely. Then it lumbered and scrambled very rapidly higher and higher with a gait that was alternately bearlike and apelike and disappeared over the ridgeline much more hastily than a man could have done. The whole episode was over in next to no time, but Sutton didn't stand up. Margaret keened. He had landed on a rock.

"It'll kill me," he mumbled slowly. "Oh, it's killing me."

He was bleeding at the mouth, gasping at the cost of each breath. His belly had struck a sizable rock that was shaped like a bulging bullfrog five feet across at the edge of the pond, and he lay motionless, with one hand in the water, splayed out where he'd hit.

"Don't touch me. Oh Jesus, it leaves you empty," he whispered, sighing at the steady flow leaving him. His words emerged only like bubbles through the blood.

"Kill me if it's long. Meg, you take the gold. Go where you want," he told her. She had one hand in his hair and held his hand.

"You can write to my sister," he told Cecil laboriously, but his body shook with an agonized effort to vomit or cough and he closed his eyes as if to admit that it was too late to give anybody her name and the details. He could move his head slightly, and his feet twitched as though of their own accord, but he soon stopped attempting to turn his head.

"We're going to do what you want. You can tell him where to write and where to send the gold. But I think you're probably going to be all right," Margaret said. "We'll stay here until you're well."

"Don't move me," he repeated, draped like a knotted towel across the rock but panicking at the prospect of more pain. "Don't put me here. Put me with Groundhog," he added. "I'm so cold. We should have stuck with the bears."

Although his eyes had opened, he had become as pale as clay and was unable to see. Cecil, remembering so plainly how his own mind had blurred in the presence of the beast—how he couldn't have concentrated on even a simple task—felt as though he himself had killed him, and glanced at Mr. Switzer for confirmation of this. But Switzer wasn't blaming anyone in particular. Switzer, apart from demonstrating his sympathy and sorrow, began to look impatient, as if Cecil and Sutton were two of a kind—impatient with himself for having stayed on, impatient to be miles away, alone and following his own star.

Sutton twice blindly moaned, and gave up the ghost. They sat by his body, while the dogs crept close for comfort. The Bigfoot never reappeared. Nor did its music sound. After a while Mr. Switzer quietly recited the Lord's Prayer and the Twenty-third Psalm.

They ended up being exceedingly glad they had brought the horses; otherwise they couldn't have returned Sutton to Ground-hog's more comfortable and comely creek for burial—Butterfly Creek, Margaret called it. She hugged Cecil, not blaming him, not cooling to Sutton's memory either, as Switzer ever so slightly had.

Lizzie, like Switzer, behaved as though Sutton's death was not Cecil's fault but only in keeping with the rest of his life. She hugged Cecil, too, to comfort him, but with a coolness acknowledging that it might just as easily have been him who had died. And this wasn't bravery to her way of thinking—daring the wrath of a Bigfoot. Facing a bear or raiding the Thloadenni Indians, braving the danger of snowslides in winter or outwitting rough river rapids was her idea of courage. Cecil remembered that the Thloadenni hunter Blizzard had suggested sarcastically that he use Lizzie herself as bait to attract a Bigfoot. And of course he hadn't done that. He'd brought her along with him one time only for companionship. But hadn't he—he thought—used first Switzer, the shaman appleman, and then his daredevil friend Sutton for bait, really, after the dogs had proven incapable of pursuing Bigfoot? There was more truth to the notion than he could deny. No animal trainer or hunter or handler could regard individual animals as indispensable. One horse herd, one dog pack, one bear act died out and you trained another, caring for them more affectionately than people who didn't know animals would ever dream of. But he had lost his head, going after the Bigfoot.

They dressed Sutton in a rose-red shirt befitting a showman to bury him, and laid in the bugle and his cobbling tools. Cecil raised a marker as tall as a man—a cross, to please Switzer—which Margaret dressed in his second-best shirt instead of saving that for herself.

"I wish we could put some color in his face," she said before they covered him up—glad, however, that he had not been disfigured. In his baggage they found twenty-two dollars in paper money and two gold eagles and several newspaper clippings with artists' renderings of Sutton's dive or Sutton's face. "Human Fly." "Man Defies Newton." When Cecil read these accounts aloud and Margaret translated, Lizzie shouted in fascination, because although she'd seen Switzer bent over his Bible, she had never asked or understood what reading was.

They left Groundhog's canyon for the open country downstream on Fourth Creek, where salmon still nested as fussily as red hens in the sand beds. But the fish died after they'd spawned, and hundreds of gulls which had followed them all the way up from the ocean were feeding on their bodies, as well as fish hawks, eagles, croaking crows and ravens, vociferous jays and magpies, and nearly every sharp-toothed citizen of the valley from timber wolves to red squirrels.

Margaret's old soldier pony had never recovered from his mauling. After limping a few painful miles he whinnied a plaintive goodbye. The four of them walked, carrying packboards. Though they hadn't enough provisions to winter in the mountains, the paint and the pig-colored horse still carried a lot of trade goods and supplies which might see them safely down the sequence of wild rivers Charley had described, clear to the coast by mid-fall, if the Indians they met on the banks were agreeable. The actual rivers didn't bear thinking about—would they be like rafting on the Ompompanoosuc for a thousand miles?

Cecil quarreled a bit with Mr. Switzer, who professed not to mind where he spent the winter, dismaying him by telling him that it was a sin to sound suicidal. For their three weeks at Groundhog's, they had about a pound and a half of gold dust, but Cecil in a burst of gaiety and determination refused to go home with no more than that. He spotted a mamma grizzly with two cubs fishing from a beach—the dry hair on her hump standing straight up, but the wet hair on her shoulders and flanks sleek around that—and rushed forward, dropped on one knee, and anchored her where she was with three shots; then dashed for the bawling cubs before they got into the creek. His dogs were reluctant to tangle with them and the bigger one reached deep water and paddled across, racing for cover, but he managed to corner and snub the second against a tree with a rope around its neck while Margaret slipped a muzzle over its nose and the sleeves he had made long ago over its feet, pinioning them.

At the Eeejookgook, loons were dashing up and down like geese, giggling in the air and from the midst of the river. Regular geese flew past with peremptory barks. Switzer planted a number of future trees at the mouth of Fourth Creek, fertilizing them lavishly with salmon flesh. He was happy to have recovered his strength and to be back on track. So was Lizzie in reentering the land of the Sikinks. Though she still liked matching her steps to Cecil's with an arm around him as they walked, she seemed more thoughtful and muted, as if already turning nostalgic. He worried that she was preparing to leave him. But when they were alone she spread her hair out, as they lay on the ground, wound his fingers in it, and punctiliously put him through his paces, reiterating their sexual games and tender pledges and making him practice her best feat, which was to have him come to a climax just when she snapped her fingers. He asked if the Indians would kill her as soon as they saw her, and she said no. How about him? She didn't say no. Instead she squeezed him.

She liked feeding morsels of fish to the bear cub and grooming it. And when Margaret was in a mood to translate, she told him that his soul lived in his eyes and he could see it if the light was right by looking into still water or by staring into her eyes. She also told him the story of how wolves had learned to eat deer: All the animals had lived peaceably in the woods and ate only plants. But one day the wolves gave a big party for everybody and made all the other animals laugh. That was when they discovered that deer and sheep and moose and caribou did not have teeth with which to defend themselves.

Salmon were dying in every eddy of the river. Such hordes of them jammed the Eeejookgook now that bears had gathered from everywhere, mountain bears and water bears, matriarchal, patriarchal and magisterial bears, boot-faced bears with low, greedy growls and fishy teeth and tongues like a razor strop in a mouth as wide as a shovel and a rancid smell as broad as a smokestack, who looked for a gun in the hands of a man, and if they didn't detect one, moved closer and closer. The currents were nickel-colored in the rains that fell. Clouds piled in white billows above black billows, and a pack of wolves probed the condition of the two horses and five dogs. The

old German shepherd Kaiser had sprained his ankle and was hob-
bling piteously, whereas each wolf had legs that spun like the spokes
of a bicycle wheel. He whined with foreknowledge that once they
caught him alone they would make a meal out of him.

With the spawning run at a crescendo like this, the big red bears
at their wet roisterous banquet hardly knew fish from flesh, and
though you could bang pots and pans to warn them you were coming, for some of them that simply added to the fun. Lizzie said the
Sikinks didn't travel when the river trail was so risky; they stayed
in their camps and fished. She helped Cecil cache a bunch of baggage in case he ever had a chance to come back for it. As they found
themselves tangled in heavier timber, the horses could no longer
hope to escape the bears with a load on their backs. Indeed, Cecil
complained that he was spending half his time climbing the trees.

He built a raft as a kind of refuge for the four of them, but got so
jittery he suddenly gave a strangled yell and dived to the side, having
been fooled by the moving clouds into supposing that the birch he
was chopping down was falling on him. When the forest appeared
impenetrable, he led the horses, and where the river rumbled between sheer palisades or tumbled past boulders that rose above the
tumultuous rapids horse high, he took charge of the raft. The oddest
part of the experience was that among the many bulky creatures he
glimpsed from the river which were either pondering the currents
or groping for fish, more than one looked like a Bigfoot, but he was
so frantically busy he couldn't be sure. He lost his steering oar when
what had seemed like a rock in the water reared out of the Eeejookgook in the shape of a salmon grizzly and wrenched it out of his
grip. Luckily he didn't run aground until two bends down.

Fish nudged his legs like puppies as he shoved with his push-pole
to free the raft, and fish hawks flapped and squabbled at head level
or hopped between fish corpses in the shallows. Tiny birds like
wrens flew right into the running water and walked on the bottom,
steering themselves with their half-open wings before flying up with
a bug in their beaks. He was scudding along three times as fast as his
friends could travel ashore except when one of these collisions with a
sandbar allowed them to catch up.

The cub rode in a crate lashed to the raft and was surviving. But the shepherd dog vanished that day. They never knew when or by whom he had been seized. His final cries must have been swallowed by river noise—a racket that was often like cries anyway—and the remnants of the original dog pack huddled closer in spite of hating the banging their masters did on the pots and pans, while a series of wolves stared at them with mesmerizing intimacy from underneath low-boughed spruce trees.

The inclines around Third Creek were more benign, the sunlight was not pinched off in the afternoon by peaks nearby, and Switzer said the soil was better drained. He praised too the abundance of bees, necessary for apple trees. He didn't want to hurry by this promising side valley. Abrupt and yet both formal and friendly, he shook hands. Cecil offered to give him the paint horse, but they hadn't located it after the last bear emergency, so Cecil gave it to him if he ever did find it, as well as the stuff that had been cached upstream.

"Aren't you scared?" Cecil demanded, still teasing him.

"*God* scares me," Switzer said, petting his faithful dog.

Lizzie and Margaret alternated with Cecil at riding the pig-colored horse or the raft for fifteen miles or more quite uneventfully, until the Eeejookgook turned boisterous again and a full-bodied new creek joined it in a smoky cauldron of currents and rocks. Past that, Cecil drifted by some rudimentary salmon weirs plaited from willow bark, and a brush hut from which a hunter might shoot ducks or a moose crossing the river. When quickwater swung him next to the bank, he was intensely alarmed, wishing Lizzie was with him to shout into the silent woods, afraid that, alone, he might catch an arrow through the throat. It didn't happen, but he was so rattled that shortly afterwards a sweeper—an uprooted aspen leaning over almost level with the river—which he hadn't noticed as he sped towards it, knocked him off the raft. To his amazement, he was swallowing water with a gash in his forehead, a headache like a sledgehammer, his boots and pants leaden, and his rifle gone. Because the raft bumped into another sweeper, he was able to catch up to it and float for another mile or two into a fat still-water, where at length he beached it and, after trying to pacify the frightened cub, lay down on a bed of moss, too tired to make a success of lighting a fire that would stay lit.

He had just shut his eyes when a body landed on him and pinned him. He struggled for his life as though in the grasp of a bear, but could free himself only enough to see that several human figures cloaked in skins were standing over him holding fish spears. He told the dogs to keep off and keep quiet so that harm wouldn't come to them.

"There," he kept repeating, and Lizzie's name, *"Xingu!"* He pointed in the direction she would be appearing from, because they might already know who he was but think he'd done away with her. A man was sitting on his rear end, and in the ignominy of his capture his mind cast about. He was going to name the bear cub Cora, and when Lizzie and he weren't touring with it they could live by one of the Penobscot Indian villages in Maine where they would excite less of a stir than at home, and despite all the distances, he would make it up to his kids also.

When they tied his hands behind his back, he couldn't gesture in support of what few Sikink words he knew. He had no language to tell them he'd fixed the eye of the old man in No Water's band of sagebrush Sikinks or that he'd greeted one of their own tribesmen in amicable fashion in the red canyon of Fourth Creek. Hearing the word for "kill," he tried to enter the argument on his own behalf but failed, which made them laugh. He saw an elkhorn bow and two guns among them. They were puzzled because he hadn't a rifle, but liked his axe, which had been strapped to the raft more securely. There were four men of different ages, with the faces of "Mountain Chinamen," as Ouddo had described them, and signs of others or of Indian women keeping just out of sight but making the brush jiggle. The talk of killing him had subsided and the man who was sitting on him got fed up with that. Lying humiliatingly tied, he waited and rested.

Lizzie, when she arrived, immediately behaved as if she had practiced in her mind for this moment beforehand. She pushed Margaret toward him, saying Margaret was Cecil's wife, shouting at the same time in surprise and anger that they were treating him in such a way after he and Margaret had saved her from the Thloadennis on the Memphramagog. She greeted several people caressingly and called for others who were in a fish camp downriver, as the Sikinks told her. She yelled for joy at being back, but yelled in outrage that Cecil was trussed up like a goose for roasting. When he had been released, she introduced him with Margaret's help to Hunts-in-a-tree, who was the boss of this temporary encampment. Hunts-in-a-tree, a well-knit fisherman with black and gray hair cut straight across his frown lines and eyebrows, continued to consider Cecil's fate without circumspection, however. At least a few white men must have been part of the fauna of the Eeejookgook throughout his lifetime—and so he seemed incurious about him—yet he seemed unafraid or even unaware of the possibility of white vengeance if he should kill him. There was an awful baldness to his deliberations on the matter.

Lizzie explained that Cecil was an animal catcher, that his friend Sutton, a gold hunter, had been killed near Groundhog's place, and he and Margaret were on their way out to the Obo River and the country of the Tlickitats. Because she scarcely glanced at Cecil as she talked, he realized with a pang of foreboding and yearning that she must think she was saving his life by not doing so. That lone Sikink who had been hunting on Fourth Creek had not seen them together, so she could pretend whatever she liked, but he remembered that her own husband was now known to be dead, and that Tom Ben's white father was said to have had several half-Sikink children here on the Eeejookgook without mishap to him, as well as Tom Ben. He wondered, therefore, if she was right. He even wondered whether maybe she wanted to be separated from him. He could see that her agitation had as much to do with him as with the relief of this reunion, nevertheless.

Around the next bend were bark huts, hide tents and many hundreds and hundreds of pounds of filleted salmon being sun-cured or fire-dried, though a couple of women had taken time out from the main task to strip a young bear of its suet. Lizzie was welcomed clamorously and commiserated with by the ten or a dozen people working there, and Cecil and Margaret were not menaced by anybody. The pig-colored packhorse and all the oddments of baggage now belonged to Hunts-in-a-tree, but in such a time of plenty no one much cared about butchering the baby grizzly. Cecil was permitted to give it food and water, as well as to repair his raft as best he could with the nails he had left, despite some grumbling on the part of an old man that the nails were too valuable to let him use.

Lizzie, while collecting her own things from the pile at Hunts-in-a-tree's tent, managed to extract and secrete the purse containing Sutton's money and gold and to pass this to Margaret, who slipped it into Cecil's hands. He found an opportunity to strap it to his right leg—which gave him a limp. But that he should limp was not suspicious when the Indians knew he had just rafted between the Eeejookgook's Fourth and Second creeks.

Margaret was itching to be gone. They could die here, she said. It was not friendly like the village of the Thloadennis. Nor had these Indians ever been "punished."

Cecil asked her if Lizzie really was going to stay behind.

"I think you're stuck with me. She did civilize you a little anyway."

The Sikinks took his coffee and the sugar that was left, but allowed him his meat and flour—after pouring water on a batch of the latter and attempting to fry it—and gave him a stack of smoked salmon to put on the raft. With all of the clothes, tools and extra guns Hunts-in-a-tree had acquired, plus the horse and four dogs, Lizzie was angrily insisting that Cecil should at least keep his axe as he floated downriver toward the lands of the white men, and that he should keep Moose. When she didn't get anywhere with the argument, she told Hunts-in-a-tree and the rest of these Indians who had been spearing fish for weeks that he could throw his axe like a lance. They were intrigued. At her suggestion they agreed he could keep his axe—and then at her urging they agreed he could keep Moose too—if in one toss he could split a specified sapling while standing in the doorhole of the smokehouse.

Cecil, without pausing for any showmanly effects or to study his small audience, simply did the feat. And it was a fine throw, except that in the heat of his effort he forgot to limp and somebody perceived the bulge in his pant leg. His clothes were taken off and the

Sikinks laughed to see the bag of gold dust fastened behind his knee.

Hunts-in-a-tree—who was known, after all, for slyly shooting meat from the crotches of trees—didn't get mad at being derided. He smiled just enough to disclose the separations between his teeth, and tied Moose to the raft and added the axe to the food and push-pole already placed there. He tied White Eye and Sally and Lizzie's Yallerdog and the pig-colored packhorse elsewhere, which promptly sent the dogs into a spasm of protests, and told Margaret in his own language that he would give the money from the purse to the "piss man." It was a puzzling announcement, until Cecil remembered Charley's telling him and Sutton when they had left his place that the next white man they would see—aside, perhaps, from Mr. Ouddo —would be a trader on the Eeejookgook or the Obo River who would whip out his penis for a pissing contest at the sight of them; that they should keep their bladders full for that.

So, the money would go for goods. The gold, however, Hunts-in-a-tree carried to a rock a little way out in the river and reached by stepping-stones, where a man had been spearing salmon, and carefully sprinkled it into the current.

"This river has no gold," he said in Sikink, smiling. "No one finds gold on the Eeejookgook."

He let Cecil get dressed and motioned him onto the raft, while Lizzie paced in the background. It was such a modest, matter-of-fact settlement, inhabited by ten or twenty adults and ten or fifteen children, that Cecil kept wondering whether she really wanted to stay and whether she really wanted him gone. Which were her relatives? And who would she marry now? She was a Sikink again, whereas Margaret was the same as a white woman in Hunts-in-a-tree's eyes and, like Cecil, in danger of getting shot.

He mocked Cecil for stalling, assuming he must be scared to embark on the river with only an axe to defend himself. "Aren't bears brothers to the white man?" he said.

No Lizzie, no Sutton, no Charley, no Roy. "You'd just as soon I take you back to Boston instead of St. Louis, I hope?" Cecil told Margaret, quite devastated, though able to joke.

"You're pushing our luck. Let's get out of here."

So they shoved off, while Sally and White Eye yowled in distress and Lizzie lifted one arm and turned to examine a net that was laid over a rock for repair. The river seized hold of the raft and spun it around and around in a fair imitation of their own helplessness and swept it into mid-channel and around the next bend almost before they were aware they had left these Sikinks behind. The clouds bulged like biceps, the river was leaden, and a red grizzly was patrolling the beach.

Cecil untied Moose so he wouldn't drown if the raft flipped over, and stopped on an island later on to cut Margaret a push-pole. The mountains on both sides of the valley grew roomy and towering, yet the river itself was not overly rugged. They passed five more Sikink fishing camps, but steering well out from shore, were not chased by anybody. Neither did the busy bears, black and caramel-colored, running along the bank with the gait of rocking horses, feel much like plunging in after them. Cecil had tightened his craft enough with his rope and nails that it could slam into a drift pile without falling to pieces. They had no accidents, no frights to compare with what they had been through earlier, and could have relaxed if they had known what was ahead.

Three times they experienced the poignancy of hearing deep bugle calls booming out of the sky and from marshes stretching alongside the river. *"Ko-hoh, ko-hoh, ko-hoh, ko-hoh!"* These were trumpeter swans, twice as big around as a large goose and as tall as a man, with wings so strong the feathers rasped as they beat the wind. But the call—hornlike and jubilant—was like Sutton blowing his music before a jump, or a celebration of poor Sutton's life.

"Ko-hoh, ko-hoh, ko-hoh!"

Their eyes filled with tears. In the vicinity of First Creek the swans were teaching their young of the year to fly, dashing into the wind to take off, and then when a baby sometimes succeeded in emulating this feat, one of the parents would fly just under it to give it a back to rest on for a moment if it got tired as it flew. The trumpet toots oompahed and clanged in such exuberant abandon that the wolves in the woods howled back and owls woke up and hooted.

At the mouth of First Creek they tied to an island, intending to listen to all this whoopee and spend the night. You could practically walk on the water, the salmon had congregated so massively at the junction—First Creek was nearly the size of the Eeejookgook's main stem. River birds and birds that had flown over from all of the lakes in the region and birds that had flown clear up from the distant sea for this feast were winging every which way overhead as if the world had been newly created.

Margaret made love with Cecil on the island's lee beach, where the dead trees from upstream weren't heaped so thickly. They did this not in spite of but in tribute to the lovers they had left behind and because they would now probably die together if either of them was unable to survive.

"Deep, deep," she exhorted him till he had swelled inside her as tumidly as she wished. "And now again."

In taking possession of the island, they'd shooed off a bunch of night herons, but were surprised to hear sounds as if the night herons had returned. Moose's hair rose. It was a bear foraging toward them in the twilight. They sprang onto the raft and floated around one, two, three, four bends, and made love a second time on another island and fell asleep, as white flames from all angles madly jerked toward a vortex at the top of the sky that was split by dark streaks like door cracks into whatever lay behind the sky.

Though the mountains downriver had expanded to the same alpine dimensions as Many Berries and the other peaks at the head of the Eeejookgook, the river looped in the bed of its valley with a generous geography that allowed wider views of what was in store. Grouse pecked sand on the beaches like chickens, and frothy streams emptied in. Moose waded and sunk their heads underwater, eating eelgrasses, till just the tops of their shoulders showed.

Cecil and Margaret saw three Bigfoots as they drifted—separate thin-haired, long-haired, box-nosed individuals placidly beachcombing miles apart. Like most of the grizzlies, they pretended not to notice the raft slowly hurtling by. Each time, Cecil naturally thought of Sutton, but he realized also that once he had left the river he would have no proof even within his own mind that these creatures had ever existed. Maybe Margaret and he would soon stop telling the story.

The bear cub was as brown as mud and utterly earthy, however. It had a vigorous appetite for salmon, had reluctantly learned to enjoy being scratched on the pit of its stomach or on the roof of its head, had chewed through the bars of its cage despite the constraints of a muzzle, so that they now had to tie it, and given half a chance, it wrestled or nuzzled or hugged them like mother and brother. Then, kneeling solemnly like a camel and copying Moose's constancy, it would study the water for fish carcasses, drowned rodents and other flotsam, riding with one paw in the water by the hour—till tempted to snap at a dragonfly or dunk its nose after a flash of silver under the surface. They called it Sweetcake, short for "Cora," because it was still too cubbish to seem very female.

Where they camped they saw a mink eating a frog, jerking the flesh off like a moose stripping bark off a tree, and Indian fire-pits and tipi rings, but no sign of a previous white tenant. The river, traveling at about the pace of a brisk walk, accumulated more islands, molded like arrowheads and forested like pincushions, spanning an acre or less. On some a moose had swum out to chew the leaders off the young aspen trees, masticating these with many droll turns of the lip and much head-tossing, which made its antlers flicker up and down among the thick branches. Often a wolf would have accompanied the moose, antic as a clown, coated in impoverished-looking gray fur and grinning. The skinnier wolves ran or swam most energetically—sprinting up a knoll to peer down at the animal, streaking down to beach level to peep up at it through the underbrush, as though a long-legged moose wasn't invulnerable to a wolf's attack in the water or on a small island.

On the afternoon of the third day they found that the Eeejook-gook, which was cannon-colored, had joined a blackwater river behind a screen of spruce islands and dead-water sloughs. They were suddenly floating due west on a rapid but flattish course between squarish mountains. Willows grew on the south bank, firs on the north. They had six matches left, no way to shoot food, and several hundred miles to go before the Obo River even entered the Hainaino—altogether eight hundred or perhaps as much as a thousand miles to salt water, from what Charley had said. Periodically the raft grated over a rock or sandbar.

They saw a bear half buried head-first that was excavating a musk-rat hole. They saw an Indian in a skin boat, but he scooted into the mouth of a slough, dropping his paddle and lifting his rifle, lest they try trailing him. They knew the railroad would probably follow this route after it crossed the continental divide from the Valley of the Tlickitats, and that the headwaters of the Valley of the Tlickitats touched the headwaters of the Valley of the Obo somewhere upriver and eastward of them. Walking in that direction, they might eventually meet white men, just as at the trading post hundreds of miles down-current from where they were.

"What do we do?" Cecil asked Margaret. "Go on or walk back?"

She said she'd rather sit than walk. She said they wouldn't starve while the salmon run lasted.

Luckily they passed a campfire before dusk. In some trepidation they struggled with the current, landed and approached, weaponless except for the axe, which Cecil held by its head like a cane.

Two Indians were sitting there. Far from threatening anybody, they didn't so much as stand up.

Margaret, speaking in Crow, finally asked them whether they were Tlickitats.

The younger one said, "Mohawk." And to Cecil: "From Buffalo. You got food? You can eat if you want." He waved at the bean pot propped over the fire and at a box of sea biscuits. "You wanna work? A guy drowned. You talk to the Major."

"You want to work?" said a louder voice from in front of a tent they hadn't seen, hidden in the trees. "The son of a bitch drowned. Do you know how to work?"

A hard-bitten little man with a foot-length beard and a barometer hung in its case on a cord from his neck and enough chewing tobacco in one cheek to make a whole supper of, emerged and handed Cecil a cup to dip a meal for himself out of the pot. When Cecil filled it and gave it to Margaret, he got him another. He had whiskers growing out of his ears.

"You can fuck her all night if you want, if you know how to work in the day. We're trying to put us a railroad through here, if the geniuses back there in Tlickitatland can ever catch up with us."

Margaret burst into a laugh. "You remember Red Town? Wasn't you in Red Town last year?"

The Major started, stared hard, blushed, turned and spit in the river. "If you can talk, you can cook beans."

Cecil explained to him that they had already met Elmer Meecham, the survey chief, in Horse Swim this spring, headed for Tlickitatland.

"Well that's where he is, one year behind," conceded the Major, becoming more reticent now that he had more information about them. "Not a bad river." He nodded at the Obo flowing past.

Cecil filled his belly with beans and told where he came from in America. He fed Moose and tended and showed off the bear cub. Then, chewing a biscuit and stretching his aching back and arms, he strolled a bit, discovering a few more tents. A burly white man crawled out of one with a Colt and a box of bullets in his hands.

"Whatchyou got for me? Where'd you come from? Are you an Obo man?" he asked.

"From the Eeejookgook," Cecil said. "Not the Obo."

"You were on the Eeejookgook? You know Isaac Ouddo?" He thrust the gun upon Cecil and stood next to him as he examined it. Cecil heard and smelled a yellow stream of piss strike the ground—and laughed.

"Ouddo, sure. And Groundhog Morris's place. We worked that for a while. We came all the way over the Hump from Charley's house."

"Old Charley Biskner? *He's* got a place," the trader exclaimed, tucking his penis back in his pants. "I like Charley. The old dynamiter with the Midas touch!" He reached in his tent and pulled out a nice sealskin coat, whitish green with gray spots, gut-sewn Indian style, and a striped woollen Hudson's Bay Company blanket.

"Maybe you got no Midas touch, but I'll tell you what. If you've walked that damn far I'll give you the gun and these on time."

Cecil laughed again. "I was trying to catch a Bigfoot," he told him.

"Oooooh," said the trader in a slow mock-falsetto. "One of those guys. I know the man before me used to try to swap stuff with one of them. He'd leave some sugar for him on the riverbank. I don't know what he got for it, really. The Bigfoot took it away, but I don't think he brought anything. I tried it myself one time for fun, but I don't think I had the knack. He wouldn't come, and the rain got the sugar all wet."

He watched the Obo's coiling currents as Cecil handled the goods.

"Tryin' to catch a Bigfoot, huh? That'd be a first, wouldn't it? That'd be something to show. Well look how much there is here that if you could catch it and ship it East you'd make a fortune, but you can't." He pointed at a surge of turmoil in the river not far from the bank. A ridge-backed slaty body three times as long as a man's and bulkier than any grizzly bear's had surfaced quietly and sunk again with only the slightest roll, like a gigantic barrel.

"Now that fellow was a fish," he remarked. "A sturgeon. But if you could catch him and hollow him out and dry him and stuff him and add some arms and legs and paint him up and sell him to P. T. Barnum, he'd call him 'The Bigfoot of the River' and make some money with him."

Cecil felt glad to be off the raft after seeing that monster. The Obo, like the Eeejookgook, seethed with ducks and other water birds landing, changing their minds, taking off, landing elsewhere.

"You shouldn't even have to fake with him—that's such a natural wonder," he said. He was grinning.

"*Ko-hoh, Ko-hoh, Ko-hoh, Ko-hoh!*" came a whole jubilant V of flying swans, bugling and trumpeting, just above the curdled water.

ABOUT THE AUTHOR

Edward Hoagland was born in New York City in 1932 and educated at Harvard. He is the author of four novels including *Cat Man,* first published in 1956, and *Seven Rivers West.* His collections of essays include *The Courage of Turtles, Walking the Dead Diamond River, Red Wolves and Black Bears,* and *The Tugman's Passage.* He is also the author of two travel books, *African Calliope: A Journey to the Sudan,* which was nominated for a National Book Critics Circle Award and an American Book Award, and *Notes from the Century Before: A Journal from British Columbia.* Mr. Hoagland has taught at Rutgers, Sarah Lawrence, Columbia and the University of Iowa, and has traveled to Alaska and northwestern Canada many times. He lives otherwise with his wife and daughter in New York, spending his summers in northern Vermont.